*In these spec... ...
Jenny Wright and Kelsey Lockhart
just can't hold on to their
innocence!*

# HIS
# UNDERCOVER
# VIRGIN

A collection of wonderfully-told
stories by two authors who write
straight from the heart.

We're proud to present

### ⊚™ MILLS & BOON®

# SPOTLIGHT

*a chance to buy collections of bestselling
novels by favourite authors every month
– they're back by popular demand!*

October 2007

## Bosses and Baby Bargains

*Featuring*

*The Nanny's Secret* by Monica McLean
*The Boss's Baby Bargain* by Karen Sandler

## His Undercover Virgin

*Featuring*

*Woman of Innocence* by Lindsay McKenna
*The Virgin Bride Said, "Wow!"* by Cathy Gillen Thacker

November 2007

## For Love and Glory

*Featuring*

*Royal Protocol* by Christine Flynn
*Her Royal Husband* by Cara Colter

## Their Little Miracles

*Featuring*

*The Cowboy's Christmas Miracle*
by Anne McAllister
*Their Instant Baby* by Cathy Gillen Thacker

# HIS UNDERCOVER VIRGIN

Woman of Innocence
LINDSAY McKENNA

The Virgin Bride Said, "Wow!"
CATHY GILLEN THACKER

⊚™ MILLS & BOON®
*Pure reading pleasure*

*This collection is first published in Great Britain 2007
Harlequin Mills & Boon Limited,
Eton House, 18-24 Paradise Road, Richmond, Surrey TW9 1SR*

HIS UNDERCOVER VIRGIN © Harlequin Books S.A. 2007

The publisher acknowledges the copyright holders of the
individual works, which have already been published in the UK
in single, separate volumes, as follows:

*Woman of Innocence* © Lindsay McKenna 2002
*The Virgin Bride Said, "Wow!"* ©Cathy Gillen Thacker 2001

*ISBN: 978 0 263 85686 6*

*064-1007*

*Printed and bound in Spain
by Litografia Rosés S.A., Barcelona*

# Woman of
# Innocence

# LINDSAY
# McKENNA

## LINDSAY McKENNA

A homeopathic educator, Lindsay teaches at the Desert Institute of Classical Homeopathy in Phoenix, Arizona. When she isn't teaching alternative medicine, she is writing books about love. She feels love is the single greatest healer in the world and hopes that her books touch her readers on those levels.

To Gonzalo E Abelenda and Ezequiel Caviglia
of Buenos Aires, Argentina. Two young,
handsome white knights who rescued us from
Agua Caliente, Peru, and got us train tickets
back to Cuzco. Thank you!
Chivalry, good manners and kindness between
North and South America are alive and well.
You are both, truly, romance heroes
of the finest kind.

# Chapter One

"Morgan, are you awake?"

"...Umphh..."

Laura smiled softly as she gazed at her dozing husband. Thin streams of moonlight filtered into their bedroom on the second floor of their log home. She could smell the scent of pine as a breeze gently blew the diaphanous white curtains beside their brass bed. Snuggling up against his back, she moved her hand in a gliding motion around his rib cage. Though the comforts of living had put a few extra pounds on Morgan, he still worked to maintain the strong, athletic build he'd had as a young man.

Placing her palm against his darkly haired chest,

she reached up and placed a kiss against his naked shoulder. "Are you awake?" she repeated.

Morgan stirred. He forced his lids open. Feeling Laura's small hand against his chest, over his heart, he lifted his own hand and pressed it against hers. "I am now."

She laughed a little breathlessly and kissed him as a reward. "I know you had a hard day. I should have talked to you about this earlier."

Morgan liked the feel of Laura's silky nightgown. The way it flowed against his nakedness made him very aware of her feminine curves. Moving carefully from his side to his back, he brought his wife into his arms. She nestled her blond head into his shoulder, her brow pressed to his jaw. Ever since her kidnapping years ago, the trauma she'd suffered, Laura had changed. Not that Morgan could blame her under the circumstances. He, too, had been changed when he and his wife, as well as their eldest son, Jason, had been victimized during the incident.

"What are you worrying over?" he rumbled as he pressed his lips to her thick soft hair. Inhaling deeply, he savored the sweet scent of kahili ginger that she'd washed her hair with earlier that night, before they went to bed.

Laughing a little, Laura eased away just enough to catch his sleepy looking eyes. Warmed by his sensitivity to her needs, she whispered, "How did you know I was worrying?"

One corner of his mouth moved upward. Her eyes shone with warmth and love—toward him. Squeezing her shoulder gently, he rasped, "Why wouldn't I know? We've been married a long time. We know one another pretty well at this stage, don't you think?"

"Even at two in the morning you have a sense of humor." She grinned a little and kissed his jaw. The sandpapery quality made her lips tingle as she sank against him.

Sighing, Morgan said, "Only for you, believe me." He'd lost count of the times he'd been awakened by a person on duty over at the Perseus headquarters about a mercenary mission. No, he savored a good night's sleep. Morgan also knew that since the kidnapping, Laura had kept a lot of her emotions in, and had lost some of her childlike spontaneity. Over time, he'd learned how to read her when she internalized things, and he tried to stimulate conversation with her, to find out what was going on inside that intelligent head of hers. Tonight was one of those nights, he realized. Laura rarely woke him up like this. He wondered if she was worried about one of their four children. Jason, their firstborn son, in particular, who was going through a very rough time the last couple of years as a maturing teen.

"What's bothering you?" he asked quietly. He felt her hand range across his chest, her touch always wonderful. Savoring the feel of her slender, feminine body against his own, he moved his fingers across her shoulder.

Closing her eyes, Laura sighed. "It's about Jenny."

His brows drew downward. "Jenny? My assistant?"

"Yes."

All sleepiness left him as he wondered why Laura needed to discuss the woman who worked for him at Perseus. "What about her?"

"You know how much we both like her," Laura began.

"Yes…" Where was this leading? Normally, Laura didn't discuss business at 2:00 a.m. with him. She helped out occasionally on hiring people for Perseus. Otherwise, she had her hands full with their four children, devoting her life and time to them, not Perseus. "She's become like a fifth child to us," Morgan agreed.

The fact that Jenny had a lot of Laura's own traits hadn't escaped either of them. With her short blond hair and pixie face, Jenny looked more like one of their children than Morgan's secretarial assistant. Jenny had been abandoned at birth, given up for adoption, and she still didn't know who her parents were. When Laura had discovered that fact, she'd automatically extended a hand to the young woman of twenty-four, and made her a part of their extended family. Morgan didn't mind. Jenny was a superb worker, highly intelligent, and had graduated from Bryn Mawr in the top ten percent of her class. She had a degree in psychology, and spoke three foreign languages fluently. Jenny was no ordinary secretary, by a long shot. She was, literally, Morgan's right-hand person at Perseus. Everything that went on, Jenny knew about. She was reliable, trustworthy and hardworking.

"You know her birthday is coming up in a week? She'll be twenty-five?"

Rubbing his face, Morgan muttered, "Oh…no, I forgot. Damn… It's a good thing you reminded me." He made it a point to remember the birthday of every one of his employees. But Jenny kept the list for him, and knowing her as he did, he realized she'd never tell him her birthday was coming up! She didn't like to take the limelight or have anyone make a big deal over her. She was almost a shadow, a behind-the-scenes player in all respects.

Laura nodded her head. "A senior moment, sweetheart."

They both laughed. Now that Morgan was in his mid-fifties, he had found out that his memory wasn't what it used to be.

"I have a special gift in mind for her," Laura said enthusiastically. "And that's what I need to talk to you about."

Raising his brows, Morgan said, "Okay…whatever it is, get it for her. She treats you like the mother she doesn't have. You don't need my okay on it." He felt Laura laugh and she hugged him.

"Don't be so quick to agree, Morgan. The 'gift' I have in mind is unusual and does require your approval."

"You're up to something...."

She laughed liltingly. "You're slow, Trayhern. Must be the time of morning I woke you up."

He grinned and squeezed Laura, placing a kiss on her smooth brow. Morgan treasured these special moments they shared. They didn't have many, not with four kids and the demands of Perseus hanging over their heads all the time. "Why is it the man is always the last to know?" he teased back.

Laura kissed his cheek and then sat up. The sheet fell away and pooled around her hips. She saw the glimmer in Morgan's dark blue eyes and reached out and skimmed her hand across his massive chest. "That's why you guys needs us girls around."

Catching her hand, he pressed a kiss to it. "Okay, I give. What's going on?" He liked the way the pale peach silk nightgown with the deep V-neckline revealed her slender body. Even after carrying his four children, she was as beautiful and desirable to him as ever.

"I've been thinking..."

"Uh-oh...now I *am* in trouble!"

She giggled and met his smiling eyes and cock-eyed grin. Despite Morgan's overwhelming work-load, when he was with her, he was more like a little boy than the serious, conservative military tactician that he was. With her, he let down his walls. He trusted her. He loved her. "Yes," she whispered wickedly, "I think you are...."

With a sigh, he struggled up into a sitting position. Leaning against the cool brass headboard, he held her hand in his. "Okay, what have you planned for Jenny's birthday?"

Laura lost her smile and turned slightly, her knees brushing against his thick, hard thigh as she met and held his glimmering eyes. The moonlight was bright, contrasting starkly with the deep shadows in the room. Morgan's face was square and large. Even in the moonlight the scar on his face stood out, a con-stant reminder of that fateful day during the Vietnam War so long ago.

"You know how desperately she daydreams of go-ing on a mission with a mercenary."

Morgan groaned. "Laura..."

She held up her hand. "Hear me out, darling."

Groaning, Morgan rumbled, "That's all it is, Laura. She daydreams. She knows she can't go on a bona fide merc mission. She's not trained for it." Scowling, he added, "Jenny is smart, bright, re-sourceful and creative, but she's not merc material. I can't put one of my men at risk to fulfill some romantic dream she has about this business. You know that.''

Sliding her hand along his jaw, Laura whispered, ''You're overreacting, darling. Remember last week, how you mentioned to me that you have a level one mission coming up in Agua Caliente, Peru? You said you needed to assign someone to interview Major Maya Stevenson's Apache pilots for that top-secret mission that will be going down in Mexico. Jenny's a psychologist. Who better to interview and help select the right three women for this? A level one assignment means no danger. Why couldn't you assign Jenny to go along? Make her feel like she's doing something important? Let her undertake the interviewing and choose the pilots. I really think if you'd do this, she'd lose her romantic visions of the business. As it is now, that's all she talks about—to be part of one of your merc teams.''

Groaning, Morgan closed his eyes. ''Laura…''

''Morgan, it's a little thing, but it'll mean so much to Jenny.''

Opening his eyes, he regarded her shadowed face and absorbed her warm, pleading look. She knew he wouldn't refuse her. He never did. How could he? Loving Laura was his whole life. Their children were proof of that, and their love had deepened and gotten even better over the years. She was his best friend. And she rarely took advantage of their bond as she was doing now.

Morgan knew that Laura felt deeply for Jenny's plight as an abandoned child. Laura had a habit of bringing in strays all the time. There was that stray kitten down at the grocers, starving, its eyes nearly matted shut, that she'd brought it home and nursed back to health. A pigeon had been hit by a car and was lying on the side of the road, and Laura had stopped and picked it up. She'd put a splint on its broken wing and nursed it back to health. Now that Laura had released it, the dumb bird made its home on the rail outside their bedroom door. Morgan wasn't very happy about that. The bird messed everywhere.

Morgan's mind ranged over the many animals Laura had rescued over the years. And he had to admit, if he was honest, that she had rescued him, too. He was a stray. He'd been abandoned in every way possible, yet, she'd opened her heart and her life to him, without question.

Morgan wouldn't make Laura beg. He respected her too much to play that kind of game. He saw that her velvety eyes were filled with love toward him. Sighing, Morgan squeezed her small hand in his large one. "Okay, okay! So who's available to go on this mock merc mission?"

Laura released a breath of air, leaned forward and threw her arms around his broad, warm shoulders. "Thank you, darling." She gave him a quick kiss on his mouth and said, "Matt Davis is coming in from Bosnia tomorrow. He's been on a level four mission, and I would imagine he'd like something a little safer and quieter.''

Morgan arched one black brow. ''Davis? Baby-sitting Jenny? Oh, brother, Laura. That is *not* a match made in heaven. That's like putting oil and water together.''

''He's the only one available,'' Laura said, biting her lower lip in thought. ''I've met him several times. He's very nice. Good-looking too. And single.''

''Is this all for Jenny's benefit?''

Laura laughed. ''It doesn't hurt that he isn't married, Morgan.''

Giving her a dark look, he growled, ''You aren't matchmaking again, are you?'' Laura had a penchant for that.

Her mouth twitched. She saw Morgan's dark, assessing gaze on her. ''Me? No. Go look at the database yourself. There's no one available except Matt. I'm sure if you explain to him the reasons for his being assigned, he'd go along with it. He's got a soft heart.''

''Humph. I've got to have a soft head to think he'd agree to it. I'm going to have to do a helluva lotta talking to get him, Laura. He's thirty years old and he will *not* like baby-sitting a rookie. Hell, Jenny isn't even *that*.'' Running his fingers through his black hair, he grimaced.

"Matt knows Spanish. And this is a Spanish-speaking mission," she reminded him. "And Jenny knows Spanish. She won't be a problem. Besides, she plans all the missions with you and Mike Houston. Just because she hasn't spent any real time on a mission, she knows how they work. I think if you tell Matt why, he'll gracefully capitulate and do it."

"I'm not so sure...." Morgan wasn't. "Grace is not his middle name."

"More than anything," Laura said, "please don't let Jenny think this isn't an important mission. Let her think that she's really contributing—that she's the best person for the job."

"I can't let Jenny think we'll do this again, Laura. She's not qualified and trained in military maneuvers."

Holding up her hand, Laura said, "I agree. Tell her that it's her birthday and that you felt she could handle this mission. You can make it perfectly clear that there will never be another. I really think that if Matt gives her a taste of a real mission, without the danger being there, she'll quickly lose that romantic veneer she's put on mercs and missions in the future. Maybe she needs to go on a mission, experience it, simply to help her to understand the rigors and stresses on our people. It could help her be a better assistant as she plans these missions with you and Mike."

Nodding, Morgan muttered, "You've got sound

arguments. Maybe we *should* put her on a safe mission. I could suggest to Matt to ham it up a little for her benefit. Level ones are usually boring as hell to a merc.''

Laura sighed. ''You've got the right idea, Morgan. I feel this will work out to everyone's advantage. Jenny will fulfill her dream. You'll get an assistant back that understands mission planning more fully.''

Chuckling, Morgan said, ''Matt's the only one who isn't going to benefit from this trip.''

''Mmm,'' Laura murmured as she moved into Morgan's arms, ''Matt's a big boy. Somehow, I think he'll roll with the situation. Jenny is cute. And she's no dummy. He'll find out very quickly just how smart and resourceful she is.''

Morgan smiled, pressing his wife closer to him. As she leaned down, rubbing like a feline against him, he murmured, ''Let's set business aside now, shall we?''

Laura laughed gently and placed her lips against his smiling ones. ''I like waking you at 2:00 a.m. in the morning, Trayhern....''

As her lips glided against his, he felt her smiling. Her body was warm and sensuous as he wrapped his arms around her. ''Yeah,'' he growled, ''no interruptions...''

''No phones, no faxes...''

"No children coming in and needing some-thing…"

Sighing, Laura whispered, "Just the two of us…. Let's take advantage of it, shall we, darling?"

"I need a special favor from you, Matt. Have a seat." Morgan gestured to the leather wing chair that sat at one corner of his massive bird's-eye maple desk in his private office within the Perseus complex. The merc, Matt Davis, assessed him critically with storm-gray eyes as he sat down.

"A favor?"

The door to Morgan's office opened, interrupting the two men. Jenny came in, bearing a silver tray with coffee, cream, sugar and those delectable Krispy Kreme doughnuts. They were Morgan's downfall. Luckily, Jenny had put only two on the tray—one for each of the men. Laura had given her strict in-structions not to serve the usual half dozen anymore, or Morgan would eat more than his fair share.

"Come in, Jenny," he murmured. "You can set the tray on the desk here."

Matt rubbed his eyes tiredly. The little blond-haired assistant gave him a cheery good-morning smile, as she had when she'd let him in to see Mor-gan for his appointment. Her blue eyes sparkled with such life. She brushed by him and he caught the scent of a very faint fragrance; maybe lilacs? He dismissed his distracting thought. Right now, all he wanted was a week or two off and some deep, sound sleep. Still, those large, expressive blue eyes of hers got to him. They reached inside of his armored heart and touched him as if he had no defenses in place. Damn. How could that be? She was all of maybe five foot two inches, and probably weighed a hundred pounds soaking wet. She was built like a bird, Matt thought, and she looked fragile. Like she might break if someone glared at her or said a bad word in her presence. Yet she was all bubbly, light effervescence. Sunshine in their dark hole of a business, he mused. Maybe that's why Morgan had hired her: she brought light to the murky world they lived in. Matt couldn't blame him. Jenny was attractive without being a raving beauty. It was her eyes and that constant, soft smile on her full mouth that were her greatest attributes.

"Thank you, Jenny," Morgan murmured as she was about to pour coffee into the delicate white china cups. "We'll do it."

"Sure…" Jenny nodded and turned. As she did, the toe of her sensible brown loafer caught the scarred, dirty hiking boot Matt wore.

"Oh!" The cry tore from her lips as she staggered forward, off balance, her arms flailing outward.

Matt saw her trip. Instantly, he was leaning forward, his arm outstretched, to grab her. He was easily able to catch her as she reeled in his direction. In seconds, her light form was in his arms, her shoulder against his chest.

"You okay?" he asked as he righted her and sat her on her feet. Matt saw her cheeks turn red with embarrassment. Morgan had come halfway out of his chair when he saw her trip, but from where he was, he couldn't have helped her, anyway.

"Oh yes…sorry! I'm so sorry, Mr. Davis…." Jenny quickly leaped away from him. She nervously smoothed her tan slacks and gave Morgan a regretful look. "I'm *such* a klutz. I'm okay, Morgan. Really." And she held out her hand to stop him from coming around the desk. The look on his face was one of genuine concern. She loved her boss so much. He treated her as an equal, not as some dumb, airhead blonde.

"You sure?" Morgan asked, halting.

"*Very* sure." Flustered, she ran her fingers through her thick, short hair. "It's just *me*." Flashing Matt Davis a slight smile, she said, "Thanks for saving me from totally embarrassing myself."

Matt couldn't help but smile back. She was such a sprite. More like sunlight dancing on the choppy waters of life than an ordinary woman.

"Don't worry about it," he murmured, and reached for the coffee.

"I'll leave you now," she said and hurried out of the room.

Morgan picked up a Krispy Kreme doughnut. "You know, these doughnuts are the best in the world." He eyed it like a jeweler eyeballing an expensive diamond.

Snorting, Matt poured them coffee. "You eat 'em. I don't need the sugar today."

"Humph, I don't, either, but... Sure you don't want the other one?"

Davis grinned and sipped the hot, fragrant coffee. "Positive." He patted his hard, flat belly beneath the white cotton shirt he wore.

Morgan bit into the doughnut, a look of absolute pleasure crossing his face. "This is one of life's little gifts," he sighed as he enjoyed every bite. "When I heard they were going to have a Krispy Kreme come to Philipsburg, I knew I was in heaven."

Davis chortled a little and sat down, sprawling his six-foot-two-inch length out again, the coffee balanced between his hands. "Better you than me. If I eat bread products of any kind, I gain weight right off the bat. In our business, we don't need that riding against us."

Patting his middle, Morgan said, "I've got about five pounds here I don't need."

"Yeah, well you're in your fifties and I'm thirty. Big difference." Matt grinned.

Good humored, Morgan took the second doughnut and sat down. He ate it with the same slow satisfaction as he had the first one. "This will be our secret. Laura thinks I'm getting one a day."

"Our secret," Matt agreed with a lopsided grin.

Dusting off his hands on the white linen napkin from the tray, Morgan picked up his coffee and sauntered back around his desk. "Now," he murmured, "I have a favor to ask of you."

## Chapter Two

"Happy birthday, Jenny," Morgan called to his assistant. He looked fondly over at her as she hurried into the war room, where all assignments were handed out. Laura stood at his side, smiling.

Jenny came to a halt in front of Morgan, who sat opposite her at the huge, oval table. Her eyes grew huge at the sight of the white frosted cake decorated with yellow roses. "A cake?" she gasped. Her hand flew to her heart when she saw the lit candles—all twenty-five of them. "You didn't have to do this," she said, touched. With a lump in her throat, she made a wish and blew out all the candles, while the Trayherns applauded.

To the left of the cake was a blue folder. She recognized the file as a merc assignment. On top of it was placed a bright red-and-silver bow. What stymied her was the fact that *her* name was on that file. Clasping her hands in nervous anticipation, she asked, ''What's this?''

Laura smiled fondly. ''Your gift, Jenny. From all of us to you. Go on, open it.''

She saw the smile that Morgan traded with Laura. They looked like they knew the punch line to a joke she wasn't privy to. Anticipation wound through her. ''B-but,'' Jenny stammered, gesturing toward the file, ''that's a merc assignment file. Did I not file it correctly?'' She took pride in her filing system and had never lost a folder yet.

''Yes,'' Morgan murmured in his deep voice, ''that's exactly what it is. And no, it's not misfiled.''

Giving them a confused look, Jenny slid her fingers beneath the bow, then carefully set it aside. Balancing the folder in her hand, she gave them a perplexed look. ''It has my name on it. That's not right. The merc who's assigned this duty should have his or her name on it....''

Morgan allowed a hint of a smile. Jenny was truly confused. ''Why don't you open it up and look at the assignment? I think a lot of your confusion will be put to rest.''

Sitting down, Jenny placed the file in her lap and opened it. Her eyes widened. She gasped. Snapping a look up at Morgan and Laura, she whispered, "This can't be!"

"Why not?" Morgan demanded.

"Why, er, I'm just an assistant to you, Morgan...for Perseus...." She stared disbelievingly at the assignment. It had her name on it as the commander in charge of the mission. Below it was another name: Matt Davis. He was second-in-command. Looking farther, she saw that the assignment was to Agua Caliente, Peru, to a top-secret military installation known as the Black Jaguar Base.

Her heart began skipping beats as she continued to rapidly scan the information. She was being assigned to interview all volunteer candidates at the Black Jaguar Base who would want to work undercover for Perseus on an upcoming mission along the Mexican-American border. She was to lead this mission! *Her!* She was to interview all the pilots and then select the three she considered best qualified for the tasks. It was a level one mission, which meant there was no risk or danger to it.

Morgan traded a warm look with Laura. He turned his attention back to Jenny, whose head was still bent over the file as she read voraciously. She nervously chewed on her full lower lip, and her thin, arched brows worked up and down as she read. She had a very open, readable face, and Morgan enjoyed watching her response.

"Jenny, we felt that you've worked here long enough to undertake a safe, but very necessary mission for Perseus," he told her in an authoritative voice. Jenny lifted her chin, her full attention on him. Morgan saw tears in her eyes. He felt Laura gently squeeze his shoulder. "We know you've dreamed of going on a mission rather than just sitting here behind your desk processing orders and reports. I felt that if you undertook a mission, that would help you understand your job here better. And Laura felt this was a worthy birthday gift to you. Is it?"

Choking on tears, Jenny fought them back. Her gaze swung from Morgan's gentle look to Laura's proud and smiling features. She knew in her heart that Laura had engineered this. "I—I don't know what to say...."

"Yes will suffice." Morgan chuckled indulgently.

"But...how do you know I'm up for it? I mean, I'm not a trained merc. I have no experience in the military. I've never picked up a pistol to fire it...." She suddenly stood up, gripping the file to her chest, and her voice went off-key with anxiety. "Oh, I know I've told you a million times I wished for a chance to go on a mission...but I know better. I really do. I know I'm a big 'fraidy-cat, not a hero or heroine like the wonderful people you employ, Morgan. I'm a mouse. A plain, dull little mouse with absolutely no military background like your mercenaries.''

Laura smiled gently. ''Not all missions require military might, Jenny. You have a degree in psychology. We felt that you were the best qualified person for this mission. You've been here a year with us and you know the routine. And you've also met most of our employees and know the type of people we're looking for.'' Laura pointed to the folder Jenny held in a death grip against her chest. ''Major Maya Stevenson has agreed to let you and your partner come down to her base and interview any interested Boeing Apache helicopter pilots who may want to take part in these upcoming missions.''

Stymied, her heart beating hard in her chest because she'd never in a million years believed she'd be given a merc mission, Jenny said in a wobbly voice, ''But, Laura, I don't know anything about the military except what I've learned here. I wouldn't know how to assess the volunteers....'' She gave Laura a panicked look.

Morgan cleared his throat. ''That's why Matt Davis has been assigned. He's ex-Navy SEAL. He knows the military and he also knows what we're looking for on this mission. He can help you with the type of questions you might want to pose to the volunteers, as well as guide you in your selection. Of course, you are the team leader and he's your assistant. In the end, your judgment, your choices, are the ones we'll go with.''

''Oh dear...'' Jenny quickly sat down before she fell down from the shock of it all. What a birthday gift! Going on a merc mission. It was one of those silly, idealistic dreams she held secret within her heart, one she never believed would come true. Shaking her head, she muttered more to herself than to them, ''All my life, I've dreamed of doing something heroic...something that would help others....''

''We felt you deserved this opportunity,'' Morgan said genially. He grinned as Jenny looked over at him. Her large blue eyes were huge with shock and wonder. ''Will you accept your birthday gift so we can get on with cutting the cake?''

Laughing breathlessly, Jenny leaped from the chair. ''Of course. Wow! I'm in shock. I mean, I really *am!* I never dreamed of this...oh, I mean I did, but I never thought my dream would come true.'' And she smiled bashfully at them. Putting the file aside, she picked up the serving knife and pulled a white china plate with gold trim from the stack at her elbow.

Chuckling, Morgan said, ''You've earned the chance, Jenny. And you can cut me an extra large piece, please.''

''Morgan,'' Laura warned lightly, ''you're trying to watch your waistline, darling. Remember?''

Giving the white frosted cake a fond look, he said, "Just a little larger than usual? Chocolate cake is my favorite."

With a short laugh, Jenny sliced him a large piece. Dropping it onto the plate, she said, "Listen, you *deserve* a big piece for giving me this chance. I promise you I won't let you down—I really won't."

And yet, as she cut Laura a much thinner slice of the cake at her request, Jenny was already feeling deep angst. Could she do this? How? She'd never done anything like it before. Yet there wasn't a day that went by when she didn't yearn, heart and soul, to take off on a mission with a merc.

Oh, she had *such* fantasies! Most of the male mercs were young, in their twenties, and they were such good-looking men! Jenny, being single, had a tough time not staring boldly at them like a dog slavering over a nice, big, juicy T-bone steak at times. It took everything she had to keep her eyes on her work, remain professional and not stare like a love-struck teenager at some of the handsome hunks who came through the office.

Her respect and admiration for the women mercs, all of whom had come from the military, was equally high. They were all so poised, and confidence radiated from them like strong rays from the sun. How many times had Jenny ached to have an *ounce* of their self-assurance and poise? In comparison, she saw herself as little more than a scared mouse underfoot. They were all intelligent, too. She knew because she often, in her spare moments, pored over their résumés. The names of the colleges, universities and military academies, were a stunning tribute. Most had graduated from the top ten schools in the United States—a fact that made Jenny that much more respectful and admiring of them. And unlike her, these women were not afraid of anything. They were simply amazing, and Jenny wished many times she had just a little of their courage, their heroism, the guts and brains they had that made their missions successful.

As she cut several more pieces of the cake, she felt her foundation shifting beneath her like quicksand. And yet she had to look strong and appear as if she could pull off this mission. Above all, she couldn't disappoint Morgan. Or Laura, who often patted her on the shoulder and told her how much she was like the women mercs who came through their office. Jenny couldn't see any comparison. What did Laura see in her that she didn't see in herself?

Biting her lower lip, she looked up. Morgan was already digging gingerly into his piece of cake. Laura had sat down next to him and was spreading a linen napkin across her lap.

"Would you like me to distribute the cake to the rest of the office?" Jenny asked.

Morgan shook his head. "No, you just sit down and enjoy your cake with us. I'm going to ask Roy to come in and do that. Today is your day, Jenny. Besides, you're no longer my assistant. You're a merc on a mission now."

With a smile she didn't feel, Jenny tried to sit there and concentrate on eating the cake. She tasted none of it, because her stomach was filled with fluttering butterflies and her heart beat erratically. Her emotions skidded from euphoria to sheer terror. Oh, what if she failed at this? She couldn't stand disappointing Morgan or Laura.

Roy came in, somber and respectful, and wished Jenny a happy birthday. She responded with a smile and thanks as she watched the tall, silver-haired man troop back and forth with plates in hand for the rest of the hard-working office staff outside the doors of the war room. Jenny saw a man, very tall, deeply suntanned, come to a standstill in the doorway after Roy had left with a final piece of cake for himself. It was Matt Davis, she realized, recognizing him as he scanned the room with storm-colored gray eyes. The very merc she'd tripped all over the other day in Morgan's office!

"Matt, come in," Morgan called, and waved him in. "You're just in time." He pointed to the last plate with a slice of cake on it. "Come and have a piece of Jenny's birthday cake. It's time you were properly introduced to your new partner."

Nodding, Matt moved silently into the room. He closed the door quietly behind him. His eyes smarted and burned. Right now, he didn't want to be here. All he wanted was twenty-four hours of uninterrupted sleep. "Yes, sir," he murmured, and turned toward the long, oval table.

Jenny held her breath. Matt Davis. The *famous* Matt Davis. He was one of Morgan's very best mercs—a level four. She'd known his résumé by heart even before he'd come to meet with Morgan. Now, as she studied his eyes, they glittered with a hard intelligence, making her nerves skitter and her pulse race. With his wide, oval face and jutting jaw, that strong nose and full mouth, he was one of the handsomest men she'd ever seen. And he was being assigned to work with her!

Jenny did everything possible to hide her feelings and not stare at him like a lovelorn teenybopper. But how could she help herself? He looked more handsome today than ever, dressed in a pair of comfortable dark brown chinos, a charcoal gray polo shirt beneath a buckskin suede sport coat and black leather cowboy boots. His hair, a raw umber color, was closely cropped in typical military tradition, and the conservative cut emphasized his rugged features. He moved like a prowling cougar across the room toward them, with a sense of tightly coiled energy surrounding him. His assessing eyes never left hers. How did he feel about working with her? Judging from the harsh slant of his mouth, he didn't like it one bit. Jenny cowered within herself, clutching the plate in her lap as if it were a liferaft on a storm-tossed sea.

"Matt, meet Jenny, your boss and teammate for this upcoming mission," Morgan said with a genial smile.

Matt halted in front of blond-haired Jenny. She could barely meet his gaze, she seemed so shy. What a tiny thing she was. He remembered her from the other day in Morgan's office when he'd come to Perseus to receive his next assignment. Hell, she wasn't a merc. Even now she was cowering before him and struggling to look confident. Her chin trembled, tearing at his heavily guarded heart.

"Good to meet you again," Matt rumbled, and he stuck out his hand. Jenny blushed at his reference to their earlier meeting.

Morgan had warned him not to make waves or let Jenny know he really didn't want this assignment with her. She was not a professional merc. She wasn't even in the military.

Jenny gathered her rapidly dissolving courage, lifted her chin and forced herself to stare up into those large, glittering gray eyes of Matt Davis. After all, he wouldn't want a coward for a partner. His hand was so large! she thought as he enfolded it around her petite one. Nevertheless, she accepted his firm, yet careful grip. Cringing inwardly, she knew her own hands were cool and damp with nervousness. His flesh was hard and warm and dry. He wasn't nervous at all.

For a brief, flitting moment, Jenny saw an unknown emotion glint in his assessing eyes. What was it? Disdain? Did he want to curl his lip because she wasn't really a merc? Not a military trained person, but a secretary fulfilling a romantic dream?

Anxiously, she searched his face for some sign of his true feelings toward her and this mission. She saw nothing except that one flicker of emotion in his gray eyes, which were focused on her. As she shook his hand, the plate containing her cake slid off her lap.

''Oh!'' she cried. Leaping up, she instantly released his hand. In leaping, she misjudged the space and bumped into the table with her hip, tottering off balance. Strong, warm hands caught her by the shoulders, lifted her off her feet and set her down again.

Gulping, Jenny couldn't look up at Matt. He must be laughing at her. She was such a klutz! ''Thank you,'' she whispered, completely humiliated once more in his presence. As Matt released her, Jenny crouched down to begin the process of sweeping the cake and frosting off the tightly woven, wheat-colored carpet and putting it back on the plate. Her flesh tingled wildly where his roughened fingers had touched her. Heat swam through her, and she felt a

bit dizzy after unexpected contact with him. Matt
had lifted her up as if she were a feather.

Laura came around the table and helped her pick
up the rest of the errant crumbs. "Accidents happen,
Jenny," she whispered gently. "It's okay. Let me
help you."

"I'm so sorry," Jenny breathed apologetically.
"I'm so clumsy...."

Chuckling, Laura said, "Don't worry about it."

Matt walked around the two women and went
over to the sideboard, where a pot of coffee was
kept warm. He picked up one of the white mugs in
preference to the flowery china cups. Giving Morgan a sideways glance, he saw his boss smile
slightly. Matt knew that look and that smile. It was
a nonverbal order for him to say nothing—and to
be kind—and patient with Jenny.

After pouring the coffee, Matt turned and stood
with cup in hand and watched the two women clean
up the mess on the carpet. Jenny was petite, like a
fine-boned bird. He saw her hands tremble slightly
as she got to her feet. Touching her flaming red
cheek, she unwittingly deposited a splotch of white
frosting on her face. Jenny reminded him of a rab-
bit—a creature without defenses, completely vulnerable. But then, Matt warned himself, no woman
was defenseless. He'd learned that lesson the hard
way.

Jenny rushed out of the room and down the hall

to the rest room, where she dampened some paper towels. Matt Davis was so tall, so strong and silent. She could feel him watching her every move. Oh, why had she wished for a mission? This was just awful. She'd embarrassed herself in front of everyone, when she desperately wanted them to think she was in command of her life and confident. Now she looked like the bumbling klutz she'd been all her life. Matt wouldn't respect her for that. Not at all.

Reentering the room, she saw that Laura had sat back down next to Morgan. She was smiling maternally toward her, and it made Jenny feel a tad better. But not much. Morgan gave her a look that said: *relax.* Matt was looking at her as if she was an alien that had stepped off another planet. She felt like a bug beneath his dark gray microscope gaze. What must he think of her? He had to be silently laughing at her.

Getting down on her hands and knees, she scrubbed the frosting off the carpet. To her surprise, she saw a pair of thick, chino-clad thighs sink down very close to her—Matt, crouching beside her.

''Here, you missed a spot.''

His deep voice vibrated through her as Jenny rocked back on her heels to meet his gaze. Wet paper towels clutched in her hands, she looked up…up into warm gray eyes that made her feel suddenly weak and wonderful. When he used his callused thumb to brush away a smudge of frosting from her left cheek, she inhaled sharply, not expecting this kind of intimacy or care from him. A tender smile lurked at the corners of his mouth as he held up the offending frosting on his thumb.

"Oh…dear…it's all over me, too…" Great! She couldn't even say anything intelligent, much less coherent. She sounded like a breathless, starstruck teenager who'd been touched by her Hollywood idol. Well, hadn't she been? Hadn't she had a crush for Matt Davis for the whole year she'd been here? Yes…but the three times he'd come to her desk for assignment details, he'd treated her coolly, without smiling. Certainly, he hadn't recognized her as a flesh and blood person sitting behind that desk. And the other day she'd practically landed in his lap!

Now, he seemed different. She saw the amusement, the warmth lingering in his eyes as he held his thumb up with the offending white frosting on it. Heat soared up her neck into her face.

"That came off me?" How had it gotten here? Her mind whirled. She was blathering, something she did when she was truly stressed. She was making an utter fool of herself in front of her boss and Matt. Jenny wanted to disappear into thin air.

It didn't happened.

"I admit you're a beautiful birthday girl, but I don't think you need this frosting." Matt gave her a slight, one-cornered smile because he could see how mortified Jenny had become. She was as red as the worst sunburn he'd ever seen. Her blue eyes, luminous and huge, reflected fear, humiliation and embarrassment at his gesture. And where had his words come from? He wasn't given to making compliments toward women. The sky blue of her eyes seemed to become dappled with gold flecks as his words registered with her. For the first time, Matt saw a tinge of hope mingle with the terror and humiliation in her eyes. It was just a simple compliment, no big deal. But he could see it affected her profoundly.

Licking his thumb, he tasted the sweet frosting. Then he grinned a little to try and relieve her of her embarrassment. "See? All gone. Not bad tasting, either." Getting to his feet, he held his hand down toward her. Jenny looked at it woodenly. She appeared frozen by his gallant gesture. When she lifted her chin and gazed up at him, he was once again struck by the childlike trust that emanated from her. Yet she was a twenty-five-year-old woman. And she'd always conducted herself with prim efficiency as Morgan's assistant. Today he was seeing a completely new side to her.

"I don't bite."

Jenny grimaced. Her hand shot out and she gripped his callused fingers. With ease, he brought her to her feet. Instantly, she pulled her hand from his, as if burned. Gripping the wet, sticky paper towels, she whispered unsteadily to all of them, "Excuse me. Let me go get rid of these. I've got to wash my hands.... I'll be right back.''

Matt raised his thick eyebrows as the door shut. He cast a questioning look at Morgan. ''Are you *sure* you want her heading up this mission?''

''I'm positive, Matt. Sit down and have some cake. Jenny's just rattled, is all. She'll settle down if you give her some space.''

Laura cleared her throat and got Matt's attention. ''Be kind to her, Matt. Jenny is a wonderful, open and helpful person. I feel if you can gently guide her, she'll do just fine on this interview mission.''

Reaching for the slice of cake on the plate, he picked up a fork and said, ''This is like baby-sitting my kid sister—not that I ever had one. Jenny's clumsy. And she gets rattled too easily.''

Frowning, Laura said, ''I know this isn't the kind of mission you wanted, Matt, but you were the only merc available. Jenny is an open book. She gets her feelings hurt very easily, and she's supersensitive. She reads body language like a pro.''

''Great,'' he muttered, eating the cake. Not only would he have to watch what he said to her, he'd have to carefully mask his reactions as well.

''There's no danger to this mission,'' Morgan noted. ''You can sort of consider it a minivacation to Peru. Enjoy the country and its people. Just be there for Jenny, support her and let her know she can handle it.''

"Well," Matt drawled as he took another forkful of cake, "at least she's nothing like my shark of an ex-wife." His mouth twisted downward. "At least I'm saved from that on this mission."

## Chapter Three

Matt tried to ignore Jenny, who wriggled like a happy puppy next to him in the first-class section of the Condor Airlines flight they were on. They'd taken a local hop from Montana over to Seattle, Washington, and gotten the international flight down to Lima from there. Jenny reminded him of the frothy, bubbly champagne. And as if sensing he didn't want to talk, she tried her best not to engage him too often in conversation. Instead she focused her attention on her laptop computer, creating questions for her interviews.

Feigning sleep, he had his eyes closed, wrapped his massive arms across his chest and spread out his long legs. Even though there was a wide arm between the tobacco-colored leather seats, he could feel her restlessness. Oh, maybe he was being too harsh toward her. Jenny was in constant movement. Maybe like a butterfly instead of a wriggly puppy. Yes, she was definitely butterfly material. Laughing to himself, Matt derided his protective instincts, which made him want to reach out and soothe Jenny's fractious, ongoing state. She was almost manic. In the airport she had clutched her large, black leather briefcase as if someone was going to steal it from her. Matt had tried to reassure her that this was a level one mission, and no bad guy was going to come out of nowhere to swipe it from her. She'd given him a dirty look that said she didn't believe him.

The corners of his mouth lifted. Jenny was on high alert as they passed through each airport facility, always looking about and studying people around her as if one of them might be "the enemy." Matt didn't have the heart to tell her that wasn't the way spies worked. This was her fantasy—being on a dangerous, undercover mission. Let her have it. Still, he couldn't remove that warmth that was lingering stubbornly around his heart every time he thought of her and her clumsiness or her breathy laughter. Her delft-blue eyes shone with such life. He wondered obliquely how someone like her, at age twenty-five, had escaped all of life's hard knocks.

She behaved as if the world were a wonderful place to be and live in. It wasn't, of course. Never had been. Never would be.

"Mr. Davis? Are you asleep?"

He stifled a chuckle as he felt Jenny's tentative tap on his upper arm. Prying one eye open, he looked at her.

"I'm not now," he rumbled.

"I, uh…well, I thought I'd like to discuss the upcoming interviews with the Apache helicopter pilots." He was looking at her as if she was a bug to be flicked off because he was bothering her. Gulping, Jenny mustered her courage and swept her hand toward the tray in front of her that held her computer. "I'm not in the military," she said, keeping her voice very low so they couldn't be overheard. No telling who might be sitting in front, beside or behind them. Glancing around and giving everyone a suspicious look, she leaned toward Matt as he opened both his eyes and uncrossed his arms.

"I just feel…well, really *awkward* about heading up this mission, Mr. Davis. I know I'm not military, and yet, Morgan wants me to interview the military pilots down there." She gave him a frown. "Over the past two hours I've been putting together some questions we might ask them. I really need your input. I'm nervous about this and don't want to mess it up." Jenny gave a short, insecure laugh. "And believe me, I can screw things up royally. If you could just take a peek at my questions?''

She picked up one page of handwritten questions and waved it in his direction. She saw his brows dip. He sat up and rubbed his face savagely. Jenny cowered inwardly, knowing he was tired. But in five hours they'd be landing in Lima, and she didn't want to try and formulate her interview questions then. She'd be tired by that time!

Matt looked at the tray in front of her. It was filled with neat piles of handwritten notes beside her laptop. Looking down, he saw at least fifteen wadded-up pieces of paper, like popcorn balls, littering the area around her small, dainty feet. Trying not to smile, he saw that she'd pushed off her practical dark brown shoes. For the flight she had dressed in a dark purple silk suit that brought out the color of her eyes and her burnished gold hair. Now he saw she had a pair of dark purple cotton socks on her feet. He'd meant to tell her how pretty she looked, especially with the dainty gold-and-amethyst earrings and matching choker, which held a teardrop-shaped amethyst pendant around her slender throat. With little effort, she looked both professional and feminine at the same time.

''Let's see what you've come up with,'' he muttered.

The male flight attendant came by and asked if they'd like anything to drink. Both said no.

Jenny sat there chewing on her lower lip, her eyes flicking from Matt's hard, unreadable face to his compressed mouth. He had a beautifully shaped mouth. She sighed inwardly and tried to contain the excitement and trepidation she felt as he went over her questions. Moving restlessly in the seat, she could barely contain herself.

"Well?" she ventured, concealed fear in her tone. "I know they're probably pretty awful, being that I've never been in the military...."

Glancing at her, Matt saw the worry and anxiety written all over her oval face. Such angst in someone her age...what had set her up to respond like this? Had she been overly criticized in her family? Had her parents been perfectionists when she was a child? Even the way Jenny held herself, so erect and stiff, as if expecting a physical blow, made him scowl.

"No...these questions are good. They're insightful." He tapped the paper with his index finger. "I like the fact that you're asking questions on a human level, rather than a military one."

Gawking at him, her mouth fell open. "You do? You mean you like them? They aren't awful?"

Setting the paper down in his lap, he focused his full attention on her. "Jenny...may I call you that? Or do you prefer Ms. Wright?"

"Er...no, call me Jenny, please. I hate standing on formality, if the truth be known...."

Nodding, he forced a sliver of a smile for her benefit. He was finding out Laura had been right about Jenny's ability to read body language big time. "Fine. Call me Matt, okay?"

She nodded hesitantly. Old habits died hard. At the office, he was always Mr. Davis. Jenny never called any of the mercenaries by their first names. When she saw his mouth curve faintly, relief shot through her. Even his gray eyes warmed a bit as he looked at her. It was much easier to deal with than his focused inspection.

"Good," he murmured. "I need to know a little about you. About your background. That will help me to help you in formulating your base questions."

The sincerity in his voice shook her, and the earnestness in his slate-colored eyes warmed her to her quaking, cowardly soul. Jenny had never expected that her questions would be worthy of the interview, much less meet with Matt Davis's approval.

Choking, she looked at him in disbelief. "You…want to know about *me?*"

With a nonchalant shrug he said, "Why not? You're my partner on this mission."

"I see…."

"You know, for all your friendliness and helpfulness, you're a closed book."

Wincing, Jenny looked down at the handful of papers in her hand. "I'm afraid I haven't led a very exciting life…Matt, and I really don't want to bore you with my life story.''

*Such a cream puff.* And a delicious one. Matt stopped himself from reaching out to stroke her hair, which looked deliciously mussed. Jenny wore no makeup and the way her blond hair fell soft and straight around her face made her look like a pixie. She looked so young. Yet he saw pain in her eyes and he wondered why. ''Want to play twenty questions, then?''

She managed a weak smile. ''No, you don't have to dig. I'll tell you. But I warn you, you'll probably be snoring like you were five minutes before I woke you up.''

His brows raised. ''I was snoring?''

Chuckling shyly, Jenny said, ''It wasn't loud or anything. Your head was tipped back, was all. A person's tongue relaxes when they sleep, and I'm sure yours was up against your windpipe, which was why you were snoring.''

Giving her a look of respect, he said, ''You're just a font of information, aren't you?''

Touching her cheeks, which were heating up beneath his dark, unrelenting inspection, Jenny felt her heart beating erratically. Did the man know he could charm even the meanest snake with those eyes of his? She wanted desperately to drown in his warm gaze. Just the hint of one corner of his mouth lifting upward sent her heart soaring with unaccountable joy. When he smiled, that hard mask fell away and she got a look at the real Matt Davis. She blossomed beneath his attention, especially when he gave her that crooked smile.

"One of my foster mothers always said I was a jack-of-all-trades and master of none," she began ruefully in answer to his question. "I know just enough about a lot of things to be dangerous, I guess." Waving her hands nervously, she added, "I have such a problem sticking with one thing and finishing it. I'm a Pisces, you see. My moon's in Gemini and I have Libra rising. I'm full of air and water, and the two don't mix very well, so I'm always at odds with myself. At least, that's what she said."

*Foster* mother? Matt scowled at how nervous Jenny was now. He saw the worry in her eyes, and the way the corners of her soft, delicious mouth pulled in. "I don't know much about astrology," he admitted.

"You're a Scorpio!" She blurted the words before she could stop herself. Slapping a hand over her mouth, she gazed at him wide-eyed as he tilted his head and regarded her in the silence.

"You got my birthdate from my personnel record?"

She nodded, her stomach sinking.

"I see."

Allowing her hand to drop from her lips, she said

in a breathless tone, "Don't worry. The information won't go anywhere. I know Scorpio people want their privacy. And they don't like people who talk about them to other people, either. They're very, very intense. Very focused. That's why you're so good at being a merc. You're a natural warrior. You know how to gauge people. Your perceptions are rarely wrong, either."

"I'm impressed. You almost make me sound like a good guy." He saw her frown and then shift restlessly in the leather seat. "So what about yourself? How about your growing-up years? Where were you born?"

Jenny's mouth quirked. Her stomach tightened. She knew Matt had come from a very prestigious and rich family. He'd been at the Naval Academy and finished in the top five percent of his class. He'd earned medals as a SEAL during the Gulf War. He'd been the head of his team until he'd quit to come and work for Perseus. She also knew, from the personal history in his file, that his parents had been married for over thirty years: the Davises were a happy family, no doubt. Matt had an older sister, a medical doctor who had graduated from Princeton University with honors. Jenny's hands hands fluttered helplessly as she answered his question. "I was born in Medford, Oregon."

"Oregon's a nice place. I've often fished for trout up in the Cascade Mountains above that little town.'' Somehow, Matt found himself wanting to alleviate the tension around her lovely mouth and erase the fear from her eyes. ''Did you ever go fishing in Klamath Lake, which is near there? Or fish for steelhead trout on the Rogue River?''

She shook her head and looked out the plane window. The sky was a bright blue, with high, filmy cirrus clouds. ''Uh, no...''

''Not a fisherperson?'' he teased. She refused to look at him. Now her hands were clenched, white-knuckled, in the lap of her dark purple skirt.

Softly, she answered, ''No...I don't like hurting anything. It pains me to even think of putting a sharp hook into a poor, defenseless little worm. It has no way of protecting itself from us...what we might do to it. Humans are a lot stronger, and sometimes brutal....''

Matt scowled. He heard a lot of pain in Jenny's voice. In fact, he could barely hear her, her voice had gone so soft. Her face had drained of color and she was pale. Very pale. And now she was sitting very, very still. His gut crawled with trepidation. Realizing he was stepping into very raw territory regarding her personal life, he said in a rasping tone, ''Don't mind me. Sometimes I'm like a damn bull in a china shop. I don't know when to stop asking questions. My ex-wife will confirm my dazzling skills in that regard.''

Turning her head, she met and held his stormy

eyes. Once again, Jenny was seeing him without that armorlike mask in place. Now he was searching and unsure of himself. She'd never have thought *anything* could rattle the heroic Matt Davis, decorated navy hero. Especially something she said. Her. A mouse. A ordinary person who had never accomplished anything of note in life. Except to be a great assistant to Morgan Trayhern. And she had also gotten a degree in psychology. She was proud of that accomplishment, too. But it wasn't the same as saving lives, like Matt did.

"My life," Jenny began quietly, "isn't anything to write home about." Shrugging, she opened her hands and said, "I was taken from my mother, who was a crack addict, when I was born. She died when I was a year old. I don't really remember anything about her.... I was turned over to the state, and over the next eighteen years, I went through five foster homes." She saw his brows gather grimly. And she saw sympathy reflected in his eyes. Heartened that he wasn't going to make fun of her, or tell her that she was less worthy in his view, she added, "I guess maybe that's why I went into psychology—to try and understand myself. I was hyperactive in kindergarten. I couldn't sit still. I disrupted the class. They said it was because my mother was a drug addict. But I never touched drugs—never wanted to. After I left my last foster home, I went to Bryn Mawr and worked to get a degree. I had to do something to prove to myself I wasn't totally a worthless human being.''

She tapped her head. ''I still have ADD—attention deficit disorder. When I was a kid they tried to drug me up to my eyeballs, in an attempt to calm me down. I just have a different way of working and thinking than most people. I thought becoming a psychologist would help me…to try and figure out who I am…or what I could be…. Oh, I know I'm a scaredy-cat. I screech if I see a spider…or a snake.'' Jenny shivered, placed her arms around herself and made a face. ''I really do leap up on a chair if I see a mouse. I'm such a coward. After all, I'm much bigger than any tiny little mouse or teeny spider or other creepy-crawly.'' She sighed sadly. ''I'm such a mess.''

''There're plenty of people who've come from broken homes,'' Matt said. ''And they go on to make something of themselves in life. That's nothing to be ashamed of, Jenny. You weren't the drug addict, your mother was. You were the innocent in all this.'' Without thinking, he lifted his hand and gently stroked her small, slumped shoulders.

Matt's touch was magical. As his strong fingers moved across her tightly knotted shoulders, she closed her eyes. His touch was healing. She felt the warmth of his hand, the strength, but also the tenderness of his touch. Amazed that such a large man could be so gentle, she released a long, pent-up sigh.

Opening her eyes as his hand lifted away, she managed a sliver of a smile.

"You're being very kind. Thank you. I know you don't have to be. You're a hero ten times over. You don't have to put up with little people, like myself." Her mouth quirked and she avoided his gaze. "I'm sure you didn't want this mission with me. Oh, not that anyone's said anything...." Jenny lifted her hands. "You're probably doing this because Morgan asked you to. I know how he sometimes puts pressure on a merc, to get them to team with someone they've never worked with before."

Just the flittery look in Jenny's narrowed blue eyes made Matt's heart wrench. "Whoa!" he murmured. "Slow down, will you?"

"I know...I talk a mile a minute. It's that Gemini moon of mine. We Geminis blather all the time. People like me don't know when to shut up."

"I'm interested in what you're saying, but you're running along at Mach 3 with your hair on fire, and I can't get a question in edgewise."

Laughing, Jenny nodded. "Fair enough. Okay, I'll shut up and you ask what you want." She couldn't believe that he didn't think less of her because of her background.

As Matt sat up, the look in his eyes set her heart palpitating for no reason. Maybe it was his unexpected touch. She would never forget that wonderful feeling of his hand sliding across her shoulders. Even now her flesh tingled.

Looking down and studying her questions more thoroughly, he murmured, ''For someone who has ADD, you've done a very nice, disciplined and thoughtful job creating these questions. Looking at your work, I wouldn't ever think you had attention problems.''

Making a frustrated noise, Jenny wrinkled her nose. ''I was so afraid that Morgan wouldn't hire me when I told him I had ADD. People like me often make a thorough mess of everything, Matt.'' She gestured nervously toward the notes he held. ''My mind works differently. I see things—letters and words—differently from the normal population. I've had to retrain and reteach myself how to think and do things your way, not mine.'' She managed a small smile of triumph. ''It was hard, but I really wanted to do it, to fit in, you know?''

''Growing up, did you stand out at school?'' Matt saw the instant anguish in her eyes. Jenny avoided his incisive gaze and clenched her hands in her lap again. He was discovering that when he hit a painful nerve in Jenny, she would naturally assume that cowering position.

''It was *awful*,,'' she admitted softly, her voice wobbly with tears. ''I was put back into a remedial class. A lot of kids made fun of me. They called me stupid. A geek. And it got so bad I just hid. I ran from them in the halls when I saw the cliques coming toward me to tease me.'' She nervously touched her hair. ''I wasn't pretty. I was such a stick compared to the other girls...and no boy would ever look at me. They called me Fraidy Cat. That was my name in school. The boys would put plastic spiders and bugs in my chair, or they'd throw them in my hair, or the girls would drop one on my tray in the cafeteria....'' Sighing, Jenny forced herself to look up at Matt. His face was thundercloud dark with anger. At first she thought he was angry at her. But when he unexpectedly reached out and gripped her hand, and she felt his gentle strength around her clammy fingers, Jenny knew different.

''Kids can be brutal,'' he growled. ''No wonder you're so jumpy as an adult.''

Matt didn't want to let go of her hand. He saw Jenny's eyes grow tender as he held and gently squeezed her damp, cool fingers. Every protective instinct he owned rose to the surface. With the pieces of information she was divulging to him, he could understand why she was excruciatingly nervous and flighty. Her ADD made her restless, so that she could never sit still for long periods of time. And he'd mistaken that for manic activity. It had never crossed his mind that Jenny might have ADD. Giving her fingers another squeeze, he forced himself to let go of them.

''Listen to me, Jenny. Will you?''

"Sure." She sat quietly, her fingers tingling in her lap. Oh, how she enjoyed his touches! Never in a million years would Jenny have thought Matt Davis, military hero, would have such a tender side to him. She felt like a wilted flower thriving beneath the sunlight of his care and concern. Her heart flooded with such joy that it took her breath away. Trying to sit passive beneath his scrutiny, she waited for him to speak.

"You know what? I like you just the way you are. It makes me respect you a lot more knowing what you've gone through." He tapped the papers in his hand. "These questions are excellent. They cut to the heart of the matter, reach the core of the interviewee. You couldn't create insightful questions like this if you didn't have intelligence and a very good grasp of the human condition. As a merc, I strive to maintain similar qualities because it keeps us alive out in the field. You've got the right stuff, Jenny. It shows here." He tapped the papers again. "You're very good at what you do. Even if you have to hang off chandeliers and do it upside down, what does that matter? What counts is the product. And it doesn't bother me that you're restless or that you talk fast. I like to hear your thoughts, what's in that big heart of yours, and how you see the world."

Matt saw her eyes widening at every statement he made about her. Then her face went rose-red as she blushed to the roots of her blond hair. "And as for being a 'fraidy cat, well, let me share this with you. I'm afraid all the time. The only thing that might be different between us is that I don't over-react in the moment. I try to handle my fear and keep thinking clearly through it." He managed a slight smile. "Where we're going, there's going to be a lot of bugs and spiders because it's jungle. But my bet is that you can use this situation to work through your fear and try to keep thinking, despite how you feel. I have faith in you, Jenny. And you know what else? I think Morgan picked the perfect person to head up this mission. I wouldn't have been able to create the questions you have. I don't have the training. I'm not a psychologist. You obviously know people, know how to touch them on a very deep, core level."

Choking back a lump that was forming quickly in her throat, Jenny stared at him. She was in shock. Finally, she whispered, "I—I've never had anyone give me so many compliments all at once. Are you sure you mean them? You aren't just saying that because you feel sorry for me?"

To hell with it. Matt reached out and grazed her flaming red cheek with his thumb. Again her eyes went a soft, velvet blue, and he knew his touch had a positive and magical affect on her. It was impos-sible *not* to touch Jenny. And it had been a helluva long time since he'd wanted to touch a woman like he was touching her. Maybe it was her vulnerability that brought out his own vulnerable side, which he'd carefully hidden from the world.

"As you get to know me better, Jenny, you'll know I'm not the most diplomatic person around. I am honest, though. To a fault. And sometimes—" Matt grimaced "—sometimes my shoot-from-the-hip honesty hurts the other person unintentionally."

"Honesty is good. Truth never goes out of style." She nodded and looked away. "You really think I'm cut out for this mission? I've had such angst about it. I worry you won't think I can carry my end of things. I worry that you'll think I'm nothing. Worthless. And I worry that you think you have to baby-sit me because Morgan twisted your arm."

Breaking out into quiet laughter, Matt raised his eyes upward. "You *are* a worrywart, Jenny. No doubt about it." When he saw her wince, he added gently, "I can handle your worry. What you have to do is put to rest all those other items. None of them are true. I'm glad I'm on this mission. And yes, Morgan did twist my arm—a little. And no, I didn't think you had what it took until I saw your questions and got more info on you as a person. Adding it all up now, I'm very confident about the mission, and you. Morgan was right—you need to be in charge. I'll be here to support you when you ask for my help. Frankly speaking, I think you're going to do a helluva good job. I think you'll be able to pick the right three volunteers for those missions.''

Jenny sat there, astonishment flowing through her. The sincerity in Matt's voice and that incredible warmth in his slate-colored eyes filled her with a happiness she'd never, ever experienced before. He believed in her. And in her heart she knew he wasn't lying. Her self-esteem got a big boost. Because of his belief in her, she felt the first trickle of actual confidence in herself and the mission.

Impulsively, she reached out and slid her hand against his sandpapery cheek. Though he'd shaved early this morning, that five o'clock shadow was there, making him look even more dangerously handsome. She saw his eyes narrow instantly as she briefly caressed him. Her heart pounded when she recognized the look in his eyes: the look of a hunter stalking his prey—*her*. Jenny didn't know what to think or say. She'd never seen a man look at her like Matt Davis was right now—with desire. Blatant, raw desire.

A warmth stirred deep within her, and that took her off guard, as well. Now her whole body was responding to his smoldering, dark look. Egads, what was going on? She felt unsure of herself in so many ways.

Jerking her hand away from his cheek, she quickly tucked it back in her lap and looked away.

"I never expected this.... You're so kind and caring...."

It took everything Matt had not to sweep Jenny into his arms and hold her. Simply hold her. That's what she needed. She needed someone to praise her. To tell her that she was a good person, capable of intelligent work. Stiffening his arms at his sides to make sure he didn't do anything he might regret, he rumbled, "You bring all this out in me. It's you."

## Chapter Four

Jenny tried to swallow her surprise as they stood in the office of Gringo Bill's Hostel with the owner, Margerite Kaiser.

"You're in room 35, Senor Williams. You and your wife will be on the top floor, with a complete view of the plaza, not to mention beautiful Machu Picchu."

A short woman with a cloud of curly black hair, Margerite smiled as she lifted a key from the box on the wall, her brown eyes sparkling.

Jenny gulped. *Wife?* Was that what the woman had called her? Frantically, she searched her sleep-deprived brain for this detail of their mission, but came up empty. They had landed at Lima at 4:30 a.m. and caught the first flight out to Cuzco, at 5:20. From there they'd taken the Inca train down to Agua Caliente. Now, as she watched Matt lean over the desk and sign a fictitious name, she tried to recall if he or Morgan had mentioned they would be traveling as man and wife. All undercover agents went by fictitious names, but posing as Matt's *wife?* And then Jenny remembered reading somewhere in the back of the report that Matt and she would pose as a couple, tourists from North America—Matt and Jenny Williams. She was no longer Jenny Wright, single woman from Montana.

"Thank you, Señora Kaiser," Matt murmured, as he picked up the key. He turned and smiled down at Jenny. "Ready for our adventure, darling?"

Blinking belatedly, Jenny realized he was using that intimate, dark tone to speak to *her.* "Why, er…yes. Yes, I am, honey…."

"Sounds like you two need some sleep," Marguerite chuckled. Looking at her watch, she said, "It's 2:00 p.m. I suggest you take a nap. You'll feel better after three hours or so of rest. And then when you get up, go over to India Feliz for dinner. It's the best restaurant we have in Agua Caliente."

Jenny thanked the warm hostess and headed out of the small office with Matt. The hostel was beautiful, in her opinion—three stories high and made from river rocks gathered from the mighty Urubamba River, which ran no more than a tenth of a mile from the main plaza, where Gringo Bill's was located. Even here in the lobby she could hear the roar of the river as it splashed over huge granite and lava boulders littering its path. Walking from the train station, she had watched the wild, frothing water swirl and bubble around the behemoth boulders. Now, as she passed a stunning oval planter filled with jungle foliage and fragrant orchids in the center of the lobby, Jenny was glad she was here. There was high humidity at this time of day and she was perspiring freely. In Cuzco, Matt had taken her shopping for some loose cotton slacks and tops to replace her silk suit, which she had no business wearing in such a climate.

Climbing the cobbled stone stairs to the third floor, she noted the colorfully painted doors to the rooms, each a different hue. "This place reminds me of a rainbow," she told Matt as they climbed steadily upward. Impulsively, Jenny skipped up ahead of him.

"This is a nice place," he agreed. Balancing their two pieces of luggage in his hands, Matt watched her run up the stairs like a graceful deer. Her hair, although straight, responded to the high humidity. Soft strands curled around her brow and cheeks, giving her a girlish look. Her eyes sparkled like deep blue sapphires, and he found himself grinning. There was nothing to dislike about Jenny Wright.

She was the diametric opposite of his ex-wife, who didn't have a spontaneous bone in her body.

Hurrying down the concrete passageway and reading the numbers as she went, Jenny finally spotted room 35 at the very end. Opening the door, she stood aside as Matt brought the luggage into the spacious, carpeted, L-shaped room. As she closed it, her heart sank. There was one queen-size bed in the room, and that was it.

Standing there, she watched Matt place the luggage on the bed and begin to unzip his suitcase. "There's only one bed," she said lamely.

Matt nodded. "When you pose as a married couple, there's usually only one bed."

"Wh-what did you do in the past when your partner was a woman?" Morgan always paired a man and a woman on Perseus assignments. He'd found that the two usually complemented each other, both providing unique and necessary skills to the operation. Just because they worked together didn't mean there was anything but a professional relationship between them, however. So how did they handle such a situation? Jenny wondered.

Her heart skittered at the thought of sleeping here, with Matt only inches away from her. She wasn't afraid of him, of what he might do. She was afraid of what *she* might do to him during her sleep! Even in sleep, she was restless and always on the move.

Opening dresser drawers, Matt deposited all his

clothes into them. "We slept on the same bed together. Why?"

Jenny moved over to her luggage and started filling dresser drawers on the opposite side of the room. "I just didn't think about this ruse of being married...what it would entail."

Giving her an amused look, Matt murmured, "Relax, you're safe, Jenny. I'll stay on my side of the bed, if that's what you're worried about." He held up a pair of blue cotton pajamas. "I even brought pj's, see? Normally, I sleep naked, but since you're along, I thought I'd better dress for the occasion."

Her eyes grew huge. She gulped. Matt decided to stop teasing her, and folded the pajamas into the bottom drawer.

"You wanted an undercover assignment. This is what it's like," he said, stuffing his empty canvas bag beneath the bed.

Busying herself, Jenny said, "Right...yes, of course, you're right." Her heart bounded. "I'm worried I might keep you up at night. I squirm in my sleep. I'm restless...I talk. Sometimes I sleepwalk...." She babbled as she quickly stuffed her three days' worth of clothes into the drawers.

"We'll work it out," he soothed. Matt went to the banks of windows lining two sides of the room, all opened to allow in the fresh, clean air. Below them was the concrete plaza, a long, rectangular school topped with a Spanish-tile red roof on one side, a gray stone Catholic church on the other, and the Inka Pizza Restaurant anchoring the third. Up the wide main street, which was littered with *touristas* from around the world, brightly painted buildings were squeezed together in an unending line, and looked like boxcars hooked up to one another. Untying the thick, dark green curtains at the side of the windows, Matt drew them closed so that there was a modicum of darkness in the room.

"You've got to be tired," he said. Sitting down on the edge of the bed, he unlaced his Ecco hiking boots and nudged them off his large feet. Well-made boots indicated to anyone who recognized them that he was a serious climber and hiker. Rich *touristas* always wore them here in Peru. It was like wearing Gucci shoes in Italy.

Jenny turned and stood by the dresser, her arms wrapped around herself. "I guess I am," she replied, studying him. Matt looked exhausted. She saw dark circles beneath his eyes and felt a twinge of worry for him. The flight had been long and stressful.

Matt finished removing his boots, placed his large, square hands on his thighs and looked over at her. "You guess? I'm ready to fall over. Come on, I'll share the bed with you." He lay down with a sigh, taking the space nearest the pale green stucco wall.

Chewing her lower lip, Jenny said, "Uh...you go ahead and sleep for a while, Matt. I'm a little too wired to try and rest right now." She hurried over to the window and looked down at the plaza. School had just gotten out, and children of all ages, looking neat and clean in their blue-and-white school uniforms, were gathering to play soccer. Their laughter drifted upward, and she smiled faintly. She loved children.

"I'll just go down to the plaza, Matt. If I stay up here, I'll fritter around and drive you crazy, and you'll never get to sleep." She smiled as she saw a group of five-, six- and seven-year-olds beginning to choose teams for the game. Their mothers, all in colorful native costumes, sat on the steps of the school, knitting or crocheting as they kept a maternal eye on their children. A number of elderly people had gathered to watch the game, too. "There're lots of benches all around the plaza. I'll just sit down there on one of them. I've got to come down from this trip. I'll watch the children and rest up that way."

He closed his eyes. "Okay, have it your way. You got the room key?"

"Yes. Go to sleep. I'll keep busy, don't worry." If the truth be known, Jenny was absolutely petrified of lying on that bed alongside Matt. She wasn't sure what she'd do tonight, but right now, at least, she'd been granted a reprieve. Hurrying to the door, she picked up her purse, and her floppy, wide-brimmed straw hat, and left as quietly as she could. Relieved that Matt didn't know why she was really leaving the room, she hurried down the three flights of stairs.

Gringo Bill's sat on one corner of the main plaza. As she walked down the sloping street leading into the plaza, Jenny noted the sky was a pale blue with white puffs of clouds here and there. She spied a green bench on the sidelines near where the children were playing soccer, and hurried to it, breathing a sigh of relief.

Looking around, she saw the magnificent loaflike, black mountain of Machu Picchu, thrusting its mighty nose upward, to a height of ten thousand feet. The sides of the black basalt-and-granite peak were covered with greenery—thousands upon thousands of bromeliads and orchids. Agua Caliente sat at six thousand, Jenny knew. She was glad that she lived in Philipsburg, Montana, which was near that same altitude. It made it easier for her to breathe, acclimated as she was.

As she sat down on the bench, a woman in a brown felt hat with a dark umber grogram ribbon around the crown joined her. Though the woman was little more than five feet tall, she was big boned and strong-looking. Her oval face and high cheekbones shouted of her Inca heritage, as did her ebony hair, plaited into two thick braids. She wore a red blouse embroidered with bright flowers and a well-worn, dark brown alpaca cardigan with white llamas on it. As she smiled and nodded deferentially in Jenny's direction, Jenny noticed that her front two upper teeth were missing.

Jenny smiled and said hello in Spanish. The woman brightened. In her hands were several colorful, hand-knit alpaca sweaters, obviously for sale. At her side was a little boy about four years old—too young for school—holding on to his mother's dark blue cotton skirt.

*"Hola,"* Jenny said warmly to him. She dug in her pants pocket. Matt had bought a couple bags of hard candy in Cuzco, explaining that the local children loved getting candy from the tourists. Producing a gold-wrapped piece of candy, she asked the woman if she could give it to her little one.

*"Sí, sí, señorita."* The woman glowed and bowed her head, thanking Jenny effusively.

*"Bueno,* good," Jenny said, and handed the candy to the shy little tyke. His dark brown hand reached out, his black, buttonlike eyes riveted on her hair. Jenny figured he probably hadn't seen many blond-haired people down here, sure Indians comprised the bulk of the population of Peru, with their black hair and darker coloring.

"Tank u…"

Surprised that he spoke English, she smiled at the mother. *"Habla inglés?* Do you speak English?"

"A little," the woman said proudly.

"Wonderful. *Bueno!* I'm Jenny. And you are?" she asked the woman.

"Maria." She looked fondly at her little boy, who had now inched forward and was sucking furiously on the piece of hard candy. "And this is Daniel, my son."

Leaning down, Jenny smiled into the child's bright, curious eyes. "*Hola,* Daniel." She put her hand out to him. "Nice to meet you."

He stuck out his sticky hand, his fingers small and fine. Jenny gently shook it and released it.

"Here, *señorita,*" Maria produced a clean damp cloth from her skirt pocket. "Your hand, eh?"

Thanking her, Jenny wiped her sweet, sticky fingers off. "It's my fault. I gave him the candy."

"*Señorita,*" Maria pleaded as she brought her merchandise forward, "would you like to buy one of my fine alpaca sweaters? I knit each by hand."

Jenny watched as the woman carefully laid out the exquisite hand-knit sweaters before her. "They're all so beautiful, Señora Maria." And soft, she thought as she ran her fingers lingeringly across the fuzzy, brightly dyed wool.

"You would look very pretty in this one," the Peruvian woman said shyly, avoiding her eyes. "The colors go with your Inti hair."

"Inti?"

"*Sí.* Inti is our sun god. Your hair is the color of

him," she said, pointing upward toward the mountains, where the sun had just disappeared. "Gold hair. It is truly beautiful."

Seeing the woman's wistful expression, Jenny smiled. "I think black hair is beautiful, too." She reached down and sifted her fingers through Daniel's short, neatly cut hair. One thing for sure, the Peruvian people were proud of their children. Nowhere in the plaza, which was hopping with life, did she see one child with dirty clothes or a dirty face. Their clothes were clean, if threadbare, and their faces had been scrubbed until they shone like polished mahogany. There were no runny noses, no matted eyelashes or dirty, unkempt hair. Matt had told her that although Peru was considered a third-world nation, the people were very progressive. They thought everything of their children and family. Cleanliness was obviously a priority.

Daniel shyly opened his hand toward her after he finished the piece of candy, to ask for more.

"Another?" she laughed, and looked to his mother for permission. Maria smiled fondly at her son and nodded.

"He is the last of our babies," she told Jenny sadly. "My other two babies, they die. The water. It is no good." She patted Daniel's head gently, her eyes holding a worried look.

Heart cringing, Jenny sat stunned. "The water?"

"*Sí, señorita.* Here, we have no good water. They

tell us to boil it. But my other two children, both older than Daniel, they drank from the river.'' She closed her eyes and wiped the tears from the corners. ''I begged them to always drink the water I had boiled. But they did not listen. Now…'' she sniffed ''…they are gone. I pray to Inti daily to watch over Daniel. That the poison water of the river does not take him, too.''

''Oh, dear…'' Jenny reached out and patted the woman's hand. Maria was in her early thirties, but already the hardness of her life had left her oval face lined and stressed. ''I'm so sorry, Maria. I truly am.'' If she'd lost two of her children, Jenny was sure she'd look as tired and sad as Maria—or worse. How could the woman go on after such a loss?

''We need wells drilled here,'' Maria confided in a broken tone. ''Wells, they say, will give us clean, safe water. And we are so poor…. But it would save our children's lives. I wish we had the money to make these wells….''

Anguished, Jenny sat there in silence. Daniel, who had now lost much of his shyness, climbed up into her lap to rest his head against her left shoulder, his eyes turned upward to look more closely at her golden hair. As she rocked the boy in her arms, Jenny couldn't fathom losing someone as beautiful and cute as Daniel. Looking at Maria's grief-stricken eyes, she felt her heart quiver with sadness for the woman.

"Well," she murmured gently as she reached out with her free hand and patted the knitwear, "I really need sweaters, *señora.* I have a good friend back home who would love one. And I certainly need one!"

Instantly, Maria's eyes lit up. "Yes? Two sweaters, *señorita?*"

"These are all sweaters for women. Do you knit any for men? I have a very dear friend who is *muy grande,* very large. Do you have any big ones?"

"*Sí, sí, señorita,* I do. But they are at my home." She pointed up the concrete street leading from one side of the plaza.

Jenny smiled. "Why don't we walk to your house? I would love to see all the sweaters you've knitted. They're so beautiful. I'd love to buy at least three." In the back of her mind, Jenny thought that Maria could use the money. She saw that her leather shoes were thin and full of holes. Although they were clean and polished, they were well past their prime.

"*Sí, señorita!*" Maria got up and gathered all her sweaters, carefully placing each into a bag before she slung it across her shoulder. She called to Daniel to climb down, but the little boy shook his head.

Laughing, Jenny rose and straddled Daniel's legs across her left hip, her arm around him. "I'll carry him, *señora.* Don't worry."

"You are sure, *señorita?*"

Jenny patted the woman's shoulder. Maria was shorter than she was, but strong and firm from all the work she did. "I'm very sure. Let's go! I'm excited to see all your sweaters."

Matt awoke with a jerk. It was nearly dark. What time was it? He groaned and rolled over onto his side. Uncovering the black nylon flap across his chronograph watch, he saw it was 1800, or 6:00 p.m.

The door opened, creaking and squealing in protest. He sat up, his eyes narrowing. It was Jenny. Her arms were loaded with goods, he saw, as she turned and nudged the door shut with the toe of her boot.

"I see I can't leave you by yourself. You'll buy out Agua Caliente," he observed in a gravelly tone.

Jenny jumped. She let out a little gasp. She hadn't expected Matt to be up, and was trying to be quiet about entering the room. Nearly spilling her cargo, she brought the plastic bags over to the bed where he was sitting.

Laughing breathily, she said, "I'm going to turn the light on. You have to see the gorgeous, hand-knitted alpaca sweaters I just bought. And what bargain prices!"

Matt smiled a little as she bounded effortlessly back to the door and turned on the overhead light. He rubbed his eyes and felt the sleep easing from him. Jenny sat on the other side of the pile of plastic bags and quickly began pulling out the sweaters for him to look at.

"You never told me we could get beautiful alpaca sweaters down here, Matt. Look!" She held up a dark burgundy one with red, pink and orange hibiscus against a dark green, leafy background. "This is for Laura. Isn't it breathtaking? Do you think she'll like it?"

He opened his mouth to speak. By the time he did, Jenny had pulled out a second one—a big one that was obviously for a man.

"And I found this one for Morgan. It's huge! But so is he. Do you think he'll like it? Señora Maria had five men's sweaters, but I loved the dusty gold, earthy browns and red and orange woven in this one. It looks like autumn to me. Does it to you? Do you really think he'll like it?"

Matt laughed. "Are you interested in my answer or are you going to keep asking me a hundred questions first?"

Grinning, Jenny said, "Guilty. I'm sorry, Matt. I'm just so excited!"

"I can see that." Matt liked her angelic smile, and her shining blue eyes, which showed every nuance of what lay in her generous heart. Her mouth, soft and parted, beckoned to him. *Hands off,* Matt reminded himself, groaning inwardly. Jenny wasn't someone to stalk and capture. No, she was a butterfly, a beautiful creature not to be caught and tamed. One could only watch it flit freely about on the air currents, moving at will from flower to flower. Such was Jenny. His butterfly.

"Well?" she pressed eagerly. "What do you think? Will Morgan and Laura like them?"

He picked up the sweaters, turned them around and studied them thoroughly. As he handed them back to Jenny, who neatly folded them, he said, "I think they'll like them. Laura, from what I can tell, wears bright colors. And Morgan wears a lot of brown and gold."

Sighing dramatically, Jenny collapsed with relief. "Whew! I was so worried, Matt. I felt so sorry for Señora Maria and her son, Daniel. They're so wretchedly poor." Her voice became strained. "You should see their house. It's nothing more than a few pieces of corrugated tin all jury-rigged together with wire. They sleep on a dirt floor. A dirt floor! Can you imagine? I can't. She was so kind. She made me coca leaf tea and offered me something to eat, but I just couldn't, Matt. I didn't want to take food out of their mouths. It was awful. I just never realized…. We're so spoiled. So rich, in comparison. My heart just bled for her. And she works all day and all night for her family. She showed me the alpaca yarn that she's dyed, for the sweaters she knits. She makes money washing people's clothes down at that smaller river that flows into the Urubamba, on the steep bank just below her hut. She works so hard! I swear, I'll never complain again when I've got to work a few extra hours at the office. I'll always remember Maria and her working conditions.''

''You're such a softy, Jenny Wright.'' He placed his hand on her shoulder and squeezed it gently. When she gave him a rueful look, Matt saw the tears in her eyes she fought to keep back. She'd tucked her lower lip between her teeth in an effort to stem them. ''I like the fact you're so deeply touched by these people.''

Sniffing, she shrugged and absorbed his warm, unexpected touch. Matt's face was open. He was, once again, accessible to her. The darkness beneath his eyes had dissolved and he looked incredibly well rested despite the long flight they'd recently endured. ''How could anyone *not* be touched by it, Matt? The Peruvian people are so friendly and kind. I just love them!''

''And so,'' he said, mirth in his tone as he forced himself to take his hand off her shoulder, ''you bought a gazillion sweaters to help her out, to put food in her family's mouth. Right?''

She gazed in awe at him. ''How did you know?''

With a shake of his head, Matt said in a rasping tone, ''Jenny, you have a heart as big as Montana.'' Looking at the sweaters, he gave her a wry grin. ''So…did you buy me one, too?''

## Chapter Five

For once in her life, Jenny decided, she was going to display courage in the face of the unknown. As she showered in their bathroom and got ready for bed after the wonderful meal she'd shared with Matt at the India Feliz Restaurant earlier, she made a promise not to act like a nervous Nellie about sharing the same bed with him. He'd made it very clear he was going to be a gentleman. Besides, he wouldn't have any interest in her. She was a 'fraidy cat, someone he probably had a heck of a time putting up with, under the circumstances. His other merc partners in the past, all women, weren't anything like her, Jenny was sure. But tonight she would show courage whether she felt it or not.

Patting herself off with the thick, yellow, terry-cloth bath towel after her shower, Jenny worked on getting her courage in place. Matt had already taken his shower and put on his pajamas. But the idea of him going to bed naked was provocative. She felt heat sweep into her face. Why did he have to be so ruggedly handsome? And he was so sensitive to her needs. He'd made a big deal over the alpaca sweater she'd bought him. The pleasure that wreathed his face had made her heart pound momentarily. The crooked, little-boy smile that came with the discovery that she'd bought him a gift had made Jenny feel warm and good all over. She was getting to know the real Matt Davis, not just the heroic military man and mercenary she'd seen a few times at Perseus headquarters. Jenny liked having him as her partner, but wasn't sure what her feelings meant.

Between the challenges she faced tomorrow morning when Matt and she would be flown by one of the women Apache pilots to the secret Black Jaguar Base to begin the interviews, and the idea of sleeping in the same bed with Matt Davis tonight, Jenny was feeling pretty stressed.

"Come on, 'fraidy cat, get your stuff in order," she told herself sternly under her breath as she shimmied into her pale green, silk nightgown. Running her fingers through her damp hair, Jenny peeked her head cautiously out the door. Thank goodness Matt had shut off the overhead light. He must have sensed her trepidation. The glow of soft sulphur lighting in the plaza below filtered into the room from behind the curtains.

Hurrying across the carpeted expanse, she saw that Matt had pulled back the sheet and light blanket on her half of the bed. Her heart began to pound. He was lying with his back toward her, facing the wall. The pillow was bunched beneath his head and jammed into position by his arm and hand. Gulping, she slid into the bed as quietly as possible. Lying down, she hugged her edge of the bed and brought the sheet up to her shoulders. It was fairly warm in the room. Matt had told Jenny that the temperature never got below fifty-five degrees Fahrenheit at any time because they were in the jungle.

"Good night, Matt," she whispered off-key. Her heart thudded with anticipation. With desire.

"See you in the morning, Jenny. Get a good night's sleep."

His deep voice soothed her anxiety. Releasing a pent-up sigh, she closed her eyes. Below, in the plaza, she could hear the kids still playing, even though it was 9:00 p.m. Maria had told her that most parents made their children come home about that time, so she knew the plaza would soon quiet down for the night.

She could hear the deep, continuous roar of the mighty Urubamba River, which ran between Machu

Picchu and Agua Caliente. Somehow the wild, rushing sound soothed her, too.

Very soon, Jenny fell into an exhausted asleep.

Matt jerked awake. What was that sound? He half
turned onto his back from his side. His arm struck
something warm and soft. Instantly, he froze. Again
he heard that mewing sound. Blinking his eyes several times, he moved quietly so that he was on his
left side, facing Jenny. The sound was coming from
her. Frowning, he eased himself up on his elbow.

In the plaza light filtering around the edges of the
curtains, he saw that she lay on her side, facing him,
and that she was literally scrunched up in a fetal
position. Her expression was tense. Her face muscles were taut, her soft mouth a tortured line. Gazing
at her hands, which were opening and closing restlessly against her pillow, he heard her whimper
again. The sounds were soft, but heartrending. Was
she having a nightmare? Matt fought the urge to
reach out and slide his fingers through the unruly
gold hair that framed her face. She moved frac-
tiously. One moment she was on her back, her
mouth working. Then she flung herself on her left
side. Again, a whimper.

He remembered what she had told him about her
life as a child, growing up. Jenny had never had any
real security, no real sense of safety, he realized.
Because she had ADD, she had been labeled a prob-

lem child to boot. He could imagine her several sets
of foster parents shuffling her off to another home
because she was simply too much to handle. Shaking his head, Matt felt anger. Didn't they realize that
foisting her off on someone else was sending her a
loud, clear message that she wasn't lovable? That
she wasn't worth sticking it out with, or worthy of
the help she needed to adjust to life and its demands? The thread of anger wound through his gut
and into his heart.

Jenny flung herself onto her back again. And then
rolled over on her right side.

Was this how she slept every night? Fitfully?
Restlessly? Matt shook his head. She looked so vulnerable and helpless in that green silk nightgown,
the boat neck decorated with bits of white lace. Lying back down, his hands behind his head, he
sighed. What he wanted to do was sweep her into
his arms and hold her. He knew he could give her
that security, that sense of safety she wanted. Every
emotion was so obvious on her face. Matt knew his
touch could soothe her. His heart expanded with the
need to touch her.

Shaking his head, he closed his eyes. *No.* He
couldn't get involved with a woman again. His ex-
wife had burned him badly enough to make him
swear off women forever. And yet this small, feisty
woman with sun-gold hair and eyes as big as a Mon-

tana sky made him long for a mate once more. Was he crazy? He was, no doubt.

He had no idea if Jenny would be well rested tomorrow morning or not. But he had to be. Rolling over on his side, his back to her, he shut his eyes and ordered himself to go to sleep. Tomorrow would come soon enough and a whole new set of demands would be placed on them. He wasn't worried for himself, but was concerned for Jenny. He wanted her to be successful on this mission because it would raise her self-esteem and give her a lot more confidence in herself. No one wanted to see her be a winner at this more than Matt. No one.

Jenny sat with Matt in the dining room of Gringo Bill's the next morning. It was 6:00 a.m. Rosemary, the cook, had brought out their bacon and cheese omelettes, sourdough toast and coffee. Today Jenny was better dressed for the climate, in a white long-sleeved blouse with the cuffs rolled up to her elbows, a sensible set of khaki cotton slacks and her hiking boots. She wore a pair of gold-and-pearl earrings in her dainty earlobes and her hair was tamed into a semblance of order despite the humidity. Outside, the sunlight was nowhere to be seen. Instead, white, wispy clouds crawled in slow, continuous motion around the black lava mountain of Machu Picchu.

As he dug into his omelette, Matt asked, "Did you sleep well last night?"

Coloring, Jenny slathered strawberry jam on her toast. "Okay, I guess. Why?" Matt looked so handsome in his dark green cotton, short-sleeved shirt, his tan chinos and brown hiking boots. She had a tough time not staring and getting lost in his warm gray eyes.

"You were pretty restless last night."

"I was?" She gave him a pained look. "Oh, no...don't tell me I kept you awake?"

He heard the consternation in her whisper. Shaking his head, he smiled slightly. "I woke up once, was all. I went right back to sleep, though." He examined her face from across the small wooden table where they sat. Around them were many other tourists and hikers getting ready to take the bus up to the Incan ruins built atop Machu Picchu.

Touching her cheek, Jenny muttered, "I'm really sorry, Matt. I know how tired you were."

Reaching out, he caught her hand, telling himself as he made intimate contact with her that they should act like a married couple in public to keep their cover intact. Squeezing her fingers, he said, "Hey, I'm more concerned about you. You've got a few shadows under your eyes this morning."

Absorbing his warm, strong touch, she reluctantly released his hand. It was the last thing Jenny wanted to do. Fumbling with the toast, she chewed off an edge of it. Swallowing, she said, "I feel rested. I'm sure I'm sleep deprived sometimes, though."

"You were whimpering in your sleep. Were you having bad dreams?"

Bowing her head, she chewed on her lower lip for a moment. "Oh…that…"

He saw anguish in her fleeting expression. "Your past?" he asked.

Shrugging, Jenny dug nervously into the omelette. She knew she had to eat heartily because of the stress of the interviews to come, even if she had lost her appetite. "Kind of…"

"Want to talk about it? I've got a pretty good set of ears on me if you do."

Just the way he said it broke Jenny's reserve. Ordinarily, she never spoke of her childhood. She wanted to forget about it, but it followed her around like an old and sometimes troublesome friend. Waving her hands nervously, she said, "I'm afraid of the dark…my 'fraidy cat stuff…."

Frowning, Matt said, "There was light coming in around the curtains."

"Not enough for me." Jenny rolled her eyes. "I'm a mess, Matt. I really am. At my apartment in Philipsburg, I have a night-light that I keep on. It helps me sleep better."

"Then," he growled, "I'll find one here in Agua Caliente and we'll put it in our room. For this mission, you need to get your sleep."

She stared across the table at him. Jenny saw the banked anger in his eyes and understood he wasn't angry at her. Grateful, she whispered unsteadily, "You are such a white knight for me…. I know I'm a pain in the butt with all my eccentricities—"

"No, you aren't, darlin'." Matt hesitated. Where had *that* come from? He saw Jenny's eyes widen at the endearment.

Heat tunneled into her face and she instantly fixed her gaze on her plate. She couldn't stand the look Matt gave her. It was a protective, loving look, if she read it correctly. Why would he worry about her? She was nothing to him. She was a nobody. Yet, in her heart, she knew that he did genuinely care, and that rattled her. He'd called her "darlin'."

Scowling, Matt ate several bites of his breakfast, the silence at the table pregnant and tension-filled. Jenny had reacted strongly to his endearment. Because she didn't like him? Considered it sexual harassment? Sometimes he got foot-in-mouth disease. Judging from the redness of her cheeks, she was shocked by it. *Damn.*

Clearing her throat, she said in a low tone, "I remember, when I was growing up, having a stuffed skunk I just loved. I called her Sarah. I don't remember when I got her…only that she'd been with me through all the homes I'd lived in. When I took her to bed with me at night, I felt like she protected me. I started getting scared of the dark when I was sent to another foster home, and my new foster mother didn't want me to have the lamp on in my bedroom. She said I needed to grow up. That a kid my age no longer needed a light or a stuffed toy.''

''How old were you when this happened?''

''Seven…I think.'' Jenny smiled gamely. ''My foster mom was right, of course, but something little and scared deep down inside me just refused to grow up or believe her.''

''Is that when you started all this tossing and turning?'' He stifled his anger and kept it out of his voice, although he was feeling it sear him inwardly.

''Yes. After my lamp was taken away, and Sarah was gone, I started getting nightmares. You know, dumb stuff like monsters hiding under my bed to get me…hiding in the closet….'' Jenny forced herself to eat the toast and jam. The moody look in Matt's eyes made her aware he was upset. ''When I got sent to my next foster family, I kept the lamp on in my room, but my foster father would always turn it off and tell me that electricity was expensive, and having a light on all night cost him too much money. By the time I was fifteen, I discovered nightlights, bought one and began to get a reasonable amount of sleep at night.'' Her smile widened. ''I forgot to bring it with me on this trip. My fault.''

''I'll see what I can do about finding one for you sometime today, after we get back,'' Matt muttered, his brow wrinkled. Finishing his food, he wiped his mouth on the paper napkin and glanced over at her. Jenny looked eager to go.

"Ready?" he asked, rising.

"More than ready," she whispered excitedly, leaping to her feet. In rising quickly, she tipped the chair over backward, and it fell with a bang to the wooden floor. The patrons in the dining room all looked up and stopped talking. All eyes centered on her standing over the fallen chair. Jenny grimaced. "I'm such a klutz!" she whispered apologetically as she turned and picked it up.

Matt's heart went out to her. He realized that the stares only exacerbated Jenny's shyness and vulnerability. Coming around the table, he slid his hand into hers and gave her a smile that said everything was going to be all right. How easy it was to pretend he was married to her, he realized in that moment, as hope leaped into her eyes. He felt her shyly return the squeeze of his fingers.

"Let's catch that flight," he murmured.

Jenny gaped as they were taken in a speeding golf cart through a dark, lava tube tunnel from the mining operation side of the mountain to the U.S. Army top secret Black Jaguar base. They had been flown to the area in a civilian helicopter piloted by one of the Black Jaguar personnel, Warrant Officer Jessica Merril. What struck Jenny about this woman pilot was that she, too, had short blond hair—with a

bright red streak dyed in it. In Jenny's opinion, it
made her look like a wild woman. Merril was out-
going, confident and vibrant. The half-hour flight
past the famous Machu Picchu architectural ruins
and deep into the jungle was made delightful by the
wisecracking army pilot. Jenny didn't know when
she'd laughed so much or so long. Indeed, if Jessica
mirrored the other female pilots here at this secret
base, Jenny was looking forward to meeting these
brave and heroic women. Matt had already informed
her that at first, the base was made up of only
women personnel. But now that was changing and
about ten percent of the base was male.

As the golf cart hummed along under the command of the driver, an army sergeant near Jenny's
own age, Jenny looked around in awe, especially
when they left the tunnel and entered a huge, deep
cavern.

"Ohh!" she gasped, turning and gripping Matt's
arm. "Look! Omigosh! This is *awesome!*"

"I agree," he murmured, impressed. The huge
cavern held not only tent and Quonset hut facilities
for the personnel, but a two-story operations building, and a huge landing lip where two Boeing
Apache Longbow helicopters and a Blackhawk helo
sat. The place was a beehive of activity with people
and golf carts coming and going ceaselessly. Matt
figured that electricity would be at a premium, and
that the base probably ran on those huge generators

he'd seen over on the mining side. It was probably that battery-powered golf carts were used to transport people and supplies from one side of the mountain to the other.

Their driver stopped at the small, two-story building with HQ painted in black on its sheet metal siding. Jenny slid out of the golf cart.

"Just go up the stairs, ma'am," the red-haired sergeant said. "Major Stevenson is in room 208. She's awaiting your arrival."

Thanking the sergeant, Jenny hurried up the outside metal grate stairs to the second floor, Matt at her heels. The loud, irritating sound of a bell suddenly clamored through the complex, echoing from the cave walls. Jenny hesitated when she saw four women dressed in black, form-fitting uniforms, helmets in hand, running toward the Apache helicopters, which were being pushed out onto the lip, beyond the cave entrance.

"They've got a mission," Matt told her as he came to a halt by her side and watched the scene unfold. "That bell is telling them to get to their helos and get into the sky. They've probably spotted drug runners on radar and are going to intercept them."

Turning, Jenny looked up at him. Now Matt's face was grim and drawn. She was seeing his warrior side once again. Gazing back at the women climbing into the dual cockpits of the Boeing

Apaches, which were painted a dark green color, she said, "They'll be risking their lives, won't they?"

Nodding, Matt turned and studied her upturned face. "Judging from the report, these pilots risk their lives every time they fly. Look at that hole they've got to fly through...whew, that's tight! One wrong move and they'd crash into the side of that lava wall."

He was right, Jenny realized in mounting alarm. They watched as the cockpit hatches were closed by the crew chiefs and the rotors began to turn. The growl and high-pitched hum of the Apaches' dual engines warming up to take off hurt her sensitive ears. Jenny knew she could never do what these women did. Her admiration for them rose steadily. Turning, she opened the door.

"I think we need to meet Major Stevenson," she told him, glancing down at the gold watch on her right wrist.

He agreed and followed her into the building, down a hallway bustling with women personnel moving to and from the various offices. He and Jenny quickly located Major Stevenson's office on the right side of the corridor.

Jenny halted and knocked on the open door. The woman behind the metal desk looked up.

"You Jenny Wright? From Perseus?"

"Yes, I am. And this is Matt Davis." Jenny moved forward with a confidence she didn't feel, but she had to pretend, for this commanding officer's sake. Maya Stevenson was more than a heroine in her eyes. She was more like a goddess—perhaps Pallas Athena, a wise woman warrior from Greek mythology.

The major's emerald eyes settled squarely on Jenny, but oddly, Jenny no longer felt anxious or worried. Somehow Major Stevenson's look calmed her nervous state. Good leaders had that ability, Jenny was discovering. At home, working for Morgan, she could be in the midst of a high-stress situation but his calm demeanor automatically soothed her, as well.

"Glad you're here, Ms. Wright, Mr. Davis. Have a seat. Let's talk. Coffee?" Major Stevenson said, turning to the coffee machine behind her desk.

Jenny cast a quick look at Matt, who drew out two chairs sitting near the wall and brought them to the center of the small, cramped room. He gave her a look at that said, *Everything's okay, darlin'.* Well, he might not have said "darlin'" but she liked to think he did.

"I'd love some coffee," Jenny said.

"Good. Woman after my own heart," the major murmured as she poured some into a white, chipped mug. "Never trust a person who doesn't drink some java." She cast a look over her shoulder. "Cream? Sugar?"

"Er…no, black, please. Matt? Do you want some?"

He grinned. "I'd better or the major is going to throw me out of here as jaguar bait. Right, Major?"

Jenny heard Major Stevenson chortle as she turned and leaned across the desk to hand her the cup.

"That's right, Mr. Davis. Black?"

"Yes, please."

Jenny saw and felt the instant rapport that Matt established with the major. It was because they were both in the military, which had its own language, slang, and above all, a unique camaraderie that was often tighter than family bonds. Jenny knew she was an outsider to their world. Still, Maya treated her as if she were a part of the group, and for that Jenny was grateful.

After handing Matt his coffee, Major Stevenson sat down. She shoved a stack of files in their direction. "I have seven women who want to volunteer for those missions, Ms. Wright."

"Please, call me Jenny? I'm afraid I don't stand much on formality."

Maya grinned darkly. "Just like your boss, I see. Okay, Jenny. You call me Maya. Fair enough?"

She smiled. "Sure." Leaning forward, Jenny asked, "These are your pilots who want to work with Perseus?"

"Yep." Maya sipped her coffee as she continued

to gauge her from half-closed eyes. "It's your job to figure out which three, Jenny. Morgan Trayhern said you come armed with a psych degree. I like that. You look like you run your life by the seat of your pants. With your intuition, right?"

Shaken by the commanding officer's perception, Jenny straightened and said, "Why, yes...yes, I do."

Nodding brusquely, Maya said, "Good. Don't trust a woman that doesn't run on her gut at all times." She waved her hand toward the files. "You pick 'em, Jenny. And then let's schedule a conference afterward and we'll go over your choices before we post the lucky three names."

"Do you have suggestions? I'd love to be aware of them."

Her grin increased. "Now...I know just enough psychology to shoot myself in the foot with it, Jenny. I feel you need to do this by yourself. You don't need me noodling in with my two cents' worth. You know the mission. You know what it requires. Any one of my pilots would do. But you and Morgan have set up certain protocols. You know the people my women have to interface with, and so it comes down to personalities, doesn't it? Who will get along with whom? And I'm out of that circle. So after you've interviewed my pilots, we'll meet and talk, okay?"

Jenny nodded and sipped her coffee. She saw a

sergeant come in and hand Maya several sheets of faxed papers. Maya thanked her, looked at them and sighed.

"Duty calls." She stood up. "Sergeant Joann Prater will show you to the room you'll use to conduct your interviews in, Jenny. If you need anything, she's your contact. Okay?"

The sergeant, a woman with short, red hair and blue pale eyes, came forward and smiled. "Let me show you to the room, Ms. Wright?"

Jenny quickly got up, balanced her coffee cup and picked up her briefcase, while Matt came forward and scooped up the personnel files. "Thanks, Maya. We hope to have this done in two or three days," Jenny murmured.

Nodding, Maya said, "That's fine. See you later."

Even as Jenny turned, she saw Maya pick up the phone with a dark and harried expression. The faxes must have been upsetting. As she and Matt followed Sergeant Prater down the highly waxed hall to a room near the end on the left, Jenny began to realize the pressure that all these women worked under continuously. Could she work with that kind of stress? No way.

The room was they entered was tiny and spare. There was a green metal desk in the middle, a small window with venetian blinds over it, and several green metal chairs. And that was all. Matt placed the files on the desk and stood back while Jenny put her coffee cup down on it and settled her heavy briefcase on the floor nearby. The sergeant left. The hum of office machines, the low voices of the staff, the ringing of phones, drifted into their space.

Looking around, Jenny set her hands on her hips. "Home. At least for the next few days."

"It could be a lot worse," Matt observed. "By the way, you made a good impression on the major."

"I did?"

"She treated you like one of her own. That's a good sign."

Lifting the briefcase to the desk, she murmured, "I thought she had. I know military people don't necessarily like civilians."

"My gut tells me she likes you."

"Then I've crossed my first bridge. I know if a CO doesn't like you, you're damned."

Chuckling, Matt moved the chairs around so that they were in front of her desk. "You catch on real fast, darlin'. Real fast." This time, he purposely used the endearment to see what effect it would have on her. Jenny lifted her chin and looked at him, her sky-blue eyes flaring with surprise...and pleasure.

"I'll bet you call every woman darlin'," she accused lightly as she pulled out her laptop and hunted for a place to plug it in. Her heart was beating erratically because the look he gave her was one of interest—and desire.

"No," Matt answered slowly as he walked to the door and looked out into the hallway, "I don't."

Flustered, Jenny sat down, opened up her laptop and turned it on. Watching Matt lean casually against the doorjamb, his hands in the pockets of his chinos, she felt a little shaky and uncertain about their relationship. Tonight, she had to go back to the hostel and sleep in that bed—with him—again. How would she handle it this time?

## Chapter Six

Fatigue lapped at Jenny as she sat down on their bed in the hostel. It was nearly ten o'clock and they'd just finished a quick meal at the India Feliz Restaurant. Matt sat at the small desk, reading the information she had typed in on the three women pilots she'd interviewed extensively today.

Untying her hiking boots, Jenny yearned to lay down and sleep. The day had been horrendously stressful on her, although she'd not let that out to anyone. No, she'd behaved confidently, as if she knew exactly what she was doing. Yawning, she stretched out on the bed, her hands tucked beneath the pillow.

Matt glanced up. He saw Jenny closing her eyes and drawing her knees up toward her body. It was dampish in the room and she was lying on top of the quilt. Getting up, he took the light alpaca blanket and spread it across her diminutive form. As he drew it up to her small shoulders, he saw her smile tiredly.

"Thanks.... I'm bushed. I think I'll take a little nap before I get my shower, Matt...."

Her words were slurring. Leaning down, he followed his desire to touch her. Threading his fingers through her short, blond hair, he whispered, "Go to sleep, darlin'. You've earned it. You did a good job up there today." He saw her lips part and realized that she was already asleep. *Good.* Last night she'd been restless, and Matt was sure she hadn't gotten very much sleep.

Tucking the brown-and-cream-colored blanket around her shoulders, he stood above her and absorbed her soft, peaceful features. What a courageous woman she was, and yet she didn't see it or recognize it within herself. Jenny had conducted the three long, intensive interviews with professionalism and intelligence. He'd seen another side to her today and he was very impressed. During the interviews, she wasn't flighty, restless or talkative. She had her questions and she asked them. And she faithfully typed each pilot's answers into her laptop. At all times, she was cordial but reserved, and kept a professional demeanor. Matt figured the degree in psychology had taught Jenny how to handle herself in such a situation.

Going back to the laptop, Matt continued to look at the answers the pilots had given during the interview. Jenny had asked him to go over the material and create comments or follow-up questions, if needed, because, with his military background, he could deduce much more than she along those lines. Jenny was a team player. Throughout the day, she'd made him feel important and part of each interview. He hadn't been relegated to a corner, to be seen but not heard from. Nope, between each interview, she'd spent at least thirty minutes, sometimes an hour, asking for his opinions, his experience, in order to gauge the prospective volunteers.

Hours later, Matt shut down the laptop and took a shower. It was nearly midnight. As he came out of the bathroom, the steam curling out the door as he opened it, he saw that Jenny continued to sleep peacefully. Maybe because he'd purchased a night-light at a local vendor's booth on the way back this evening? It burned brightly and steadily in a wall socket. When he'd taken his shower, he'd turned off all the lights with the exception of the night-light.

As he approached the bed, his heart expanded. Matt felt such tenderness toward Jenny. She slept like the angel she was. He recalled how, on their way down the dirt path from the helicopter landing pad, she'd wanted to go visit Maria and little Daniel, to see how they were. Matt and Jenny had gone to the part of town next to the soccer field, where most of the poor lived in shabby tin shacks, with rocks on the roof to hold them down during thunderstorms or on windy days. Maria was just coming back from the roaring tributary that cut through the small town on its way to the mighty Urubamba. She had a load of wet clothes in her huge basket.

Smiling softly, Matt shook his head as he remembered Jenny's kindness. As tired and hungry as she was, she'd followed Maria to her humble home and helped her hang the laundry on several lines outside the shack or down at the river. And she'd also brought Daniel a piece of chocolate cake they'd been served at the base cafeteria. The little boy's eyes had lit up like Christmas tree lights. It was painfully obvious that Jenny dearly loved children. She'd hugged Daniel, kissed his silky black hair and given him the small gift. Maria's husband, Juan, had thanked them for their generosity.

Crouching down now, Matt placed one hand on the side of the bed near Jenny's drawn-up knees, which were tucked warmly beneath the alpaca coverlet. "You're an incredible person, Jenny Wright," he whispered as he trailed his fingertips across her firm, warm cheek. "What are you? A beautiful fairy? A pretty butterfly? You're more a figment of my imagination than real, aren't you?" Matt spoke softly, not wanting to rouse her from her badly needed sleep. When he grazed her cheek, she moved slightly in response. She was so sensitive. So fragile. And yet, despite her difficult years growing up, she pushed courageously forward.

Matt found himself wanting to help Jenny continue to grow, to evolve out of her imprisoned past. She brought out his natural desire to help others. For so long, Jenny had been alone. Matt had discovered earlier today that the few relationships Jenny had had with men had all been negative. She blamed herself, of course, for the outcome of each. However, she never said anything negative or disparaging about men. From Matt's view, knowing only what she shared with him, the men she'd known had been first-class jerks who didn't have a clue how to appreciate someone like Jenny. They couldn't get beyond her restless flightiness, her talkativeness when she got nervous, or her lack of self-esteem.

"No," he whispered softly, "you don't tame a butterfly, do you, darlin'? You just give her her freedom, and appreciate her for what she is and is not...."

Rising slowly, Matt moved around the end of the bed. He pulled back the covers on his side and eased his bulk down, not wanting to disturb Jenny. Once in bed, he lay with his face toward the wall, because if he didn't, he was going to turn on his side, reach out and gently pull Jenny into the curve of his arm. His heart wanted that more than anything...and yet Matt brutally reminded himself that women were trouble with a capital *T*. His ex-wife had taught him that.

Tomorrow was another day, and he found himself looking forward more than ever to working with Jenny. She was mesmerizing to him; she had so many facets, like a gleaming, brilliant diamond. And he was enjoying discovering the many scintillating and wonderful sides to her. Yes, tomorrow was another day. A delicious day full of possibilities....

Jenny held her breath momentarily when Chief Warrant Officer Akiva Redtail walked into the interview room. She was copper-skinned, with gold, slightly tilted eyes. Though she wore the same black, body-hugging uniform the other pilots did, several things set her apart from the women Jenny had interviewed yesterday. Mostly it was the invisible yet powerful energy that Jenny felt surrounding the nearly six foot tall, big-boned woman pilot. It nearly knocked Jenny over as Akiva Redtail soundlessly entered the room. Akiva's hair, thick and black, hung straight and shining down across her breasts. She wore a bright red headband that brought out her obvious Native American looks. What caught Jenny's attention was a small braid started at the center part and tucked neatly behind her right

ear. Around her waist, tucked in her belt, was a very
old-looking ax covered with leather, the aged handle
knicked and well worn. On her right side, near her
pistol, she wore a beaded Indian scabbard with short
fringe that held a huge knife.

"Hi, Ms. Wright," Akiva Redtail said, thrusting
out her hand across the desk. "I hear you're the
woman who's gonna pick the lucky three?"

Jenny couldn't help but smile at this bold, confident pilot. She gripped her hand and shook it
warmly. "That's right, but Mr. Davis, my partner
here, was in the military, and will be helping me
make the final choices. Have a seat? I'll try and
make this as fast as possible."

The pilot released Jenny's hand and went over to
Matt and shook his. "Yeah, I've got the dirty duty
today. Let's hope the cowbell doesn't ring." And
she grinned wolfishly as she sat down. Taking a
huge wad of bubble gum out of her cheek, she threw
it in the wastebasket nearby.

"I chew bubble gum when I'm on duty. Reduces
my stress level," she explained as she sat comfortably, one booted leg across the other.

"I'd probably drink," Jenny said wryly. "I admire what you pilots do. It's dangerous work."

"Thanks. It's nice to get a compliment from the
outside. Not many know about us, or what we do,"
the woman agreed good-naturedly. She looked
around the spare office. "But it's home and we love

it here. We're good at what we do and we know it." She flashed a huge smile. "I like being in trench warfare. It's where the action is, and I was born for action."

Smiling, Jenny typed in the pilot's name into her laptop. She liked Akiva Redtail immensely. There was such warmth and joviality in her shining golden eyes, which missed nothing. Opening her personnel file, Jenny studied it for a moment and then looked up at her.

"I'm going to hang myself out on a limb here and tell you I'm completely ignorant of Native American people. Could you help me understand where you've come from? Your background? That way, I'll have a better idea of how you might fit into this upcoming mission with Perseus."

"Absolutely. What do you want to know? I'm an open book," Akiva said, and she laughed heartily.

"I hope you don't think I'm insulting you," Jenny said, "but you have a beautiful name. May I call you Akiva? And can you tell me about the name? How you got it? As well as your back-ground."

Raising her thick, arched brows, Akiva nodded. "Sure, no problem. I'm half Charicauha Apache and half Santee Lakota. On my mother's side, the Apache side, my great-great-grandmother rode with Geronimo. She was one of his women warriors."

"A woman warrior?" Jenny gasped. "Really? I didn't know Apaches allowed women to fight."

Chuckling indulgently, Akiva gave her a wry look. "My dear, Apaches are a matriarchal society. If a woman has what it takes to be a warrior, then she becomes one. Warrior blood runs in my veins. And my great-great-grandmother rode for years with Geronimo, until they were suckered into a trap by the U.S. Army and she was shot in the back, paralyzed, and eventually died, months afterward. She was his greatest warrior and he relied heavily on her. After that attack, Geronimo fled back to Mexico."

Akiva pointed to the ax and the knife in her belt. "See these weapons? They belonged to my great-great-grandmother. She used them, too. And they've been passed down through our family. My mother gave them to me when I entered the U.S. Army. Just before I joined, I became an Apache warrior. It involves a long, tough endurance test." She pointed to the braid on her head. "See this? This is what is known as the third braid of the warrior. Only an Apache man or woman can wear it, after they've passed many, many grueling, life-and-death tests to earn it. I earned my third braid at age seventeen."

"Wow!" Jenny whispered, caught up in Akiva's story. "What a wonderful family background. Women warriors...and look at you now."

"Yeah, instead of a horse, I ride a Boeing Apache

Longbow around instead. Extreme, dude, isn't it?"
She chuckled. "But I love it. I just have a horse of
a different color, is all. I'm still doing what I do
best, which is to fight for right and light."

"And your name? Does it mean something?"

"Native American names always mean something, Ms. Wright. Akiva is from my Apache side.
When we do ceremony, we create a kiva, or a place
where the sacred ceremony can be held. My grandmother and mother were both medicine women.
They had jaguar medicine. You know, back in their
day, jaguars roamed the Southwest freely. Each of
my relations confronted and traded spirits with their
jaguars." Akiva smiled lethally. "And I got 'em
now, myself. Can you feel them around me?"

Jenny sat back, amazed. "Jaguar medicine?"

"Sure. My grandmother gave me her jaguar spirit
guide when she died. My mother recently passed
over and gave me hers. Now I have two, and believe
me, I use 'em all the time in my business. Their
eyes and ears alert me to Russian Kamov helicopters
that are out there lurkin' around and wanting to
shoot us out of the sky. They warn me. Sorta like a
strong gut intuition, you know?"

Fascinated, Jenny absorbed Akiva's intensity and
fell captive to her narrowed golden eyes. She could
easily fantasize that Akiva was more jaguar than
woman, and Jenny almost swore for a fleeting moment that she saw the face of a jaguar superimposed

over Akiva's own features. Blinking, Jenny laughed awkwardly and chided herself for her overactive imagination. "There's no doubt, I sure feel power around you. Now I know why."

Nodding as if pleased with herself, Akiva said, "Extreme. That's me. If you're looking for someone to carry out an impossible mission, then you've got to think of me first."

"No doubt," Jenny said. "If Akiva comes from your Apache side of the family, is your last name, Redtail, from your Lakota side?"

She crossed her legs and leaned forward. "Yes, it is. My father's family are Santee Lakota and live in Nebraska. Redtail is his family name. They took the name when the U.S. Army made them come up with a first and last name. The red-tailed hawk is our family totem." She grinned and pointed to her eyes. "I have hawk eyes, too. I can see things a lot of other pilots can't. I don't miss anything."

"And so you have hawk medicine, as well." Jenny guessed.

"You got it." Akiva smiled hugely. "I think Major Stevenson ought to keep you around, Ms. Wright. You got the right stuff. You're fast on your feet and you fit right in with us rebels with a cause."

Jenny felt heat flood her face at the pilot's sincere praise. The look in Akiva's eyes reminded her of a hawk measuring its competitors. It was clear the pilot desperately wanted this mission. And at the same time, Akiva had the good grace to admire Jenny herself, for what she brought to the interview. Feeling a flood of confidence flowing into her at Akiva's words, she glanced to her right to look at Matt, to see his expression. He was gauging Akiva as he had all the others—with his poker face intact.

Jenny looked back at the pilot. "Tell me why you'd want this mission, Akiva?"

Getting up, she smoothed out her uniform. "I'm good at what I do. I understand there're three positions open. I want to be considered *only* for the undercover assignment. I don't care about the one on the border, and training those guys how to fly at night and pick up drug planes comin' to the U.S." She waved her hand and shook her head. "I want the undercover assignment. I speak five languages besides English. Spanish comes easy to me." She pointed to her skin and grinned. "I *look* Mexican, don't you think? I pass for a South American all the time. I understand that mission will be based in Mexico, although I know little else about it. I feel that, with my keen intuition and my ability to think on my feet, I could successfully fulfill that mission's requirements."

"And going undercover doesn't scare you?"

Shrugging dramatically, Akiva said, "I'm scared all the time, Ms. Wright. I live scared. The difference between me and most people is that I can *think through* my fear and know what to do to get the job done. That is what separates me from most others.''

Admiring her strength, her beauty and confidence, Jenny said, ''You make good points, Akiva.''

''I always do.''

Jenny smiled. How she wished she could have just a cup of Akiva's confidence, which radiated from her like rays of sunlight! Not only was Akiva empowered as a woman who fully embraced who and what she was, she thrived on her power, as well. Jenny couldn't fault her for having a healthy ego. Under the circumstances, with the danger these women faced daily, one needed a strong ego and a boatload of confidence, to boot. Akiva was honest about herself and her skills, but she could also reach out and praise others.

''Do you prefer to work alone or with a partner?''

Akiva moved around the room, her hands on her hips as she hung her head in thought. Walking slowly in a circle, she came to a halt in front of the desk and looked at Jenny.

''It would depend upon the circumstance. As a woman, I'm naturally inclined toward teamwork. But there's a side of me that is perfectly happy running the gauntlet alone, too. Maybe it's my Apache blood.'' And she flashed her a white, even smile of pride. ''I'm easy either way, Ms. Wright.''

''What if the mission required you to work on

your own? You wouldn't have a partner. No backup. No help if things turned bad.''

Akiva lifted her strong chin and looked around. ''Sounds like my life around here.'' She chuckled derisively, then became serious. ''We're always on the slats because we can't ID the Russian Kamov attack helicopter radar signature on our equipment. If things turn bad out there, then it's them against us. There's no U.S. Cavalry arriving. Just Perseus and Morgan Trayhern.'' She smiled thinly. ''Isn't this a hoot? Two generations later, I'm a part of the very U.S. Army that chased down and killed my great-great grandmother. How's that for karma?''

''It is,'' Jenny agreed, quickly typing in her answer. ''So, it wouldn't bother you to live alone, on alert every day in a remote site in the jungle, with no help at all?''

''No.'' Akiva's eyes narrowed to slits. ''I have my own backup from another world, Ms. Wright. I know you Anglos in North America don't believe in spirit guides, but we Indians do. And they are just as real as you and I. You don't have to believe that. But I do. I've had it proved to me time and again that my spirit guides not only help me, but guide me, and have more than once saved my butt from a sling.'' She punched the air with her finger. ''I have my spirit jaguars—two extra sets of eyes, ears, noses—to keep me alive and fighting.''

The energy swirled and shifted dramatically

around the room. Jenny felt it. So, obviously, did Matt. He moved uncomfortably, but said nothing. Akiva stood there, hands on her hips, defiant, self-assured, that unseen power palpable. Jenny felt as if a lightning bolt had struck the desk between them. She felt addled and confused in the wake of it.

"I believe you," she told Akiva, faithfully typing in her answer.

Just then, the alarm bell rang. Jenny jerked her head up at the sound. She saw Akiva's face go hard and her eyes narrow to predatory slits. In one smooth, unbroken motion, she whirled around, her black hair a swirling cape around her shoulders as she sped out the door and down the hall.

"Whew!" Jenny said as she stood up. "She is *something else,* Matt!"

Rising, he moved to the door and watched the flurry of action as the bell continued to ring throughout the complex. Once a drug plane or helicopter had been spotted by the base radar operator, the bell was rung and the two Apaches and supporting Blackhawk lifted off in pursuit soon after. Such a response entailed a lot of fast action on the part of the ground team, as well as the pilots.

Turning, Matt saw that Jenny's eyes were huge with excitement. He smiled a little and leaned against the door. "You almost look like you want to run out there with Akiva and jump in that Apache and take off with her."

"Don't I wish!" Jenny touched her cheek, her voice filled with awe. "I wish...oh, how I wish I possessed that kind of raw courage and confidence. She is just so incredibly strong and self-assured about herself and what she can do."

"Don't be so quick to condemn yourself," Matt warned her darkly as he pushed away from the door and ambled toward the desk. "Not everyone needs to be a warrior on the front lines like these women are. The support group behind them is equally important. Without them, those helos wouldn't be serviced, fueled up—they wouldn't go anywhere. And the office people are handling the traffic, the phone calls, the in-house operation that coordinates everything from bombs to bullets that those big rigs are outfitted with."

Nodding, Jenny said, "You're right." She realized he was referring to behind-the-scene people like her—who helped Morgan keep Perseus running effectively. The look in Matt's eyes was one of admiration for what she and others like her did, and it made her heart soar. Shutting off the laptop, Jenny sat back down. "We haven't even had a chance to talk about last night."

He grinned and sat on the edge of the desk. "Oh? You mean your falling asleep and not taking a shower before you hit the hay?"

Wrinkling her nose, she said, "Yes."

"I didn't notice any odor, if that's what you're gnashing your worrywart teeth over."

She laughed at his gentle teasing. "You're reading my mind!"

"Well, when every expression flits across that beautiful face of yours, it's kinda hard not to know what you're thinking or feeling."

A delicious warmth infused her heart, and Jenny felt euphoric as he gave her that special look. She could drown, literally, in Matt's gray eyes.

"Beautiful? Me? Hardly. Now, if you want beautiful, look at Akiva. She's gorgeous! She's so primal and wild-looking, a very earthy, sensual woman."

"That's one kind of beauty," Matt agreed, crossing his arms and watching Jenny fiddle with her paper and pencils. He saw the look in her blue eyes and recognized how much she really *wanted* to believe he thought she was truly beautiful. She *was* beautiful. All he had to do was convince her of it. "Your beauty, on the other hand, is not so dramatic, but it's just as moving to a man, believe me."

"Oh?" Jenny met and held his smoldering look. Her skin prickled deliciously as his gaze slid to her mouth, lingered there and then moved down across the rest of her body. She had never felt this way about a man before—as if his gaze was a physical touch grazing her heightened, sensitive flesh. It was a wonderful feeling. One that made her ache to kiss him, to slide her hands in a ranging, exploratory motion across his powerful, darkly haired chest. Gulping unsteadily at her wild thoughts, she felt it must be Akiva's primal presence that was making her feel like a wild woman!

"Your beauty is quiet, warm sunlight to a man's starving, cold soul," Matt told her quietly. "Your warmth, your spontaneity and generosity of heart would melt the hardest of hearts, darlin'." He wanted to add, *And you've melted my heart to the point to where all I can do is think about touching you, kissing those petal-soft lips of yours, making you mine in every possible way.... want to feel you breathe. I want to breathe with you and flow into your welcoming body and feel your arms wrap around me and heal my wounds. Heal me....* But he didn't. He said nothing as he absorbed her gentle blue gaze, which glinted with gold in the aftermath of his warm praise of her.

Matt wondered how he was going to maintain his distance from her in bed each night. Because of the pilots' schedules, and their sporadic and unexpected flight missions due to drug trafficking, the interviews were going to take much longer than first anticipated. That meant more nights with her. How in the hell was he going to keep his hands off her?

## Chapter Seven

"I can't sleep," Jenny sighed as she twisted to look to her right. Matt lay with his hands behind his head. In the dull light that filtered in through the window and the glow of the night-light, she could see his rugged profile and the set of his mouth. It was nearly midnight, according to the luminous dials on her watch.

"Me neither," he rumbled.

"I keep running those interviews over in my mind. Darn, the pilots we've interviewed so far are *all* up to handling the missions that Mike Houston designed for Perseus."

"Especially Akiva. She's good merc material. I

know Morgan would love to steal her away from here and offer her a job at Perseus.''

''Ohh,'' Jenny whispered in an admiring tone, ''she is so unique! You're right—Morgan would fall all over himself trying to get her to join us. I love her rock solid confidence. It's so nice to see that in a woman. I mean, all the women pilots have it, but she's *really* got it.''

One corner of Matt's mouth lifted. ''You have it, too, you know.''

She turned onto her side and allowed herself the complete luxury of staring at him in the gray light of their room. Jenny had come to look forward to these nights shared with Matt. She was sleeping well now. Maybe it was the night-light…or maybe it was Matt, who gave her such a sense of safety.

Jenny saw him slant her an amused look. ''I feel more confident since coming here,'' she admitted. ''I think it's because of you, as well as how the women pilots treat me. They respect me.''

Moving onto his side, Matt propped himself up on one elbow. It took everything not to reach out and graze Jenny's ruffled hair or slide his aching fingertips across the smooth slope of her cheek. As his gaze dropped to her parted lips, he groaned inwardly. What would she feel like beneath his mouth? How would she taste? Tearing his mind from below his waist, he murmured, ''What you don't realize is a lot of people respect you. You're just the last to see it.'' He saw her give him a funny, sad smile.

''Maybe...'' With her fingertip, Jenny drew an invisible pattern on the sheet, between them. Her heart was starting to pound again, and she knew why. She wanted to reach out and touch Matt's hard, dark jaw. Even though he shaved each morning, by this time of night his beard darkened his face once more, giving him a very dangerous, dark look that thrilled her.

''What about you, Matt? You always want to know about me. You never speak about yourself...your past...or what brought you to this point in your life.''

''Uh-oh,'' he teased, ''here comes twenty questions.''

Giggling, Jenny held his warm gaze and felt a luscious sheet of heat flow downward, to pool languorously in her lower body, where a throbbing ache was centered. ''I know you're a merc, and I know you value secrets. But couldn't you share just a little bit about yourself with me? After all, I was an open book to you. I trusted you enough to tell you about my embarrassing life, thus far.''

To hell with it. He reached out and cupped Jenny's chin and held her widening blue gaze. ''Listen to me, darlin'. You have nothing to be ashamed of about your past or your childhood. You had it rough. And you've survived. I'm really proud of you, Jenny. You've come a long way. You were handed nothing but rags and yet you made a rainbow quilt with them.''

His fingers were gentle as they curved against her cheek and jaw. Closing her eyes, she trembled as she absorbed his tentative touch. When he withdrew his fingers, she slowly opened her eyes. A feeling of dizziness, of craving him, of wanting more than she deserved, gnawed through her heart and body.

''A rainbow quilt,'' she said quietly. ''Is that how you see my life?'' She watched his smile form; it was a smile of a wolf hunting its chosen prey. Yet it didn't make her feel uncomfortable. Rather, she felt wanted and desired. Jenny had never had a man look at her quite the way Matt did. Was she reading the signals wrong? If he really desired her, why didn't he kiss her? Why didn't he speak of how he felt about her? Or was he just into having a one-night stand? Jenny wouldn't go for that...ever. She'd made mistakes with men before, but she'd learned from each of them. There had to be a lot more than raw sex to a relationship. There had to be a genuine enjoyment, a friendship, between two people, too. The thought flitted through her head that she wasn't brave enough to pursue a relationship with Matt. In her mind's eye, she imagined he would be drawn to a woman from the military who had the same kind of background, plus that similar raw courage that Jenny certainly didn't possess. A little saddened over that thought, she absorbed his growing smile.

"You're a rainbow, all right," Matt said as he forced his hand to rest between them on the sheet. The ache in his lower body was intensifying—rapidly. He wanted to take her. To drown in her soft blue eyes, worship those petal-shaped lips and feel her womanly arms around him, holding him as only a woman could do.

"That's nice," Jenny said with a sigh. "Do you know how I see you?"

Matt saw the unsureness come into her expression as she boldly blurted her questions. Jenny tucked her lower lip between her teeth, a sign that she was nervous about putting out a tentative feeler in his direction. "How do you see me?" In order to ease her tension, he teased, "Like a clam? Armored up? Like a wall?"

Laughing breathily, she said, "No, not at all! I see you..." she lifted her eyes toward the darkness of the ceiling momentarily "...as a wonderful knight in shining armor."

Groaning, Matt said, "Jenny, I'm not. Just ask my ex-wife. I might have been the Don Quixote type of knight in her eyes, but that's about it." He chuckled derisively.

Jenny had been waiting for him to open up to her, and she knew this was her chance to gently delve into his past. "What was she like—your ex-wife?"

Matt rolled his eyes. "Marilyn is a red-haired attorney. A criminal trial attorney. A shark of the first order."

"You must have seen something in her you loved?"

With a grimace, Matt muttered, "Yeah, I did. I liked her passion, her fire, her belief in battling for the underdogs of life and helping people who couldn't normally afford a lawyer like her. She was a top gun at a big law firm, and what I liked about her was that she cared for the little people of the world. Always. Marilyn never looked down on them." Rubbing his face to wipe away the tiredness that was lapping at him, Matt added, "I make her out to be a demon, but she's not, really. She just raked me over the coals when we got divorced, and I'm still smarting from it."

"I've seen some divorces turn awfully nasty," Jenny agreed glumly.

"Ours was. It didn't have to be, but we were both hardheaded and stubborn. Neither of us would give in to the other. I ended up on the short end of the stick, and I guess, being honest about it, I'm a sore loser. I need to let it and her go."

"Did you have any children?" Jenny asked. She saw the anguish and pain in Matt's darkening eyes.

"No, thank God we didn't."

"Did you want any?"

"Yes, but we decided we'd wait until we were in

our mid-thirties. Marilyn had her career, and I was shifting from the U.S. Navy to Perseus at the time. We didn't feel it would be fair to bring a child into a home where both parents were fighting for new, higher-paying career slots.''

''That's great that you thought of those things. A child could suffer under that kind of situation.'' Jenny liked the idea that Matt was sensitive to what it would take to raise a child.

''Yeah, you would be especially sensitive to that issue, since you were traded around from one foster family to another,'' he replied. ''I know you like kids. Daniel thinks you're his second mother,'' he chuckled. Even tonight, after they'd been flown back to Agua Caliente, Jenny had walked to the river, where Maria was washing the clothes of her many clients. The older woman was methodically pounding the wet garments with a large, smooth stone while Daniel played nearby in a pool that had been created by the townspeople for small children. No one would dare to try and swim, much less cross, the wild hundred-foot-wide tributary, which poured like a rabid, frothing dog into the Urubamba downstream.

Jenny had once again brought the child the dessert she'd gotten at the Black Jaguar Base mess, and Daniel had been thrilled. And she had bought Maria several worn, dark green wool blankets that Major Stevenson had said she could distribute to the poor.

Maria had stood there, blankets in hand, with tears of gratitude in her eyes. Little Daniel had toddled up, his hands covered with chocolate frosting after having eaten the cake, and gripped Jenny's slacks. She hadn't cared that the little boy was messy, and had picked him up, kissed him on the cheek and hugged him lovingly.

"Someday," Jenny whispered now, giving Matt a dreamy smile, "I want children."

"How many?"

"Two, I think. Two is plenty. It takes so much money to raise them, nowadays. I'd like to give them the opportunities I never had. To make their lives a little easier, so that they can follow their dreams, whatever they may be."

"You'll be one hell of a mother," Matt rasped, meaning every word. He itched to reach out and touch her. Matt saw the languid look in her darkening eyes as she stared across those scant inches at him. Her lips parted.

Taking a deep breath, he closed his eyes. "I think I'd better tell you that you're in danger, Jenny."

Her eyes widened enormously. "What?" Instantly, she sat up. The sheet slid and pooled around her hips.

He stared up at her. The white cotton nightgown she wore was simple, yet feminine, with lace around the scoop neck. She had clasped her hands against her breasts, her expression truly one of concern.

"Calm down," he told her heavily, and he reached out and slid his hand along her arm. Her skin was soft and warm. Inviting.

"What's the danger?" She began to look around the room. "Spies?"

"No…me."

Snapping her head to the right, Jenny stared down at him. He reminded her of a cougar lazily stretched out on a boulder. The powerful feelings around him, and what she saw in his eyes, helped her make the connection. "Oh…" Gulping, she said, "I think we'd better talk."

Nodding, Matt gave her a grim look. Jenny was like a startled, beautiful deer in that moment. The look in her eyes was one of shock and disbelief. Why? Didn't she know how beautiful she was? How precious to him? How achingly desirable?

"I'm having one hell of a time keeping my hands off you, if you want the truth," he growled. "I don't know what's happened, Jenny. You have a way of getting under a man's armor. Reaching out and touching his heart. At least, that's how I feel about it. I don't know when or how it happened, but it has. And I'm looking at the fact that we're sharing the same bed and that I want to share a lot more than just the space on it with you."

Her breath jammed in her throat. Staring at him, Jenny opened her mouth in amazement. "Y-you like me?"

Giving her a lazy, amused look, Matt said, "Like? That's an understatement, Jenny. I *want* you. In every conceivable way. But I'm not sure about you...about how you feel toward me. There's just something magical about you. You're a butterfly, you know? Beautiful. Distant. And I feel like if I reach out to drag you into my arms and kiss you until we melt together, that I might scare you—destroy you—in the process. In some ways, I see you as being so fragile...." His brows dipped and he stared down at his darkly haired hand, resting on the sheet between them. "This has got to be mutual or it isn't going anywhere. And I don't know where it might lead. I don't have a damned clue. All I know is that I want you. I like listening to you talk. I like sharing life stories with you. You make me laugh—did you know that? I wake up in the morning looking forward to the day with you, and I haven't felt that way in a long, long time. I enjoy your company. I like seeing the world through your idealistic eyes, because the way I look at life, it's a helluva lot uglier. You make me feel clean inside, Jenny...I don't know how else to explain it. I know I'm not very good with words and all...."

Jenny sat very still. His words cascaded across her like warm, unexpected sunlight. "I—it's so hard to believe what I'm hearing, Matt. I mean..." She cleared her throat, her voice wobbling. "I never thought you'd be interested in someone like *me*. I thought you'd be more interested in one of those women pilots we're interviewing. A strong, confident woman. Not someone who shrieks over seeing a spider.''

He gave her a cutting smile. ''I see you as confident. I see your self-assurance blooming. And so what if you screech over a spider? I'm afraid of things, too. We all are.''

Placing her hands on her reddening cheeks, Jenny whispered rawly, ''I didn't know, Matt. I didn't think I was... I didn't think that you...'' She closed her eyes. Her stomach turned, not from fright or fear, but from a wild desire that coursed through her in that moment. Heart fluttering, all she could do was sit there and feel her way through Matt's unexpected admittance.

''Listen, this is *my* problem, Jenny. I just wanted to warn you, so that if some night I accidentally, in my sleep, turn over and pull you into my arms, you won't be shocked. Just give me an elbow in the chest and I'll wake up and let go of you. Okay?''

She could feel her heart pounding beneath her palms, which were pressed to the center of her chest. Looking over at him, Jenny saw how unhappy he appeared. ''This is so shocking, Matt. I never thought you'd have the *least* interest in me!''

''No man in his right mind wouldn't be interested in you, Jenny.'' He saw pain reflected in her eyes.

As she placed her hand on the sheet between them, Matt put his hand over hers in a protective gesture.

"Well, that's not been my experience. They haven't exactly been beating down my door, Matt. I've had two relationships and they were disasters...at least for me." She hung her head and felt his hand move gently across hers in a soothing motion. It gave her the courage to go on. "You might as well know the rest of my life story. I fell hard for a guy name Mark, in college, when I was working toward my degree. I was a lot worse than I am now." She gave Matt a wry look and a weak laugh to try and make a joke of it. But her attempt failed.

"What do you mean?"

"I'm ADD, remember? Ants in my pants. Can't sit still. Constant motion. Restless. Talkative. I warned Mark about my...lacking, and how I was. He didn't seem to care, but as our relationship developed, it did bother him. The night-light bothered him. And he didn't want to talk. Oh, I know men in general aren't good at communicating...but he said I never shut up. That hurt."

"Sure it would." Matt wanted to find Mark and rearrange his immature face for him. "Go on..."

Grimacing, Jenny pulled her hand from beneath his and drew up her knees. She wrapped her arms around them and rested her chin on top. Her voice was hesitant and riddled with confusion. "I just couldn't be what Mark wanted, so I broke up with him."

"That was a healthy thing to do. If he couldn't accept you as you are, then you weren't going to have many positive things left between you."

"Right. Well, that burned me but good, and I swore off men for a long time. I just kept my nose to the grindstone for a couple of years. In my senior year, I met Bobby. Actually, he chased me for months before I gave in and had a date with him. Oh! This is so embarrassing to tell you, Matt...." She shut her eyes tightly for a moment.

Sitting up, Matt leaned against the headboard and rearranged the sheet around his waist. The agony in Jenny's voice tore at him. Lifting his hand, he moved it lightly across her tense, drawn-up shoulders. "Was he just chasing you to get you in bed? A one-night stand?" he guessed.

Nodding, Jenny turned and looked at Matt, relishing the feel of his hand as it moved slowly across her shoulders. "Yes. I fell for it. Me. At twenty-two, I fell for it. I knew better. I guess I was hoping that Mark was wrong. He said no one would want someone like me in their life. I'd drive them crazy." Matt's features darkened and a flash of anger sparked to life in his narrowing gray eyes. His hand left her shoulders. Inwardly, Jenny cried out for his continued touch.

"So I'm gun-shy. That's why I find it hard to

believe you'd be interested in me. You're a hero, Matt. A genuine hero, with ribbons and medals to prove it. You're a true warrior. And yet you're so kind and sensitive underneath that armor you wear.''

"And you think that what I just shared with you means I want a one-night stand with you, right?"

Jenny avoided his sharpening gaze. His mouth stretched into a thin line. Hurting, she barely got out the whispered word, "Yes..."

"Because you don't think you're worth a long-term relationship, right?"

Cringing inwardly, she nodded. "Who wants a coward in their life, Matt?

"Listen to me," he said roughly as he settled his hands over her shoulders and turned her toward him, her knees pressing against his hip. Her eyes widened. "How about deleting 'coward' and inserting 'survivor' instead?" Matt tightened his fingers around her small shoulders and leaned down until his face was inches from hers. His emotions took hold of him and his voice lowered to a vibrating growl. "You have survived more adversity from birth onward than most people are ever given. You didn't become a drug addict like your mother, and you could have. You have ADD, but you've learned how to live your life and get along in the world with it, regardless. And you've got a degree in psychology, which clearly shows your discipline, endurance and drive. In my eyes, Jenny, you're a heroine of the first order.'' He gave her a small shake to emphasize the fiery words, which tore out of him in a blaze of frustration, anger and desire. He wanted so badly for her to know how wonderful a human being she really was, that others didn't see her as she saw herself. ''You want to know what *real* courage is? It's living life, day in and day out, the best you can, darlin'. It's about trying to be a decent human being even if you're tired, you're feeling rotten or life has been kicking the hell out of you. It's about struggling to always treat others with respect, with kindness and as your equal.''

Matt eased his grip on Jenny as he drowned in her tear-filled eyes. ''You *are* those things, Jenny! You're a heroine in my eyes and my heart. You're a true survivor—*not* a coward. I want you to take what I'm saying to heart. Please. If I have any influence at all on you, let my honesty replace how you see yourself, okay?''

Hot tears squeezed from her eyes. ''Oh, Matt...'' She lifted her hands and placed them on his broad, powerful shoulders.

Unable to bear seeing her cry, he whispered raggedly, ''I want to hold you, Jenny. Please? I want to give you a safe place. I promise, no funny stuff. Just let me hold you for a little while? I can't stand to see a woman or kid cry. It just tears the hell out of me...''

She crawled into Matt's opening arms. How wonderful it felt, Jenny decided, as he leaned back against the headboard and drew her deeply into his strong embrace. Resting her cheek against his shoulder, his jaw against her hair, she closed her eyes and shyly slid her arms around his torso. Just feeling his hand move protectively across the back of her nightgown, then up to sift gently through her hair, brought more tears to her tightly shut eyes.

"I...never knew.... I just never knew...." she sobbed.

Gruffly, he whispered against her silky hair, "What? That you're a good person, Jenny? That you're courageous already, even if you're the last to realize it? Why do you think Major Stevenson and those pilots respect you? Not one made fun of you. They *admire* you, darlin'. You just don't see it." Breathing out savagely, Matt continued to hold her soft form against his harder one. Sweet mercy, how he wanted to kiss her. But he couldn't...he didn't dare make that move unless Jenny made it first. He swore he would not take advantage of her like Mark and that other jerk had. Right now, as she wept unashamedly in his arms, her small body trembling with each sob, he wanted to give her a safe harbor from the rugged life she'd endured alone thus far.

Grinding his teeth with anger, Matt glared up into the grayness of the quiet room. If he had anything to do with it, Jenny's days of being alone, feeling as if she were a loser and a coward, were over. Matt wasn't exactly sure how he would make that happen, only that his heart told him to do it. Jenny was worthy of love. She was one of the most outwardly giving, loving people he'd ever run across. Matt knew, without a doubt, that he wasn't perfect. Far from it. But he wasn't like the men of her past, either. He valued a long-term relationship. Was there hope for them? Would she consider him more than just a working partner on this mission?

Matt was scared. As he closed his eyes, sighed raggedly and simply absorbed the warmth and fluid feminine length of Jenny in his arms, he was more scared than he could ever recall being. And he was unsure of what else to say. Or do. Or how far to go with her. What it all boiled down to was that Jenny had to make the next move. He had to wait and be patient. To let the shock and trauma and beauty of tonight's honest baring of their souls settle within her heart and mind. That would take time.

Did they have it? How many days were left here? Matt knew that as soon as they got back to Perseus HQ, he had another mission waiting for him, and he'd be gone for another three months. Dammit, anyway. Life was not fair.

## Chapter Eight

It took everything Jenny had the next morning after they arrived at Black Jaguar Base, to set aside thoughts of the incredible tenderness and care that Matt had shared with her earlier. Her body still sang from the way he'd held her, as if she were a priceless, delicate and beautiful vase that would surely shatter if he clasped her too tightly in his strong, warm arms. Oh, she wouldn't break, Jenny knew. What Matt didn't realize was that she had a ribbon as strong as steel winding through her.

Matt was sitting to one side in their small cubicle of an office, sipping his hot coffee, when the first interviewee of the day came to the door. A woman with eyes to match the sable color of her shoulder-length hair came and knocked lightly on the opened door. She was about five foot six inches tall, firmly muscled and with a narrow face. Although she wore no rank identification on her black uniform, Matt knew it was Captain Sarah Klein, the XO—executive officer—of the base. She was Major Stevenson's right hand, and a big part of why the base ran so successfully. He watched covertly as Jenny stood and offered her hand to the XO.

"Hi, Captain Klein," Jenny said. "Come in, please. I know you're busier than a one-armed paper hanger around here. Have a seat and we'll get this interview done as fast as possible so you can get back to work."

"Thanks, and call me Dallas, will you? It's what everyone calls me." She turned and nodded in Matt's direction. "Good morning, Mr. Davis."

Impeccable manners. Conservative and diplomatic. Matt nodded and kept the analysis to himself. "Good morning, Dallas. You had your java yet?" He pointed to the coffee machine located on the sideboard near Jenny's desk.

Laughing huskily, Dallas said, "Oh, yes. My day started at 0400 when one of our maintenance crews had an unexpected mechanical problem with our Blackhawk. I'm running full bore on my wire-walking coffee routine, thanks. One more cup and you'll have to scrape me off the ceiling,'' she added with a chuckle.

Jenny grinned. She liked Dallas immediately. The XO position required a lot of hard behind-the-scenes work, judging from what Matt had told her earlier on their flight from Agua Caliente to the base. The commanding officer created the orders and the XO catalyzed them and made things happen. It was the hardest job in a squadron, from what Matt had told her. And looking at Dallas, who relaxed, one leg across the other, her long, spare hands in her lap, she could see the care-worn quality to her face, the tiredness lurking beneath her sparkling sable eyes.

Still, there was a softness at the corners of the pilot's mouth, and Jenny found herself liking the woman without really even knowing why. Dallas inspired her simply with her quiet, easygoing, steady presence. Maybe it was the woman's face, which was narrow and oval, with a strong chin, aquiline nose and large, liquid, deerlike eyes, that bestowed a sense of calm around Dallas and made Jenny feel at ease.

Quickly opening up her personnel file, Jenny asked, "Why do you want to volunteer for the border trading mission, Dallas? Aren't you busy enough around here?''

A smile lurked on her well-shaped mouth. Opening her hands, she said, "Even an XO needs a change of pace every once in a while. I asked

Maya—Major Stevenson—what she thought of me thinking about volunteering for such an assignment because of the heavy responsibilities and duties I have around her. I asked her if she could get along without me for three months."

"And could she?"

Dallas shrugged. "She said she could. Maya lies well." She chuckled indulgently. "But she also knows I've been XO for three years now, and I need a mental health break from all this…" she waved her hand toward the door "…crazy activity."

"So, you see this mission up on the Mexican-American border, and the required training of U.S. Army Apache helicopter pilots," Jenny asked, "as less strenuous than what you're doing here?"

Tunneling her fingers through her loose, slightly wavy hair, Dallas said, "Absolutely. That will be fun compared to the nonstop tension that we operate under here."

"The mission requires someone with a lot of diplomacy. I note here from our mission analysis that the person chosen for this assignment must be able to get along with men even though there will be prejudice against a woman being in command of the training." Jenny looked up. "Are you prepared for the male Apache pilots to give you problems because you're a woman, Dallas?"

She leaned forward, her elbow on her knee. "That's a good question, Jenny. My answer is yes,

I can. After all, I'm an Israeli pilot on loan to the U.S. Army. I went through Apache rotorcraft training at Fort Rucker, Alabama, some time ago. We had a *lot* of prejudice thrown against us because we were the first class of women to go through that male bastion. We learned well from that experience.'' She smiled slightly, then her eyes narrowed. ''I believe my age, which is twenty-nine, and my three years of experience in a combat zone, will eventually get these younger pilots to come around and respect me and what I have to teach them. They might not like the fact that I'm a woman. But they will respect the fact that I'm a combat veteran. It's one thing to have been in the two-day Gulf War. It's completely another to be operating daily on a wartime footing such as we have here, and live to tell about it.''

''I see. And why would you want to put yourself into the same situation that you endured before with U.S. Army Apache helicopter pilots?''

Dallas grinned and leaned back, relaxed. ''You're very good at asking the right questions,'' she murmured. ''You should be an XO.''

Laughing, Jenny nodded and blushed. ''Thank you.'' She glanced over to see admiration shining in Matt's eyes, and an I-told-you-so look on his face. ''But I don't think I have the moxie, the courage that you women display here daily every time you fly against those Kamov Black Sharks that are just waiting to try and destroy you.'' Shaking her head, Jenny patted the laptop. ''I'll stick to being an interviewer, fair enough?''

Dallas smiled fully. ''Okay…suit yourself. We can always use someone like you down here, though. Your insight and perceptions are bang on, and in my job as XO, I'm more a personnel manager than anything else, making sure things work smoothly and fluidly around here. You have that same kind of people awareness in you. And that's a gift an XO needs just as much as training.''

Glowing inwardly, Jenny nodded. ''Thanks, Dallas. And do you see your abilities to handle and manage people as one of the reasons why you want this mission?''

''Yes. I feel I can smooth over rough spots, and I can deal with challenge and adversity better than most.'' She grinned a little more widely. ''I was raised in a kibbutz in Israel. My father was a military pilot.''

''And he was highly decorated,'' Jenny noted, looking at the personnel record.

''Yes. And my mother is in the Mossad, the secret service of our country.''

''So, you come from a military family.''

''If you live in Israel, the military is a fundamental part of your life, Jenny. Everyone gives two mandatory years to it.''

''What made you want to become a combat helicopter pilot? Over in Israel, they have no women in that arm of their air force.''

"Exactly." Dallas pursed her lips. "I was born to fly. Growing up, I remember seeing the eagles and hawks around our kibbutz. I wanted to soar, to feel the lift of that hot desert air taking me up into the blue of the sky.'' She aimed her hand upward. "My father was a military jet pilot. He taught me to fly when I was fourteen years old. Later, I grew to love helicopters, and by the time I was eighteen, I had hundreds of hours flying them. It was natural for me to want to fly helos. He suggested I apply to the U.S. Army, as part of their foreign pilot exchange program, for training.'' With a shrug, she said, "I got lucky...well, maybe that isn't the right word. My father, because of who he is, was able to open that door for me. The U.S. Army allowed me to come and train, and that's where I met Maya. After we received our wings, I applied to come down here to be a part of this clandestine operation. They accepted me and the rest is history.''

"That is so impressive," Jenny murmured. "You've done so much to open up the possibilities for women in Israel to fly combat.''

"I hope so." Dallas smiled warmly. She looked at the watch on her wrist. "I'm sorry, I've got to go—I've got to be at a tact and strat meeting in five minutes. Do you have any other questions?'' she asked as she rose.

Jenny nodded. "Just one. Why are you called Dallas and not by your real name, Sarah?"

Chuckling, Dallas halted at the door, her hand resting on the jamb. "Oh, that. I think you know every pilot gets a nickname or handle during flight school?"

"Yes."

"Do you remember the American television series, *Dallas*?"

"Of course."

Her eyes crinkled with amusement. "In my younger days, I had this wild obsession about the American West. Cowboys. Indians. And my favorite show was *Dallas*. So my women squad mates chose the handle Dallas for me."

"Have you been to Texas? To Dallas?" Jenny wondered with a smile.

"Oh, yes." She rolled her eyes. "That's another story, for another day." Lifting her hand, she said, "Thanks for taking the time to see me. I'll keep my fingers crossed that you'll consider me for that training opening up on the border."

After she left, Jenny turned to Matt. "What a difference in personalities!"

He sat up and put his coffee mug on the edge of her desk. "You're seeing the difference between just being a pilot in the squadron, like Akiva, and someone whose collateral duties are much more critical. Being a CO or XO are the two hardest positions to be in.''

"What is your feeling about Dallas?"

Matt grinned. "Judging from the shining look, the excitement in your eyes, I'd say you've found the perfect woman to head up that border mission."

Touching her cheek, Jenny mumbled, "I can't hide a thing from you, can I?"

Gloating, he said, "No...but you know by now that whatever you reveal is safe with me." More than anything, Matt wanted Jenny to feel comfortable around him. This morning, when he'd held her as she sobbed out her heart to him, he knew that they'd taken an important step in that direction. He'd held her. He hadn't tried to take advantage of the situation. Oh, it was hell on him, no doubt about it. Even now he positively itched to slide his fingers around her smooth, small breast, to nuzzle his face into her sweet-smelling, silky blond hair, or kiss the nape of her slender neck, which probably would feel like a soft, fuzzy peach beneath his lips. It was a damn good thing she couldn't read his mind. And even better that he could put an unreadable mask across his face so she couldn't discern the lurid, selfish, greedy thoughts he had about her.

Reaching out, Jenny touched Matt's hand, which rested on the side of the desk near his coffee cup. "You make me feel safe," she said quietly. "This morning, when I cried…you have no idea how wonderful it felt to be in your arms… to be held…."

"I'll always be a safe harbor for you, Jenny," Matt replied, gazing at her intently. "And that means beyond the scope of this mission. We've been thrown together for now, but I'd like to think that when we get home, what we've got, what we've shared, won't be over."

There, he'd said it. He'd put his biggest hopes into words. Judging by the widening look in her blue eyes, the way her black pupils enlarged, Matt knew he'd struck a sensitive chord in Jenny. Her thin blond brows knitted for a moment and, hands fluttering, she busied herself with the files. Matt knew her well enough by now to know that was a nervous reaction. Her brows dipped and her mouth went thin. What was she thinking? Feeling? Had he gone too far? Probably. *Damn.*

Licking her lips nervously, Jenny cast him a quick glance. "Gosh, Matt…everything seems so crazy for me right now, so different…." Her heart pounded at the idea that Matt wanted to continue to explore their relationship once this was over. She was thunderstruck by that. Hope warred with the silly idealism that she brought to every relationship. In her experience, Jenny had found she'd expected too much from the man. And yet Matt's sincerity, the burning look in his eyes, made her heart skitter with such elation that she could not ignore it.

Muttering, he said, "Yeah...I didn't mean to pressure you, Jenny."

Before he could say another word, the intruder alarm bell rang noisily throughout the cave complex. He saw Jenny jump in response to the loud, harsh sound, and then physically force herself to sit and relax in the aftermath.

Mind and heart in tumult over Matt's admission, Jenny didn't know what else to do or say at the moment. Lamely, she offered, "There goes our next interview," and she held up the personnel file of Chief Warrant Officer Cam Anderson, a green-eyed, redheaded twenty-five-year-old from Montana.

"She's got the duty?"

Nodding, Jenny stood up. "Yes, and so does the other perspective volunteer, Captain Dove Rivera." She hesitated, deep in thought over his declaration. How often had she dreamed of a man saying those wonderful words to her?

Standing, he said, "Might as well call it a day, then? There's no telling how long they'll be gone." Giving her a glance, he saw Jenny standing there, a pensive look on her face, the file clasped in her hands.

"Yes, we might as well fly back to Agua Caliente," she murmured.

Matt smiled slightly as he met and held her blue eyes. Was Jenny going to dodge his admission? It looked like it. Disappointment flowed through him.

Looking at his watch, he stated, "It's almost noon. How about a picnic down by the Urubamba River? Maria was telling me yesterday about a sweet spot with plenty of shade that's ideal. It's close to Agua Caliente, too. How about it?"

"A picnic?" Jenny liked the idea and drowned in the burning look he gave her.

Seeing the interest and excitement in her eyes as she placed the laptop in her black nylon carrying case, Matt said, "Yeah. Are you game?"

"Just you and me?"

"Yes." He saw the corners of her mouth pull upward. "Am I pushing you?" His heart thudded hard in his chest as he asked the question. If Jenny felt pressured, then it was a no go as far as he was concerned.

Zipping the case shut, Jenny lifted her chin and gazed the short distance to where he stood, his brow wrinkled with concern. "I'd love to, Matt." And she would. Her heart skittered. Where was this leading? He was so incredibly handsome, strong and self-assured. Why would he see anything in her? And then Jenny caught herself and stopped that old tape from the past from playing itself out in her head. No, she was worthy of someone like Matt Davis. She told herself that sternly a number of times as she shut off the light and left the office with him. A part of her did believe there was hope for them—a very small part. Another part of her wondered whether such a dream could ever come true. And then the sick, wounded side of her that had yet to heal said that she was being a fool once again, that she wasn't worthy and that he was only after her to get her into bed for a one-night stand.

As they walked down the hall, Jenny's heart lifted with joy. Euphoria swept over her. Suddenly, the healing part of her *did* believe that Matt was genuinely interested in her, warts and all. Even a toad with warts could have a lifelong mate, she reminded herself as she took the metal grate stairs down to the black lava floor of the cave. As they walked toward an awaiting golf cart that would zip them through the tunnel to the mining side of the mountain and the world beyond, Jenny smiled. It was the smile of a woman finding the door to her prison, opening it and walking outside for the first time in her life.

"Llama cheese sandwiches," Matt murmured appreciatively as he reached out and handed Jenny the huge slices of dark brown bread stuffed with peeled tomatoes and white, crumbly cheese. He had brought one of the old wool army blankets along and they had just settled comfortably on it to enjoy their picnic. Thanks to Maria's directions, they'd located the small sandy spot beneath the protective branches of a silver-barked eucalyptus tree towering on the bank. A hundred feet away, the Urubamba splashed and thundered. There were gargantuan boulders of all colors and sizes out in the river, large enough that they couldn't be swept away by the strong, relentless current. The river actually looked like a garden of stones more than water. Over the eons, the boulders had tumbled from cliffs in the rugged Andes, from which the Urubamba was born. The sky had cleared to a powder-blue hue, and was strewn with hundreds of cobalt-colored swallows with cream breasts, flitting and diving along the restless, churning river, snapping up dragonflies, mosquitoes and moths unlucky enough to be spotted by the birds.

Jenny took the sandwich in both hands. "This is huge! I can't possibly eat all of it, Matt." Kannie and Patrick, the owners of India Feliz, had ordered their chef to make them a "wonderful" picnic lunch. Wonderful it was—and huge.

"Eat what you can," Matt said, setting out the green bottle of Peruvian white wine. He popped the cork and poured the golden liquid into awaiting plastic cups. "Kannie tends to think you're too skinny." The woman had thoughtfully added tasty, thinly sliced, deep-fried potatoes with their special herbs and salt sprinkled across them. Matt could overdose on them, they were so good. But then, potatoes in Peru tasted like none other worldwide. This was, in his opinion, the potato capital of the world. And if that wasn't enough, Kannie had included two thick slices of chocolate cake with white frosting for dessert.

Munching on the delicious sandwich, Jenny sighed. She sat on one side of the blanket with her legs crossed, the picnic spread between her and Matt. The dappled shade of the eucalyptus above them cut the heat and humidity, which always increased between noon and sunset. The riverbank was about five to ten degrees cooler than the jungle itself because of the ice-fed stream churning and tumbling rebelliously in front of them. The water, as a matter of fact, had felt like ice cubes to Jenny, when she'd tested it earlier with her hands. She didn't see how Maria or any other Peruvian woman could constantly work in that chilling water from the tributary. Maybe that was why Maria's hands were so leathery and thick—to protect them from hypothermia.

Looking up at Matt as he eagerly bit into his own sandwich, Jenny gestured to the river. "I have never seen a river that rages like this one."

"This is what they call a '5' river," he told her. Taking one of the red linen napkins, he handed it to Jenny and then got one for himself. She looked so young and relaxed here by the water. A picnic had been the perfect idea. "Guys who run rapids rate rivers from 1 through 5," he told her. "The more dangerous it is—the faster it flows and the more rocks or boulders you have to try and navigate around—the higher the number." With a shake of his head, he sipped the fruity wine. "Frankly, I consider anyone who even *thinks* of trying to run the Urubamba insane. No one could do it. They'd kill themselves with the speed this river has and end up smashing into one of those huge boulders out there."

"No disagreement from me. Plus the water is so cold, Matt."

"That's why it's great trout fishing." He grinned. "Trout thrive in icy water. I was born in Ketchum, Idaho. My dad ran an outfitting company. I grew up hiking and fishing all the time." His father had a small company that he'd built into a multimillion-dollar business.

"What a wonderful childhood." Jenny studied the river for a long moment before speaking. "Maria was telling me that a boy who works at a local hotel was swept away in that tributary where they wash their clothes. He slipped on a rock while carrying luggage across it with several other young men. She said it happened so fast that no one reacted soon enough. The boy was dragged out into the center by the strong current, and in no time was washed out into the Urubamba." Her voice lowered. "Maria said they found his body three days later, washed up far below the town. That's so sad, but that tributary and this river are nothing to mess with." She shivered.

"I'm not going to argue that point at all," Matt murmured, taking another hefty bite of his sandwich. The sunlight played upon her blond hair, dappling it with spots that reminded him of gold coins. Jenny *was* a treasure to him. In all ways.

"Do you know how long it's been since I took time out for a picnic? Just to sit and watch the world go by?" he asked.

She smiled and sipped her wine. "No. Tell me."

Stretching out to his full length, his legs off the blanket and resting across some small, smooth rocks, he said, "I can't remember the last time. When I was growing up I used to like to go down to the creek on our property, go fishing and just lie under that big, spreading oak's arms."

"Sounds nice," she ventured. "You look like you wish for more of that now?"

"You're astute."

"Thank you. Well? Are you wanting to rest from your dangerous, intense lifestyle? To just spend time watching the world go by?"

Matt's mouth pulled slightly as he popped several salty slices of potatoes into his mouth. "Yeah, maybe I am. I'm older now. Feeling like I want to settle down."

"And before?"

"Footloose and fancy free, as they say. That's probably what destroyed my first marriage."

"Being away so often?" Jenny knew that many

of the missions Perseus ran were three to six months in length. Sometimes longer, especially undercover ops. And that was a long time to be gone unless there was a very understanding spouse at the other end, which wasn't often the case.

Nodding, Matt sipped the wine and then set it down in front of him on the blanket. "Yeah, my being gone really put the marriage on the skids. Everything else that helped push it over the edge was secondary. When I finally 'got it'—that my being gone so often and so long was really at the core of our problems, I tried to change. But—" he scowled "—it was too late, only I didn't want to admit it. I had quit the SEALs and joined Perseus, thinking that it would somehow save what we had. But…it didn't."

"Life from where I stand is an endless classroom," Jenny told him gently. "We all make tons of mistakes. It's what we do with what we learn from them the next time around that counts."

"Wise words from a wise young woman," he granted as he finished off the sandwich. Reaching for the chocolate cake, he removed the plastic film. Taking a plastic fork, he dug into it.

The silence stretched between them. It wasn't really silence with the roar of the Urubamba right next to them. Matt enjoyed watching Jenny eat. She took small bites. After every bite, she'd suck on her fingertips, which got messy with the llama cheese. Of late, he'd noticed that a lot of her restlessness and frenetic, almost manic activity, had ceased. She seemed much calmer. Happier. Or was it his imagination? Was it him? Peru? Or was she becoming more confident in herself and her skills as these interviews progressed? Matt wasn't sure. Finally, he got up enough courage to ask her a question that had been begging to be voiced for a long time.

"Jenny?"

"Yes?"

"What are your dreams? What do you want out of life? Where do you see yourself five years from now?"

## Chapter Nine

Jenny thought for a moment and then slowly wiped her fingers a final time on the red linen napkin. She saw the seriousness and interest in Matt's eyes and knew that his question wasn't small talk. Her heart skittered, and she was unable to drag her gaze from the tender flame burning in his gray eyes.

"Well…you know, I never had a template for my life." With a slight shrug, she continued, "Maybe being passed around to different families was upsetting to me and I just never got attached to anything…or hardly anyone. But I knew I wanted to make something of myself, come heck or high water. I had to prove to myself that I'm not the dummy they called me all through the different schools I went to. Getting that degree was really my only goal.''

Looking toward the roaring, massive Urubamba, Jenny said with deprecation, ''My life has been like that river, in a lot of ways, Matt. Look at all those huge boulders, hundreds of them, scattered across the expanse. I feel like I've been a Ping-Pong ball, hitting life's boulders and being bounced to the next ever since I was a child.'' Her mouth curved ruefully as she turned and met his hooded gaze. ''And if I ever fell in that river, I'd be bounced around like one, too.''

''Perish the thought,'' Matt growled. ''You wouldn't last five minutes in it. No one would. Not even me, and I'm a trained SEAL. If smashing full speed into one of those boulders didn't kill you outright, then the hypothermia would get you in ten minutes or less.''

Slowly folding the napkin in her lap and then smoothing it out against her thighs, Jenny said, ''No argument there. Anyway…my goals? Dreams? I just kinda hang loose, you know? Getting this job and working for Morgan was an unexpected joy. I love him so much. He's like a gruff old teddy bear, sorta growly, but he has such a tender, caring side to him. And Laura…well, she's wonderful.'' Giving him a slight smile, Jenny added in a whisper, ''Sometimes…sometimes in a moment of weakness, I fantasize that Laura and Morgan are my *real* mother and father. Oh, I know that's stupid…but that's how I feel toward them. And because of how they treat me, kind of like another daughter, I want to stay with Perseus for as long as they'll have me. Morgan giving me a chance to take this assignment is a huge plum, I know. I don't want to screw it up. I want to do well and show him that his faith in me is justified."

"Jenny, you're not going to screw up this mission. You can see now that you're good at what you do. I know Morgan will be happy with how you're handling everything, and who you choose for these three missions."

Nodding, she moved her finger in a circle on the napkin. "Yes…I'm beginning to see that." Lifting her chin, Jenny beamed at him. "Thanks to you… and to the pilots who, in their own way, support and encourage me, too."

"Well deserved," Matt murmured. "What about your personal life? You've told me what you want careerwise, what about the private Jenny Wright? What are her dreams? Her yearnings?"

Closing her eyes, she smiled and clasped her hands in her lap. "Oh! What a dreamer I am!"

"Can you share some of them with me?" Matt sat very still. Jenny looked in that moment like a golden angel as the sunlight lanced across her hair, stirred by the breeze along the river. The expression

of joy on her face expanded his heart. How badly he
wanted to rise up on his knees, lean across that basket
and plant a hot kiss on those smiling lips of hers.

"I *love* being a part-time baby-sitter for Laura. I
love children. Well..." Jenny opened her eyes and
laughed "...you can see that by how much I adore
Daniel and the other children here in this town. I'd
love to have a family of my own someday." Her
brows moved downward. "I'd like to have a chance
to undo what was done to me, and to give my children a stable, secure, caring environment. I'd like to
have a man who *wants* to be a father, not just someone who comes home at night and is available on
weekends to his kids." Opening her hands, she added
wryly, "I know this is a dream. I know it's not reality. But I see Morgan and Laura. He's over at their
house almost every noon, for an hour. And sometimes, when things aren't hectic, Laura will bring the
twins to see him on weekends if he's got to work
over there. She makes sure he's not pressed for time.
I love to see Peter and Kelly, who are twelve now.
They're curious and fascinated with the HQ being
underground. They love all the big screen displays
that show the satellites, and the colorful pictures that
show where across the globe our mission teams are
located."

"So, you want a man who's really involved in
raising the kids?"

"Absolutely. Otherwise, why have them? Why put it all on the woman to raise them, while he gets to be an absentee dad? I don't agree with that, Matt. I'm probably expecting too much of a man I might want to marry someday, but it's too important to gloss over. I won't do that to a child. I see how wonderful Katy—their second child, who's seventeen now—has turned out, with Morgan's daily influence on her. She's such a stunning and beautiful young woman. She looks so much like Laura."

"Jason is a little different," Matt noted as he sipped his wine.

"Well," Jenny said worriedly, "you know he was kidnapped by a drug lord when he was very young? Although he was rescued over in Hawaii by two of Morgan's best, he was old enough to remember those events, and I'm sure it's scarred him. He was torn from his family. Held hostage. And even though he's nineteen years old now, and going into his second year at the Naval Academy as a midshipman, Jason is withdrawn. Being firstborn, he's following in his dad's footsteps and wants to become a marine upon graduation. But he isn't trusting and open like the other three children. I can understand why. I wasn't stolen out of my house by a drug lord, but I was passed from one family to another, and the feelings are the same—like being abandoned."

"I think you're right about Jas," Matt said as he

set the empty glass aside. "There's a lot of turmoil deep inside him. He's become a loner as a result and doesn't trust anyone or anything outside himself."

"I know." She sighed unhappily. "I watched Morgan and Laura when he came home for the Easter holiday. They love him so much. They want him to be happy, but he isn't. Somehow, since that kidnapping, some deep connection between Jas and his parents has been broken. It's so sad, Matt, to see him. I wanted to cry. Jas just went off to his room, to be alone. And when Laura tried to get him involved in the family Easter egg hunt, he went for a hike into the mountains, instead."

"The boy has emotional wounds," Matt agreed. "Maybe being at the academy will help him understand commitment and teamwork. At least, we can hope that."

"Yes, and that as he gets older and experiences more of life's hard knocks, he'll be able to get in touch with his emotions and feelings and bond again with Morgan and Laura. I know, from being a psychologist, that on some unconscious level, Jas blames his parents for being kidnapped and abandoned. He's got a lot of unconscious rage aimed at them because of it. I'm sure he's not aware it's there or that he even understands his actions are hurting everyone. It's only natural for a small child to see separation from his parents as some sort of punishment. And no matter how much love, praise and support Morgan and Laura have lavished on Jason since his rescue, he's rejected it. The experience made him feel too vulnerable, and he's built a hellacious armored wall around himself to keep that from ever happening again.''

''Did your childhood affect you that way, Jenny?'' Matt said, enjoying the way the corners of her mouth lifted at his observation.

''No. But although I felt abandoned like Jason did, I wasn't kidnapped, and there's the difference. I mean, poor little Jas was literally snatched out of his bed. During the rescue, Sabra, the woman operative, held him, while Craig Talbot, the helicopter pilot, flew them out of the drug lord's villa. Only the helicopter was shot up and they crash-landed halfway to their destination. Jas had to endure that trauma, too. Sabra used her own body to shield him after they made the emergency landing. And if she hadn't run away from the site with him, Jason would have been killed.''

Shrugging, Jenny said more softly, ''Jas remembers all of it. And what's worse, he considered Sabra his 'auntie'—he was very close to her as a young one. That's why Morgan put her on that mission to locate and extract him. Sabra was wounded by a piece of flying shrapnel when the helicopter blew up. Jas was found sitting next to her, crying his little eyes out, while she was bloody and unconscious.''

Shivering, Jenny gave Matt a soulful look. "He's endured a lot. Those kinds of memories are like a brand on your heart and brain, as far as I'm concerned. They are life-altering events that affect a person forever."

Nodding, Matt said, "Jason has suffered a lot, there's no question. Maybe being in the naval academy will help him. He so badly wants to carry on the family's military tradition. I think he wants to erase the stain on the family's honor, too."

"Oh…that." Jenny sighed and sipped her wine with pleasure. "I think Morgan has more than shown the American public that he wasn't the traitor they thought he was during the Vietnam War."

"Still," Matt said, "I saw it in Jas's eyes sometimes in the year before he left for the academy. You know Laura and Morgan throw a huge, five-day Christmas party every year for those of us home from missions at the time."

She smiled. "Oh, yes! Laura goes all out. She loves to entertain and see people have a good time. She knows the stresses and demands on the mercs and their families. I helped her with some of the decorating last year, and drove to Helena with her to shop for gifts. The celebration was a lot of fun, and I got to meet a number of people who work for Perseus."

Matt's eyes crinkled. "I missed the last one because I was out on a mission, but I heard from a number of the guys who were able to attend that it was the best ever. The women mercs like it because they got to dress up.''

Sighing, Jenny said, ''It was wonderful, Matt. I loved it. Laura is so good at pulling people out of their shells and getting them to mix and mingle. Morgan is good, too, but Laura's heart and soul goes into this extravaganza. For five days, we were wined and dined while we celebrated and danced the nights away. On Christmas morning, they opened up their beautiful log house to about fifty people or so. There was a huge twenty-foot-tall Christmas tree, which we all helped to decorate on the first evening, and then everyone gathered for brunch. Afterward, we got to open gifts.'' She clapped her hands with delight. ''You wouldn't believe how wonderful it was! Laura knows every person who works for Perseus—and what they would like. It was great to see men and women who risk their lives become like animated children during the celebration. There was so much laughter and warmth. I just loved it. Laura calls it her Five Days of Christmas celebration.''

''And seeing the glimmer in your eyes, I can tell you're a big kid at Christmas yourself.'' It was one of the many things Matt had come to appreciate about Jenny. When she needed to be an adult, she was. But the moment she could slip out of those traces, she became spontaneous and childlike, filled with awe and wonder at the world around her. He found that refreshing and realized she made him feel more like a kid himself.

Laughing pleasantly, Jenny reached for her cake, unwrapped it and eagerly began to consume it. "That's one thing I really like about myself—being able to be a kid still. Maybe that's why I love children so much. They haven't lost the ability to be flexible and spontaneous in the moment."

He regarded her from beneath his short, thick lashes. "So, we're back to my original question, Jenny Wright. What do you want out of life?"

Hesitating fractionally, Jenny placed the plate in her lap, her hands around it. "The same thing everyone wants. I'd like to be married someday. I'd love to have two kids."

"Would you balance career and kids?" Matt asked.

Jenny shrugged. "I feel very strongly that children need a full-time mother for the first seven years of their life. I got to experience both sides of this. I had some foster mothers who stayed at home full-time. I had others that worked full-time, along with my foster fathers, while I had a procession of baby-sitters."

"You've been able to develop a unique perspective on this," Matt noted. He saw Jenny frown.

"I've thought a lot about this...I chew everything to death," she admitted with a giggle. "I'd hope that my husband would make enough money to allow me to stay home with our child. If he didn't, then I'd try to have some kind of job I could do at home, so I'd be there, anyway. And if that didn't work, then I'd look at taking a night job so I could at least be there during the day for the baby." Her brows rose and she gave him a playful look. "Of course, the dad would be hauling his fair share of the load of raising this child, too. It wouldn't all be on my shoulders. He'd learn how to wash the baby, change diapers and care for him or her just as I would."

"That's a fair expectation," Matt agreed.

"What about you?" Jenny asked, spooning more of the delicious cake into her mouth.

"Me?" Matt shrugged and played with the napkin in front of him. "After my divorce, I swore I'd never marry again. But now…I guess age and time have worn me down on that statement." He grinned a little. "I don't like the loneliness, to be honest. I don't like coming off a mission, going to the condo in Philipsburg where the mercs stay between assignments. The condo is beautiful and has all the amenities…but it's lonely."

Finishing off the cake, Jenny placed the paper plate and wrapper back into the pack. "That's the great thing about a good marriage. You have your best friend to do things with, to talk to, to share with."

"Yes, and in a bad marriage, none of those things are in place."

"You speak from experience," Jenny offered gently, seeing his gray eyes darken with old pain from the past. Reaching out, she squeezed his hand, which rested on top of the crinkled linen napkin between them. "Looking at how marriages are so disposable nowadays, I think a key to a successful one is that you become best friends, that you share a love of things together."

Turning his hand over, he lifted her fingers and pressed a tender kiss to the backs of them. Her eyes flared with surprise, and then turned languid with pleasure. Smiling up at her as he reluctantly released her hand, Matt asked, "Can we be friends?"

Jenny smiled in response. It was almost too much to hope for! Matt wanted her friendship. The thought filled her with happiness—and, she mused, a flutter of anticipation. What would it be like to *really* get to know Matt?

Jenny sat expectantly behind her desk at the Black Jaguar Base. Chief Warrant Officer Two, twenty-five-year-old Camilla Anderson, was due any minute for her interview. Matt sat in a relaxed position in the chair near the wall, coffee in hand. He gave Jenny a slight smile.

Matt thought Jenny looked even more beautiful this morning. Had the picnic down by the river done it? His kissing her hand? Or maybe he felt that way because they had finally taken the time to sit and explore one another on a deeper personal level? The answer was probably all of the above. Today she wore a pale pink, short-sleeved cotton blouse with a colorful scarf around her neck, khaki shorts and her hiking boots. Her hair was slightly mussed, as it always seemed to be, but on her it looked fetching. There was always a chaotic energy about Jenny, but he was growing to enjoy that aspect of her. Her hair, he realized now, seemed to symbolize her restless nature. She tried to tame it into place, but something—the helicopter blades, the mountain breeze— was always thwarting her efforts, and finally she'd give up let it be tousled and windblown—and lovely.

Maybe that was the key to Jenny, he mused, as he sipped the hot, fragrant coffee. Letting her be who she was. Two immature men had hurt her by trying to force her into a mold of what they thought she should be instead of prizing her as the unique flower she was.

Last night had been pure, unadulterated hell on Matt. She had slept soundly, like a baby, beside him. And he'd barely slept at all, inhaling the scent of the spicy ginger shampoo she'd used to wash her hair earlier. How badly he'd wanted to reach out, slide his arms around her and bring her against him.

Still, Matt acknowledged that simply sleeping together was helping Jenny. Each night she was less and less restless. She slept more deeply. Those dark circles beneath her eyes had disappeared and she was blooming like one of the breathtaking orchids that grew in such proliferation all around Agua Caliente.

CWO2 Camille Anderson came thunking down the hall toward the opened door, interrupting Matt's thoughts. As he shifted his attention to the Apache helicopter pilot who raced in the door, breathless, the young woman gave them a quick smile of hello and took the seat in front of the desk.

"Whew! Sorry I'm almost late." She glanced at the watch on her left wrist. "I've got collateral duty in the maintenance section with Major York, and we ran into some problems with one of the Apaches... thing unexpected." Blowing out a breath of air, she quickly moved her fingers through her thick, naturally curly auburn hair.

smiled and said, "Don't worry about it. We've learned that things around here are like a cork bobbing on the ocean, and we've got to be flexible."

Cam grinned and nodded. She smoothed her black uniform across her long, strong-looking thighs. "Yes, ma'am, that's the name of the game."

"Call me Jenny. What do you like to be called?"

"Cam." She grinned broadly. "Or you can call

me 'Tree Trimmer,' which is my new handle around here.''

Smiling, Jenny said, ''Tree Trimmer? What kind of a name is that?''

Opening her long, artistic-looking hands, Cam laughed deeply. ''About two years ago, I put the skids of our old Cobra, when we still had it, into the tops of the jungle trees and whacked off a bunch of branches. There was a thunderstorm approaching, and a gust of wind, a strong one, pushed the helicopter downward. I compensated for it, but not soon enough, and we ended up eating some jungle real estate. Major Stevenson was with me at the time, and gave me the name.''

Jenny smiled. She liked the tall pilot. Cam Anderson had lively forest-green eyes, a square face and short auburn hair that barely stayed tucked behind her ears. The ruddiness of her cheeks and the hundreds of freckles sprinkled across her fine, thin nose made her look decidedly Irish. There was a quiet alertness about Cam. Five foot nine inches tall, she was solidly built and large-boned. Glancing at her file, Jenny saw that she weighed a hundred fifty-five pounds. She was all legs, Jenny realized, with wide hips. In the back of her mind, Jenny applauded women who carried some weight on them. This skinny-as-a-rail stuff was for the birds. Cam was physically strong-looking, and Jenny knew that, like all the pilots and most of the other women personnel of the base, she worked out at the gym that was set up on the mining side.

"What was your handle before you turned those trees into salad?" Jenny teased with a smile. She saw Cam brighten as she sat before her, both booted feet on the floor, her hands relaxed on her thighs.

"Coming out of Fort Rucker training, they called me Cougar." She shrugged, a grin edging her wide mouth. "I come from Montana. I was born up in the Rocky Mountains. We have cougars and black bears all over that area. When I was very young, my mother had left me out in our backyard, which butted up against the national forest. When she came back a few minutes later, she saw a cougar sitting no more than ten feet away from me. Just watching me."

"Goodness," Jenny exclaimed. "I'll bet your mother just about had a heart attack!"

"I was six at the time. I still remember the incident. I wasn't scared, either. I kept saying, 'Here, kitty, kitty, kitty!' and that's what freaked my mother out."

"Amazing. What happened next?"

Cam grinned. "The cougar leaped up and left as soon as she saw my mother running toward me."

"Was it going to eat you?"

Cam's eyes lightened with laughter. "No, I don't think so. I still remember the feeling of that meeting.

It was like seeing an old friend again, odd as that sounds. I was happy to see the cougar.''

Jenny touched her cheek. ''I feel for your poor mother. She must have thought the worst.''

''Oh, my mother was pretty cool about it. I remember her picking me up and saying that the cougar was too big to be a house cat and that I shouldn't try calling it, because it wouldn't come. That it belonged in the wild.''

Jenny smiled. ''Is that how you see yourself, Cam? A woman who belongs in the wild?''

''Great question. Yes, I do. I've always been very confident about myself, and that's probably due to my parents telling me from the earliest I can remember that I could do anything I wanted in life, and be successful at it.''

''Good for them,'' Jenny murmured, writing down the information to be put into her laptop later. ''So tell me why you want to volunteer for one of these three assignments.''

Cam became very serious. She crossed one leg and frowned. ''I'm going to level with you, Jenny. It will probably cost me the possibility of getting one of these missions, but I owe you—and Major Stevenson—the truth on why I'd like to be considered.''

Jenny saw pain in Cam's eyes and in the way her mouth thinned. ''I'm listening.''

With a heavy sigh, Cam opened her hands and

lowered her voice. "A year ago Major Stevenson and I were flying the Cobra on a mapping mission, looking for new trails that the druggies were cutting in order to get their cocaine to drop-off points. We were at tree height." Her voice turned sad. "We got attacked by a Kamov out of the blue. Neither of us saw it coming. It shot us down."

Jenny frowned. "Oh, dear..."

"Yeah," Cam muttered, "bad news. *Really* bad news. I'm sure you've heard this already...it's an old story around the base."

"What story?"

One of Cam's thick brows moved upward. "How I abandoned Maya after the crash? The druggies were coming. I could see them in their trucks, hightailing it toward us. The Cobra was burning a hundred feet away from us. I managed to drag Maya out of the burning helo because she was unconscious. She'd taken a hit on the helmet from a branch as the helo twisted and fell down through the trees." Rubbing her face, she muttered, "Damn, this is harder than I thought it would be. Anyway..." she sighed with resignation "...I abandoned Maya. I ran away. I ran into the jungle to escape the druggies who were coming."

Jenny's heart contracted. She saw the anguish in Cam's face and heard it in her husky, low voice. Slanting Matt a quick glance, she saw him grimly studying the pilot. Although his face was unreadable, Jenny could feel he was suffering for Cam, as well.

"Wait…" Jenny murmured, holding up her hand. "No, I haven't heard this story from anyone, Cam. And I don't have the kind of military background to judge your decision."

"I do," Matt stated quietly. He set the coffee mug on the desk and folded his hands between his thighs as he studied Cam. "You might give Jenny your reasons for what you did, Cam. I think I know, but you need to share it with her so she understands the context of your decision—why you decided to do what you did under those circumstances."

Nodding, Cam blew out a painful breath of air. "Right…of course." She turned her attention back to Jenny. "I had a military decision to make. Maya was my commander. You've seen how thick the jungle is, right?"

"Yes, it's very dense, nearly impossible to walk through," Jenny replied. "I've heard the only way you can get through it is to hack a path with a machete."

"Correct," Cam whispered. "Well, Maya was out cold. The druggies were less than a quarter mile away and coming at high speed down that dirt road toward us. I knew they would capture both of us. I also knew that no one here at the base knew we'd been knocked out of the sky. I—I had a decision to make—leave Maya or try and take her with me."

"But," Jenny said quickly, "if she was unconscious, how in the world could you carry her through that wall of jungle? That would be impossible."

Nodding, Cam whispered, "That was the dilemma I faced. I wasn't hurt except for my arm being injured. I could get away. I felt I could escape deep enough into the jungle and eventually, over a day or two, make it back to the base to tell them what had happened. From there, we could mount a rescue effort for Maya."

"Under the circumstances," Jenny said gently, "I don't see that you had any choice in the matter. Did you escape?"

"Yes…reluctantly, let me tell you." After rubbing her face, Cam dropped her hands and stared down at the floor between her black flight boots. "I've never felt so horrible…leaving Maya. I didn't know how badly hurt she really was. I knew, from a military perspective, the right thing to do was get out, but damn…I didn't want to leave my fallen comrade in harm's way. I didn't want to leave Maya in the hands of druggies who I knew could hurt or kill her."

Jenny's heart contracted with anguish for Cam, whose face was tense with torment. "I don't see that you had a choice."

"Well," Cam said quietly, "that's why I'm here. Eventually, I did get found by Major York and Wild

Woman, and I got lifted out of the jungle and taken back to the base, where I told them what had happened. Lucky for us, things worked out okay in the end, and Maya freed herself eventually...but it still hurts here.'' She pressed her hand to her heart region. "I still feel like I abandoned her. My head tells me that what I did was right. But I was taught never to leave someone who was sick or hurt. And I feel that I should have stayed with her...." She compressed her lips and gave Jenny a quick look.

"And that's why you want to volunteer for one of these missions? In some way, to make up for that incident?"

"Bingo. You got it.'' Cam straightened up and threw back her proud shoulders, as if to try and shrug off the invisible weight she carried to this day. "I want a shot at one of those missions. I want to somehow make up for the past. I know Maya would be proud of me, maybe forgive me, if I could be successful at one of them. And that's what I'd like—a shot at the night border work. I have a lot of reasons to do it, to show her that she can have renewed faith and trust in me.''

"I see...'' Jenny murmured. "I'll take your desire to make things right once again into consideration, Cam.''

She brightened. "Thanks...it would mean a lot to me. I owe the major. I'd really like to repay her this way.''

# Chapter Ten

Jenny gave Matt a searching look after Cam left. She got up and quietly shut the door to their office. Turning, she leaned against it, her arms across her breasts.

"I'd value your feedback on her, on the reasons she states, Matt. Right now, I don't feel Cam's the right person for that border mission."

He stood up and rubbed his jaw while he gazed out the small window that overlooked the rear of the cave. "You're not wrong to feel that way," he murmured. Turning, he moved to the front of the desk and sat down on the edge, his hands resting on the cool metal. Jenny looked concerned, and he could see the frustration in her eyes.

"Cam is fueled by guilt," he told her. "Guilt that would plague *any* military person, and that's what you need to put into perspective here. We're trained *never* to leave a fallen comrade in the field. It just isn't acceptable in the SEALs. The Marine Corps has a similar tradition. I really felt for her when she was sharing that experience with us. I'd be torn, too. But under the circumstances—" he hooked a thumb over his shoulder "—with that dense jungle out there, Cam wouldn't have gotten ten feet, carrying Maya over her shoulder. It's one thing to be able to move, it's a whole 'nother thing to be carrying an unconscious person. And at six foot tall, Maya isn't any lightweight."

"So, you think Cam did the right thing?"

Giving her a pained look, Matt said, "You know what? The only person who can really answer that is Cam. Her training told her not to leave Maya wounded, alone and in the hands of the enemy. Another part of her, the survivor, saw that if she didn't escape, then no one back at the base would even *begin* to have a clue as to what happened or where they were. At least if she escaped and made it back to base, there'd be *hope* that Maya could be rescued."

"I see both sides of the issue," Jenny murmured. "What would I do in her place, I wonder?"

Matt nodded. "Right. You have to put yourself in her shoes, with her training and mind-set. The other factor, which is the wild card in all this, is the personality involved. Frankly, knowing what I know about this incident from her, I'd say she made the correct call. Escape and live to fight another day. Escape to get word back to your team as to what happened, and then mount a rescue effort for the fallen comrade. I think she did the right thing. And as for her thinking Maya holds the decision against her, I know that's not correct. Cam is holding it against herself. Maya understood her decision—I know, because I talked to her about it earlier this week, when I saw Cam's name on the list. In fact, Maya has told Cam to her face that she'd have done exactly the same thing if she'd been in her shoes.''

Jenny moved toward Matt, until she stood less than a foot away from him. The sleeves of his light blue chambray shirt were rolled up to just below his elbows, and the dark hair on his massive, well-muscled arms made her ache to reach out and slide her fingers across them. Fighting the urge, she studied his frowning features and darkened gray eyes as she pondered Cam's dilemma. ''It's good to know you talked with Maya about this.'' She slanted him an amused glance. ''If I was in trouble, you'd come after me, wouldn't you?''

Matt met her warm gaze. ''Of course I would. And so would you, if the tables were turned.''

Jenny nodded. ''Yes, I would.''

''Even if the deck was stacked against me? Even

knowing in advance that you might be killed in the process of trying to rescue me?''

"Without a doubt."

Matt gave her a long look. "People like you are the ones who, when a grenade from the enemy is rolled into a squad bay filled with people, throw themselves on it to save everyone else. But then, you die because of your actions."

"That is an act of ultimate courage—to put your life on the line for another, not knowing the outcome," Jenny agreed quietly as she chewed on her lower lip. She saw him roll his eyes. "What? What would you have done differently?"

"I'd probably kick the grenade out of the area with the toe of my boot, or pick it up and throw it. I'm not an idealist." Matt reached out and grazed her cheek, which instantly turned a flaming red. He saw the pleasure come to her eyes at his unexpected touch. How badly he wanted to kiss Jenny, to feel those soft lips beneath his hungry, greedy mouth. "You are."

Even though she was afraid, Jenny overcame her fear and boldly reached out and ruffled his hair in a playful motion. "You be the realist. I'm happy to be the idealist on our team."

Catching her hand, he smiled wolfishly. She grew still and relaxed within his warm, strong grasp. Matt saw the enjoyment, the gold flecks in her blue eyes as they glinted in merriment. With his other hand, he opened her smaller one and grazed her palm with his callused thumb. Instantly, he saw her lips part in surprise…and obvious pleasure.

"You know what?" he murmured as he held her tender gaze. "I like you just the way you are." Giving her hand a final squeeze, he released it. "Just don't find any grenades to go throw yourself on. I want you around me for a long, long time."

Shaken by his smoldering look and the grazing touch of his thumb upon her tingling palm, Jenny tried to smile, and failed miserably. "A 'fraidy cat? You want a mouse like me around? I don't believe it." She had said it partly in jest, part seriously.

"Then," Matt growled warningly, "believe this…" And he stood and placed his hands on her shoulders. Jenny looked up at him, surprise and desire written clearly in her eyes. Automatically, she placed her hands on his arms. Leaning down, he nuzzled her soft, silky hair, which smelled of wild ginger. "I want to kiss you so damn badly I ache, Jenny. But I won't do it…can't do it, unless you want me to." He rested his lips against her hair and felt her sudden intake of breath. Her hands hesitantly slid up to his elbows and she shyly leaned closer to him. There were scant inches between them now. Matt could feel the feminine heat of her body, the courageous heart beating beneath her small breasts.

Her world spun to a halt. Jenny hadn't expected

Matt to do this—to take her into his arms, to draw her so agonizingly close to his hard, male body. To press his mouth against her hair, so close to her left ear. She released the breath of trapped air from her lungs.

"I want you," he rasped unsteadily. "For all the right reasons, darlin'. You're precious to me, do you hear?" He slid his hands across her shoulders and forced himself not to pull her hard against him. This had to be mutual or it would never work. His heart was spilling over and he wasn't sure why. Maybe it was Cam's tortured story. Maybe he was fearful of losing Jenny because she was such an idealist. She'd give her life in a moment if need be, and he knew it. And then she'd be gone. Ripped out of his life forever. As a mercenary, as a SEAL, Matt knew how quickly life could be snuffed out. How fast it could be taken away from a person. His heart thundered in his chest with his desire to make her his now, immediately.

Jenny felt Matt's warm breath against the side of her face. She hungrily absorbed the feel of his roughened hands against her blouse. Her body was swept with a fire of intense longing. With a need so overwhelming that it consumed whatever fear or hesitancy lingered from her past. Matt deserved a woman who was as brave and courageous as he was being right now. Jenny understood the cost to him to admit what lay in his heart. More than anything, she believed him.

Lifting her chin, she met and drowned in his stormy gray gaze. Shivering with anticipation, she whispered unsteadily, "You're a man of honor, Matt. I know you mean it when you tell me you want me for all the right reasons." Lifting her hand, Jenny placed her palm against the side of his recently shaved face. There were so many small scars across his flesh. It hurt her to think how he'd received them. She knew there had to be some traumatic story behind each one, and that made her stomach clench in hurt.

When she touched him, his face grew tender... with love? What was she seeing in his eyes? Gulping, she couldn't be sure. Could he love her? Was she worth loving? Judging from his intent expression, the answer was an undeniable yes. She saw his strong lips part. His hands ranged upward from her shoulders to her face and framed it gently.

"I'll never be the warrior that you are, Matt."

"In my eyes, my heart, Jenny, you're already a heroine, a survivor, and I admire and respect the hell out of you for that. I don't care how you see yourself. What matters is how you really are. Do you understand that, darlin'?"

She closed her eyes and nodded slightly. His hands were so warm and comforting against her cheeks. "You deserve someone brave. Someone you can count on, Matt. You've helped me be stronger, and believe more in myself. You've been such a wonderful friend to me that I don't know where to begin—''

"Shh," he rasped, "don't tell me, Jenny. Show me how you feel about me. That's the place to start. We have a friendship. We respect and admire one another. Let's build on that. What do you say?'' He held his breath as he saw the effect his roughly spoken words had on her. The languid desire in Jenny's eyes as she opened them made him groan. Her lips were parted, and he saw the lower one tremble slightly as she boldly stepped forward, melted against him and placed her hands around his neck, drawing him downward…to kiss him.

Matt whispered her name like a prayer as he felt the first, tentative brush of her lips against his. A groan ripped from him. Instantly, he drew her close. She was soft, rounded, and seemed to flow against the harder angles of his tense body. Her arms wound around his neck and she stretched upward, her mouth opening to his hungry, searching lips. She tasted of sweet cinnamon and coffee. Her breathing came in chaotic bursts, warm and tingling against his sensitized flesh.

Inhaling deeply, Matt dragged in the gingery, womanly scent that was hers alone. Jenny was in his arms! She was kissing him! Wanting to reward her courage, her boldness, because he knew that she had to overcome a lot of fear to open herself up to him, Matt softened his mouth against hers. When he ran his tongue across her lower lip, a small moan trembled from her—a moan of pleasure. Satisfaction roared through him.

Desperately wanting to make her part of him, Matt ranged his hands across her slender arms and shoulders. He wanted to cup his fingers around her breasts, but stopped himself. This was a kiss of introduction, of mutual exploration, he sternly reminded himself. Yet his body was hard with need. Hot like fire itself, Matt was sure that Jenny was more than a little aware of his aroused state as her hips brushed naively against his.

Jenny drowned in the splendor of Matt's mouth. She hungrily drank from him. He was strong and sure, and shared that with her. It gave her the courage to boldly return his ardor. Her lower body throbbed with a smoldering fire that exploded violently to life as his mouth glided commandingly against her waiting lips.

Lost within the splintering sunlight and heat his mouth evoked, Jenny entrusted herself entirely to his strong, hard body. Matt's arms felt incredibly secure around her. Pressed against him as she was, she was wildly aware of his need of her. Intense, melting heat flowed through her like a river of lava. Never had a kiss spun her into a realm of such beauty and joy as this one was.

All too soon, he drew away. Jenny was confused. Her heart hammered violently in her chest as he reluctantly eased her away from him, his hands firm on her upper arms. Yet the predatory look in his silvery eyes sizzled through her, awakening her senses, and her mouth throbbed with the male power of him claiming her as his own.

"Your next interview is in ten minutes," he rasped. A deprecating smile pulled at one corner of his mouth as he reached out and tamed her hair back into place. "I think we need to get ourselves together for it, okay?"

Matt was right. With a slight moan, Jenny held on to his arm for a moment more. "Y-you're right...yes..." And she took a deep, shaky breath as she gazed up at him. "You kiss so wonderfully...."

Matt's returning grin was that of a peacock who was very pleased with himself, and she laughed breathlessly. She could still taste him on her lips. It was a heady discovery filled with promise.

"Me? A good kisser?"

"Yes, you," she declared. Finally, Jenny let go of him and stepped away. She didn't want to. She wanted to kiss Matt again and again, and explore him slowly. So slowly and deliciously, with her hands, her body, her lips. Matt was bringing out a decidedly sensual side of herself she'd never encountered before. Although surprising to Jenny, she reveled in it. "You make me feel intensely. I feel my body more than I ever have."

Her blush was demure and her honesty heart-wrenching to Matt. Sliding his hand along her jaw, he whispered, "You do the same thing to me, Jenny. I think there's a lot we have in common, don't you?"

"Oh, yes," she answered with a slight, embarrassed laugh. Moving awkwardly around the desk, she sat down before she fell down, her knees feeling suddenly mushy. Her mind and focus weren't on the coming interview at all. She opened the desk and pulled out her purse. After brushing her hair, she tried to pat her blouse back into place, and hoped she looked unmussed and presentable.

Matt sat on the edge of the desk, a predatory smile on his mouth and a gleam in his eyes that said *You're mine. All mine.*

It was late afternoon as they walked away from the helicopter pad and ambled down the dirt path parallel to the railroad tracks that would take them into Agua Caliente. This time Jenny slipped her hand into Matt's. He carried her briefcase in his other hand.

Jenny gave him a tender smile and Matt felt joy rise in his chest as never before. That one, perfect kiss had told her what lay in his heart. Matt knew he didn't have fancy words. Women often did a great job of communicating, but he felt like he had two left hands and a tongue to match when he tried to tell someone how he felt. His feelings for Jenny had been translated through that life-altering kiss he'd shared with her earlier.

As they walked along the path, Matt spotted bright yellow orchids with luscious red lips. One day, as Jenny had played in the shallow pool along the tributary, where all the children were safe from the strong, powerful currents, Maria had told Matt in a confidential voice about this flower. It was the marriage orchid, she'd whispered. She'd had a wicked glimmer in her chocolate-brown eyes as she looked pointedly downstream to where Jenny was crouched next to Daniel, playing with his dearly beloved red rubber ball. Maria confided conspiratorially to Matt that a man who was thinking of marrying the woman of his heart would always give her this orchid, for it was a symbol of his intent to ask her for her hand and heart, to be his wife someday soon. At the time, Matt had wondered if his feelings were that transparent. They must have been.

Leaning down now, he pulled Jenny gently to a halt. "Hold on," he told her as he snapped off the round, green stem of the orchid. Straightening, he turned and put the briefcase down beside him. Placing the orchid stem in the top buttonhole of her blouse, he arranged it so that the blossom lay against her shoulder, just beneath her chin.

The orchid was fragrant, and Jenny closed her eyes and drew in a breath. "How beautiful," she whispered in awe, and reached out, sliding her hand down his forearm. Opening her eyes, she said, "Thank you, Matt...that's so sweet and thoughtful of you. I've never had a man give me flowers before."

He stared in shock at her comment, then swallowed his surprise. Picking up her briefcase, he turned and led her down a well-worn path to the tributary. "Well, expect them often from me."

Matt liked the daily schedule they'd fallen into. Jenny always saved her dessert from lunch at the base to bring back to Daniel. Maria was always down at the tributary this time of day, pounding the soapy clothes for her clients. Little Daniel, who always waited anxiously to spot them, would wave and jump up and down. He knew the dessert was coming.

Jenny touched the orchid. "It's beautiful, Matt. Thank you." He was so tender. So thoughtful. And yet to look at him, at that hard, warrior's face and mouth, no one would ever suspect he had such a romantic side to him. Jenny smiled. "This day is perfect, Matt. Perfect in every way."

As they made their way down the steep part of the path to the roaring tributary, he said, "The first day of the rest of our lives."

His meaning wasn't lost on Jenny. She saw the

burning desire in Matt's eyes as he turned and looked at her on the path, which was only wide enough for one person to traverse at a time. Long, hip-high grass grew luxuriantly on either side of the trail. The sun was shining brightly between powder-puff white clouds. The constant, throaty roar of the Urubamba filled the air around them.

Keeping a steadying grip on Jenny's hand, Matt led her to the shelf of rock where at least twenty Peruvian women toiled away with their laundry. Halfway down the bank, little Daniel, dressed in a bright red shirt and shabby, brown cotton trousers, his feet bare and muddy, waved gleefully toward them. Matt grinned as Jenny moved ahead of him, waving gaily back at the youngster. He saw Maria down on her hands and knees at her favorite flat rock on the edge of the churning water, the clothes wet and soapy as she beat them methodically with the smooth, gray stone in her hands. She looked up and nodded, giving them a wide, welcoming smile.

As they approached, Matt noted the long coil of white hemp rope near Maria. When she was finished washing the clothes, she'd string the hundred feet or so of rope from one spindly tree on the bank to another, and then hang the dripping garments there to dry overnight. In the morning, she'd come down and collect the clothes, fold them and carry them in baskets to her clients, who would give her a few soles for her efforts.

Maria's eyes danced as she saw Jenny approach. Her smile increased immensely and she called to her, commenting on the orchid she wore.

Matt realized Jenny didn't know what the orchid symbolized. That was all right. In time, he'd share that with her.

The bank of the tributary was mostly rock, and a little grainy sand. Daniel ran brokenly along the edge of the roaring tributary, on small, brown, spindly legs, his ball in his left hand. His eyes were wide and he was calling Jenny's name as he hopped and leaped over the gray, black and speckled boulders.

Matt stopped near Maria to say hello. Then he put the briefcase down and looked up in time to see a horrifying sight.

Daniel was hurrying across the rocky terrain toward Jenny when his muddy feet slipped on a smooth rock. The boy yelped and the red ball he carried in his hand flew out into the swirling water as he tried to regain his balance. Daniel turned and cried out, reaching for the ball, which bobbed only a few feet away in an eddy of icy water.

Matt started to shout. Maria shrieked and leaped to her feet, her cry echoing over the noise of the river. But it was too late. Her son vaulted into the river to retrieve his ball. In seconds, he was swept out into the wicked current.

Matt's voice was drowned out by the roar of the Urubamba as he saw Jenny drop the cake plate she carried. Without hesitation, without even thinking, she leaped into the water to try and grab Daniel's small, extended hand. Instead, the deadly undercurrent yanked her booted feet out from under her! In a split second she disappeared into the foaming blue-green water.

## Chapter Eleven

The instant Jenny hit the water and felt her feet ripped from beneath her by the raging current, she screamed. It wasn't a scream of fear as much as it was a response to the icy coldness of the water, which sucked her breath out of her in a millisecond.

She heard Matt's voice above the roar, the absolute fear in it. There wasn't even time to look, for the current hurled her out into the frothing, twisting waves and into the path of a huge, ocher-colored boulder the size of a small car. To her horror, she saw little Daniel strike the side of it, bounce off and go under. Instinctively, because she couldn't fight the raging, angry current, Jenny drew her feet up close to her body, wrapped her arms around herself and took a deep breath of air before she struck the looming boulder full force.

Pain arced along the right side of Jenny's body. The violent flow dragged her beneath the water as she ricocheted off the rock. An unseen but deadly whirlpool hauled her under again.

*No!* Jenny kicked violently. Popping up to the surface with a gasp, she saw Daniel just ahead of her. He was shrieking and flailing awkwardly, his small mouth contorted. Fear made his eyes bulge. Jenny kicked outward and lunged for all she was worth, her hand stretched toward him.

*Yes!* Her whitened fingers wrapped strongly around Daniel's small wrist. As the tributary twisted her around and around, she hauled Daniel against her body with all her strength. The child stopped shrieking, his eyes pleading and anxious. His small arms clasped in a death grip around her neck.

Jenny went under. *No! Oh, no! Not like this!* She lunged hard and resurfaced. Trying to get oriented, she heard Matt's voice roaring above the river's thundering. Flinging her head to get the hair out of her eyes, Jenny saw him running parallel to them, fifty feet away. His face was set, his mouth a slash. In his hands he carried the hemp rope that Maria used to hang her clothes with. He was running hard, dodging the larger boulders, slipping and flailing as his booted feet hit the rocky, uneven surface of the bank. In an instant, Jenny realized what he was going to try and do. Wrenching around till she faced the upcoming opening in the Urubamba she realized there was less than a hundred yards to go before they were vomited into that relentless, unforgiving river.

Daniel's hand clawed in panic at her face. He was shrieking with terror. Jenny gripped him hard. She tried to pull his fingers away from her eyes so that she could see as the current spun them around once more.

Going under again because the icy temperature was sucking the heat and strength out of her body, she found water flooding violently up into her flared nostrils and opened mouth. Darkness closed around her as she struggled to push upward once more, to the surface. To life-giving air. Her boots, now waterlogged, were becoming deadly weights on her feet. They tugged her downward. There was no time, no way to get them off, for they were laced tightly. If she tried, she might lose Daniel, and she couldn't do that.

As she shot to the surface, she grabbed Daniel under the arms and held him high so that he wouldn't go under and drown. Everything was beginning to slow down. Jenny felt as if her life was a movie, being shot in sluggish, slow-motion frames. To her right, running hard and screaming, was Daniel's mother. Behind her, about ten or fifteen villagers were hot on her heels. All of them were trying to catch up to Matt, who was well ahead of them.

Daniel's sobbing screams of unrelenting terror tore through Jenny. The river ripped at her, once again contorting her sense of direction and twisting her around. Without warning, because she couldn't see it, she was smashed savagely into another boulder.

A cry ripped from her as she slammed into the obstacle. Again her right side took the brunt of the blow. Jenny felt something give way there and pain arced up into her chest. She shrieked in agony, but her hands tightened around Daniel as she continued to try and hold him up out of the grasping, greedy water churning and bubbling around them.

Again, as she bounced off the side of another boulder, the undertow around it hauled her down. Down, down, down. She felt Daniel struggling. He was below the surface. Water tunneled up into her nose as she fought the deadly whirlpool. They would both die if she didn't fight back!

The thought of Daniel dying was too much for Jenny to accept. From somewhere deep within her, she found strength. Adrenaline streaking through her body, she kicked. Kicked savagely. Kicked upward. Air! Oh, God, they had to have air!

Jenny shot up and out of the water with a cry. As she vomited violently, water regurgitating from her lungs and up through her mouth and nose, she heard Daniel whimper. His clinging grasp on her neck was weaker. She saw the fear in his dark brown eyes. He was gasping for air and choking.

Fifty yards to go.

Using the last of her strength, Jenny righted herself so that she was facing the Urubamba, which seemed to be rushing to them. On the edge of the bank where the tributary met the river, she saw Matt skid to a halt, mud flying around him. She saw the terror in his eyes as he began to make a loop on the end of the rope. And then he gathered it up in his large hands and began to twirl the loop around and around his head like a cowboy getting ready to rope a steer.

Her mind was groggy now, the cold water making her hypothermic to the point where she couldn't think clearly. Yet Jenny sluggishly realized what he was going to try and do. He was going to throw the loop out to them. If she could catch it in time, Matt could haul them to safety before they were carried into the Urubamba River.

Jenny knew she was dead. She knew it in her heart, in her soul. Yet she also knew Daniel had to live! If only she could catch that rope Matt was going to throw! He would have only one chance. *One.* For if they were swept into the Urubamba, they would both die. The current was unforgiving, swift and deadly.

Her heart rebelled. She couldn't die! Daniel couldn't drown! He was too young! He had his entire life in front of him! As Jenny was spun around again, slammed into another boulder, she realized something else. Something so precious, so life-giving, that it created an inner fire of determination that she'd never experienced before in her life. She loved Matt Davis. Unequivocally. Forever. And dammit, she wanted a chance to pursue that love with him!

Like a race horse floundering toward the finish line despite the fact that he had absolutely no strength left, Jenny resolved not to quit no matter what. Her determination, her desire to live, exploded through her like a nuclear bomb detonating within her heart and soul.

In those seconds that crawled by, Jenny gritted her teeth. She kicked hard and fought the sucking, grasping current. Her strength was gone. She could feel her life being stolen by the icy water, the cold sucking it out of her like a greedy vampire. *No! No, I won't go down without a fight! I won't! I love you, Matt! Oh, I love you! Please...please, give me the strength, help me! I want to tell you that! Oh, please, help me!*

As she popped up to the surface, her feet pointed downstream, she heard Matt hoarsely calling her. Instantly, she lifted her hand high, preparing to try and catch the rope that was swinging above his head. The relief in his eyes was momentous as he saw that she understood what he was going to try to do. There was no way, even though he was a SEAL, that he could just jump in and rescue her, Jenny knew. No one could beat this river, with its deadly currents and icy temperature.

For an instant, Jenny bobbed on the surface of a quiet place between two huge boulders. She kept her hand held high, her numb, white fingers stretched outward like claws.

It was then that Matt threw the loop. He'd seen that quiet space between the boulders and had prayed that the current would carry Jenny and Daniel into it. It was the only smooth water in the whole tributary. His aim had to be precise. If the rope landed too far in front of them, it would be whisked away instantly by the current. If it landed too far behind, Jenny would be unable to swim upstream to try and reach it.

He saw how white her face was. He knew she was suffering from deep hypothermia. No one knew better than Matt what hypothermia could do to a body. It robbed victims of their mind, their ability to think. They became confused. Disoriented. Worst of all, the icy water sucked the life out of a person. First it stole the heat out of the muscles, then the muscles slowed down. Finally, they stopped working, because the cold literally froze them in place. And that was when a person drowned.

He saw Jenny's distorted mouth, the cry on her pale, bluish lips. Little Daniel was clinging to her neck in a death grip. Matt was sure she wasn't getting adequate air. And judging from the amount of water she was swallowing, it was only a matter of time before she'd run out of oxygen and slip quietly, forever, beneath the waves of the violent, angry water.

One chance. He had one chance. His heart thundered in his chest as he saw that her hand was still raised upward. *Yes!* She was still coherent. Still able to think. Maria and the rest of the villagers gathered around him, panicked and anxious. They halted, panting, and clasped their hands together in prayer. He swung the loop high above his head, steadying it as best he could. One chance...

More than anything, Matt realized he loved Jenny in that moment. And his anger and need of her were heightened knowing there was a good chance she would drown with Daniel and be swept away by the Urubamba. Anguish seared his chest, and it felt like a branding iron was burning his heart. He'd just found her! He'd just realized how wonderful she was. And he needed her. More than any person in his life, he needed her.

Hand tightening on the rope coils in his left hand, he timed his throw. The moment Jenny drifted between those boulders and the water smoothed, he sent the loop snaking out powerfully toward her raised hand.

Everyone held their breath.

Someone cried out.

Jenny's hand was up, her fingers grasping toward the sky, her flesh white, her fingertips blue. She saw the loop skittering in their direction. The current turned her sideways. No! Fighting the exhaustion, fighting the weariness that was seeping rapidly through her body now, she forced herself around.

She twisted back just in time to have the rope strike her clawing fingers. Yes! The loop settled over Daniel—*good!* She was so tired. The current started to pull her away from the eddy and out into the frothing, bubbling waters. *Get the rope around herself!* Her mind kept screaming at her to do it, over and over again. But her hand wouldn't obey her mind. The loop was around Daniel. She tried to pick it up and drag it across her wet head, but the hemp tumbled out of her nerveless grasp. She had seconds to go before they'd be swept into the Urubamba.

At least Daniel could be saved—that was what her mind told her. Jenny fumbled again with the loop, her fingers numb. She could feel nothing. With her other arm, she held Daniel protectively against her. The loop dropped again. With a weak cry, Jenny felt a huge, tugging sensation. A powerful current snarled around her legs as she wearily continued to kick to keep them afloat.

Looking to her left, she realized they were now being sucked into the Urubamba itself. Crying out, her lips contorted, she closed her eyes. This was it. She was going to die. At least Daniel would live....

But then, as they made the turn and began to flow into the Urubamba, Jenny opened her eyes. A resolve, deep and surprising, flashed through her. In that moment when everything seemed to be moving with such anguished and excruciating slowness, she picked up the loop one last time. She forced her fingers to close around the rope, though she couldn't feel the soggy line.

Matt was roaring at her. His voice was drowned out by the thundering Urubamba as they were swept out into it.

A bolt of energy flashed through her. Jenny felt it crackling and moving like hot, boiling lava down her arms and into her frozen, unresponsive fingers. That surge of heat gave her the strength to pull the loop up and across her head. The rope slipped around her shoulders, with Daniel within it as well.

Matt cried out. He needed help! Instantly, several village men came down the hill and were on that rope behind him. He jerked it taut and saw the loop tighten instantly around Jenny and Daniel. They were being swept out into the mighty river so fast that it boggled his mind.

The moment the rope grew taut, Matt hauled back on it with all his weight. Jenny and Daniel were drifting out toward a massive set of boulders. If they struck them, they would be knocked unconscious by the fury and speed of the current. Five men hauled back with him at the same time. Grunts and groans broke out. He watched, his breath snagging in his chest, as they fought against the current. Two lives dangled on the end of that line. What if the rope broke? How strong was it? He didn't know. His lips curled away from his clenched teeth.

*"Pull!"* he cried out in Spanish. *"Pull hard!"*

The villagers grunted and groaned again. Backs bent. Feet dug into the muddy bank, then slipped. Fingers groped savagely as the escaping rope sizzled through their hands. *Stop it! Stop the rope from escaping!*

Matt dug the heels of his boots into the rock and mud, and leaned backward with his full weight. The rope pulled taut! They'd stopped it from escaping. He watched helplessly as Jenny went under with Daniel in her arms. *No!* He knew why she had gone under. He knew this would happen.

*"Faster. Faster!"* he screamed at the others.

Every man was pulling as hard as he could on that rope to try and bring them to shore. But as the villagers pulled, Jenny and Daniel were dragged underwater. The very act of rescuing them could kill them now.

Tears of rage and frustration stung Matt's eyes. He saw the current raging over Jenny's blond, limp hair. He saw her holding Daniel's head above the water the best she could, even though she was beneath the suffocating flow herself. Tears washed into the sides of his contorted mouth. He could taste the salt of them. His eyes were narrowed to slits. His heart pounded frantically in his chest.

*There!* Jenny's head bobbed to the surface as they finally hauled them closer to shore. They dragged her nearer, up across the hidden boulders and rocks at the river's edge. He saw her hands fall away from Daniel. She was unconscious. He knew she'd taken in a lot of water. Luckily, the rope kept Daniel against her as they hauled them the last ten feet to safety.

When they were close enough to shore, Matt dropped the rope and lunged forward. The bank was steep. He skidded down the rocky slope toward where Jenny lay on her side, unconscious, half out of the water. Daniel was screaming. He was flailing and trying to keep his face out of the water.

The men of the village were on Matt's heels. They tumbled and leaped to get to them, as well.

Matt reached them first. He splashed out into the knee-deep water, slipping and sliding on the algae-covered rocks. He nearly lost his footing. With one hand, he gripped Daniel by the scruff of his shirt. With the other, he grabbed Jenny beneath her right arm. Lifting their dead weight, he fell backward with both of them in his arms.

As he hit the shallow water, Matt bruised himself against the rocks. One of the villagers—Daniel's father, Juan—reached him and grabbed his sobbing son from Matt's grasp. The child was swung upward, passed to another man closer to shore, and then lifted by a sea of outstretched hands to the safety of the bank and his mother's open arms.

Matt felt strong, supportive hands sliding beneath his armpits. Two men dragged him upright as he held on to Jenny. She was unconscious. Her face was bluish colored. Her once-beautiful, sun-colored hair lay limp and clinging to the icy flesh of her face.

Once on shore, Matt managed to stand with the help of the men who protectively surrounded him. In one ragged motion, he lifted Jenny against him and turned. The villagers realized he had to give her artificial respiration, but couldn't do it on this rocky slope. He had to have a smooth, uncluttered area where he could lay her out and work on her. Without a word, they turned and helped him struggle up the rocky, slippery bank to the red clay bank above.

Gasping and panting, Matt laid Jenny down on her belly. He quickly pulled her arms above her head and straightened out her small, precious body. Turning her face to one side, he quickly straddled her. With his hands, he pushed on the middle of her back in a forward motion toward her shoulders. The villagers crowded around in a circle. Many prayed out loud. Others watched, their eyes huge, their mouths open in silent distress.

With the first savage effort, water came gurgling out of Jenny's slack, parted lips. Again Matt pushed. More water. He growled her name.

"Jenny! Come back to me! Dammit, don't you die on me. Not now! Not like this!"

He pushed again. More water.

How much had she swallowed? The little fool! She'd gone under to keep Daniel above the waves. She'd knowingly given her life for his. Tears stung Matt's slitted eyes as he worked feverishly over her. Pumping the water out of her didn't guarantee anything. When no more came out, he quickly got off her and rolled her over. Jenny was like a limp, wet rag doll.

As he leaned over her, his ear near her nostrils and slack mouth, he could feel no breath. Jenny wasn't breathing! He felt for her pulse with shaking fingers. *Nothing*. She was dead.

*"No!"* he howled. *No!* Not like this!

Leaning down, Matt eased her head back, propped her chin up and cupped it with his shaking hands. He pinched her nostrils closed with his fingers and settled his mouth firmly against her lips. He was alarmed at how cold she was. It was then that Matt realized the courage she'd had to stay coherent, to stay conscious that long. Not even a SEAL could have survived that river and that temperature without a wet suit, and Jenny had. She'd survived long enough to know that Daniel would live.

Pumping two breaths into her, Matt watched her chest rise beneath the wet, clinging material across her breasts. Then he straddled her again and put his hand on her sternum, pumping it five times, hard and solid, to shock the heart into starting. He heard a *crack*. He knew he'd just broken her sternum with the force of his hands, but it was unavoidable. He *had* to save her!

Again he breathed his breath into her. Again he shocked her heart. She had to come back to him! She had to!

Grayness began to replace the darkness that Jenny found herself floating within. She saw a tunnel of light and recognized people she had loved, who had died, standing in the middle of it. And then she saw two white figures. They were indistinct, and yet the sense of love that emanated from them was overwhelming as they floated toward her in that glowing tunnel.

*Go back.*

She stood there, confused by their telepathic order. The figures, which towered over her now, were luminous and filmy-looking as they spoke to her once more.

*Go back. Your time is not yet. You must return.*

The moment those words echoed through her

mind, Jenny felt herself being sucked downward into what felt like a swiftly moving, circular tornado of energy. As she was whirling and spinning downward, the light dimmed and grew black...and then...colors. She was seeing rainbow colors.... Her lids moved. She felt heat. She heard gasping. She heard people talking in low, stressed voices. What was going on?

Her lids fluttered. Jenny felt warm, strong hands lifting her upward. Her head lolled against someone's shoulder. And then she felt the first stab of pain in her right side and in the center of her chest.

It was the pain that brought her to consciousness. Yet as she came to, she felt as if she were being cradled in loving arms. She felt the trembling touch of someone's fingertips across her brow, felt them brush her hair from her eyes and cheek. What had happened?

After a struggle, Jenny finally opened her eyes. The first thing she saw was Matt leaning over her, his eyes wide with fear and anxiety. He was holding her in his arms. And Jenny saw another emotion in his narrowed gray eyes: love. Love for her. It was the oddest moment of her life, as she felt strung between that tunnel of light and here, back in her body. She could read his mind, feel what was in his heart. It was the most astounding revelation to her, for she'd never experienced telepathy before.

Jenny clung to his stormy looking gaze and felt

his arms tighten protectively around her. How safe she felt! And when she dragged her lids open even more, she saw the tension in the slash of his mouth ease. She saw his lips part. And then she heard words she never thought she'd ever hear from him.

"Jenny? Jenny, are you all right? It's Matt." His voice cracked. Tears flooded his eyes as he continued to caress her damp hair with his trembling hand. "I love you. Do you hear me? I love you. Don't you leave. Don't you ever leave! You hear me?"

# Chapter Twelve

"Are you warm now?" Matt whispered against the damp hair near Jenny's ear. He was lying on their bed, his back against the headboard. She was tucked in a thick, warm alpaca blanket, her head resting tiredly against his chest. A soft sigh broke from her, and he squeezed her gently because she'd suffered a set of very badly bruised ribs. The doctor who had examined her had said that the cartilage portion of the sternum was cracked, as well. That would heal up in about three weeks. The ribs would take as long, or maybe a little longer.

Closing her eyes, Jenny whispered, "Yes, I feel *much* better." The last two hours had been the most horrifying and the most joyous of her life. Never had Jenny experienced such care and tenderness from a man. She'd barely been conscious when Matt had hoisted her up in his arms after she had nearly died. So many other hands—of village women who passed alpaca blankets to her to keep her warm. Village men who helped Matt—had touched her as well.

Nearly half the village had followed Matt as he walked quickly to the plaza and into the small medical clinic. Right behind him were Daniel and his parents. Jenny was worried for Daniel, but compared to her the little boy seemed unharmed by his brush with death.

She couldn't stop crying as the doctor examined her behind the cloth curtain. Luckily, Matt never left her side, never allowed his hand to slip from her shaking shoulders. Since she had been nearly hypothermic, Matt had stripped her out of her wet clothing, nearly tearing off her boots and heavy socks. He'd wrapped her tightly in several blankets and then sat her up on the gurney and begun to briskly rub her back, shoulders and arms to force the blood to flow.

The nurse had given her coca leaf tea to drink, because it was warm. But most of all, Matt's care had brought her back to life. Now Jenny wondered if she'd heard things as she lay on the bank near death. Had Matt really said he loved her? Her heart contracted. Snuggling beneath his hard, unforgiving jaw, she tucked her bruised hand beneath her chin and felt the lull of exhaustion creeping over her. Just the way his hand trembled lightly on her drying hair made her want to start crying all over again.

Matt closed his eyes and held her gently. "You almost died out there today," he said in a low, rasping tone against her ear. "Jenny...I was so scared. Scared of losing you." Compressing his lips, his brow wrinkling, Matt knew he had to get out how he felt toward her. Would Jenny push him away? Was his love one-sided? Would she become scared and run? He had no way of knowing, but in his gut he sensed that Jenny was far stronger and more resilient than he'd ever given her credit for. Anyone who would leap into that icy coffin called a river to save another's life was heroic beyond his scope of understanding. She was a real-life heroine. And she had a heart as huge as the universe. More than anything, he wanted to share his own heart with her. Would she feel the same way?

Matt felt her stir at his murmured admission. He eased her back just enough so that her head rested on his shoulder and she could look up at him. Her eyes swam with tears, but the flecks of golden sunlight in their depths gave him the courage to go on. His hands tightened slightly on her shoulder and the hand he held. Such a small, delicate hand. But what a courageous heart she had. Giving her a slight, unsteady smile, he added, ''Did you hear me out there earlier? You may not have. You were going down for the count. Maybe you weren't conscious enough....''

Jenny felt her heart began to skip beats. She saw the stormy, narrowed look in Matt's eyes and knew...knew what he was going to say. Her heart expanding like a flower opening, she held her breath and waited.

''Hell...Jenny, I love you.'' There, it was out on the table. Now she could either accept or reject him. Matt felt suffocated in those seconds as he saw his words register. Her eyes widened enormously. Her petal-perfect lips parted. There was shock and...something else in her eyes. What it was, Matt wasn't sure.

Matt's strained features blurred. Since becoming conscious, all Jenny could do was weep off and on, having no control over her ragged, tattered emotional state. Huge tears formed and rolled down her cheeks as she held his anxious gaze.

''Y-you do?''

Licking his lips, Matt growled, ''Yes. How do you feel about me?'' His heart bounded once. Hard. Never had he been so scared as now—and he was an ex-Navy SEAL, who had encountered hundreds of situations where he'd been scared to death. But not like this. Her tears tore at him. He lifted his hand from her smaller cooler one and tenderly wiped her tears away with his callused fingers.

Choking on words that stuck in her throat, Jenny closed her eyes as his gentle touch caressed not only her flesh, but her aching heart, and made it expand with euphoria. As he drew his hand away, she caught it, her still-white fingers wrapping around his thicker, stronger ones. "I can't explain it, Matt," Jenny began brokenly. Gripping his hand, she confessed, "I feel like such a coward. You've got more courage than I do. I—I've been feeling so strongly toward you since I met you that it's been driving me crazy. I was afraid to call it love because it seemed too soon. I was scared…that maybe how I felt about you wasn't how you might feel toward me." Gulping unsteadily, she could barely hold his burning gaze. "Does that make sense?"

Whispering her name, Matt carefully turned Jenny so that she was facing him fully. Cognizant of her bruised ribs, he maneuvered her so that her drawn-up legs settled against his hip. With one arm around her blanketed shoulders, he released her hand and cupped her face.

"Do you know how priceless you are to me, sweet woman? How I look forward to waking up with you beside me every morning? I've been fighting myself every night not to drag you into my arms and love you until your body sang with joy along with mine. So many times your melodic laughter had flowed through me and lifted me up. You make me feel happier than I've ever deserved to be.''

Sighing audibly, Jenny closed her eyes. ''You're so beautiful with your words, Matt…a poet.'' Touching her heart with her hand, she reopened her eyes and stared warmly up into his. ''I think I've loved you from the beginning.''

Nodding, Matt felt an avalanche of fear melting off his tense shoulders. Jenny loved him! Heart soaring, he tried to keep it in perspective. Grazing her cheek, which was now damp with tears and rosy with emotion, he said, ''I think I did, too. I think it took this incident to drive it home—to both of us.''

Nodding, Jenny closed her eyes and absorbed his continuing touch. ''Yes…yes, it did….'' As he caressed her, his fingers created a pleasant, building fire from her temple and cheek, down to her neck. In that moment, she felt like a sacred vessel—much loved, hotly desired.

Swallowing hard, Matt kept his caress light and tender. He saw the pleasure in Jenny's sweet face and smiled inwardly as her lips parted. He continued to explore her face, neck and small, proud shoulders, but he told himself not to go too far. She was in no condition to make love. Bruised ribs were as bad as broken ones, as far as he was concerned. She couldn't even take in a full breath of air because of the pain. Luckily, the bruises were low on her rib cage, and she was able to wear a tight spandex wrap to keep them protected and stable. No, right now, all he wanted to do was let her know how much he loved her. Touch was one form of communication, one he was very good at. And Jenny needed to be cradled, cared for, nourished and held as never before. After all, she had died back there on the banks of the Urubamba. She had told him earlier about the tunnel of light and how she was told to go back, that it wasn't her time yet. When he'd heard that, fear shot through him like an icy pick stabbing him through his thudding heart. His breath had brought her back. Back to him. Now everything else could wait. They had time now. Precious time.

"Kiss me, Matt?"

Her voice was trembling. He saw her lovely blue eyes open. Saw the tears, the joy, the shining light in her gaze that was meant only for him. This time, he realized her tears were happy ones. To be shared. Giving her a very male smile, he cupped Jenny's face with his hands and leaned down. Above all, he wanted her to know that he worshipped her. That she was priceless, and beyond anything he'd ever imagined for himself. Matt had thought love was a four-letter word that could only wound and hurt. Well, he was wrong. The woman whose lips he now grazed, whose breath he inhaled deeply into his heart, his needy soul, had shown him he was wrong.

A little moan moved through Jenny as Matt's strong, sure mouth covered her lips in a butterfly light caress. His hands were steadying as she leaned upward, wanting more, desiring much more from him. Seeming to understand what she was asking, he pressed his lips firmly against hers, rocking hers open and moving his tongue languidly against her own. The effect was so surprising, so potent, that Jenny quivered.

"Like that?" Matt whispered raggedly against her ear. He opened his eyes and saw her grow languid beneath his stroking caress. Something told him Jenny was not all that experienced in lovemaking, and until he knew for sure, he was going to take his time with her. He would teach her, share with her, find out what she liked and what she was ready for.

"Umm..." Jenny melted completely beneath the heated onslaught of his very male mouth. Just the brush of his bearded face against her cheek created wild tingles within her. Jenny lost herself in his strength, in his tender assault upon her senses. She felt him holding back, as if she would break if he was too rough with her. Under the circumstances, her reeling mind told her, she was in no condition to make love to him right now. Not with her cracked sternum and bruised ribs. Matt had more sense, more control than she did presently.

Gradually, Matt eased his mouth from hers. As he opened his eyes, his hands still framing her rosy cheeks, he saw the slumberous quality of Jenny's gaze as she peered wonderingly up at him. His lips curved ruefully. Moving his fingers across her un-marred brow, trailing them down the sides of her clean jaw, he whispered, "I love you, Jenny Wright. And I'm looking forward to the day when I can love you totally...."

She trembled at his husky tone and the caress of his fingers against her face and neck. Her breasts ached to be touched. The throbbing fire in her lower body was almost painful. Hungering for him desper-ately, she managed a soft, strained laugh as his hands settled back on her shoulders and he eased her around so that once again she lay against his warm bulk.

"I don't know if I can last that long," she mur-mured shyly. No man had ever looked at her and made her feel so feminine, so wanton, as the way Matt did. For whatever reason, he made her feel bold—deliciously so. At her comment, she saw that wonderful mouth of his crook in a kind of little-boy smile that melted her soul.

"Yeah?"

"Yeah," Jenny replied, grinning and putting a frisky note in her voice.

Laughing deeply, Matt hugged her, but carefully. He kissed her brow, her nose and dipped quickly down to capture her smiling mouth. "You know what, sweet woman? I think I've got a bead on you now. You go around with this meek, mild, shadowy facade.'' He tapped her nose teasingly. ''And you're really Princess Xena underneath—courageous, strong and invincible.''

Giggling, Jenny caught his hand. She basked in his tender teasing. ''Invincible? Oh, I think not. If you hadn't had the presence of mind to pick up that rope and toss it to me, I'd be dead now. No, I'm not invincible, darling…but with you, I feel that way. You're such a role model for me.''

Losing his smile, Matt cupped her chin. ''Listen to me, Jenny. Don't you ever think you aren't heroic, because you are. I'm a trained SEAL, and I'm not sure I would have survived that river. That water would freeze the strongest SEAL in minutes.'' Matt gave her a grave look. ''You were in that ice water for nearly three minutes, Jenny. Plenty long enough to go completely hypothermic, and you didn't. You held Daniel up above you so he wouldn't take in water until the very end. By that time, we had you in the shallows. You are so strong. You're passionate. It was that huge heart of yours that gave you the courage, the physical strength and doggedness to save that little boy.''

His words fed her. Nourished her starving soul as nothing else ever could. Matt was completely sincere in his analysis of her attributes, and he honored her decision to jump in after Daniel in spite of the danger. Suddenly she saw herself in a way she never had before. Sliding her fingertips across his raspy face, Jenny whispered, "Your belief in me, that I could be courageous…a heroine…helped me believe in myself. Believe that I could do what I did." She gazed up at him, knowing he was her role model. "Isn't that what love is really all about, Matt? One partner supports and helps the other become all that they can be? Love means building up, not tearing down."

Nodding, he rasped, "Yes. Yes, it is, Jenny." Catching her hand, Matt pressed a warm, long kiss to the center of her palm and watched her eyes grow slumberous with pleasure again. "I think a couple of days of rest are what you need now. I'm going to talk to Major Stevenson, ask her for some time off to let you heal up before we finish these interviews. Okay?"

Her brows shot up. Jenny sat up, too quickly. She grimaced and tenderly held her ribs with her hand. "No! No…don't do that! I promised her I wouldn't take up a lot of her time. She simply doesn't have it. I'm fine, Matt. I want to go to the base tomorrow morning just as planned."

"Okay, tiger woman," he sighed. Giving her a charged look filled with love, he said, "You stay here. I'm going to go down to the plaza for a minute."

As he eased away and stood up, Jenny frowned. "Why?"

"Kannie and Patrick, owners of the India Feliz,

are making you your favorite meal, and they're walking it down here for you. It's their way of honoring and thanking you for saving little Daniel." He grinned. "And it's supposed to be a surprise, nosy."

She smiled softly. "That's so nice of them! They didn't have to do that."

Matt opened the door to their room and smiled back at her. "Expect to get a few accolades over your rescue, sweet woman. Well deserved, I'd say. I'll be right back."

Jenny was stunned when the civilian helicopter, flown by one of the Apache pilots masquerading as a civilian, flew them into the military side of the base instead of to the mining side, which was general protocol. She gripped the seat, her knuckles whitening, as Chief Warrant Officer Akiva Redtail whipped the small Bell helicopter through an opening in the black lava wall that led to the military complex. Jenny sucked in a sharp breath as Akiva moved the chopper through the hole, barely large enough to accommodate the whirling blades, as if she were on a Sunday drive. One wrong move, and Jenny saw all too clearly that the blades could smash into that unrelenting black basalt and they'd die in a fiery inferno. She felt Matt's hand settle over hers for reassurance.

No sooner had they cleared the hole than Akiva

said cheerfully over the intercom, "We call it the Eye. Extreme, eh?"

"Uh, yes…extreme…." Jenny whispered, fear lumped in her throat. She heard Akiva laugh huskily as she adroitly guided the helicopter to the lip, a smooth basalt slab at the edge of the gargantuan cave.

"Why are we landing on the military side?" she asked Akiva, frowning. They always flew to the mining side, their cover. And flying the Eye was a frightening experience for Jenny. Something she never wanted to do again.

Akiva maneuvered the Bell helicopter around, hovered and then descended to the deck of the cave. "Major Stevenson ordered me to bring you in this way," she told her enigmatically. She lowered the helicopter to the lip, settling gently on it. Immediately, Akiva cut the power and the blades began to slow. She turned and grinned at Jenny. "Take a look out there." And she pointed inside the cave.

They had to wait until the blades stopped turning before the ground crew could forward to place chalks beneath the tires of the helo and put the blades in a sling that would stop them from turning in the breeze.

From the grin on Matt's face, Jenny knew something was up. But what? Frowning, she leaned down and looked out the window toward the cave. Just about every single person who worked at the base was standing at stiff attention, in a rectangular formation. Everyone was in dark green, U.S. Army dress uniforms, not their normal workday clothing. She saw Majors Stevenson and York at the front of the ranks looking toward them expectedly, smiles of welcome on their faces.

"What's going on?" Jenny asked as Matt opened the door once the blades had stopped.

"A formation," Matt told her. He helped her out of the helicopter, taking care to lower her gently to the basalt floor so she wouldn't jar her taped ribs. Today, despite a little shyness on her part, Matt had helped Jenny to dress, because she couldn't raise her right arm far due to her painful ribs. He'd pulled out an apple-green blouse and khaki slacks for her this morning. She'd managed to wriggle into everything by herself, except she couldn't button the blouse. Matt tried not to make her feel embarrassed when he saw that she wore a simple white cotton chemise and not a bra beneath the blouse. Jenny had blushed furiously as he awkwardly fumbled to close all the buttons on the shirt, plus work the snap closed on her slacks. It was obvious Jenny didn't like feeling helpless.

Now she stared at the military formation, mystified. Akiva came around the helo, grinning like a jaguar who had sighted her quarry. Her cinnamon eyes shone with happiness. She looked over at Matt.

"Ready?"

Matt nodded and smiled down at Jenny, who was completely perplexed as to what was going on. She was not familiar with military procedures or protocol. As he slid his fingers beneath her left elbow and guided her toward the others, she hung back a little in trepidation.

"It's okay," he whispered as he leaned down, his lips near her ear. "This is for you, Jenny. It's a celebration of sorts."

Reluctantly, she fell into step with Matt. As they approached, the two commanding officers of the base came to attention and saluted her crisply. Confused, Jenny saw Akiva also come to attention and snap off a smart salute to her, as well.

"What's going on?" she asked Maya.

The CO smiled a little. To her left stood a woman at attention who was holding two items in her hands.

"Jenny? Why don't you come forward? We want to honor you."

Honor her? Why? Her head swam with even more confusion as Matt gently eased her forward so that she stood between Maya and ranks of uniformed personnel. Matt had a proud look on his face, his teeth even and white as he smiled at her.

"Jenny Wright?" Maya Stevenson's husky voice rang throughout the cavern.

Startled by her name being called so loudly, she gasped. And then Jenny gathered herself. Maya picked up an official-looking piece of paper and stepped smartly in her direction. Stopping in front of her, she faced the formation and began to read from it.

"Let it be known that civilian Jenny Wright is being honored for her bravery in saving the life of a little boy yesterday at the tributary in Aqua Calien- te." Maya lifted her chin and nailed Jenny with a narrowed look. "As commanding officer of the Black Jaguar Squadron, it gives me great pleasure to award you the Purple Heart Medal, a medal reserved for someone wounded in action who turns and helps her comrades instead of thinking solely of herself."

Stunned, Jenny watched openmouthed as the bru- nette sergeant stepped up, carrying a small, gold vel- vet pillow that had a purple heart with a purple-and- white ribbon draped over it. Maya picked up the medal, and turning, moved briskly over to Jenny. Gently, Maya pinned the medal on the left side of her blouse. Stepping back, she saluted her, as did the other officers who stood nearby.

"At ease," Maya ordered her squadron.

Immediately, everyone relaxed and placed their hands behind their backs, alert to what their CO was going to say.

Jenny felt embarrassed. Maya had a slight smile playing across her full lips. The power this woman had was immense, and Jenny felt benign warmth flowing from her. Maya's emerald-green eyes softened. Her voice lowered a bit, but it still rang clearly and strongly throughout the cavern, so that everyone present could hear her speak.

"Jenny, we like to honor anyone who places their own life secondarily to saving another. That's what this squadron is all about. Our lives are the line for the betterment of the world in general. When I was informed of your courageous act of bravery yesterday, I told my officers about it. We felt, to a person, that you should not only be publicly honored for what you did—and nearly died doing—but also given a military medal for your heroism."

Maya smiled a little and pointed to the medal. "We don't have civilian medals, but we wanted you to have one of ours so that you knew how much we honored your bravery. This medal happens to be one of too many that I have of this type...."

Polite laughter rippled through the formation. Jenny turned and looked at the smiling faces of the women squadron and the glimmer in their eyes as they looked at their CO. Clearly, Maya's leadership here was unquestioned, and her people loved and respected her.

Maya continued in a warm tone, "You suffered many wounds and nearly died rescuing that little boy. In our eyes and hearts, you are brave and heroic. We want you to keep this medal, the Purple Heart, as a token of our appreciation, esteem and respect for who and what you are. We're proud to have you as one of our own.''

Maya held out her hand to Jenny, smiling hugely.

In shock, Jenny looked over at Matt, who stood off to one side with Akiva. Jenny brought up her hand and shook Maya's. The CO's grip was like a steel trap. "Th-thank you, Major Stevenson...." And she released Maya's hand. Turning, she lifted her hand, a small smile on her lips. "Thank you, everyone. This is so...so unexpected. I really don't know what to say...." And she turned back to Maya, who was smiling over at her husband, Dane York.

They were honoring her! Jenny realized. They were celebrating her act of bravery in rescuing little Daniel. A lump formed in her throat. Everything blurred. Automatically, Jenny's badly bruised and cut hand went to the medal that hung on her blouse. Maya was giving her one of her own medals. A medal given for being wounded while in action and under fire. She smiled bravely through her tears at the tall woman warrior.

"I'm honored that it came from you and your squadron. I'll never forget this, Major. Not ever. Thanks so much. I never expected this...."

With a brisk nod, Maya lost her smile. She came up and handed Jenny a small piece of cloth. "When someone in a squadron gives a person the squadron patch, it's like saying they're family. They're one of us." Pressing the round patch, which had a head of a snarling black jaguar on it, encircled with red and blue rings, into Jenny's palm, Maya added, "Welcome to the base, Ms. Wright. You're now one of us, a black jaguar."

Jenny's gaze clung to the patch, until the emblem blurred. Sniffing, she blinked through her tears. Matt approached and slid a tissue into her hand. She thanked him and wiped her eyes and blew her nose.

"This is all so wonderful," she said, strengthening her voice so the formation of smiling, nodding women could hear her. Lifting up the patch, Jenny said, "I know none of you know me, but for so long, I never belonged to anyone, anywhere. I was a foster child. I don't want you to feel sorry for me. What I want you to know is how great it feels to finally be a recognized member of a larger family."

There was instantaneous clapping and cheering. Some of the women whistled. Others cried out her name. Some smiled. And some had tears in their eyes.

Jenny turned and looked up at Maya, who had a tender look on her face. She could look very stern and official at times, but now Jenny could see deep emotion in her eyes, and in the smile lurking at the corners of her well-shaped mouth.

"I feel like you know what you've just given me."

Nodding, Maya whispered, "I do, Jenny. Now

you have a home. And we're all your sisters and brothers. From now on, you have a family. A big one.'' She gazed over at Matt, and stepped aside so that he could join them.

Jenny showed him the patch that lay in her palm. She saw the pride and love shining in his eyes for her. The applause continued. It was overwhelming to her. Wonderful. Unexpected. Exhilarating. As Matt put his arm tenderly around her shoulders and embraced her carefully, Jenny heard cries, yells, Indian war whoops from Akiva and wolf whistles from the men in the group. Matt kissed her lightly on the mouth and then eased away.

As he did, he rasped, ''Soak it all in, Jenny. You deserve this. They're honoring you because you are a real, live, honest-to-God heroine. I love you so much. You've got a heart as big and wide as the state of Montana.''

It was all too much for Jenny. After nearly dying yesterday afternoon, and then to have this raucous, sincere celebration in her honor, she couldn't stop the tears that trickled from her eyes. Oh, she knew she probably shouldn't show her tears in front of all these military people. But as she self-consciously wiped them away, she saw many of the squadron wiping moisture from their eyes, too.

No longer would she ever consider herself a coward. And she swore to never call herself a 'fraidy cat again. Her spirit lifted and then spread its wings and flew. Matt's arm around her shoulders was like sunlight to Jenny. The look of pride mixed with love in his expression was all she would ever need. Now, she could come to his side a whole person, not a frightened shadow as she'd been before. With Matt's love, his belief in her supporting her strong, confident side, she would grow into a more balanced human being. And wasn't that what love was all about? Partners nurturing one another so they were always growing, with each other's help?

## Chapter Thirteen

"I'm so excited!" Jenny whispered wickedly as she walked arm in arm with Matt toward Morgan's sprawling two-story log cabin. In truth it was a beautiful place that he and Laura had added on to over the years as they had more and more children. Now there was an octagon-shaped living room at one end of the structure. The rest of the cedar home looked more like a standard cabin one would find in the Rocky Mountains of Montana. It was snowing, and she lifted her face to the softly falling flakes as they walked up the recently swept brick path.

Matt grinned. "What about? The Five Days of Christmas party that's going to start tomorrow?"

Jenny was like an exuberant child as she stuck out her tongue and tried to catch the huge snowflakes spiraling lazily downward from the soft gray sky above. He kept his arm around her waist to keep her from slipping.

Smiling up at him, Jenny stopped and threw her arms around his neck. Matt wore a corduroy jacket with a cranberry-red shirt beneath it. Snow lightly covered his short, thick hair. She wasn't disappointed as he lifted her off her feet and captured her smiling mouth.

As they stood kissing hotly on the walk, the silent, mighty Douglas firs like green sentinels around them, Matt eased his mouth from hers—reluctantly. In the weeks since they'd returned home to Montana after the mission, he'd found his life more happy than he could ever believe possible. He had also deferred his upcoming mission in order to spend more time with Jenny. Instead, he had taken over the job as mission planning coordinator and worked with Mike Houston. It gave him the best of all worlds, but more importantly, he had time to be with Jenny to cultivate their deepening relationship.

Now, drinking in her sparkling blue eyes, he gently deposited her on the path.

"What was that sudden, bold attack on me for?" Matt demanded as they turned and began to walk toward the entrance.

"Just because," she answered coyly.

Giving her a skeptical look, Matt grumbled, "When I see that expression on your face, I know I'm in trouble, sweet woman."

Laughing, Jenny stopped and faced him. "The doctor said my sternum is all healed up now, and my ribs are fine. You *know* what that means, I hope?" Her eyes danced with deviltry as she saw his mouth pull into a crooked grin. "Yes, I can see you do!"

"Really?" The last six weeks had been a special hell for both of them. With Jenny's sternum and rib injuries, Matt wasn't about to try and love her, and possibly reinjure her. No, they'd decided to wait until the doctor cleared her. A sweet warmth flowed through him as he saw the glint in Jenny's eyes. How much she'd changed since coming back from Peru. All good changes.

"Really," she murmured. "Come on! We'll be late for the final meeting! There's so much to do for each day of the party!" She grabbed his hand, raced up the steps and opened the ornately carved cedar door. The symbol on it was of the sun and moon entwined with a colorful rainbow. Morgan was the sun. Laura, his moon. And the rainbow, as far as Jenny was concerned, shouted of the love between them and their four beautiful children. She wanted a marriage just like theirs.

Once inside, they shed their coats, hanging them on hooks in the foyer, and removed their boots, placing them on an awaiting rug nearby. Jenny quickly ran her fingers through her blond hair, now damp from the snowflakes. She caught Matt watching her through narrowed, thoughtful eyes. Her body ached to touch him, hold him and love him. The past six weeks had been incredible for her. No longer was she a 'fraidy cat. Morgan liked her new boldness and take-charge attitude. Laura applauded the obvious confidence that she'd brought home from Peru with her. Jenny herself was getting used to this new persona and she liked it—an awful lot. Even better, Matt loved her.

The delicate scent of heated apple juice with cinnamon in it wafted through the cabin as they hurried across the highly polished cedar floor toward the living room, where everyone was to meet. Jenny knew Laura would have cups of the warming cider waiting for everyone.

Christmas music floated through the house, low and joyful. This was Jenny's second year at the five-day celebration that Morgan and Laura threw for all the families of Perseus who lived in Philipsburg. Even better, returning mercenaries were welcome as well. It was five days of nonstop celebration, of making Christmas something special and memorable not only for them, but for the needy, the poor and the sick of the area. Jenny loved it! There was so much fun for everyone, especially the children of the families.

Entering the octagon-shaped room, Jenny spotted everyone cloistered on the thick, comfortable, butter-yellow leather couches that sat in a semicircle around a low oval table made of cedar and glass. Jenny saw red-haired Abbie, a local schoolteacher who was Laura's right-hand woman in decorating for this wonderful event. Next to her sat Colt Hamlin, a mercenary who had just come in off a harrowing mission. Several wives of mercenaries, including Shah Randolph and Susannah Killian were in attendance, as was Sarah Harding, who mined sapphires in the mountains nearby with her mercenary husband, Wolf.

Laura warmly welcomed Jenny and Matt and asked them to come and sit down. She passed around notebooks and pens for all and launched into the coming week's list of activities.

Throughout the two-hour meeting, Matt couldn't keep his mind off Jenny. He had bought a beautiful emerald engagement ring and wanted to ask her to marry him when the time was right. Tonight, he would.

As he sat there, Matt's heart expanded with a love so deep and wide that it made him in awe of the emotion Jenny evoked so easily in him. They'd been living at her condo since they'd come home. Every night, after work, he looked forward to the evenings with her. They made dinner together, then ate it in front of the fireplace, on a soft black alpaca rug she'd brought back from Agua Caliente. More than anything, he enjoyed their deep, exploratory talks. In many ways, Matt thought, the past six weeks had been perfect—a chance for them to get to know one another without sex being a part of their relationship.

Not that he didn't want to love her; he did. But bruised ribs were so very painful; he'd had them once himself. Matt didn't even want to entertain the idea of crushing Jenny with his weight or hurting her by holding her in his arms. The last thing in the world he wanted to do was cause her pain.

Jenny lifted her chin and gazed over at him, a soft smile of welcome on her mouth. He smiled back and caressed her shoulder as she hunched over the notebook and scribbled away. Coordinating this five-day event, Matt was discovering, was like moving an army from point A to point B. Still, he could hardly wait until this meeting was over and they were done for the day. He had a special night planned—for just the two of them.

Slivers of moonlight filtered through the Victorian lace curtains of Jenny's bedroom, where Matt lay waiting for her to emerge from the bathroom. He'd surprised her with a catered dinner, complete with champagne, red roses and a bottle of her favorite perfume, piki-piki, made of white ginger

blossoms from Hawaii. It was all part of his telling
her he loved her.

The door opened.

His eyes narrowed. Tonight, he had draped the
dark green flannel sheet across his hips to hide his
lower body, because he wore nothing to bed. Usually, he did, out of respect for Jenny. Tonight, everything was different.

Jenny stood there uncertainly, a fluffy yellow
towel wrapped around her. The color complemented
her damp blond hair. Her slender hands held the
terry-cloth material across her breasts, and she was
obviously naked beneath it.

Matt's breath hitched. An ache, so deep and filled
with such yearning, flooded his heart and fed his
soul as he saw her huge blue, smoky-looking eyes.

Lifting his hand, he murmured, ''Come here...''
His fingers stretched outward and she moved like a
graceful deer, her hand extended toward him. As
soon as their fingers touched, he curled her hand
into his. Lifting the flannel sheet, Matt guided her
into the bed beside him.

''I'm nervous.... I know I shouldn't be, but I
am,'' Jenny whispered. Giving him a pleading look,
she added with a twisted smile, ''And I'm supposed
to have such confidence now because of everything
that happened down in Peru.''

''You have courage. You always have,'' Matt
said in a rasping tone. Jenny removed the towel and

allowed it to drop to the floor, then snuggled beside his long, hard length. "Saving Daniel's life was no little thing, sweet woman," Matt said as he curved his arm around her shoulders and brought her firmly against him.

"I—just feel so inadequate right now," she whispered, closing her eyes and frowning. Matt's body was powerful. More powerful than she had ever realized. As she sank against him, her softness against his granitelike angles, she slid her hand shyly across his flat, hard torso. "I'm worried I won't please you…that my breasts are ugly-looking…or too small…or I won't look good enough for you…." There, the truth was out. Jenny pried her lids open and, risking everything, looked up at Matt.

The tenderness burning in his eyes was her undoing. How could she worry about such things? She saw the love for her reflected in his gaze. And as he moved his hand in a caress across her damp hair, down her cheek to cup her chin, Jenny realized that her anxiety had been for nothing.

A rumble of laughter vibrated within his chest as she met and held his gaze. As her lips parted, Matt guided her chin gently upward and rested his mouth lightly against hers.

"Listen to me, will you?" he whispered across her lips. A hot, throbbing ache centered in his loins, but he ruthlessly controlled it for her sake. "There is nothing ugly about you, Jenny. You're perfect to me. In every way. I'm just as scared, just as worried as you are, sweet woman.''

''You are?'' Jenny's eyes widened enormously as she met and held his smoldering gaze. Shimmering tingles radiated through her, head to toe, as he kept touching her lips like a butterfly, teasing her and letting her know how much he cherished her.

''You see, you aren't the only nervous Nellie around here.'' As Matt's arms moved around her, pulling her against him, Jenny sighed. He was just as scared as she was. He wanted to please her, give her as much pleasure as she wanted to give him. Even though he was a man of the world, a hero in her eyes, he was terribly human—just like her. That evened out the playing field.

Her racing pulse settled a little. The fear that had held her hostage quickly dissolved beneath the exploratory touch of his mouth gliding slickly across her lips. Jenny responded to his tentative kiss, her breath quickening as she pressed herself wantonly against him.

The groan that reverberated through his taut, hard body resonated like a drum within Jenny. As Matt turned and lowered her against the mattress, his arm cushioning her head and shoulders, she closed her eyes and uttered a soft, tremulous sigh. She allowed herself to begin a bold exploration of him, her fingertips trailing languidly from his thick, powerful neck, down across his bunched shoulders to his tense, darkly haired forearms.

"Look at me," he commanded roughly.

His moist breath feathered across her cheek as she slowly opened her eyes. Jenny smiled up into his smoldering, narrowed gaze and saw the love he held for her. Yes, there was no doubt: Matt *did* love her. She saw his mouth curve faintly as he traced her brow with his index finger. There was such tenderness in his expression. Her skin tingled wildly as he move his fingertip downward, across her cheekbone, to the corner of her mouth.

"You are the most beautiful, most precious person in the world to me," he told her in a husky tone as he glided his fingers across her lower lip. "And all I want to do is kiss you senseless and feel myself within you. I've never wanted anyone more than you, Jenny...." And he dipped his head and settled his mouth firmly across her parted lips.

The warm strength of his lips cajoled hers, and a hot fire exploded deep within Jenny's lower body. As he leaned over, pressing her solidly against the mattress, she took his full weight and gloried in his strength as a man. Feeling the rigid hardness of him against her abdomen, Jenny responded boldly by pressing her hips more surely against him. Again Matt groaned. Her heart sang with joy, with the power she had as a woman. His mouth was worshipful against her lips, sometimes teasing, sometimes tempting and always heated and hungry. He wanted her on every level.

Lost in the mindless beauty of the pleasure beginning to throb through her, Jenny felt him tear his mouth from hers. They were both breathing heavily. As his lips settled against the ripe peak of her nipple, Jenny quivered and cried out with pleasure, arching beneath him as he suckled her. Her hands opened and closed in a frenzy as a delicious river of sunlight radiated from her breasts throughout her moving, twisting form.

Helpless beneath his onslaught, Jenny could no longer think. All she could do as he eased one knee between her thighs was to feel herself spiral into a fiery cauldron of desire for him on the most primal, animal level. Sliding her hands over Matt's slick, taut shoulders as he moved across her, she opened her eyes and drowned in his burning gaze. Just as she lifted her hips to meet and meld with him, his entire body momentarily froze.

A low moan of absolute joy slid up her throat as he eased slowly into her tight, slick confines. She felt his arms holding her, cradling her as if she were the most priceless, fragile and beloved being in the universe. There was concern on his perspiring face, and silent questioning in his eyes. Was he hurting her? Was he moving too quickly? Her answer was instantaneous as she arched her hips and drew him deeply, very deeply, within her. Matt hissed, the breath coming between his clenched teeth. Raising his head, he closed his eyes, a grimace making a tortured line of his mouth.

Jenny moaned again as he leaned down and took her lips hotly and commandingly. She felt him thrust into her, a man claiming his woman. There were no words for the sensation, for the powerful movement of his male body against her softer, more giving one. With each rhythmic movement, she felt fire building to a white-hot blaze within her wildly throbbing body. Curling her smaller legs around his massive ones, she clung to him, her face pressed against his sweaty neck. She clung to him with all her womanly strength and felt the cradle of his arms holding and rocking her in an ever-deepening rhythm.

A powerful sensation, like a galactic sun exploding within her, surged and then swept through her, a tidal wave of heat and pleasure. Arching like a bow against him, she released a startled cry of raw gratification. No longer was she the meek, mild Jenny Wright. No, beneath the tutelage, the guidance and supporting love of Matt, she became a woman of wild, primal desire.

Moments spun into a vortex of sun-gold colors, a rainbow of stars shimmering through her sleek, hot body as she climaxed a second and third time in the space of minutes. Matt knew how to please her, how to engage her body and her heart in a way no other man had ever done before. Jenny felt like a violin, her moans of desire and satiation keening out of her throat and whispering from her lips. He played her like a master, her taut body the instrument under his experienced direction.

Jenny felt Matt stiffen. His low animal growl—one of possession, of loving her and making her his in every way—permeated through her. She felt his arms tighten like bands around her, pushing a rush of air out of her lungs. Clinging to him, Jenny realized his life, his love were flowing deep within her welcoming body. Sliding her arms across his torso and arching back, she smiled softly and prolonged his release by moving sinuously against him over and over again.

Finally, he uttered her name and collapsed against her, his head next to hers. Their breathing was labored and chaotic. Jenny kissed his sandpapery jawline, and then his parted lips, and clung to Matt's mouth as he tenderly ravished her in return. His hands moved lovingly across her shoulder, cupping her small breast and then sliding down the line of her hip to her thigh.

"You are so giving," he rasped. Beads of sweat matted his dark hair against his forehead. He felt Jenny's hand move across his cheek to his brow and smooth his hair to one side.

"You are," she said. Then she laughed throatily and met his opening eyes, which were silver with satiation and joy. "I've never felt like I do now, darling. It's you," Jenny whispered, her voice tremulous. Framing his face with her hands, she held his bold, narrowed stare. "I feel like a very rare, beautiful violin that has just been played by a master— you."

Chuckling, Matt eased off her. He didn't want his weight crushing her small form. "A violin?" Rolling to his side, he brought Jenny up against him, one arm behind her neck. With his other hand, he brought up the sheet to their waists. "You're a beautiful woman, Jenny. Beautiful to me in every way."

Her heart fluttered with unparalleled joy. "Really? I wasn't too bad? It was good for you, too?"

Seeing the anxiousness in her eyes, Matt smiled and kissed the tip of her nose. "I feel adored, loved and very, very satisfied, sweet woman." Instantly, he saw all the worry disappear from her huge, blue eyes, which once again danced with gold flecks. As Matt caressed her mussed hair, he smiled down at her. "You're my life, Jenny. You're all I'll ever want or desire. We might have rough times ahead, but just know that through it all, I love you. And together, we'll get through them like the good team we were down in Peru."

Glowing beneath his praise, his heartfelt, rumbling words, Jenny closed her eyes and relaxed against his damp body. His heart was thundering beneath her ear as she pressed her head to his chest. Never had she felt more desired, more loved, than she did now, as he held her in the aftermath.

She felt Matt sigh deeply, the sound coming from his very soul and shuddering out of him. He relaxed with her in his arms. As she opened her eyes, she saw the moonlight shimmering in through the delicate lace curtains and creating a pattern throughout the room. Light and dark. Happy and sad. Joy and grief. Life was all of these things. With Matt at her side, she could weather them all.

"Marry me?"

The words rumbled from him. Jenny's eyes widened. She looked up at Matt. He was studying her tenderly in the moonlight. His wonderfully chiseled mouth curved ruefully as he gazed down at her. She couldn't help but smile in return. Lifting her hand, she moved it against his cheek.

"Yes..."

"You won't be sorry."

"I know...and you won't be, either..."

"I know..." He reached across her and opened the drawer on the bed stand. Fumbling for and finding the ring box, he retrieved it. Easing Jenny upward so that she could lean against him as he rested against the headboard, he placed the small green velvet box in her hand. "Here, this is for you...."

Heart pounding momentarily, Jenny gave him a wide-eyed look and then slowly pried the lid open.

"Oh...Matt!" Jenny looked at the dainty gold ring that had small, rectangular, channel-cut emeralds across it. Even in the moonlight, she could see the stones sparkling as she eased the ring from the box.

Proudly, he watched her expression as she held it up. Jenny was like a child in that moment, amazement written on her face, her well-kissed, softly swollen lips parted in awe. Turning, she met and held his gaze.

"Do you like it?" he asked in a husky voice.

Her face softened. "Like it? I love it, darling." She held it out to him. "Will you?" And she extended her left hand.

How easy it was to slide that engagement ring on her small, slender finger. Matt grinned bashfully as he held her hand and looked at her. "What do you think?"

The corners of her mouth curved upward. She saw the hope, the love, burning in Matt's stormy gaze. Heart bounding wildly, she whispered unsteadily, "Yes...yes, I'll marry you, Matt...."

It took every bit of control he had not to crush her against him. Instead, Matt leaned down and tenderly slid his mouth against hers. As the moonlight bathed them in silent radiance, Matt promised Jenny that he would cherish every moment of life with her from this moment forward—forever.

\*     \*     \*     \*     \*

# The Virgin Bride Said, "Wow!"

## CATHY GILLEN THACKER

## *CATHY GILLEN THACKER*

is a full-time wife, mother and author who began typing stories for her own amusement during her children's "nap time" when they were toddlers. Twenty years and more than fifty published novels later, Cathy is almost as well-known for her witty romantic comedies and warm family stories as she is for her ability to get grass stains and red clay out of almost anything, her triple-layer brownies and her knack for knowing what her three grown and nearly grown children are up to almost before they do! Her books have made numerous appearances on bestseller lists and are now published in seventeen languages and thirty-five countries around the world.

# Chapter One

"They turned us down again, didn't they?"
Brady Anderson guessed, as Kelsey Lockhart
strode across the sunny pasture toward him, her
cheeks pink with temper, her tousled hair glowing as cinnamon-red as the leaves in the maple
trees around them.

Kelsey's long slender legs continued eating
up the ground until she reached his side. Tip-
ping her flat-brimmed hat back off her forehead, she met his searching gaze and reported
unhappily, "Yep, they sure did. That's the fif-
teenth bank that's said no to us because we
didn't have enough collateral."

Brady grinned, trying, as always, when he
was this close to her, not to notice how very
pretty Kelsey was in an outdoorsy, lady rancher

sort of way. Personally, he'd never been much
for redheads. They were a bit too temperamen-
tal for his taste. And Kelsey Lockhart, the
youngest of the four delectable Lockhart sisters
of Laramie, Texas, was that, for sure. But there
was something about the pale gold freckles dot-
ting her smooth golden skin, the lusciousness
of her full lips that had his gaze returning to
her face again and again. Chuckling, he looked
into her dark green eyes, which were now flashing with both frustration and impatience, as he
commiserated humorously, "You'd think we'd
get the hint, wouldn't you?"

Kelsey leaned against the part of the aging
wooden fence he hadn't yet treated with wood
preservative. Unlike him, she refused to take
this latest rejection in stride. She folded her
arms in front of her contentiously and glared at
him, wanting answers. Now. This instant.
"What are we going to do?" Her expressive
red brows slammed down over her long-lashed
eyes. "We can't buy the rest of the horses and
cattle unless we get a loan. And since no bank
will give it to us, and we haven't had the resources to make a killing in the stock market

again…'' Kelsey's voice trailed off in discouragement.

Brady shared Kelsey's frustration about that, since it was a talent for investing that had drawn them together initially and enabled them both to come up with the cash for the down payment on their ranch the previous summer. If they had another six months and enough seed money to get started, maybe they could do it again. Maybe. But they didn't have either the time or the seed money. Which left them fewer options. Brady put down his brush and wiped his hands with the cloth he had looped into his belt. The rest of the painting would have to wait. "Then we look for a venture capitalist to underwrite the rest of our setup expenses," Brady said, having already anticipated just such a move being necessary. He put the lid back on the bucket of wood preservative, picked up his brush and gave Kelsey a confidence-inspiring look. "And I know just the one."

An hour later, Kelsey and Brady were sitting in Wade McCabe's office on the Golden Slipper ranch that he shared with his wife, Josie.

A stellar businessman himself, Wade listened

patiently to their plans for expanding Kelsey's horse-riding stables and Brady's cattle operation, and reviewed their business plans, which Brady knew full well were solid as a rock. And then Wade zeroed in on the same thing all the bankers had. "Unfortunately, the two of you aren't married," Wade said, with a disapproving frown.

"So?" Kelsey said, spoiling for a fight about that—one of many they'd had with literally everyone who had learned how they'd impulsively pooled their resources so they could make their individual dreams of owning their own ranch come true, sooner rather than later.

"That's true," Brady interrupted coolly, putting up a hand before Kelsey could go all contentious and argumentative on them. He looked Wade straight in the eye. "But we did buy back the ranch that belonged to her folks. We've been in partnership for four months now. That ought to count for something." Especially since most people in Laramie hadn't thought he and Kelsey would last more than a few weeks together, at most.

Wade sighed and handed back their business

plan. "Look, Brady, I know you're a good man and a talented cowboy—otherwise my brother Travis wouldn't have hired you to work on his ranch—but that doesn't mean I approve of what you're doing with Kelsey here."

Brady had an idea what Wade was hinting at—that he was somehow taking advantage of the six-year age difference and Kelsey's youth to get what he wanted. "We're business partners, Wade," Brady told him. "Pure and simple."

Wade nodded. "Yeah, I heard you've been sleeping in the tack room in the stables since you moved out to the ranch, and have even rigged up a little bathroom and outdoor shower for yourself there."

"Nothing untoward has gone on between us," Kelsey interrupted, beginning to look very ticked off that anyone could even suspect there had been. "Not that it would be any business of yours or anyone else's if there had been!" she finished angrily.

Wade lifted a brow in a way that said "The lady doth protest too much."

Brady knew how Wade felt. If he didn't

know better, he'd think by Kelsey's defensive reaction and the blush in her cheeks that there *was* something going on between them. Not that it would have been surprising if there had been, from a strictly physical perspective. Kelsey was one very sexy woman. She was half a foot shorter than Brady, with a slender, athletic body that curved in all the right places. Very much a tomboy. Notoriously fickle. But somehow very innocent, nevertheless. She had a way about her that somehow made her everybody's kid sister. And yet there was nothing siblinglike about the increasingly lustful feelings he was beginning to have for her, Brady knew.

Was that what Wade McCabe was picking up on? Was that what had Wade, and everyone else who knew them, concerned about the partnership between him and the black sheep of the Lockhart family? Brady wondered, his glance taking in Kelsey's snug-fitting jeans and red cowgirl boots. The man's denim work shirt she wore knotted at her hips was loose enough to conceal the abundant curves of her breasts and her slender waist—the figure-hugging tank top she wore beneath was not.

"Kelsey," Brady finally said, before Kelsey could make the two of them look even guiltier with her hot-tempered protests, "Wade is not interested in our love life or lack thereof. Not that there is one, you understand," Brady finished firmly, looking at Wade. Regardless of how much he desired Kelsey, he had never once so much as tried to kiss her. For one thing, he didn't want to be another notch on Kelsey's belt. He figured to date and then be dumped by her, as she apparently dumped every man sooner or later, would be the kiss of death for their partnership. Because he doubted he could ever get over that. For another, he didn't think he should get involved with her when he still had some very sticky problems of his own to deal with—a secret debt of his own that was coming due in two weeks. A debt that could change the way she felt about him, permanently, once she realized all he had been keeping from her and everyone else in Laramie. She might understand him not telling everyone about the rash promises he had made and the debt he owed. A debt he still had no way to effectively settle, without a loan from a venture capitalist like Wade McCabe. But she wouldn't understand him not telling her. Not when his earlier actions could leave her partnerless in another two weeks.

"That's good to hear," Wade continued with a warning look at Brady, picking up their conversation where Brady had left off, "because Kelsey is like a kid sister to me and I wouldn't want to think you or anyone else had taken advantage of her."

"Wade, could you please just forget about my personal life and concentrate on business. I'm trying to get a loan from you here—not advice to the *not* necessarily lovelorn."

Brady grinned at her cute play on words.

Wade was amused, but he didn't grin. "Kelsey, I am a businessman, pure and simple," he told her firmly, standing to signal the meeting was over. "I don't make bad investments. If I had I never would have been a millionaire by the time I was thirty. And the bottom line is, this partnership of yours and Brady's does not look like something that is going to stand the test of time to me."

"Thanks, anyway." Brady stood, too, and

held out his hand, to let Wade know there were no hard feelings. Maybe the trick here was to go to a venture capitalist who didn't know them personally. Someone who didn't feel so protective of Kelsey.

Ignoring Brady's hint that they cut the meeting short and make a dignified exit, Kelsey glared at Brady, who was still shaking hands with Wade McCabe. She slipped her hands in the pockets of her jeans. "Oh, really, and how do you figure that, Wade?" She lifted her chin, the look she gave Wade as contentious as the rising tenor of her voice. "Do you have some sort of businessman's crystal ball?"

"No," Wade returned evenly, abruptly looking as if he were an exasperated father talking to a wayward child. He clamped his lips together. "But I do know your history with men and jobs, Kelsey."

Oh, man, Brady thought, having heard this same spiel or something like it from everyone in Laramie County.

"And you never stay with either very long," Wade continued flatly, not about to back down from his stance any more than Kelsey was.

"The bottom line? The only way I'd loan you and Brady money is if you were married."

"WELL, THAT'S IT THEN," Kelsey said as she and Brady walked back out to the Lockhart-Anderson Ranch pickup truck. She thrust out her chin defiantly. "We'll just get married. Today."

Brady rolled his eyes. "Kelse, be serious."

"I am." She stomped closer. "We need the money to expand. You need more cattle, fence and feed to start turning a profit on your side of the ranch. And I need more horses, another stable to house them, and the money to hire some instructors so I can teach all those kids and adults who want riding lessons from me. The only way that will happen is if we get a loan."

"I agree we need more money as soon as possible," Brady said. He opened the passenger door for Kelsey.

Instead of getting in, she leaned against the side of the truck. "Then let's get hitched and get it," she suggested in her usual carefree manner.

Brady frowned. As much as he hated to admit it, he could see himself married to Kelsey. He could also see them in bed. Making love. And doing any number of things that would lead to nothing but trouble. He had just sworn to Wade McCabe he would keep Kelsey out of trouble. Not lead her into it. "Marriage is serious business, Kelse," he reminded her sternly.

A mixture of curiosity and devilry sparkled in her dark green eyes. "You say that as if you know," Kelsey taunted.

Brady hated being the responsible one in any relationship. But when he was with Kelsey, that was exactly what role he usually found himself playing. "Well, I do," he retorted evenly.

Kelsey's lips parted slightly in an "oh" of surprise as she continued to study him carefully. "Have you ever been married?"

"No." Deliberately, Brady pushed aside the memory of his near-miss. "You?"

"No," Kelsey replied rapidly, the look she gave him letting him know she had never been anywhere close. Which wasn't a surprise, given her notoriously fickle history with men. "But that doesn't mean I couldn't be if it were necessary for business reasons," Kelsey continued. "And let's face it, it is." She stood, legs braced, heels dug into the gravel driveway beneath her feet. "The only way anyone, whether it be bank or venture capitalist, is going to give us any money is if we first demonstrate enough stability to prove to them it will be a sound investment, either by cohabiting on our ranch for a very long time, like a matter of years, or going the traditional route and already being happily married. Besides—" she shrugged "—it will get everyone who thinks I shouldn't be partnering with you, because it will prevent my ever falling in love and/or getting married to anyone else, off my back."

She had a point there, Brady admitted reluctantly to himself. He braced a hand on the roof of the pickup, next to her head. "I thought the wedding fever that had swept town last summer had sort of died down," he countered, looking down at her.

"Hah!" New color swept Kelsey's cheeks, making the golden splattering of freckles across her cheeks and nose stand out all the more. "It's only gotten worse since Sam McCabe and

Kate Marten got married last week. John and Lilah McCabe are dropping hints about me marching down the aisle.'' She looked at Brady, her frustration as evident as her determination to do something about it, something reckless, something they wouldn't want her to do. ''My sisters make no secret about how much they want me to marry,'' she continued hotly.

''But you've told everyone under the sun you are never getting married, ever, no matter what.'' As far as Brady was concerned, that should settle it. But it didn't. Not for the Lockhart sisters, the McCabes, or even, it seemed, Kelsey herself, who had seemed to get more and more antsy about the subject as time went by, Brady noted.

Kelsey bent her knee and propped the sole of one boot against the side of the pickup. ''So?'' she shot back mischievously. ''I'm notoriously fickle, remember? I change my mind all the time. I've had several dozen different jobs in the past six years, and many, many more boyfriends. This will be just another indication of my flightiness.''

Brady regarded her in exasperation. He couldn't deny being involved with Kelsey—even as merely business partners—brought an endless array of surprises. But there was a limit as to what he was willing to do, even to achieve his dreams of being a successful rancher and self-made man. With a great deal more patience than he felt, he explained, "Kelse, we can't just say 'I do' and then move in together and live under the same roof and have everything magically work out."

Kelsey looked shocked. Abruptly, she moved away from him. "Who said anything about living under the same roof?" she spouted, looking abruptly as irritated with him as he was with her. She poked a finger against his chest. "I'm talking about a marriage of convenience here, a business arrangement, Brady. I just want to get hitched long enough to get our money."

Brady released his breath in a whoosh of frustration. "Doing something purely for the sake of money is always a bad thing, Kelse." He knew, having already done so himself. In fact, it was the agreement he'd made two years ago that was likely to be the end of life as he wanted it, yet.

"But building up our business isn't." Kelsey turned pleading eyes to his. She grabbed both his hands and squeezed them in hers. "Please, Brady." She looked up at him in a way he was hard-pressed to deny. "Let's get hitched. Now. Today."

"YOU DID WHAT?" Wade McCabe asked two hours later.

"We got married at city hall," Kelsey announced, still carrying the bouquet of Texas wildflowers Brady'd gotten her before they'd gone into the courthouse.

"This isn't funny," Wade said, after studying the marriage certificate they'd handed him, for proof. Wade glared at Brady.

"Believe me, it's no joke to us, either," Brady replied. He was pretty sure it was the overbearing, intensely protective nature of all those around her that had pushed Kelsey to be the wildly reckless woman she was.

"So let's talk money," Kelsey said, grabbing Brady's hand and plopping herself down in a chair in front of Wade's desk. "Brady and I were thinking prime plus one, in terms of interest rates."

"Payable in six months, max," Brady added firmly, as he took the chair next to Kelsey's. He didn't want them beholden to Wade any longer than possible.

"There's no way you can do that," Wade argued.

Actually, Brady thought silently, there was. Although even Kelsey didn't know about the way he was going to do that....

"By then, we figure we'll have established enough of a history and a business to be able to get another loan, from either a venture capitalist or a bank," Kelsey said seriously, looking and acting like the top-notch businesswoman she was.

"Okay. I'll give you the money you want," Wade said, "but I've got some conditions, too."

Although he wasn't anxious to learn what they were, Brady had expected as much.

"Such as...?" Kelsey prodded.

"If this marriage of yours proves to be a fraud, I get the deed to your ranch, free and clear." Wade gave that a moment to sink in, then continued, even more seriously, "It's not too late to back out. Because unless I miss my guess,'' Wade continued, looking from one of them to the other, ''this is still at the stage where it can all quietly be undone, maybe without even an annulment if you're lucky enough. People will know what happened, of course— since you went to city hall—but the mistake won't be a permanent or long-lasting kind of thing, and you'll still have your ranch.''

''Just not the loan money from you,'' Brady guessed quietly.

Wade nodded. He looked at Brady as if he thought Brady should have known better than to get sucked into one of Kelsey's wild ideas. Unfortunately, Brady knew that was true.

''Fine. Draw up the papers,'' Kelsey said heatedly.

''I mean it, Kelsey.'' Wade frowned all the more. ''If you insist on doing this…on trying to pull something over on me and everyone else, I'll take your ranch,'' Wade warned.

Brady had only to look at Wade to believe him. This was the only way Wade thought he could protect Kelsey from herself. Not surprisingly, Kelsey kept her hold on Brady's hand.

"I married this man. I'm staying married to him," she announced boldly. "Now, draw up the papers, Wade. 'Cause as soon as you do, we're signing on the dotted line."

KELSEY AND BRADY WENT straight to the bank, then headed back to the ranch. They were still wearing the boots, jeans, denim work shirts and hats they'd had on earlier in the day. The only difference were the matching dime-store wedding rings on their left ring fingers. "See," Kelsey said after a while, trying not to worry about what she'd recklessly insisted they get themselves into, "I told you it'd be fine."

Brady's black brows drew together. To Kelsey's consternation, he didn't exactly look as if he agreed with her.

"Absolutely nothing has changed," Kelsey continued, as she studied Brady's strong, six-foot frame. Although he tended to be a little mysterious—he never talked to anyone about the life he'd had before he had landed in Laramie, Texas—there wasn't a finer-looking cowboy or more capable cattleman around, as far as she was concerned. He was solidly muscled from head to toe and had shoulders that were broad enough to lean on. Not that she'd ever really done so. A suntanned face, and a smile that was sexy and reckless enough to make her heart skip a beat. And he made a good partner, too.

Brady turned his pickup truck into the lane, the fading afternoon sunlight casting shadows along their path. "Well, I wouldn't say that, exactly," he said, nodding at the proliferation of cars and trucks in their drive. As she turned her gaze in the direction of his, it was all Kelsey could do not to groan out loud. It looked like a convention of the Lockharts and the McCabes. He turned to Kelsey expectantly. "Are we having a party I didn't know about?" he asked.

Kelsey frowned, then allowed hesitantly, "Maybe a wedding reception."

Brady's lips came together firmly. He slanted her a glance. "What?"

"Well, you know my sisters." Kelsey shrugged off the concern in Brady's midnight-blue eyes. "And now that the word is out, they probably want to throw us a party or something to welcome you to the family." As well as chew her out, big time, for not inviting them to witness the ceremony when they were all right there in town and could easily have attended and or tried to talk her out of doing such a reckless and impulsive thing in the first place.

Brady cut the motor on the pickup. "Sounds like fun," he said unenthusiastically.

Judging by the surly look on his face, Kelsey guessed, the duplicity of what they had done was beginning to get to Brady, too. But knowing there was no going back and undoing anything, especially now that they had the money they needed sitting in the bank, Kelsey pushed open her door and jumped down from the truck. "I just hope they don't have our family minister in there," Kelsey said. If she had to say her vows in front of clergy, she'd really feel married. And she didn't want to feel linked to Brady in that way. It was going to be hard enough as it was, pretending to one and all they were truly head over heels in love when they were in public. Noting Brady looked as alarmed about that prospect as she was feeling, Kelsey quickly reassured him. "They probably just have a cake or a wedding dress from my sister

Jenna's shop that they want me to wear for pictures. I'm sure we won't have to say our vows
again.'' It had been hard enough rushing
through the words the first time, without really
meaning or even concentrating on the promises
they were making to each other.

''Good.'' Brady released a short sigh of relief. He lifted his hat and ran his hand through
the inky-black layers of his hair, straightening
the tousled layers as best he could. '''Cause,
uh…''

''I understand perfectly,'' Kelsey said, cutting him off and letting him know with a quick,
decisive look that it wasn't necessary to say
more, as he slammed his hat back on his head
and circled around the truck to join her. She
knew he didn't want to have to fib to people
about the nature of their relationship any more
than she did. ''And I quite agree.'' She linked
hands with him—as much for moral support as
show—and drew a deep breath, still holding her
bouquet of Texas wildflowers and their certificate of marriage close to her chest. ''There's
only so much pretending a body can take in one
day.'' Drawing strength from both his touch

and the look in his eyes, she said, "Ready to go in and face the music?"

"Sure." Brady grinned, abruptly looking as determined and devil-may-care as Kelsey had felt earlier. He shrugged and tightened his hand on hers. "Why not?"

## Chapter Two

"I can't believe you did this," Meg Lockhart said the moment Kelsey and Brady walked in the door.

"So much for any hopes of a wedding reception," Kelsey said lightly, as she looked at the faces gathered around her. Her oldest sister, Meg, was there with her doctor-husband Luke Carrigan. Second-oldest Jenna stood next to her, looking fashionably pretty in one of her own designs, with her rancher-businessman husband, Jake. Dani, who was closest in age to Kelsey and could usually be counted on to understand her little sister, was seated on the sofa, with her movie-star husband, Beau Chamberlain. Lilah and John McCabe rounded out the party. All looked grim, worried and very, very concerned about the nuptials that had just taken place, sans festivities of any kind. "This feels like an intervention," Kelsey continued joking, hoping to bring a little levity to the situation.

"It is," Jenna said. "And I called it."

"Thanks, heaps." Kelsey took off her hat and hung it on the rack next to the front door. She strode across the polished wood floor. "Just what Brady and I needed on our wedding night, a lecture times eight."

"Believe it or not," Dani said as she stood and put her right hand on her rounded tummy, "we just have your best interests at heart."

"We're all worried about you," Meg agreed gently but firmly.

"Well, you needn't be," Kelsey shot right back. She linked her arm through Brady's and put her head on his shoulder. "Because Brady and I are happy as can be."

Everyone in the room sighed and frowned at that.

"You know we promised your parents we'd watch over you girls," Lilah McCabe said.

"I'm not sure a business arrangement called a marriage is what they would want for you, Kelsey," John McCabe added.

Kelsey's conscience ignited like a match to a flame. Stubbornly, she pushed any doubts she had about what she was doing aside. In this case, she told herself firmly, the end did justify the means. "On the contrary, Dr. McCabe, I think they'd be very happy to see the ranch back in the family, and looking so good again."

"I don't think that's what John and Lilah mean," Jenna said a little testily.

Kelsey glared at her sister.

"We want you to have love, Kelsey," Meg added.

"Passion," Dani agreed.

"Not to mention a relationship that will stand the test of time," John elaborated bluntly. He looked at Brady.

"Well, thank you all for your vote of confidence," Kelsey said, more irritated than ever at the depth of familial interference going on. "But Brady and I want to be alone now, so...if you don't mind..."

"Kelsey—" Meg started.

Knowing there was only one way to end it as quickly as she wanted to end it, Kelsey turned to her new husband, grabbed him by the shirtfront and tugged him toward her. She barely had time to register the surprise in his eyes before she planted a big kiss right on his lips.

BRADY HEARD THE GASPS around him as Kelsey's soft, luscious lips pressed against his. He had two choices. He could push her away, which would humiliate her even more than she already had been that day by her own actions and the words of others. Or he could play along. Given how good, how right her lips felt molded to his, Brady decided to play along. Not content to be a passive participant at anything he did, he wrapped his arms around her waist and pulled her up on tiptoe, so she was pressed even closer to him. And then the world faded away, as it became just the two of them. Locked together.

Only the sound of a collective "ahem" brought them back to reality. Reluctantly, Brady lifted his lips from hers and looked down at Kelsey. Her lips were dewy and pink, her eyes dazed with the same kind of wonder he felt. Heck of a first kiss, he thought. *Heck of a first kiss.*

"You know, maybe there's a little more going on here than we realized." Lilah McCabe was the first to speak.

"I think we should go and leave the newly-weds alone," John McCabe concurred. He and Lilah led the way out the door, followed by the Lockhart sisters and their husbands.

"You hurt her," Jake said to Brady, "you deal with us." Beau and Luke nodded their confirmation of that threat. "You call if you need anything," Beau told Kelsey sympathetically, before he exited with the group.

Jenna came back in. She put a key on the table beside the door. "My apartment above the shop is empty right now. Should either of you need it, for any reason, you feel free to use it." She left again, too.

Motors started up. One by one, the vehicles headed down the lane to the highway. Kelsey looked at Brady. Brady looked at Kelsey. She had never looked more beautiful or desirable to him than she did at that very moment. He sighed. This was going to be a lot harder than he'd thought. A lot harder. Given the way she had just felt in his arms, he didn't know how in the heck he was going to keep their relationship platonic. "I hate to say it, Kelse," he drawled, "but I think we've just gotten ourselves into one heck of a mess."

KELSEY COULDN'T HELP BUT notice the mixture of derision and regret in Brady's low tone. Suddenly, it seemed the Lockharts and the Mc-Cabes weren't the only ones worried about what she and Brady had done. Determined not to let herself fall prey to the same pessimism, Kelsey propped her hands on her hips and lifted her chin. "Why in the world would you say that?"

Brady rolled his eyes and continued to pace. "Besides the fact I've got the whole Lockhart-McCabe 'army' breathing down my neck?"

"They're a little excited." Kelsey plopped down on the sofa as if she hadn't a care in the world. She shrugged, and continued, "They'll get over it."

Brady's lips curved up on either side. "Before or after they pulverize me?" he asked. His probing glance made a leisurely tour of her body before returning to her eyes. "And speaking of pulverizing me, what was that kiss about just now?''

Kelsey had hoped he would be too nice a partner to bring that up. Guess not. Again, she pretended a lot more self-confidence and courage than she really felt. ''I know we promised no sex.''

Brady's midnight-blue eyes narrowed. ''That was part of the deal, all right.''

''But we had to make it look good,'' Kelsey persisted as she leapt to her feet once again. Unfortunately, Kelsey thought, it had felt good, too. Much more so than she had expected or ever experienced. But Brady didn't need to know that.

Brady clamped a hand on her shoulder and spun her around to face him. His fingers were as warm and strong as the rest of him, his manner every bit as stubborn and headstrong as hers. ''Are we going to have to keep on making it look good?''

Kelsey flushed and stepped back, out of reach. ''What do you mean?'' she demanded, still able to feel the impression of his touch, even though he was no longer holding on to her.

Brady's eyes narrowed as he reminded her seriously, "Wade McCabe said if our marriage is nothing but a ruse to get his money—which, by the way, we've already taken—then he's going to take the ranch from us."

"I remember," Kelsey said irritably.

"So how are we going to get around that?" Brady adapted a no-nonsense stance, legs braced apart, arms folded in front of him, that would have been very intimidating had Kelsey allowed it.

She didn't. Kelsey ran a hand through her tousled hair, pushing it off her face. "The way I see it, there are all kinds of marriages that are real as can be and yet...well, you know how it is after a while," Kelsey continued as if she knew what she was talking about when she damn well didn't have a clue. "The husband and wife don't seem at all romantic anymore, or even much involved with each other physically, and yet they stay together."

"There's a difference between being together and being happy," Brady pointed out sagely.

"That's true," Kelsey said, "but we could be together and be happy without having sex."

Brady lifted a brow and looked straight into her eyes. "Speak for yourself," he said.

KELSEY STARED AT HIM in silence. Brady wasn't sure why he had started this. He just knew someone had to shake up Kelsey's cock-eyed view of the world. It looked like it was going to be him. He edged closer. "I don't know any man who is living under the same roof with a woman he lusts after, who is happy when the two of them aren't sleeping together at least every once in a while," Brady continued, and watched the way Kelsey's freckled cheeks turned an even pinker hue.

Kelsey studied him suspiciously as she slightly tilted her pretty head to the side. "Are you saying you lust after me?"

Brady shrugged, seeing no reason to lie about it. Not that he could. Surely, she'd felt his arousal, pressed up against him the way she had been. "After that kiss, I sure do." He hooked his thumbs through the belt loops on either side of his fly and rocked back on his heels. "And now we're going to be living under the same roof."

Kelsey's green eyes shot sparks. "Says who?" she demanded.

"Says me." Brady strode closer. No way was he going to be her puppet on a string and it was high time she realized that. He lifted a hand and brushed an errant strand of cinnamon-colored hair from her cheek, then cupped her face with his palm. The silky heat of her skin warmed him through and through. "We can't make this look like a real marriage if I'm still sleeping in the stable and you're sleeping in the house."

"Oh. Well." Kelsey jerked in a breath and stepped back, away from him. "You can have one of the other bedrooms, then. There are three to choose from."

Brady knew that would only make things worse. After that kiss, he was going to keep wanting her. And not just as a platonic partner, either. And unless he missed his guess, even if she didn't want to admit it to herself, Kelsey was probably going to keep wanting him, too. "That doesn't solve the problem of lust," he told her frankly, meaning it.

KELSEY KNEW WHAT HE expected here. Like Wade McCabe and everyone else who knew her, Brady expected her to cry uncle, and declare this impetuous marriage of theirs a mistake. Sooner, rather than later. He may have even figured that she would beg Wade McCabe's forgiveness for trying to pull one over on him, and possibly even get it. Well, she wasn't going to do that. People thought she was fickle enough as it was, without adding fuel to the fire. Which left her only one option. Which, under the circumstances, wasn't nearly as untenable an idea as she would have expected it to be.

Kelsey shot Brady a glance, letting him know she was as reckless and impulsive as ever, and proud of it. "Fine then, we'll sleep together once, and then that will be it. At least until we decide it's necessary to do so again. It'll be a good thing," Kelsey continued, picking up steam as she went along. "I'm no good at lying. Everything I feel or think is right on my face, anyway."

Brady rolled his eyes. "No kidding about that," he said dryly.

Kelsey lifted her shoulders in an indifferent shrug and kept her eyes on Brady's. "Now that we're married, everybody is going to be trying to figure out if we've slept together or not, anyway," she told him with as much outrageous brazenness as ever. "So we might as well do it, get it over with, and out of the way, so to speak."

Brady narrowed his eyes at her thoughtfully. To Kelsey's disappointment, he didn't back down one bit, either. "That's a very typically *male* view of things," Brady said, mocking her too-casual tone to a T.

"What?" Kelsey propped her hands on her hips. The way he was challenging her was making her mad. Worse, it was exciting her, too, in a way unlike anything she'd ever felt before. Stubbornly, she kept her eyes locked with his, even as her heart began to race like a wild thing in her chest. "You don't believe I'm serious?" she asked very softly and coolly.

Brady clamped his lips together. A new, worried light came into his eyes. "I'm not sure what to believe right now," he said seriously, after a moment, suddenly seeming all of his twenty-nine years. "I mean, I know you're a tomboy—"

"Thank you." Kelsey flashed him a tight, mocking smile.

"But this…" Brady continued, clearly at a loss as to what to do next.

Kelsey shot him a sultry smile, already toying with the top button of her shirt. "Don't you want to satisfy your curiosity?" she goaded playfully.

Brady's chest and shoulders suddenly looked hard as rock. "Well, sure…"

Telling herself she didn't need or want to look below his waist, lest she lose her nerve, Kelsey challenged, "Then let's go. Upstairs. Now. You and me."

Brady laughed. Kelsey could see he didn't take her any more seriously than her sisters or the McCabes had. She slowly unbuttoned her shirt and started up the stairs. When she reached the top, she shrugged it off, whirled it lariat-style over her head, and then rocketed it Brady's way.

BRADY STARED AT THE SHIRT fluttering past the stairwell to the floor. The next thing he knew Kelsey had turned the corner into the upstairs hall and a very lacy, surprisingly transparent black bra had followed.

Feeling as if he were in the middle of the wildest, most erotic dream he'd ever had, he moved to pick up the bra. It was still warm from her skin and scented with orange-blossom perfume.

Brady swallowed around the sudden dryness in his throat. Lower still, there was an insistent ache he sure as heck didn't want to be feeling. His fingers closing on the fabric, Brady stared in the direction Kelsey had gone. Damn it all if this new wife of his wasn't serious.

He couldn't believe it.

Not once in the entire time they'd been partners had Kelsey so much as offered him even a handshake. In the space of a few short hours she had proposed marriage, rushed him to city hall, held his hand and kissed him like there was no tomorrow. Now she was taking off her clothes. He swore again as a boot clattered to the first floor. Then another. Then her belt and jeans sailed down from the upstairs hall. A pair of socks followed. Brady swallowed. The only thing she had left was her panties. Before he could even make a move, those followed, too, and they were just as lacy, just as transparent as her bra.

He heard her laughing, then the sound of her footsteps moving toward her bedroom. His lower half surging to life, Brady headed for the stairs.

KELSEY WAS ALREADY BENEATH the covers in her bedroom. Her cheeks were flushed but there was a telltale devilry in her eyes, and a challenging tilt to her chin. "Are we going to get this over with or not?" she said.

Brady looked at the elegant line of her bare shoulders, and her satiny smooth skin. She had the covers tugged well above her breasts, but what little he could see, coupled with the kiss they had exchanged not too long ago, had him already hard as a rock. "I'm not the kind of guy who plays around," he warned, wanting there to be no mistake about his intentions. "If we do this, if we begin a sexual relationship with each other, there's no going back. I expect exclusive rights to your bedroom and I'll give you the same to mine."

"Fine," Kelsey said as she watched him methodically take off his shirt, boots and jeans. Her pretty green eyes widened as he stripped off his socks and low-slung red briefs, too.

"But I reserve the right to say when and where it'll happen."

Brady had no problem with that. Once she was his woman, he figured he could convince her to make love with him anywhere, anytime the need struck. And if not, he thought as a smile curved his mouth, he'd sure have fun trying.

Naked, he climbed beneath the sheets.

To his frustration, although she was naked, too, Kelsey kept her arms on top of the blankets, the covers pressed tightly against her. She had a funny look in her eyes, too. Sort of excited and scared and nervous and yet ridiculously brazen and full of bravado, too. "If I didn't know better," he teased, "I'd think you'd never done this before."

"Ha, ha, very funny." Kelsey gave him a withering look. "Can we just get on with it, please?"

Irritated at the way she kept calling all the shots and ordering him around, Brady frowned. "Sorry for the delay, ma'am." And with that, he lifted the barrier of sheets still between them, shifted over top of her and lowered his head to hers.

THE FEEL OF HIS LIPS against hers was even more tantalizing and electric than before. Kelsey gasped as Brady's mouth brushed against hers. She quivered all over as he slipped his tongue inside her mouth and rubbed it against hers with lazy, sensual strokes. His hands moved to her breasts, and still kissing her, he shifted his weight, so he was lying beside her, one arm beneath her neck, one leg thrown over hers. When he'd brought her nipples to hot, aching peaks, he let his hand trail lower still, across the flat of her abdomen, and that was when panic, unlike Kelsey had ever felt, set in. Kelsey broke off the kiss and, hands splayed against his chest, pushed him away with all her might. "Stop!" she said. "I can't do this!"

# Chapter Three

"What the...?" Brady said, looking every bit as shocked and upset as Kelsey would have expected him to be, given her abrupt change of mind.

"I'm a virgin." Kelsey tugged the covers to her chin and scooted as far away from him as she could without leaving the bed. She hated to disappoint him, but she knew she couldn't go through with it, not feeling the way she did. "I thought I could," she continued, trembling from head to toe. "But I can't. I—" She swallowed hard around the growing ache in her throat. "I'm sorry."

"A virgin," Brady repeated, still looking as stunned as if she'd hit him over the head with a board.

"Yes." Keeping the sheet wrapped around her like a shield, Kelsey eased from the bed. "So now you know." She took a breath, and kept her eyes from Brady's naked, gloriously sexy body. Doing her best to build on what little dignity she had left, she said, "I trust you won't tell anyone else."

Brady shook his head. "Then what…what was that striptease about?"

"I thought it might be nice to go to bed with you." Kelsey tried her hardest but could not keep her eyes from straying to his long, sturdy limbs and glowing golden skin and the wealth of curly black hair. He was solid muscle from head to toe. And lower still, below his waist… Oh, my. My!

Aware he was still glaring at her, waiting for her to continue, she moved her eyes from his arousal, back to his face. She gulped in great amounts of air. "After all, we're married," she said hastily, wishing he would do something besides lounge there, so expectantly, on her bed. "And it would solve some problems. And…and I've never done it before and all my sisters obviously have, so…"

"So you thought you'd use me to get some experience," Brady said grimly. "And in a roundabout way keep up with all of them." Lips set, he bounded from her bed and snatched up his jeans.

Not about to let him make her into some villainess, when all she had done was make a simple error in judgment, Kelsey stomped closer and shot right back, "Listen, cowboy, it's not like you weren't using me, too. To...to..."

"Experience some pleasure?" Brady filled in the blanks.

"Right." Kelsey tore her eyes from his rigid lower half.

"Only we didn't get anywhere near that, Kelse." Brady stomped closer yet, his strong, tall body exuding so much heat he could practically have started a prairie fire all on his own. "All we did was frustrate ourselves."

Like she didn't know that? She was still tingling all over, still wanting something indescribable, still scared. But she would be damned if she would show Brady Anderson, her new husband, any of that, especially when he was being so sanctimonious. So Kelsey merely went over to her vanity and sat down on the bench. Aware he was watching her every move even as he tugged on his jeans, she crossed her legs at the knee beneath the toga-wrapped sheet, and offered him a sassy smile, pretending an ease she couldn't begin to feel. "Better luck next time?"

"There's not going to be a next time," Brady vowed, grabbing his shirt.

Panic filled Kelsey's soul. She'd gotten used to having Brady around. "What do you mean?" Despite what had just happened between them, she still wanted him in her life.

But, oblivious to her feelings on the matter, Brady jerked on his boots, one after another. "I mean I don't enjoy being played for a fool," he stormed.

"I didn't do that!"

Finished, Brady stood and advanced on her so deliberately and methodically he took her breath away. He didn't stop until he towered over her. "Then what do you call it?" he asked very softly, looking down at her.

Kelsey swallowed but didn't back down. "A mistake."

His lips compressed thinly. "I agree with you there."

Remorse filled her, followed quickly by the need to behave responsibly and make amends. "Brady…"

He put up both hands before she could touch him. "Just don't, Kelse. Just don't."

Without another word, Brady stormed from the room. Kelsey had just started to run after him when the phone rang. Frowning, she went to get it. Rafe Marshall was on the other end of the line. An old school chum of Kelsey's, and former boyfriend, he was now principal at the elementary school and father of eight-year-old twins. "I really need to talk to you," he said. "I've got a big favor to ask. Do you think you could come over to the school and meet me?"

"Now?" She couldn't imagine what Rafe would need to see her about.

"Well, yes," Rafe said, "if it's convenient."

Why not? Kelsey thought, her curiosity piqued. All she was going to do here was sit around and feel bad about what had *not* happened with Brady. "Be right there," Kelsey said.

She went to her closet, put on a fresh set of clothes, retrieved her boots from the bottom of the stairs and headed out the door. She saw Brady come out of the barn just as she was climbing into her pickup truck. Ignoring the way he was looking at her—as if he'd had second thoughts and wanted to talk to her after all—she gunned the truck and sped off.

Rafe was waiting for her when she entered the empty halls. He led her into his office and gestured for her to have a seat. ''Shouldn't you be home having dinner with your twins?'' Kelsey asked. Since his wife had died a couple of years ago, Rafe had tried to give his kids as much stability as possible. Most nights that meant he was with his kids.

''My mom is visiting and with them. I told her I'd be late.'' Rafe sank down behind his desk. He was a handsome man, given to wearing his shirts and ties in the exact same color, but the stress of the past few years had left him with wings of gray just above his ears, and at his temples, and a hint of sadness around his eyes. Lately, Kelsey had noted happily, that sadness had been disappearing, bit by bit.

"Kelse, I need your help." As usual, Rafe got straight to the point. "You know Patricia Weatherby?"

Kelsey nodded. "She works at the chamber of commerce, has a little five-year-old girl named Molly." As she recalled, they had stopped in Laramie en route to California when Molly had to have an appendectomy, and liked the town and the people so much they decided to settle here permanently.

"Right. Well—" Rafe paused and drew a deep breath, as if already working up his nerve "—I want to ask her out."

Kelsey shrugged, not sure where she fit into all this. It wasn't as if Rafe needed her permission. The two of them had been over for a long time. "So what's stopping you?" she asked.

"I'm afraid I'll mess it up." Rafe frowned, worry darkening his eyes. "I haven't had a date since I got married and that was years and years ago. I'm afraid if I go out with her, without a little practice, I'll mess it up and blow my chances with Patricia permanently."

Rafe could be a little physically clumsy at times, but Kelsey didn't hold that against him and she couldn't see a nice woman like Patricia Weatherby doing so, either. "You're being a little hard on yourself, aren't you?"

He didn't think so. He picked up a pencil and turned it end over end. "Do you know how many other guys have asked her out since she settled here? Fifteen. No one's made it past a first date. She won't go out with them after that—she says she'd like to be friends, but beyond that, she can tell it's not going to work out. She's real nice about it, from what I've heard, but she's firm. Once she has decided you're not the one for her, you're not the one."

Ouch, Kelsey thought, taking off her cowgirl hat and laying it in her lap.

"And since you sort of operate the same way... Well," Rafe amended quickly when he saw he had offended her. He leaned forward urgently. "You know what I mean. You've dated a lot of guys, Kelsey, and turned 'em all down eventually, usually after just a date or two or three yourself, so...I figured maybe you could clue me in as to what it is exactly that turns women like you and Patricia off to men in the first place. Then I would know what not to do and I could just not do it."

Kelsey could see he was dead serious. "Well, it really isn't any one specific thing, Rafe," she said, being careful not to hurt his feelings, even though she did think he was worrying about this unnecessarily. Still, she figured it wouldn't hurt to help him build up his self-confidence. She sat back in her chair and fingered the brim of her hat. "A lot of things turn a woman off to a guy."

"Such as…?" Rafe pressed.

Kelsey shrugged and did her best to explain. "Sometimes it's a chemistry thing. I get that kiss at the front door at the end of the night, and I know…we haven't got a shot." Unlike with Brady. When he had kissed her, she had known they not only had a shot…that it was damned likely they'd end up together at some point, for at least a certain length of time.

"But it's not always as simple as a lack of chemistry," Rafe said.

"No." With effort, Kelsey forced her mind away from Brady and his kiss, and their near tumble, and back to the conversation at hand. "Sometimes it's the way a guy forgets to open a door for me," she said.

Rafe looked stunned. "*You* want guys to open a door for you?"

"Well, not always. Sometimes. Why?" Kelsey found herself getting defensive. "You got a problem with that?"

"No. I'm just surprised. That's all." Rafe paused. "What else?"

"Well, honestly, Rafe, I don't know." As restless as could be, Kelsey shot out of her chair and paced his office, slapping the brim of her hat against her thigh as she moved. "I haven't even had a date in a while, not since the guys in town stopped asking me out."

"Well, yeah—" Rafe was quick to jump to the other men's defense "—none of them thought they had a chance." He stopped and made a face when he saw he had offended her again. "Sorry. Listen, would you do me a favor? Would you have a secret date with me?"

Kelsey sighed and sat down in her chair again. "Why does it have to be secret?"

"Because I don't want Patricia to think I'm interested in any woman but her when I do ask her out. Besides, what I want you to do is sort of give me a dating lesson. Let's just go somewhere where nobody knows us, and we'll pretend we're on a date, and I'll do all the things I intend to do for Patricia, you know, like holding the door and having dinner table conversation and maybe even asking her to dance if you think that's a good thing. You can critique me. And that'll give me a chance to get all my ducks in a row and build up my confidence before I actually do ask her out. I really, really don't want to blow this, Kelsey. I think Patricia's the woman for me, and I haven't felt that way about a woman since my wife died.''

Rafe seemed so sure about what he wanted. Kelsey could only admire him for that. Besides, she figured she owed him. He had steered a lot of kids who wanted riding lessons her way. ''I would be happy to help you with that, Rafe,'' she said.

''How about tomorrow night then?'' Rafe asked.

Kelsey hesitated. ''Tomorrow's pretty busy. Brady and I are going on a buying trip and I'm not sure how long it will take, or when we'll be back, but Wednesday evening is definitely free.''

"Wednesday evening is good for me, too." Rafe smiled. "Meet me at the Gilded Lily, around seven."

Kelsey frowned at the mention of the restaurant he had selected. "There are a couple of waiters over there who are known to be a little snooty, Rafe." In Kelsey's opinion, it was not the place to be if you were as nervous as Rafe was likely to be on his first date with Patricia Weatherby.

"It's also the only true five-star restaurant in the area and I want to impress Patricia and show her a really memorable time."

Kelsey could see he had his mind made up. Far be it for her to try to change it. "All right, then. The Gilded Lily it is. Oh, and Rafe?" Kelsey paused as she headed out the door. "I probably should mention one more thing. As of this afternoon—I'm married. So your idea about keeping this little dating lesson of ours a secret? It's a good one."

"WHERE HAVE YOU BEEN?" Brady demanded the moment Kelsey sauntered in the front door. He was dressed in his usual dusty brown cowboy boots and jeans, but he had changed into a clean blue denim work shirt that brought out the blue of his eyes. Trying not to think what it might be like to go on a date with Brady, Kelsey walked right past him, into the kitchen.

Even though she knew she owed him an apology, she didn't want to think or talk about what had happened between them earlier. She still felt pretty embarrassed at the way she had lured him into her bed and then chickened out at the very last minute, before anything really momentous could happen. But she figured he did not need to know that.

"And hello to you, too, husband dear." Adopting her most carefree air, Kelsey put the bag containing a take-out beef barbecue dinner down on the table. "I hope you're hungry. I bought this especially for you."

His scowl faded as the aroma of tender, mesquite-flavored beef and spicy barbecue sauce filled the air. "If you'd have asked me, I'd have gone with you."

Kelsey brought out containers of vinegar-based slaw, potato salad and beans, and snapped the lids off those, too. She held his gaze for a moment, before she went to get the plates and silverware. "I thought we both needed some cooling off time."

"You can say that again." Brady brought two cold drinks and a stack of paper napkins to the table and held out a chair for her before he sat himself. As casually as if they ate dinner as a couple every day. If she didn't know better, she'd think he'd been talking to Rafe about the things she really wanted from a man. One thing was for sure. Brady'd never held a door or chair for her before, not even when they got married this afternoon. In fact, he'd gone out of his way to steer physically clear of her.

Kelsey waited until they had both filled their plates with a generous amount of food, then said, "Listen. About what happened earlier, I'm sorry."

Brady sighed in a way that let her know he had as many regrets as she did. He reached across the table and took both her hands in his. "I'm sorry, too." He looked at her deliberately. "I scared you and I sure didn't mean to do that. If you'd just told me you were a beginner..." His voice trailed off.

Despite her desire to remain in peace-making mode, Kelsey couldn't help the rise of temper insider her belly. He made her sound so inept. She tugged her hands out of his. "A beginner?"

"A beginner in bed," Brady corrected himself hastily. "Okay?"

Kelsey frowned. She hated the fact he looked so at ease when she was still tied up in knots. "Well, if I am, it's not for lack of trying this afternoon."

"If I had known how inexperienced you were," Brady huffed in an irritated tone of voice Kelsey was beginning to know all too well, "I would have said no."

Kelsey rolled her eyes. "Exactly why I didn't tell you," Kelsey sassed right back, determined not to let him get the better of her in this or any other way.

"But had I agreed," Brady added as if she hadn't spoken, continuing to look at her in a very sexy, very determined way, "I would have indoctrinated you slowly. I wouldn't have rushed you into it. I would have—"

"Seduced me?" Kelsey guessed hopefully as the two of them began to eat.

"Yes." Brady nodded.

Abruptly, Kelsey's mind was filled with images of the two of them in bed. All night. "Well, we could still do that," Kelsey murmured offhandedly, her curiosity mounting as her innate recklessness took over once again and pushed her to explore this life to its limits. What would it have been like, she wondered, if she hadn't panicked, but instead had regained her courage and let Brady's hand move lower, more intimately still? Would he have made love to her, the way he had wanted to make love to her? Would they still be in her bed now? Despite her fear, she tingled just thinking about the possibility of losing her virginity with Brady. Here. Now. Tonight. After all, he was her husband....

Brady, who was still watching her intently, guessed at the nature of her thoughts and made a rude, guffawing sound in the back of his throat. "Oh, no, Kelse. Not on your life are we trying that again."

Kelsey's brows knitted together in consternation. The disaster this afternoon aside, she had never been one to give up on anything she really wanted, and neither, she sensed, had Brady.

"Why not?" she asked. Wasn't that what you were supposed to do when you fell off a horse, so to speak? Get back on?

Brady took a thirsty gulp of his drink and forked up some tender beef. "Because I am not all that fond of sexual torture and cold showers, that's why not."

Kelsey watched him chow down for several long seconds. "That's what it felt like to you?" she asked after a moment. "Torture?"

Brady rolled his eyes and gave her an annoyed look. "Honey, hours later, I'm still hard. And I figure I'm going to be that way for a while."

Kelsey was glad the tabletop obstructed her view of his lap. Otherwise, she might have been tempted to look to see if that was, quite literally, true. One thing was certain—this discussion they were having looked like it was making him as physically uncomfortable as it was making her. She paused and wet her lips, then asked curiously, "Is that natural, for you to still be...?"

Brady silenced her with a hand to her lips. "Please," he groaned out loud, as if he were in pain. "No more questions. And no more talk of us going to bed together because it is just not going to happen," he said firmly.

Now that Kelsey was getting her nerve back, she was beginning to get excited all over again. She hated being excited about something with no opportunity for follow-through. And her feminine instinct told her that if the time and place were right, Brady could show her a very good time. She thrust her lower lip at him contentiously. "I think you're being unfair." Maybe this could work out after all. Given a little time and a lot more tutoring and patience on his part. "Couldn't we just, um, experiment a little, see where things lead?"

Brady sighed and looked as if he were praying for patience. "Didn't anyone ever tell you not to play with fire, Kelse? You might get burned."

That was just it, Kelsey thought, she wanted to get burned—by Brady. Before either of them could say anything further, there was a knock at the front door. "I'll get it." Looking relieved at the interruption, Brady bolted from the room.

Her mood glum, Kelsey stayed where she was. Seconds later, Kelsey heard the front door open. Then voices—both male and female. Too soon, Brady was back in the kitchen, Kelsey's sister Dani and her husband, Beau, with him.

"Can you believe it?" the six months pregnant Dani was saying, as she set down a small wedding cake from Isabelle Buchanon's bakery. "Tonight of all nights, our plumbing goes out. Sorry, Kelse. Beau and I are just going to have to sleep here at the ranch with you and Brady tonight. I hope you don't mind."

How naive did people think she and Brady were? Kelsey wondered. Even a five-year-old could have seen through a ploy like this. "Would it matter if I did mind?" Kelsey asked Dani facetiously.

"I know you've had a busy day, although I was surprised to see that you and Brady didn't exactly spend it all together. I saw you getting out of your truck over at the school earlier this evening. You were alone." Dani spoke as if that were a grave indictment of the marriage already.

"I'm not alone now," Kelsey said, refusing

to explain what she had been doing at the school. "And if you want to know the truth, you and Beau are interrupting our first night as man and wife."

"Well, you could always put it off then until you are alone," Dani said blithely, as if that were the best idea in the whole wide world. "Just sleep in separate bedrooms tonight," she advised with a smile. "Brady at one end of the hall. You at the other. Beau and me in my old room, in between. Perfect."

Kelsey looked at Beau, Dani's husband. He was never this quiet, except when it came to family conflicts. Then, he tended to step back and let the sisters work out their problems largely unassisted. "How did you get dragged into this?" Kelsey asked Beau.

Beau flashed her his movie-star grin. "I know when Lockhart fireworks are coming up. Figured I'd be here to keep the peace. Besides, we can't sleep at our house tonight, remember? Anyway—" Beau shot a look at both Kelsey and Brady, as if trying to decide for himself if this marriage was a hoax or not "—I hope the two of us aren't imposing too much."

Kelsey could see that was true. Beau, who'd only been a member of the family a short time, was willing to give both Kelsey and Brady the benefit of the doubt, as well as a chance to make things work. Her usually a lot-more-understanding older sister harbored no such generosity.

Kelsey gritted her teeth and hung on to her temper with effort. "It really isn't necessary to chaperone us, you know," she said evenly after a moment. She stood and fit her hand into Brady's much larger one, loving the way his callused fingers immediately closed around hers. "I'm perfectly safe here at the ranch with Brady," Kelsey continued, without an ounce of her usual recklessness. "He's a good guy."

"I don't doubt that at all," Beau said firmly, giving Brady a man-to-man glance that seemed to speak volumes.

"He's not going to do anything to hurt me," Kelsey added firmly.

"I'm quite aware of that," Dani countered, catching the brunt of Kelsey's withering glare. "It's your own impulsiveness that is the problem."

Kelsey frowned, her urge to throw a full-fledged temper tantrum growing. "What's that supposed to mean?" she demanded icily.

Dani sighed and put a gentle hand on Kelsey's shoulder. "Honey, I know how competitive you are, but this is not the way to go about catching up with the rest of us."

"Don't even start." Kelsey pushed her sister away. "What do you know." She shook her head at the half-finished meal on the table. "I've lost my appetite." She stormed away from the table, pausing only long enough to look at Dani. "You know where the sheets are." As far as Kelsey was concerned, her uninvited chaperones could make up their own bed. "Meanwhile," she continued stormily, ignoring the thick silence that had fallen over the room, "I'm going on to bed. And Brady—" Kelsey looked at him long and hard, letting him know this was one loyalty test she expected him to pass with flying colors "—I expect you to join me."

# Chapter Four

"Well, isn't this cozy," Brady said, joining Kelsey in the master bedroom a few minutes later, shaving kit in hand.

Trying not to feel self-conscious in the ribbed knit undershirt and loose-fitting men's pajama pants she typically wore to bed, Kelsey went into the adjoining bathroom and plucked her toothbrush out of the holder. "Don't look at me like it's all my fault," she warned as she squeezed toothpaste onto the brush.

Brady tossed his shaving kit onto the counter next to her orange-blossom shampoo. "Isn't it?" Arms folded in front of him, Brady lounged in the doorway and watched her brush, rinse and spit. His lips set, he unzipped his bag and pulled out his own toothbrush and paste.

"You could have done what your sister so clearly wanted you to do and offered to put off our *wedding night* until we were alone."

"Which is going to be never, in case you haven't figured that out," Kelsey whispered back, pausing to blot her mouth with a towel. Unable to get by him, because his tall frame was blocking the only exit out of the small bath, she bided her time impatiently as Brady brushed his teeth.

Able to see he still didn't understand what was really going on here, Kelsey continued to whisper, "Ten to one, Meg and Luke, and Jenna and Jake, would be here, too, if they didn't have kids at home. But they do. So obviously Dani and Beau have been elected—"

"—or volunteered," Brady interrupted, following his tooth-brushing with a swish of mouthwash.

"—to play chaperone for me and you," Kelsey finished haughtily.

Brady straightened and gave her a look. "Maybe it's not such a bad idea, given what they think is the reason you married me today." He led the way back into the bedroom.

Kelsey stormed after him. "I am not competing with them!"

He turned to face her and continued unbuttoning his shirt. "Not even a tiny little bit?" he demanded, towering over her.

"Well, okay." Reminded of what had happened, or nearly happened between them that afternoon, Kelsey backed up a step. She swallowed hard around the sudden parched feeling in her throat and forced herself to look up at him as if being here with him like this did not bother her in the least. "I wouldn't mind it if I had already found the love of my life, but I haven't so..." She let the thought go unfinished. Then, deciding she was much too close to him, she went around to her side of the bed and climbed in.

Looking unhappier than ever, Brady stripped off his shirt, boots and jeans, and climbed in beside her. "So you 'made do' with me," he theorized grimly.

Unwilling to lie down just yet, now that they were actually in bed together again, Kelsey propped herself against the headboard. She pulled the sheet up to her chest and held it against her breasts. "That isn't it and you know it."

Brady gave her a hard look that challenged her veracity as he settled back against the headboard, too.

"We're partners," Kelsey continued stubbornly.

Brady tugged the covers no higher than his waist. "And man and wife," he muttered in a low, disgruntled tone that carried no further than their bed, "who—thanks to your impulsiveness—are now sharing a bed for the night."

"What choice did we have?" Kelsey railed right back at him in the same highly irascible manner. "If I'd not slept in the same room and the same bed with you tonight," she shot back quietly, "then Dani and Beau might have told Wade McCabe there was nothing to worry about after all. Wade would have concluded that this wasn't a real marriage, and there goes the deed to the ranch." Still holding on to the covers, she clamped her arms in front of her and stared straight ahead. "I am not giving up this ranch."

"Well, there we agree, anyway," Brady said,

abruptly lying down and stretching out beside her.

Was it her imagination, Kelsey wondered, or was this bedroom of hers getting smaller and more intimate by the minute? Beside her, Brady shifted around and sighed loudly. Kelsey rolled her eyes and refused to look at him. "Now what's wrong?" she whispered stonily.

Brady shifted again. His shoulders were so broad, they took up his half of the bed, and his legs were so long, his feet were hanging off the end of the mattress. He grimaced and continued to try to get comfortable. "This bed is awfully small."

Kelsey shifted a little farther away from him, so they would no longer be touching, and nearly fell off the edge of the bed. He was making this harder than it had to be, she thought, glaring at him. "It's a double." It should sleep two.

"Which would be fine for me alone," Brady conceded, sighing and staring at the ceiling again, "but with you in here...it's going to be awfully darn hard to sleep here without touching each other."

"So what if we do touch each other?" Kelsey challenged. ''Nothing's going to happen we don't want to happen. Unless—'' Kelsey paused, grinning, as the next idea—and it was a brilliant one—hit.

As the silence strung out between them, Brady rolled toward her. ''What?'' Brady demanded suspiciously, searching her face.

Kelsey shifted onto her side to face him. She snapped her fingers and flashed him a mischievous grin. ''Never fear, cowboy. I know how to get rid of Beau and Dani faster than you can say 'We're outta here!'''

BRADY DID NOT LIKE that look in Kelsey's vibrant green eyes. That look always guaranteed trouble. ''What are you up to now?'' he demanded.

Kelsey raised her knees beneath the covers, braced her arms on either side of her, and began to rock back and forth suggestively. ''Let's see how loud we can get this bed to squeak.''

Brady swore, rolled and grabbed her shoulders, hard enough to temporarily stop her. ''Are you out of your mind?'' he said, ignoring the tantalizing warmth of her skin beneath his fingertips.

"No." The flush in Kelsey's cheeks increased and the soft edges of her lips curled up merrily. "Actually, if you want to know the truth—" she paused and waggled her eyebrows at him teasingly "—when it comes to bright ideas, I'm 'in the zone' today."

Brady ignored the clear definition of her breasts beneath the clinging blue cotton undershirt. Kelsey might not realize how sexy she looked, dressed for bed, but he did, and it was driving him crazy. The last thing he needed was her emulating the sounds of the two of them making love. "That is definitely a matter of opinion," he said, pushing away images of their erotically entwined bodies.

Kelsey scowled at him. As the seconds drew out, her lips formed a delicious pout. "It makes perfect sense," she countered in that soft, determined tone he knew so well. "And if you would just stop and think a minute, Brady, you would know that."

Deciding holding her that way was courting danger, Brady let her go and shifted away from her.

Kelsey sighed and elaborated in a low, exasperated voice. "Dani and Beau are here to prevent us from making love, if we haven't already done so."

"So?" Brady said.

"So—" Kelsey frowned at him impatiently, looking as if she were irked that she was still having to explain her thinking to him. "The two of them would be here with us until their baby was born if they thought they could prevent our consummating our marriage with their mere presence."

Given the possessive, protective way he was beginning to feel about Kelsey, maybe that wasn't such a bad idea, Brady thought.

"I love my sister and her new husband," Kelsey continued to explain resolutely, looking Brady square in the eye, "but I don't want them in residence with me for the next three months."

Put that way, neither did Brady. Although, up until this afternoon, he and Kelsey had been only business partners, he had come to relish his time alone with her.

"Now, on the other hand," Kelsey theorized softly, with a very wicked grin, "if my nosy sister and her husband discover we're already making love, the horse is already out of the barn. There would be nothing they could do to invalidate our marriage, and they'd likely leave. So what we need to do, fast, is make it sound like we're making hot and heavy love in here. So come on," Kelsey whispered, pausing to utter a long, sultry moan that swiftly had Brady groaning softly, too—for a completely different reason. "Help me here," she whispered as she began to rock back and forth.

For a virgin, she was remarkably adept at simulating the sounds of lovemaking. Too adept for Brady's comfort. The hard-on he'd had earlier sprang back to life, with near painful consequences. He knew much more of this and they'd both have reason to regret her impetuousness. She thought she'd been shocked before...

"Cut it out, Kelsey," Brady warned grimly.

"No." Kelsey threw her head back against the pillows, exposing the long slender column of her throat and, beneath the scooped neckline of her undershirt, the tempting uppermost curves of her breast and the jutting imprints of her nipples. Shutting her eyes, she rocked all the harder and moaned again, even louder. Down the hall, he could hear the sounds of Dani and Beau moving around, stepping out into the hall.

Brady knew he had to stop her—now. Before her sister and husband came to investigate, and discovered this for the ruse it all was. Because she wasn't about to *listen* to him, there was only one way to do that.

Brady moved swiftly, so he was on top of her. As abruptly as his weight covered hers, she went still. The sultry moan came to a strangled end as her green eyes opened wide. She looked first startled, then furious as—unable to rock the bed even the slightest, with his weight stopping her—she moaned again, even louder, and whispered feistily, "You're not stopping me."

"The heck I'm not," Brady threatened, and then he quickly shut her up the only way he knew how. He lowered his lips to hers and delivered a traffic-stopping kiss.

She uttered another moan of strangled passion, and then to Brady's dismay, instead of stiffening in shocked resistance—the way he expected her to—or trying to fight him off, she wreathed her arms around his neck, opened her mouth to the plundering pressure of his, and let her body melt against his. He thought kissing her earlier, in this bed, when they'd both been naked and willing as could be, had been arousing. It was nothing compared to the way he felt now. His body ignited. And so did his soul. Despite the reckless way she had behaved all day, baiting him and driving him crazy, he wanted her. Damn, how he wanted her...

Kelsey had known, after the way she had panicked earlier, that Brady expected her to fight him off. Which was, precisely, why she hadn't. She didn't want him thinking he could second-guess her, when the truth was, he just couldn't. And...she had also had all day to think about what she had walked out on when she had cut and run from this bed. Fiery kisses. Heart-stopping passion. Not to mention the possibility of actually climaxing for the first time in her life. It infuriated her to realize she was as old as she was, and still had no earthly idea what all the fuss was about. If all the romantic books and movies, not to mention the glowing happiness of all three of her sisters, were anything to go by, what she had been missing up to now was pretty darn sensational.

But not as sensational as the feeling of Brady's lips, moving over hers, or the intoxicating pressure of his tongue twining with hers. He tasted hot, male and forbidden. He smelled even better—like soap and cologne. His body was warm, strong, solid. And the way he was pressing against her created a delicious, tingling ache.

The fear she'd felt earlier gone, Kelsey gave herself over to the steamy embrace completely. And that was when Brady stopped, lifted his head and swore again.

"DAMMIT," BRADY WHISPERED, rolling onto his back, his every muscle—and he had a lot of them—tensed and flexed. "I told you we were not going to do this, Kelsey."

Trembling, Kelsey stared at him. "I don't see why not," she told him breathlessly.

"Obviously." Brady shut his eyes and lay his arm across his forehead.

Kelsey rolled onto her side and studied him

in the dim bedroom light. Despite the fact it was rather cool in there, a light sheen of sweat had broken out on his body. He was breathing as hard as if he'd just run a six-kilometer race at top speed. "Are you okay?" she asked after a moment. She thought she was all worked up, given the way her body was tingling and aching with frustration, but Brady almost looked as if he were in pain.

Brady swore again, not moving in the slightest. "If I head for the shower, will they be able to hear the water running from down the hall?" he asked.

Kelsey thought a minute. "Yeah."

Brady swore again.

Kelsey brightened. "I could go with you," she offered. "You know, talk and moan a lot. If they thought we were in there together, it wouldn't look so suspicious. In fact, from what I gather, showering together is a pretty newly-wed thing to do. So…"

Brady groaned again, even more miserably than before. To Kelsey's consternation, rather than take her up on her rather brilliant suggestion, he reached over and turned off the light.

Dropping back onto the pillows, he continued breathing as if he were in dire pain. "Kelsey?"

"Hmm?"

"Stay on your side of the bed," he ordered gruffly. "Be quiet. And go to sleep."

KELSEY HAD NEVER BEEN ONE to take orders, but something in Brady's voice told her she had better do what he said. So she turned onto her side, away from him, and tried not to think about what had almost happened, what most certainly would have happened, had she not chickened out earlier that day.

The next thing she knew it was morning, there were sounds of people moving around downstairs, and Brady was nowhere in sight. Trying not to feel disappointed she hadn't gotten to see what it would be like to wake with him sleeping next to her, she got up, pulled on a robe over her pajamas and headed downstairs. To her surprise, Brady was at the stove, cooking breakfast for Beau and Dani as if he owned the place. Which, Kelsey had to admit reluctantly, now that they were married, he sort of did.

"Morning." Brady smiled at her as if absolutely nothing had happened before.

Kelsey resented him for that. She had expected him to act as physically frustrated and out of sorts as she was. But maybe it was better that he didn't, she decided quickly, given the fact they had a very nosy audience who were intently watching everything she and Brady did and said. "Morning." Kelsey nodded at Brady, then at Dani and Beau. Since when had the three of them become such good friends? she wondered suspiciously.

"Pancakes or eggs?" Brady asked.

"Both," Kelsey said, just to be obstinate.

"Coming right up." Brady turned back to the stove.

"Brady was just telling us he thought it would be okay if I did some location shots here for the movie I'm working on," Beau said. "Is it okay with you? The film company would pay you for the use of your cattle and horses and pastures, of course."

"Of course." Kelsey nodded, feeling like a fool because this method of making money to further expand the ranch hadn't occurred to her before.

Dani smiled, looking a lot more at ease with Kelsey's marriage to Brady than she had the night before. To Kelsey's further aggravation, breakfast continued, pleasant as could be, with Brady playing the cheerful host, and Beau and Dani talking up the new film project Beau was working on and the recent movie reviews she had written, plus the book of movie reviews Dani was about to publish, until it was finally time for them to head to their respective offices.

"I imagine our plumbing will be fixed this evening," Beau announced as he exchanged a meaningful glance with Dani. Dani nodded, too, and Beau continued, "So we won't be coming back tonight. You two lovebirds will be on your own."

Thank heavens, Kelsey thought. But for once did not speak her mind.

Dani and Beau left. Kelsey slapped her hands on her hips and turned on Brady. She hated being protected or excluded and it looked like the three of them had just done both. "Just what the heck did you tell them before I woke up?" she said.

BRADY LOOKED HER RIGHT in the eye. "The truth. That I'd cut off my right arm before I'd do anything to hurt you," he said quietly.

The wind went out of Kelsey's sails as quickly as it had come in. "Well, apparently they bought it hook, line and sinker," Kelsey said as she finished her coffee in a single gulp.

"I mean it." Brady took her by the shoulders and held her in front of him. The truth of what he was saying was in his midnight-blue eyes. "You're not just my partner now, you're my wife, Kelse. We're building something pretty darn important here and I don't want to lose that."

Kelsey swallowed around the sudden lump of emotion in her throat. "I don't, either," Kelsey said cautiously. To her amazement, she felt oddly protective of him, too.

"Good." Brady nodded as if that settled that. To Kelsey's disappointment, he stepped back and returned his attention to the eggs cooking on the stove. "Now that we've got money in the bank, I think it might be a good time for us to go and look at those additional horses and ponies you've been wanting to buy, and put a bid in on some more tack for your riding stables.'' He filled two plates with eggs and pancakes, and then sat down at the table with her.

Kelsey realized without wanting to that she could quickly get used to taking all her meals with Brady. Maybe even sleeping with him, too. Not that she needed to be thinking about that at all, given the fact he had chosen not to make love to her the previous night, even when she had changed her mind and said it would be okay.

She swallowed around the sudden parched feeling in her throat, and tried to think about business instead of the incredibly wonderful and satisfying way Brady kissed. ''We can get a better deal on some used tack if we go to the auction house,'' she said, as if their business were all she had on her mind.

''Good idea,'' Brady said as he added butter and syrup to his stack of fluffy golden hotcakes. ''I want to cut our expenses as much as possible to make room in the budget for the cowboys I'm intending to hire.''

Kelsey noted he needed to shave. She liked the way he looked with a morning beard, sort of dark and dangerous, maybe even a little bit like an outlaw. A very handsome, sexy outlaw. Aware she was letting her thoughts digress again into forbidden territory, Kelsey forced herself to straighten up and get her mind out of the bedroom. It was funny, what a little thing like a marriage license and ceremony could do to a woman—even a formerly nonromantic tomboy like herself. She'd been married to Brady less than a day, and already she could feel herself changing—for the better.

"When will that be?" she asked, aware she wasn't looking forward to a time when she and Brady would no longer inhabit the ranch alone.

"As soon as I can find qualified cowhands and staff up," Brady told her, looking as if he were longing for that day as much as she was dreading it. "I asked them to put up a Help Wanted sign for me at the feed store and also posted a notice with the Cattle Raisers Association. Hopefully, calls about working for me won't be long in coming."

# Chapter Five

Brady finished the dishes and threw some corn in his pickup and drove out to feed the twenty head of Black Angus cattle he already had while Kelsey showered and got ready to go. When she came downstairs, he was still out on the ranch somewhere. But there was an older man she had never seen before walking around their front yard. He was standing next to a late-model luxury sedan. He had on an elegant suit that was very much at odds with his craggy, rough-hewn appearance. Frowning, Kelsey went out to see who he was and what he wanted. As she got closer, he swept off his dove-gray cowboy hat, revealing a full head of silver hair that was badly in need of a trim.

"Can I help you?"

He nodded at her politely and put his hat back on his head, before striding toward her authoritatively. His dark eyes zeroed in on hers. "I'm looking for Brady Anderson or Kelsey Lockhart," he said in a raspy voice.

"I'm Kelsey." Kelsey held out her hand—it was immediately swallowed up in his much larger, very callused palm. "What can I do for you?" she continued, noting the expensive gold rings he had on each hand. The diamond, onyx and ruby stones looked to be genuine and expensive. Not the kind of thing an ordinary cowpoke or someone from Laramie, Texas, would wear. The same went for his shiny alligator boots.

"My name is Hargett," he said.

"Pleased to meet you," Kelsey said. Was it her imagination or was their unexpected caller giving her a particularly close—almost suspicious—scrutiny, too?

Before Kelsey could ask Hargett anything more, Brady roared back into the yard. He jumped out of his truck and strode toward them. It was clear by the extremely irked look on Brady's handsome face that he knew who Hargett was even if she didn't. "What are you doing here?" Brady demanded, ignoring Kelsey and going straight for Hargett.

"Nothing yet," Kelsey said, not sure why Brady was being so rude to this man.

Ignoring her, Brady looked at Hargett. "We had a deal," he stated tightly, abruptly looking like he wanted to punch someone or something. "You weren't to come near me."

Hargett shrugged, not the least bit apologetic. "Time's up," he said.

Brady clenched his jaw and, still glaring at Hargett resentfully, pushed the words through his teeth, "Not for two more weeks it's not."

Brady wheeled around abruptly. Putting his hands on her shoulders, he propelled her toward the ranch house. "Kelsey, wait inside."

Kelsey's jaw dropped open at the unprecedented autocratic timbre of Brady's tone. She dug in her heels obstinately and refused to comply with his rude order. She glared at Brady. If there was something going on here, she wanted to know what it was. "You don't tell me what to do!" she spouted off.

Brady was not in the least amused by her

rebellious attitude, but Hargett chuckled. "I like a gal with spunk," he said.

Brady shot Hargett a lethal look before turning back to Kelsey. "In this case," he countered firmly, "I am telling you what to do." When she still refused to budge, Brady took Kelsey by the arm and led her to the porch steps, well out of earshot of Hargett, who was still sending them both interested looks. "This doesn't concern you."

Kelsey arched a warning brow of her own. "Need I remind you that we are partners and as such everything you do on this ranch concerns me?"

"This doesn't." Brady enunciated each syllable in a way that had Kelsey's own temper flaring sky-high. "Now, go inside and wait for me there." He waited, expecting her to do his bidding. Kelsey still didn't budge. "Fine," Brady said, swearing beneath his breath. "Hargett and I will just leave and have our conversation elsewhere."

Exasperated by Brady's unexpected secretiveness, Kelsey blew out a gusty breath. "You don't have to do that. I'll go inside," she grumbled ill-temperedly, figuring at least she could spy on them and gather what information she could that way.

"Thank you," Brady said, clearly hanging on to his patience by a thread.

Kelsey rolled her eyes and stomped off. She didn't know what was going on, but she did not like the way Brady was behaving. He was going to pay for this.

BRADY WAITED UNTIL KELSEY was safely in the ranch house before he walked back to Hargett. Then, moving so they were on the other side of the pickup truck and facing away from the windows, Brady stated roughly, with what precious little patience he had left, "You shouldn't have come here."

Hargett shook his head at Brady sadly. "That sweet little wife of yours doesn't know anything about the deal you made with me, does she?"

"No." Brady tensed as he thought about what would happen if he couldn't follow through on his half of the bargain he had made. "And I don't want her to know, either." Brady paused, wondering how best to protect Kelsey from the choices he had made in his desperate attempt to change his life for the better. Now that he thought about it, he should have realized Hargett would show up here as soon as he learned about the marriage. But he hadn't thought about it, because he hadn't really wanted to face the fact that this day of reckoning was coming, and soon, whether he liked it or not. Brady blew out a short, restless breath. "How did you know we were married, anyway?" Brady searched Hargett's face.

Hargett took a cigar out of his pocket and lit the end of it. "My people do a search of the state records every day." He paused to draw on the end of it, then put the lighter away. "Your name came up on a marriage license yesterday. When they brought it to my attention, I figured I had better check it out."

Brady sighed and rubbed the tense muscles in the back of his neck. "Yeah, well, I wish you hadn't." He shot a look at the window, and saw Kelsey standing there in plain view. Brady's frown deepened as he realized his wife was taking in everything she could about his little set-to with Hargett. "Now she's going to be full of questions," Brady complained.

Hargett took another long drag on his cigar. "Perhaps rightly so, if she's your wife."

Brady fell silent. He refused to feel guilty about keeping his past from Kelsey. What was important was not the life he had been born into or the man he had been, but the man he was now.

"She has a right to know about your past, Brady," Hargett insisted.

"I'll tell her when the time is right," Brady retorted stubbornly, "and not before."

Hargett studied Brady, as always seeing far more about what Brady was thinking and feeling than Brady wanted. "In two weeks—" he began.

"I'll have met my conditions for my freedom," Brady interrupted.

"If not, you know you're going to have to come back to work for me," Hargett said sternly. Still puffing away on his cigar, he inclined his head toward the ranch house. "A deal is a deal whether you are married to that pretty gal or not."

BRADY WAITED UNTIL HARGETT had left before he headed for the ranch house. He walked in to find Kelsey sitting in a chair, her arms behind her, a bandanna drawn like a gag across her mouth. He raced to her side and tugged it off. "What happened?" he demanded worriedly.

Lazily, Kelsey brought her hands—which were not tied after all—around to her lap. "Oh, I can talk now?" she queried innocently.

Too late, Brady wished his "gag order" had stayed in effect.

He rubbed at the back of his neck again. "I'm sorry I had to order you inside like that," he said.

"Are you?" Kelsey repeated in the same mocking tone.

"I didn't want you talking to him," Brady continued, doing his best to appease her while at the same time telling her as little as possible.

"That was apparent." Kelsey studied him. Slowly she rose from her chair to square off with him, a little less hot-temperedly. "Who is Mr. Hargett, anyway?"

*Good question. And one I am not about to answer all the way. At least not right before I get my permanent release from his service worked out with him,* Brady thought. "I used to work for him," he said finally, telling her as much as he could, without abruptly ruining the rapport he and Kelsey had built up over the five months they had known each other and the four months they had been partners.

"As a cowhand?" Kelsey asked pointedly, still scrutinizing his face.

Brady shrugged, uncomfortable with lying to Kelsey or anyone else even a little bit, but not willing to divulge the complete truth to her or anyone else, either. The life he'd had in the past was over. He didn't live that way anymore. Unfortunately, his past wouldn't remain in the shadows if he started talking about it to anyone who was curious. "More of a jack-of-all-trades," he allowed eventually, telling her only what he was comfortable with.

"And you quit," Kelsey guessed.

"Yes."

Kelsey's brows knit together, her expression perplexed. "Why?"

Brady sighed, wishing like heck this new wife of his was not so persistent. "Because I didn't like what I was doing for him,'' Brady explained.

"Why not?''

"Because I wasn't suited for what he wanted me to do.'' Brady tried but could not quite keep the exasperation from his low voice.

"Then why did he show up here today?'' Kelsey continued, moving even closer to Brady. She didn't stop until they were toe-to-toe. "Does he want you to work for him again?''

"Yes,'' Brady said firmly, as he drank in the clean and sexy orange-blossom smell of her hair and skin, "but I'm not going to do that.''

The soft edges of Kelsey's lips turned up in a slight smile. "So why couldn't I hear you tell him that?'' she asked casually.

It was all Brady could do not to roll his eyes and/or beg for mercy. "Because Hargett and I don't get along all that well. He's a pretty blunt-spoken man and there's never any telling what he's going to say. I didn't want you to be witness to any unpleasantness.''

Kelsey thought about that for a minute. "And that's all it was.''

"Yes.'' He had been protecting his wife from

Hargett's pushiness, plain and simple. She hadn't been in any physical danger. But she could easily have had her heart broken—had Hargett had more of a chance to disillusion her by telling her everything Brady had not.

Brady had known he was going to have to tell her all he'd done and why, for a while now. But he had wanted to wait until his past debts were cleared and they had money in the bank. That would not happen for another two weeks.

"So I wasn't in danger," Kelsey said.

Brady frowned. It was time this conversation took another tack. "Only from me," he teased her lightly, "if you don't stop talking."

Kelsey rolled her eyes. "You are one of the most difficult men I have ever met."

Doing what he had wanted to do from the first moment he had laid eyes on her that morning, Brady wrapped his arms around her. "The same goes for you in the female category."

Kelsey narrowed her eyes at him as she splayed her hands across his chest. She tilted her head up, to better search his face. "I know you're not telling me everything," she insisted worriedly.

Brady could feel her body melting against him, even while her will remained as feisty and difficult as ever. He grinned as he realized he wanted her to surrender to him heart and soul. Pushing her hair back away from her face, he brushed his thumb across her lips and told her softly, "A little mystery is good for every marriage, haven't you heard?"

"Brady—"

He kissed her deliberately, rubbing his lips across hers, then with growing intensity, until nothing was held in check. He had counted on her mouth to be soft and sweet. He hadn't expected her to rise up on tiptoe, thread her hands through his hair, press her slender body against his and kiss him back passionately, wildly, wantonly. He could feel the surrender of her body in the trembling of her knees, and the way her soft, delicate hands caressed his shoulders with slow, seductive strokes. And yet there remained an innocence to her as she met him boldly, kiss for kiss. He wished he could take her upstairs and make up for the calamity that had happened the day before, when she had lured him there unexpectedly. But he knew he couldn't do that.

Reluctantly, Brady drew back. There would be time for more kisses. Maybe even time for wooing her and making her his woman, as well as his wife. But it wouldn't be this morning. Not when they still had so much work to be done, a ranch to outfit, and only two weeks to finish making this ranch the roaring success he knew it could be. He let his arms fall to his sides and stepped back. Ignoring the faint but unmistakable look of disappointment on Kelsey's face, he tugged the brim of his hat low across his brow, so it shadowed his eyes from her searching gaze, and said, "We better go if we're going to look at those horses and ponies today."

FORTUNATELY FOR BOTH of them, the schedule of appointments they had made for that morning kept them plenty busy. There was no more time for kisses. Only serious looking and hard bargaining. "No way are we paying that price for those horses," Brady said, when they finally found what they wanted, midafternoon. He stepped forward to negotiate with the owner, a crafty man who reminded him very much of his former "boss."

"They're worth every penny," the rancher said.

"Individually," Brady concurred, before Kelsey could give in and just agree to pay the owner the inflated price he wanted. "Since we're taking them all off your hands at once, saving you all that time, effort and feed, we should get a better deal."

The rancher shrugged indifferently. "The price stands."

Beside him, Kelsey tensed. Brady remained unconcerned. He knew a bluff when he saw one. "Then we go to the next ranch on the list," Brady said, taking Kelsey's arm.

"Okay, okay, wait," the rancher said before they could depart. "I'll lower the price by five percent."

"Twenty," Brady insisted.

"Ten," the rancher countered, frowning.

"Twelve and we'll call it a deal," Brady said.

The rancher sighed. "Done." He shook hands with Brady, then Kelsey. They talked about the transfer of the horses, which would be done in forty-eight hours, and completed the bill of sale. In silence, they walked back to Brady's pickup truck to go to the auction house and look at the used saddles and bridles that had come in from a ranch west of there.

"I could have handled the negotiations on my own, you know," Kelsey said as soon as Brady turned back onto the highway.

Brady knew Kelsey was irritated with him, and for good reason from her perspective. She was an equal partner, and hence should have had fifty percent of the say in what was going on. Knowing by the look on her face, however, that she was going to cost them money they didn't have to spend if he let her in on the bargaining, he had cut her out of the negotiations. Brady was sorry he had hurt her feelings. He wasn't sorry for the business stance he had taken. "You were ready to just give him the money he wanted, and I knew he'd take less," Brady said.

Kelsey scowled. "But if he hadn't…"

"Then we would have ended up paying full price," Brady reassured her.

Silence fell between them. After a while, Kelsey asked, "How'd you get to be so good at negotiating?"

Brady frowned. They were headed into dangerous territory again. "My dad was a notorious skinflint. He didn't pay one penny more than he had to for anything. I guess some of his frugality rubbed off." Brady paused, reflecting how little he still knew about big portions of Kelsey's life. He slanted her a curious glance. "What was your parents' attitude toward money?"

Kelsey rubbed the soles of her boots restlessly across the rubber floor mat. "Well, we never had enough of it, I can tell you that."

Brady had worried about a lot of things, growing up. Having enough money had not been an issue, however. He studied the brooding look on Kelsey's face. "And that experience has made you…?"

"Not want to count pennies," Kelsey said firmly, looking resentful again and staring straight ahead. "Not if I can help it."

They arrived at the auction barn and went inside. The tack from the big spread was in miserable condition over all. Kelsey took one look at it and was ready to forget it, but Brady was instantly intrigued. He fingered a bridle that was dirty and rough with age, seeing the possibilities, not just what was. "This stuff is awful," Kelsey said.

"Yeah, it is in deplorable condition," Brady agreed readily enough, going on to inspect a saddle that was in equally bad shape. He was getting excited despite the way Kelsey was turning up her nose. "But it's good-quality gear—some of the saddles in this group go for close to two thousand dollars each."

"When they're new and in good condition," Kelsey allowed.

Brady grinned and told her with a confidence he hoped would rub off on her, "These could be cleaned and treated with saddle dressing. A little elbow grease and they'll look like new. Same for the bridles, and the rest of the tack."

Kelsey still looked skeptical. "Half the buckles on this tack are broken, Brady."

Brady took her elbow and steered her over to a deserted corner of the auction house. He looked down at her, wondering how she could still manage to look so pretty and fresh when they'd been on the run all day. "A new buckle costs sixty-nine cents, and a solid brass alligator locking snap is six dollars. Compare that to a hundred dollars for each brand-new headstall, or a hundred-fifty for each brand-new breast collar—when between us we're going to have some forty horses to completely outfit—and you begin to see the wisdom of buying this in bulk at a greatly reduced price and repairing it. We can save literally thousands of dollars this way, Kelsey, and still have some darn fine gear for you and for me."

"Only one problem with your plan, Brady. I don't know how to repair tack." And, Brady could see, the thought of messing up some two thousand dollar saddle terrified her.

"It's not hard if you have the proper tools," he said amiably, reassuring her with a glance. "I'll teach you." It would be a good excuse to spend time together. A lot of time together. "Meanwhile," he continued amiably, "we ought to snap up that bin of horse blankets over there, too. A good washing and air-drying and they'll all be good as new."

"Okay," Kelsey sighed. "You've sold me." She looked deep into his eyes. "But you have to promise to help with all the extra work it entails."

Wishing he had the privacy to kiss her again, as thoroughly and completely as he wanted to kiss her at that moment, Brady put a hand across his chest. "Word of honor."

By the time they got back home it was nearly suppertime. Together, Brady and Kelsey carried the stacks of horse blankets and several piles of tack from the back of his pickup truck, into the barn. The rest of the saddles and the horses they'd bought would be delivered on Thursday. Then Brady went out to feed and care for the horses they did have. When he got back, he had hoped Kelsey would have washed up and started supper. He wanted to spend the evening together—and the time to do a little kissing, too.

Instead, the ranch house was empty. Her pickup truck was gone. On the coffee table in the living room she had left a note that read simply, "Back tomorrow. K. L."

Frowning, Brady looked around and found one other thing missing as well.

# Chapter Six

Dani was cooking dinner with Beau when Kelsey rapped on their back door and walked in. "Sorry about my appearance," she said at her older sister's aghast look.

"What have you been doing?" Dani gave the chicken-and-rice dish another stir and set her spatula on the spoon rest. "You're covered in ranch dust from head to toe."

Kelsey washed her hands at the sink, then filched a slice of tomato from the salad Beau was making. "Brady and I bought some saddles and horses and stuff, and we carted some of it— like the horse blankets—home with us. They weren't washed yet and I got as much dirt on me as the back of his pickup truck."

"Where's Brady now?"

Kelsey paced the kitchen restlessly. "At the ranch, taking care of the horses and cattle we do have."

"Everything okay?" Dani asked.

"Yeah, sure," Kelsey fibbed, not about to tell her sister she didn't dare spend another night at the ranch alone with Brady, for fear of what she might want to happen, if she were left alone with him for too long. "It's just been a busy day." She didn't want to cap it off with another romantic rejection from Brady. "And I need to ask you a favor."

"Whatever we can do for you, we will," Beau said as he wrapped his arms around Dani's ever-expanding waist, and kissed her neck with husbandly affection. "You know that."

"Yeah." Kelsey tried not to notice how happy the two of them looked—how happy all her sisters looked, now that they were married to the men of their dreams. There was no reason for her to envy them. One day soon she would find her bliss, too. "Well, I just need to borrow a computer. Hopefully a laptop if you guys have a spare."

Beau frowned. "You're welcome to use mine, but it's over at my office on Main."

"I've got mine here. You can use that," Dani said. She stood on tiptoe to kiss Beau's cheek and reluctantly extricated herself from his arms.

"Can I take it with me and bring it back to you tomorrow?" Kelsey said. "Maybe print some stuff then?"

"Absolutely. Whatever you need." Dani led the way to her study and packed it up for Kelsey in the carrying case.

"Well, I better get going," Kelsey said.

"And think about getting a shower while you're at it," Dani teased. "Or at least changing your clothes."

At the reference to her grubby state, Kelsey stuck out her tongue. Dani laughed. Both she and Beau waved as Kelsey drove off.

Instead of going home, Kelsey drove over to Jenna's apartment, parked behind the shop and, Dani's laptop in tow, headed up the stairs. Once inside, she stripped off her clothes and headed straight for the shower. Dani was right, Kelsey thought. She wouldn't feel great until she had washed off some of this grit.

BRADY SHOWERED AND SHAVED, and put on a clean set of clothes. Following his hunch about where his errant, unpredictable wife had gone, he drove into Laramie. Kelsey's pickup truck was right where he had expected it to be— parked behind Jenna Remington's boutique on Main Street. He left his truck right behind hers, and took the exterior steps to the apartment two at a time. When she didn't answer his knock, he strode on in anyway and found Kelsey walking out of the bedroom. She was wearing one of the sexiest negligees he had ever seen. The powder-blue satin gown had a plunging back and pretty low front and was held up by a pair of very thin spaghetti straps. It clung to her curves like a second skin, clearly delineating breasts, waist, hips and thighs. Her long hair had just been washed and blow-dried—it tumbled softly to her shoulders. Her face looked freshly scrubbed, and the complete lack of artifice gave her an innocent look that was even sexier than the nightgown she wore.

Kelsey scowled at him. ''I came over here to work,'' she said.

Brady grinned. She looked as ready to make

love as he was to give it. "As what...?" he
quipped. "A lady of the evening? Because if
it's companionship you're looking for—" he
tipped his hat at her and winked "—I volunteer."

"Very funny."

"It's no joke, Kelse." Brady took off his hat
and set it on the table beside the door. He sauntered over to join her on the sofa. "I came to
find you because I wanted to be with you tonight."

Kelsey did not look at him as she opened up
the laptop computer on the coffee table and
turned it on. "Well, I've got to work on my
schedule of riding classes, and start pulling together some instructional packets for the stu-
dents to take home. Rules of Riding Do's and
Don'ts and things like that. I borrowed Dani's
laptop computer and Jenna's apartment to do it,
so if it's an evening of fun you're looking for,
I suggest you go on down to Greta McCabe's
dance hall and kick up your heels there."

"Without you? I don't think so. And that still
doesn't explain the negligee you're wearing."
He would've liked to think it was just for him,

but since she clearly hadn't expected to see him tonight…

Kelsey sighed. "I left in such a hurry I forgot to bring any clothes with me. And this is the only kind of nightwear Jenna had in her closet. She's not exactly a T-shirt and jeans girl, you know, unless she's out at her and Jake's ranch. When she's in town, she's all sophistication. The only things in that closet are dresses and nightgowns like this."

"Well, you look…really nice…." Brady said at last, knowing that didn't begin to cover it. She looked sensational. He didn't know how he was going to get through the evening without making her his.

Kelsey gave him a brisk smile. "You look really nice, too, Brady." She pressed her lips together. Her shoulders drew tight as a bow as she focused on the laptop computer screen in front of her. "But that doesn't change the fact I've got work to do."

"Maybe I can help you," Brady offered.

Kelsey began to type with the hesitancy of a novice computer-user. "I don't think so."

"Okay, have it your way." Brady shrugged

and headed for the refrigerator. They had all evening to get closer and figure out where this marriage of theirs was leading.

Kelsey sighed loudly as he opened the refrigerator door. "Now what are you doing?" she asked, clearly perturbed.

"Getting something to eat. I'm hungry." Brady hunkered down to survey the interior. He was not enthused about what he saw inside the refrigerator. "Unfortunately, there's not much in this refrigerator except diet soda and yogurt."

"Works for me just fine," Kelsey said. "But maybe you should hit one of the restaurants before you head back to the ranch." Not waiting for his reply, she began typing on the laptop computer again.

Brady watched her move the mouse with the same awkwardness she typed. At this rate, he thought, it was going to take her all night. Which maybe was the plan? "I could bring us something back, if you want."

"No, thanks. I'll be fine with the yogurt and diet soda."

Brady continued standing there. It didn't take

a genius to see she had put him in the deep freeze. He had hoped this evening would be the start of their getting even closer. Instead, she looked like she couldn't be more miserable. "Did I do something wrong?" he asked, after a moment.

"No." Kelsey made a panicked face. "I did. Darn it, I can't get this graphics program to work!"

Glad they were now in an area he excelled in, Brady crossed to her side. He sat down beside her, so close their thighs were touching, and looked over her shoulder at the screen. "What are you trying to do?"

Kelsey lifted the laptop computer from the coffee table to her lap. "I wanted to make a big blue box, with red lettering inside it, but every time I attempt the red the blue goes away and now the darn thing has completely locked up." Kelsey tapped on the computer keyboard, trying several different things. She wiggled the red mouse key in the center of the keyboard. Nothing worked.

Brady leaned across her to see what he could do. "Let's use the escape key." Nothing.

"Maybe this will work," he said, finally shifting the laptop onto his lap and taking over the keyboard. He typed in several variations and tried entering the commands into the computer. Still nothing.

As every effort to unfreeze the keyboard failed, Kelsey grew tenser and more worried. Finally, Brady sighed. "I think you've got a hardware problem here."

"You mean the computer is broken?"

"Yep, looks like. Because you can't exit any of the programs, and it won't even turn off."

Kelsey buried her head in her hands and looked all the more miserable. "Dani is going to kill me."

"It's not your fault," Brady soothed as he set the malfunctioning laptop on the coffee table once again.

"Well, it sure seems like it. The thing was fine when I picked it up." Kelsey gestured at it angrily. "I use it for half an hour, and now it's broken." She leapt up from the sofa and began to pace the small apartment.

Trying not to notice how the satin gown delineated Kelsey's ample curves, Brady returned his glance to her face. "We can get it repaired. She's probably got other computers at her house, right? Since she's a film critic and works at home?"

"Actually—" Kelsey bit her lip and swung back around to face Brady "—Dani's got several."

"Then it's no big deal." Brady shrugged. "I suppose, though, you and I should be getting a computer of our own. That way you could work at home." *And I wouldn't be chasing you all over Laramie County at night, just to spend time with you.*

Abruptly, the computer screen went blank. Noticing, Kelsey said, "Hey, it shut off all by itself."

But it didn't turn on again.

Nor, to Brady's disappointment, did Kelsey.

"YOU'RE REALLY GOING TO BED at eight-thirty at night?" he asked, when she had packed up her computer and the scribbled notes she had made.

Trying not to notice how he was looking at her—as if she were a forbidden dessert he would very much like to devour in one sitting— Kelsey smiled. "Yes. I'm very tired." She finished zipping up the carrying case, then straightened. "It's been a very long day. I just want to go to sleep." *Before I inadvertently screw up anything else. Like my "marriage."*

Brady shrugged, clearly disappointed. "Okay."

"So you can feel free to go home now," Kelsey continued, doing her best to get rid of him in as polite a manner as possible.

Brady stood and checked to see how much money was in his billfold. "I think I will go out and get some supper for us," he said.

Kelsey didn't like the possessive note in his low tone or the presumption in his eyes. That this was going to turn out to be some romance- or sex-filled evening after all. He had already turned her down twice. She wasn't giving him a chance to go all gallant on her and turn her down again. "I told you I'm not hungry."

"I'll bring it back. Just in case."

Kelsey rolled her eyes. She did not understand why this man would not give up on the idea of their spending the night together. It wasn't as if he had romance in mind, or would miss her if she weren't there. Besides, she needed time alone to collect her thoughts in a way that would prevent her from falling in love with someone who saw her only as a business partner and means to an end. "You're not sleeping in the same bed with me tonight," she warned him. Sleeping with him made her feel really married. And they weren't. Regardless of what Wade McCabe or her sisters thought. She needed to remember that before she found herself wanting to make love with him again.

Brady smiled at her matter-of-factly. "The sofa looks fine."

Kelsey tried not to think of the passionate kisses he had given her both times they had been in bed together. "There's a bed at the ranch," she said. It had been a little cramped and uncomfortable for two people who were trying to sleep without touching each other all night, but for one, it would do just fine.

Brady scowled and came closer. "If I sleep at the ranch tonight and you sleep here, as far as Wade McCabe and everyone else is concerned our marriage will be over, at least as far as appearances. Which would mean we'd be turning over the deed to the Lockhart-Anderson Ranch to him, pronto, and I'm not doing that. Hence, wherever you go, I go. Got it?''

Slowly, Kelsey let out the breath she had been holding. ''Unfortunately.''

''So back to dinner,'' he said. ''Anything special you want?''

''No.'' She flashed him a tight, humorless smile. ''Thanks.''

''Okay.'' Brady grinned as if she had welcomed him warmly and shrugged. ''I'll just wing it then.'' He grabbed his hat and put it on. ''See you in a while.''

FIVE MINUTES LATER, Brady walked into Callahan's Pizza and Subs. Mac Callahan, a stocky, friendly guy in his mid-twenties, was standing behind the counter. One of the young entrepreneurs in Laramie, he had opened his restaurant right out of college, and thanks to Mac's attention to quality and service, his business had been thriving ever since. ''Hey, Mac,'' Brady said.

''Hey, Brady. Heard congratulations are in order.''

"Thanks. Listen, you wouldn't happen to know how Kelsey likes her pizza, would you?"

Mac grinned the way everyone who knew they were newlyweds grinned. "Trying to surprise her with a honeymoon special, huh?"

Actually, Brady thought, he was trying to lure Kelsey out from behind a locked bedroom door. But that was another matter. One Mac didn't need to know about. "Here's hoping," Brady said casually, taking off his hat and hanging it on the rack next to the door. "So if you could help me out, I'd appreciate it."

"No problem." Mac picked up his order pad. "Kelsey's favorite is pepperoni, sausage and onions. Double cheese. Easy on the sauce."

"Sounds good to me. Make it an extra large. Add an order of buffalo wings, extra hot, and a hot Italian sub with everything in case she's of a mind to try that. We didn't have time to eat much today, we were so busy, so she's got to be as hungry as I am." For food, and other things as well...

While Mac began preparing the order, Brady leaned against the counter and watched. "You known Kelsey long?"

"I dated her. 'Course, near every guy in town can tell you that, too."

So Brady'd heard.

"She's a nice girl," Mac continued conversationally. "Hopelessly fickle, of course. Can't stay with anyone or anything for long." Mac slanted Brady a hope-filled glance. "Maybe that will change, now that she's got the ranch and you."

And maybe not, Brady thought, as he considered the way she was running hot and cold with him, recklessly inviting him into her bed one minute, kicking him out of it entirely the next. Hoping Mac's experiences with Kelsey could give him some insight into her behavior, Brady asked, "So how long did the two of you date?"

"Two weeks."

Brady warned himself not to jump to conclusions. "Did you dump her or did she dump you?" he asked casually.

Mac slid the pizza into the oven and started on the hot Italian sub. "That's not the way it works with Kelsey. She doesn't like ugly or emotional scenes. She just sort of eases away from a fella."

"Eases away," Brady repeated uncomfortably, not sure he understood.

"Well, starts losing interest," Mac explained further. "The signs are real subtle at first. She doesn't quite seem to be listening to what you're saying. Finds excuses to stay apart or spend time away from you. Before you know it, she's looking to somebody else." Mac snapped his fingers. "Then it's over. Just like that." Mac peered at Brady in concern. "Say, it's not happening to you already, is it?"

*It better not,* Brady thought grimly.

KELSEY WAS TOSSING and turning in bed, wishing she'd thought to smuggle in some of that yogurt for dinner before she had flounced off, locking the door behind her. Now it was too late, Kelsey thought as her stomach rumbled even louder. Because Brady was back. He was out in the living room. And worse, he had obviously brought food back with him, just as he promised. And not just any food. Mac Callahan's pizza.

Well, she had two choices. She could stay in here, pretending to be asleep, and starve to death. Or she could go out there and chow down. As always, the tomboy in Kelsey won out.

She threw back the covers and marched out into the living room to join Brady, hopelessly sexy negligee and all. He was sitting with his feet up on the coffee table, a plate of food in his lap, watching a popular sitcom.

Brady glanced over at her, taking in her tousled hair and irritated expression. For once, his eyes did not stray to her breasts. "That was quick," he said. "I haven't even had time to go to sleep yet and here you are already up, after a good...oh, thirty-five minutes' sleep."

Kelsey gave him a look that let him know she did not appreciate his attempt at humor at her expense. "Are you still sharing?" she demanded, getting right to the point.

Brady frowned as if that was a huge problem. "You told me you didn't want any dinner," he reminded her, squinting thoughtfully.

Her mouth was watering, her taste buds begging for even a smidgen of the food he'd brought back. "I changed my mind, okay?" Kelsey told him irritably, pushing the tousled hair off her face. "Now, can I have some or not?"

Brady flashed her one of his sexiest smiles. "Help yourself, darling. I figured you'd cave as soon as you smelled Mac's cooking—which I have to say is far superior to either yours or mine—so I got plenty."

She scowled at him—if this was his way of playing hard to get, and even harder to hold, it was working. Kelsey went to the kitchenette where he had left the food, and helped herself to a slice of pizza, a generous portion of wings and half the sub. She opened the fridge and found a six pack of cream soda. Regular, not diet. "You bought cream soda...."

"Mac Callahan said it was your favorite."

It was. Only problem, she could never remember to buy it when she was at the grocery store, and most vending machines didn't carry it, so she rarely had it. She paused to flip open the top and take a swig of the deliciously sweet soda. "You talked to him?"

"The whole time I was there," Brady affirmed in a smug know-it-all tone that had her alarm increasing by leaps and bounds.

Kelsey came over and sat down beside him on the sofa. "What did he say?"

Brady flashed her a wickedly mischievous grin. "Oh, lots of things. Most compelling were his tips on how to keep you interested in me." He winked. "Cream soda was right up there on the list."

Kelsey had a funny, sinking sensation inside her that for once had nothing to do with her desire for Brady. "You are joking, right?"

"Nope." Brady finished off one fiery-hot chicken wing and started on another. "Mac thinks, as does everyone else in town, that you are one fickle gal."

Kelsey broke off a chunk of pizza with her fingers. "That's just because we used to date and it didn't work out."

Brady narrowed his eyes at her. "It didn't work out with a lot of guys," he pointed out quietly.

Kelsey flushed. "Is that a criticism? Because, I'm telling you, Brady Anderson, if it is—"

He held up a staying hand before she could bolt to the relative safety of the breakfast room. "I'm just trying to understand you."

Kelsey blotted the corners of her lips with her napkin. "Not to mention how and why I got my reputation as a heartbreaker."

Brady shrugged, as if it didn't matter to him one way or another, when she could tell it did. "Well," he allowed, with a sexy wink, "now that you've brought it up, I wouldn't mind hearing your side of things."

To her surprise—usually she didn't give two figs what anyone thought of her—Kelsey wanted to confide in him. More than that, she wanted Brady to understand her the way no one ever had. "I have dated a lot of guys, but it wasn't because I wanted to set a record or anything. When I started out, I was just trying to find my own Mr. Right. And as soon as I realized the guy I was dating wasn't my Mr. Right, I ended it."

"Makes sense," Brady said, the gentleness in his eyes giving her the courage to go on.

"Usually someone else would ask me out straightaway, and I'd go, and then after a week or two, sometimes more, sometimes less, I'd find out he wasn't it for me, either," Kelsey said softly.

"And the more guys you rejected, the more of a challenge you became," Brady guessed.

Kelsey nodded, the bitterness and hurt she felt about that turn of events surfacing. "I sort of became the Mount Kilimanjaro of the fairer sex here in Laramie, and the guys around here began to want to go out with me, strictly for the challenge. It became a test of manliness, the quest to conquer me and take me to bed and steal my heart—and not necessarily in that order." She sighed, hating the way that had made her feel. She turned and looked deep into Brady's midnight-blue eyes. "That may not have been what they told themselves they were doing, you know. But it was what was happening nevertheless, and every time I realized I was just an object to be conquered, that rather than being themselves, the guys were doing everything and anything to please me, so they could go where no man had ever been before. Or worse, they were pretending to be something or someone they weren't, just so I'd think the two of us were a perfect match and I'd succumb to their charms. Each time, it was like a switch turned off inside me, and that was just it. It was over. I couldn't feel anything for them anymore, so then it was easier to break up with them.''

Kelsey paused, hating the hopelessness she heard in her voice. She hadn't realized until now how much all the jockeying for her attentions had influenced her.

"Anyway, that's what I liked about you, Brady,'' she continued firmly, taking his hand in hers. "From the beginning there hasn't been any pretense. You are who you are, and that's that. There's no pretending anything with you. No ulterior reason on your part for being my friend and partner and now husband, and I appreciate that, more than you can know.''

Abruptly, Brady looked uncomfortable. "I'm no saint, Kelse,'' he told her gruffly, extricating his hand from hers.

"But you're not using me,'' Kelsey persisted, letting him know with a look that he was different from all the other guys she had dated. "You haven't lied to me or pretended to be anything you're not, just so you could claim me and get me into your bed. The majority of those other guys did, whether they were conscious of it or not.''

The way Brady looked at her then, as if there was nothing he wanted more than to make love to her, then and there, had Kelsey's pulse racing.

She swallowed. "Anyway, I think that's enough questions for one night," she said casually, putting her plate aside. "And I know I've had enough pizza." Enough rejection, in a sexual and romantic sense, too.

"Running out on me?" Brady said as they carried their plates to the kitchenette and set them there.

"Going to bed. Alone," Kelsey clarified, quickly putting the leftover food away, and letting him know with a look that despite how she was dressed there was not going to be any hanky-panky in that apartment that night.

Not just because they had nothing better to do. She had figured out the first time she had tried to go to bed with him, just for the heck of it, that she wasn't cut out for meaningless sex, even with someone as sexy and wonderful as Brady Anderson.

No, when she finally made love with a man it was going to have to be because she loved him, and he loved her, and for no other reason. She might be falling for Brady, big time, but all he felt for her concerned business, with an occasional dash of lust and guilt, which wouldn't make for a satisfying sexual relationship, she was sure.

"Thanks for the dinner." She brought back a pillow and a blanket and set them down on the coffee table. Feeling reckless and mischievous again, she said, already backing toward her bedroom door, "Sweet dreams, cowboy. The sofa is all yours."

"And so is this," Brady said, taking her into his arms abruptly. Ignoring her soft gasp of surprise, he delivered a long breath-stealing kiss that had her middle fluttering weightlessly and her nipples aching. She surged against him, and he kissed her again and again, so thoroughly and completely that her knees went weak and she moaned her pleasure despite herself.

When he finally let her go there was no doubt he desired her. And intended to have her, as soon as the time was right. "Good night, Kelsey," he said.

"Good night."

# Chapter Seven

Kelsey's mood was blue the next morning as she took her clothes out of the compact washing machine in Jenna's apartment, and shook out the wrinkles as best she could. And it was bluer still after she'd gotten dressed and ready to go. "What's the matter?" Brady asked when she walked out into the kitchen to help herself to some of the coffee and blueberry muffins he'd brought back from Isabelle Buchanon's bakery down the street.

Kelsey sat down next to Brady at the small round table in the breakfast nook, between the kitchen and the living room. She spread her napkin across her lap, broke open her muffin and spread it with butter. Her expression still glum, she said, "I have to tell Dani I broke her laptop computer."

"You didn't break it," Brady corrected her, sipping his coffee. "It broke while you were using it. There's a difference, Kelse."

Kelsey warmed to the understanding she saw in his eyes, even though she knew it wasn't that simple. "Dani may not see it that way," she warned.

Brady frowned. His dark brows knit together in confusion. "Why wouldn't she?"

"Because—" Kelsey drew a long, steadying breath "—it wouldn't be the first thing of hers that I've borrowed and returned in less than stellar condition. One time I got barbecue sauce on a cashmere sweater. And then there was the blender that I borrowed for a party that didn't stand up to the amount of crushed ice I needed...."

"Even so, she's not going to be upset with you."

Kelsey sighed and gave Brady a skeptical look. She wished that were the case. But this computer had contained work Dani did for a living. Dani took her job as a movie reviewer very seriously, and so did Kelsey. If anything were to happen to any of Dani's work because of something Kelsey had done or not done, Kelsey would never forgive herself. Nor would Dani.

"Want me to go with you?" Brady asked. "I was here. I saw what happened. I can talk to her about the problem."

Kelsey hesitated. She wasn't accustomed to leaning on anyone. Never mind a husband of her very own! But in this case, it would be good to have him by her side. Especially if things were as bad as she feared they would be. "If you wouldn't mind..." Kelsey said.

Brady shrugged his broad shoulders affably as he went over to rinse out his coffee cup and plate, and slid them into the dishwasher. "What are husbands for? Besides standing guard over you and sleeping on the sofa, that is."

Kelsey shot Brady a droll look and didn't respond to his teasing quip.

Looking determined to coax a smile out of her, no matter what it took, Brady put a hand to his spine and stooped over to walk like an eighty-year-old man with back trouble.

"'Course, I may never walk straight again," he complained comically.

Truth to tell, Kelsey hadn't slept much better in the comfort of the bedroom, knowing he was in the next room, tossing and turning, just as she was. Trying not to think how sweetly and soundly she had slept when they'd been forced to share a mattress out at the ranch, she advised, "Next time aim for a bed."

"I will."

She caught her breath at the heat in his gaze. No doubt about what he was thinking there. No doubt about what she still wanted. Even if she'd come to her senses and realized it wasn't wise.

She had waited this long to make love with a man she loved. She could wait a little while longer for it to be right.

Why, then, did she keep wishing, deep inside, that it was him? Kelsey wondered. And why, then, did she keep wishing it would be soon?

"SHE'S GOING TO TAKE the news about this well. You'll see," Brady continued encouragingly as he and Kelsey walked up to Dani and

Beau's house and rang the bell shortly after breakfast.

Kelsey tucked her hand in his and held on to Brady as if it was the lifeline he was quickly turning out to be. She hoped he was right. She hated disappointing her sisters and/or being the cause of turmoil in the family. It was hard enough being the black sheep of the family.

Unfortunately, Brady was wrong about her sister taking the news well.

"You're sure it's broken?" Dani said, looking more panicked than she'd been about anything except her hasty marriage to Beau Chamberlain some months back. Of course she'd had good reason to be in a tizzy about that, Kelsey thought, since Dani hadn't initially believed she was married to Beau, never mind been able to remember the two of them saying "I do."

"Positive," Kelsey replied wearily. She leaned against a case of videotapes in Dani's home office, and folded her arms in front of her like a shield against the criticism sure to come.

"It completely froze up and then it went dead," Brady added.

"Let's just have a look," Beau said calmly,

getting the laptop computer out of its case. He plugged it in and turned it on. As Kelsey had feared, absolutely nothing happened. No lights came on. No clicking or beeping sounds were heard.

"Oh, Beau, what am I going to do?" Dani asked as tears welled in her eyes. She sank into a chair and put her hands on her pregnant tummy. "I've got most of the book I've been writing on that computer's hard file!"

Kelsey had been afraid of that. "But you've backed them up on diskette, haven't you?" Beau said.

Tears fell down Dani's cheeks and splashed onto the desktop in front of her. "Not most of them. I meant to do it, but I just…"

Noting Brady looked confused, Kelsey turned to Brady and explained, "Dani's writing a book of film reviews for movies that are out on video."

"Months of work are on that computer!" Dani said, crying all the harder, making Kelsey feel worse.

"I'm sorry." Feeling as if she could not sink any lower, Kelsey burst into tears, too. "I'm really sorry.'' Unable to bear seeing her sister hurt any more, Kelsey spun around and ran out of the house to the pickup truck at the curb. She would have driven away, but she didn't have the keys. So instead she started walking blindly down the street, furiously blinking back a steady flow of new tears all the while.

She was halfway into the next block when a pickup pulled along beside her. Brady rolled down his window. He looked as calm as she was upset. ''Kelsey, get in the truck,'' he said quietly.

Ignoring the compassionate gleam in his midnight-blue eyes, Kelsey shook her head and kept moving. She needed to be alone. She needed time to pull herself together. Couldn't he see that?

To her frustration, instead of heeding her request, Brady stopped the truck, got out and came marching down the sidewalk after her. Kelsey stiffened her spine, prepared to elbow him away from her. She wasn't prepared to have him drop down in front of her and circle an arm around her knees. Or pick her up and sling her over his shoulder, like a sack of feed.

Kelsey struggled to free herself and was rewarded with a tightened grip around her hips and thighs. She flailed her arms against his spine in a way that demanded he pay attention to her. "Brady Anderson, you put me down this instant!" she said as the ground swam before her eyes and she continued to look at the world upside down.

"Gladly." Brady continued striding along back to his truck. "As soon as I'm sure you'll listen to me."

Kelsey hated the smug male confidence in his low tone. Attitudes like that always brought out the worst in her, and this was no exception. "There's nothing to say," she countered rebelliously. As Kelsey struggled for balance, she put her hands around his waist.

Brady stopped beside the passenger door on his truck and set her down as abruptly as he had picked her up. He put his arms on either side of her, and using his torso, backed her up against the passenger door. "Sure there is," he said easily, looking down at her.

"No," Kelsey countered breathlessly, looking up into his dark blue eyes and wishing he would kiss her again, "there isn't."

He merely grinned and chucked her on the chin. "How about—" he paused to let his gaze rove her face, slowly and sensually "—we're going to Dallas, because I have a friend there who can repair any computer ever made?"

Even as she tingled at his nearness, Kelsey felt a brief ray of hope. It was quickly snuffed out by the reality of the situation. "Even if your friend can fix it, that may not help restore the data that was lost when it crashed," Kelsey answered him.

And if she had single-handedly destroyed, even inadvertently, months of her talented sister's work, Kelsey would know everything she and everyone else in the family had ever felt about her was true. It would mean she was and always would be a disaster waiting to happen.

"Well," Brady said, so gently it made her want to start crying all over again, "we'll never know until we try, will we?" He took her elbow and steered her aside, so he could open the passenger door for her. He brushed his lips against her temple. "Now, get in the truck so we can go."

AN HOUR AND A HALF LATER they were in the suburban home office of Maria Gonzalez. A pretty young woman with dark hair and even darker eyes, she led them into a well-equipped workroom containing computers of all shapes and sizes. Pictures of her family decorated the wall. As Kelsey looked at the photos of Maria and her clearly adoring husband and teenage daughters, she couldn't help but feel envious. What she wouldn't give for a little of this domestic bliss herself. Not that anyone needed to know that, of course, Kelsey thought. Because if they knew how much she wanted to love and be loved like that, they might start feeling sorry for her.

She'd had enough pity at the time her parents died to last a lifetime.

She didn't need any more.

"Thanks for fitting us in," Brady told Maria.

"No problem." Maria smiled. "You know I owe you. And Hargett, too. Without the two of you, none of this would be possible."

There was that name again, Kelsey thought.

And there was that look on Brady's face— the one that said he didn't want anything to do with Hargett.

It wasn't like him to be afraid of anything.

But, for some reason, he was afraid to have Kelsey learn much of anything about the rough-looking, very well-dressed man who had appeared, uninvited, at their ranch the day before.

Before Brady could stop her, Kelsey asked, "What exactly did Hargett and Brady do for you?"

Maria sighed as she set the laptop computer on her worktable and opened it. "I wanted to set this place up and work from home, but I couldn't get a loan from the usual channels. Brady heard about it and hooked me up with Hargett and I got as much money as I needed, right on the spot, no questions asked." She shrugged, allowing ruefully, "Of course the interest rate was a little higher than I would've paid at a bank, and the way Hargett kept checking in with me constantly to see how I was doing was a little—oh, unnerving—but I had so many referrals so quickly, I was able to pay the loan off within a year. And that was that."

Kelsey shot Brady a curious look. He gave her a look that said, "No more questions, Kelse." Then he stepped between her and Maria. "About this computer," Brady said firmly.

While Maria listened raptly, Brady explained how the laptop had frozen and then crashed.

Maria got out her tools and opened up the guts of the computer. The next hour and a half were devoted to a thorough check of the computer, and it was clear from Brady's constant involvement that he knew almost as much about how computers worked and stored information as Maria Gonzalez did.

Had it been Brady's hobby, Kelsey would not have been surprised. But he didn't even own a computer these days. Or if he did, she had never seen it.

So how, she wondered, had he gotten so knowledgeable?

Was this another part of his mysterious past?

The mysterious past that Hargett and now Maria were both connected to?

Kelsey understood Brady not wanting to talk about Hargett. Hargett seemed to make Brady very tense.

But she didn't understand him not wanting to talk about people like Maria. Maria was very nice, and still seemed to consider Brady her friend. Yet Brady had pretty much cut her out of his life, too. Why? Was it because of what Maria knew and accepted about Brady's connection to Hargett?

"It's a faulty switch," Maria explained to Kelsey, who was pretty much lost as to what the two were talking about, it was so technical. "All I have to do is replace it, and—" she finished putting it in "—voilà, power again."

Kelsey beamed. So far so good, then. "Can we tell if we lost any information when it crashed?" she asked nervously.

Maria nodded. "I'll let you know as soon as I finish checking the hard drive."

While Kelsey paced the workroom, and Brady watched over Maria's shoulder, Maria typed in a lot of complicated commands.

"Apparently, all you lost was whatever you were working on yesterday after 5:00 p.m.," Maria told Kelsey seriously, "because until then, the records show all the information entered into the computer was saved and is still in good shape."

Kelsey breathed a sigh of relief. "Then it's just my stuff that was lost, and that was not important." She felt like dancing a jig.

"Thanks a lot, Maria. We really appreciate this," Brady said as he pulled out his wallet.

Maria stopped him from paying her. "I owe you, Brady. Big time. I'm just glad I got to see you again. I thought—when you and Hargett had that big falling out—I might never see you again."

Briefly, sorrow creased Brady's handsome face. "I'm sorry I haven't been in touch," he said as he put his wallet back in his pocket.

"Well, don't let it keep happening," Maria scolded warmly. "I want you—and Kelsey here—to come over and have dinner with the whole family soon."

Again, that reluctant look on Brady's face. "We'll try," he said.

"Do better than that. Do it. And by the way—" Maria glanced at the wedding rings both were wearing "—isn't there a little something else you neglected to tell me?" she teased. "Like just how long the two of you have been married?"

Brady grimaced. "Three days."

Maria's eyes widened. "What about your honeymoon?" she asked, aghast.

"Long story," Brady said.

"And then some," Kelsey agreed, figuring there was no need to get into all that now.

"Hmm." Maria studied them both, this time seeing a lot more than Kelsey would have liked. "Well, I'm just glad you got married, Brady," Maria murmured, after a moment. Her dark eyes softened sympathetically. "Given the way you felt after your break-up with Rexanne—"

"Water under the bridge," Brady interrupted.

"Yeah." Maria got his hint, loud and clear, and did not continue with whatever it was she was about to say. "I guess it is."

# Chapter Eight

"So who was Rexanne and when were you engaged to her?" Kelsey asked curiously the moment the two of them got into Brady's pickup truck to head back to Laramie.

Brady kept his eyes on the road. "It was a couple years ago," he divulged in a way that let Kelsey know he would appreciate it if she didn't ask any more questions. "And she was just somebody I worked with."

Kelsey knew she would never understand Brady unless she understood whatever it was that had made him run from his old life. She wanted to understand him. Not just as his "temporary wife," but as his friend and his partner. She studied his handsome profile and the brooding look in his midnight-blue eyes.

"Did she cheat on you?"

For a long moment, Brady was silent. "It's a lot more complicated than that."

Kelsey waited, hoping he would explain. Finally, he did. "Rexanne was very pretty and very sought after. She'd had dozens of boyfriends, and even several failed engagements before I met her, and as much as I hate to admit it, I think that was even part of the attraction between us."

"Sort of like the guys I've been dating," Kelsey interrupted.

Brady nodded. "Right." A remoteness she hadn't heard before crept into his tone, as he continued self-effacingly, "I liked the challenge of making a woman like that mine. And up until then I'd been pretty restless. Dating a lot of women. Hoping to find The One, but finding none of them interesting enough to hold my attention long-term."

Kelsey understood that. She had done her share of fruitless searching, too. She knew what it felt like to constantly have everything turn out wrong. It was very frustrating and disappointing, to say the least. "But Rexanne did keep your interest," she surmised.

"Looking back, I think it was more the challenge of making her mine than anything else. She had such a reputation for being unattainable."

Kelsey tensed, uncomfortably aware of how the two situations mirrored each other. "Rexanne played hard to get?" Kelsey guessed, aware she was beginning to feel just a tad bit jealous for the first time in her life. Usually, she didn't care who the other women had been in her boyfriend's life.

Brady nodded. "Oh, yeah. She made me work for that first date, and every one after that. And I'd be lying if I said I didn't find that exciting at the time, 'cause I did." He paused to shoot Kelsey a brief, honest look before returning his attention to the road. "Here, I had all these other women lined up, wanting to marry me. Whereas Rexanne wouldn't give me the time of day."

"But she did finally agree."

"Yep." Brady turned on his left signal. As soon as it was clear, he guided the pickup into the far left lane of the freeway. "And that's when the problems started on my end," he admitted as he accelerated to keep up with the fast-flowing traffic. "I felt so trapped. Restless. I guess deep down I knew I didn't love her, not the way I should, not enough to make a marriage last, but I'd made this commitment to her. I didn't think I could or should back out."

Brady paused and shrugged his broad shoulders affably. "Anyway, the wedding plans continued full steam ahead all the way till the week of the wedding. And that was when I began to get the feeling something was wrong on her part, too."

He sighed unhappily as he continued to recollect. "Rexanne denied it, of course. She was determined not to let her family down again, determined to prove she could remain faithfully devoted to just one man. And I know she didn't want to hurt me. But my uneasiness persisted, and the night of the wedding rehearsal I caught this glimpse of her looking at Zeke, my best man, and him looking at her, and there was such longing there, such connection, I knew—even though neither of them had done anything about it—that she'd fallen in love with Zeke. So I confronted them, and they admitted it was true, and we called off the wedding that very evening to the great disappointment of family and friends. And Rexanne married Zeke the next day—in my stead."

Kelsey stared at him, unable to believe he was so matter-of-fact about it all, after suffering what had to have been a major humiliation, being left at the altar that way. Her heart going out to him, she asked softly, "Is that when you sort of dropped out of sight?"

Just that quickly, the expression on Brady's face closed down. "Let's just say the whole experience made me seriously reevaluate my life," he said carefully after a moment. Seeing their exit coming up, he turned on his right signal, checked to make sure it was clear, and began getting over into the far right lane. "I knew I wasn't happy." His lips pressed together as he steered the pickup down the exit ramp. "I'd been counting on my marriage to Rexanne, the acquisition of a wife and kids and a satisfying family life of my own, to make me happy. But in retrospect, I realized the vague sense of dissatisfaction I had was more deeply rooted than that," he told her seriously. As they stopped at a traffic light at the bottom of the ramp, he turned to face Kelsey. "I needed to do some soul-searching of my own and figure out where I belonged, what kind of life I wanted, before I made a commitment like that to anyone else."

Kelsey searched his eyes. "Are you happy now?"

"With ranching? Yeah." Brady smiled, and the joy he expressed then seemed to radiate from deep inside his heart. "Happier than I've ever been in my life."

When the light changed, Brady drove a quarter mile down the road and pulled into the gas station on their right. "Do you still want a wife and kids?" Kelsey asked as he parked in front of the pump and cut the motor.

"I've got a wife, remember?" Brady took her hand in his and lifted it to his lips. He pressed a tender kiss into her palm. He shot her an intent look that took her breath away before continuing, just as contentedly, "And I wouldn't mind a few kids."

Kelsey blushed and tried not to think about how those kids he wanted would likely be made. Knowing Brady, it wouldn't be in some test tube or medical lab. She swallowed hard and tugged her hand away from his. Blushing, she grabbed her purse, got out of the truck and walked around to where the gas gauge was. "Let's not put the cart before the horse, okay?" She slid her credit card into the slot on the pump that allowed them to pay for their purchase outside.

Brady laced his arm around her shoulders and leaned down to whisper in her ear. "We could always adopt if you don't want to do it the old-fashioned way," he teased.

Kelsey's flush deepened, despite her efforts to remain cool, calm and collected. That was the problem, if she ever had children with Brady, she did want to do it the old-fashioned way. And judging from the look on his face, he knew it, too.

Unfortunately, they couldn't do that unless, or until, they had a real marriage, and right now they were far from that. They hadn't slept together. And they certainly hadn't mentioned being in love with each other. Although, she was beginning to think, on her part, that was exactly what was happening....

Determined to change the subject, to something even more important to her and less comfortable for Brady this time, she said, "Were you working for this guy, Hargett, when all this happened?"

Brady's expression shifted from good to bad, just as she had suspected it would. Clearly, this subject was not welcome. He dropped his hold on her, punched a couple of buttons on the pump. "Yes," he said abruptly, the look he gave her, as he opened the fuel door and took off the gas cap, forbidding her to ask anything more.

Kelsey paused, wondering what the source of the tension between Brady and Hargett was.

Knowing there was only one way to find out, she ignored Brady's warning look and asked idly, anyway, "Hargett doesn't happen to own a savings and loan, does he?"

Brady shot her a look as if wondering where on earth she had gotten that idea. "No," he said flatly. "He's an independent businessman."

*An independent businessman. That could mean anything—and not necessarily good, either.*

''What does he sell?'' Kelsey asked, her sense that Brady was deliberately shielding her from something unpleasant or shameful stronger than ever.

Brady shot her a sharp look that seemed resentful of her nosiness. ''Why does it matter?''

*Because,* Kelsey thought to herself, *whatever is going on between you and Hargett is wedging a distance between you and me.* But wary of revealing the extent of her feelings to Brady, lest she ruin their partnership because he didn't feel anywhere near the same way about her, Kelsey fell silent.

She thought a moment more, about the rough-hewn man in the expensive suit. He loaned out money at higher than usual interest rates, to people like Maria who couldn't otherwise get a loan for what they wanted to do, and then came around and checked on them to the point it was unnerving to them.

She knew of only one job that fit that description.

She watched as Brady replaced the nozzle on the pump and screwed the gas cap back on. ''Is he a loan shark then?''

Brady burst out laughing, as if the whole idea were absurd. "I never thought of it that way," he answered finally, still grinning at what was apparently an insider's joke.

And to Kelsey's frustration, that was all he would say on the subject, even after they'd taken their credit card receipt from the slot and had gotten back on the highway home.

THEY STOPPED EN ROUTE to Laramie to see a bull and some Black Angus cows Brady was interested in. With the last of the money Wade McCabe had loaned them, Brady negotiated a pretty savvy deal for both cattle and bull. All would be delivered to their ranch the following day.

"You know, you'd be a pretty good businessman," Kelsey said, unable to help but be impressed, although she was still a little ticked off he wouldn't tell her more about this mysterious Hargett. But that was Brady. He was always playing his cards close to his vest. She just wished his secretiveness about his past life wasn't beginning to hurt so much. She wanted him to trust her enough to be able to tell her anything and everything. Because without that kind of intimacy, there could be no real and lasting love between them, that much she knew.

Brady drew up alongside the mailbox. The red flag was down, so that meant the postman had already come. "A rancher is a business-man, Kelse."

Kelsey leaned out across the open truck win-dow and got the mail out of the black metal mailbox and their afternoon newspaper out of the newspaper carrier underneath the box. "You know what I mean," she said as she set it all on her lap then rifled through a stack of mostly bills and a few catalogs. It was all for her. Brady had his delivered to a post office box in town.

"Yeah, I do." Brady turned his truck into their gravel lane, kicking up clouds of dust be-hind them. "And the range is the only place I want to be," he said, staring straight ahead, both hands clenching the wheel. "So forget try-ing to make me into the next Texas billion-aire."

Kelsey caught the edge in his voice as he whipped the pickup around to a rather fancy stop, next to one of the barns. It was the first time Brady'd been really short with her in the five months they'd known each other. Which told her just how close to the bone she'd cut.

"Sorry," she said after a moment. "I didn't mean to get under your skin." She hopped down from the truck and circled around the back. Together, they stood there, admiring the crisp fall weather and the blue Texas skies overhead. It was close to seventy degrees. A light breeze ruffled the turning leaves on the trees. Kelsey looked down at the scuffed toes of her boots. "I know how it is to have people wishing you were something you aren't," she told him. And it hurt, no two ways about it.

Brady took her elbow with one hand, and carried Dani's repaired laptop computer in his other as he steered her toward the back stoop. "You talking about your sisters?"

Kelsey shrugged, pretending as if it didn't matter to her in the least. "Everybody who knows me, actually," she said as Brady unlocked the door and ushered her inside the mud room, and from there into the ranch house kitchen. "Everybody had an idea what I should

be. Secretary, flight attendant, saleswoman—
you name it, I've not only been pushed to those
jobs, I've held them.''

Brady set the laptop on the table, then took
two soft drinks out of the refrigerator. The
house was a little stuffy after being closed up
all day, Kelsey noted. She watched as Brady
went over to open up the window above the
kitchen sink.

''Twenty-four jobs in six years, isn't it?''

Kelsey tilted her head to study him better as
she leaned against the opposite counter, wary
of getting overly comfortable with him.
''How'd you know that?'' Now that she was on
the receiving end of the nosy questions, she
found to her surprise she wasn't any happier
about them than he had been.

Brady's lips tipped up ruefully at the corners.
''Let's just say I was warned not to get involved in any kind of partnership with you, by
just about everyone,'' he said.

Kelsey found herself bristling at the implied
criticism of her past. She regarded him steadily
over the rim of her soft drink can. ''Why did
you, then?''

"I don't know exactly," Brady said, shrugging as if some things weren't meant to be looked at too closely. "It was just something I wanted to do," he explained.

Kelsey nodded and turned her glance away. She couldn't help but wish he had given her a more poetic reason for the two of them being together, instead of just out-and-out gut instinct and stubbornness, but at least he was honest about what he was feeling.

That counted for a lot.

She couldn't imagine being involved with someone who wasn't honest with her.

Because without truth, what was there?

Brady frowned as he looked at the feed store calendar hanging on the wall. "I can't believe the week is half over," he said, shaking his head. "Wednesday night already!"

Wednesday night!

*Oh, no,* Kelsey thought. Quickly, she glanced at Brady's watch. "What time is it?" she said anxiously.

"A little after six, why?"

Because she had a date with Rafe Marshall tonight, that was why! Figuring however, that

Brady might not cotton to that idea, given the way it might appear to others, she decided to spare him any worry as she took a big gulp of her drink and then tightened her fingers around the can. "No problem, really. I just have to be somewhere at seven."

He scanned her from head to toe, taking in her red chambray shirt, jeans, hat and red cowgirl boots. "You want me to go with you?" he asked cheerfully.

Kelsey wished he could, but in this case, three really would be a crowd. "Nope," she shot back, just as agreeably. "Just stay here, take care of the ranch, and get ready for all the horses, cattle and tack we're having delivered tomorrow." Thursday looked like it was going to be a good day. And once it was over, they would have everything they needed to turn this homestead from an iffy operation to a first-rate spread.

Brady stepped close enough for her to take in the tantalizing masculine fragrance of his skin and hair and the warmth of his body. Was it her imagination or did he have loving her on his mind?

"You going to be here for dinner?" he asked, running a hand lightly down her arm, eliciting delicious tingles everywhere he touched and some places he didn't, as well.

*I'd sure as shootin' like to be,* Kelsey thought, *given the sexy new light in your eyes.*

As she tried to figure out how to handle this very tricky situation, Kelsey made a vague, noncommittal sound in the back of her throat.

She really didn't want to hurt Brady's feelings by shutting him out this way, but Rafe Marshall had sworn her to secrecy, and a promise was a promise.

"Um, no." Now that she was the one deliberately shutting him out of a part of her life, she found she couldn't quite meet his eyes.

The heat of a self-conscious flush in her cheeks, she made a big show of sorting her mail and stacking it neatly in the letters rack beside the kitchen telephone.

"Listen, would you mind taking the computer back to Dani?" Kelsey said as she grabbed her catalogs and put them on the bookshelf where the cookbooks should have gone, if she'd had any. She turned and looked at Brady directly. "I know we were going to do that together this evening, but now I really don't have time," she said honestly.

"No problem," Brady said with an affable shrug.

"Thanks." Ignoring the mounting curiosity on Brady's face, Kelsey rushed up the stairs to get ready for her secret date.

*Chapter Nine*

She was not cheating on him, Brady told himself firmly, the entire time he was outside taking care of the horses. And there was no reason to think that might be so. Kelsey wasn't even all that interested in having a fling with him. She hadn't had the time or the inclination to go after another man. Besides, they were married. The deed to her beloved family ranch was on the line. She wouldn't do anything to screw that up.

But when he saw her run out of the house in a dress and high heels, looking pretty enough to pose for wedding pictures, he was no longer sure of anything.

His options were limited. He could deliver Dani's computer to her, and then return home and sit here at the ranch and wait for Kelsey to come back. Or he could follow her and find out what she was up to tonight. Even before he emerged from the barn, Brady knew what he was going to do.

For a while, as the two of them drove the country roads, Brady was worried Kelsey might realize he was behind her. But she didn't. And when she turned into the Gilded Lily and parked in front of the nicest restaurant in a thirty-mile radius and was helped out of her car by none other than a dark-haired man in a suit and tie, he understood why she had dressed up so much.

She was having a secret rendezvous!

Teeth gritted, Brady watched as his wife was escorted into the restaurant by her "date." When they had disappeared inside, he guided his truck all the way into the parking lot. He didn't know why he was so hurt. It wasn't as if he and Kelsey were really man and wife. Brady just knew that he was hurt. But maybe that was his fault, too, he conceded. For not following through on what she had obviously wanted and making her his woman as well as his wife from the beginning.

The question was, was it too late to go back and do what he should have done on the very day they married?

"YOU'VE GOT TO RELAX, RAFE." Kelsey smiled as he helped her into her seat.

"Sorry. I'm just so rusty at all this. I feel like I'm all thumbs."

"Patricia is not going to mind if you eat your salad with your dinner fork and your dinner with your salad fork, or forget to put your napkin on your lap before your first sip of water."

"But she will mind if I do something stupid like close her dress in the door," Rafe said.

"I think you should just be yourself," Kelsey soothed. Seeing how nervous Rafe still was, she reached over and took his hand in hers. "Honestly," she said, staring deep into his eyes with as much confidence-inspiring intensity as she could, "everything is going to be fine. You'll see."

At the door there was a commotion. A shadow fell over them. Kelsey looked up to see Brady glaring at both of them. "So this is what you're up to tonight," he said grimly.

"It's not what it looks like," Kelsey said quickly, standing, too.

"Oh, isn't it?" Brady volleyed back. He crossed his arms in front of him and his jaw hardened all the more.

"No," Kelsey spelled out, just as plainly as her heart took on a rapid, thudding beat. "It is not." She propped her hands on her hips and gave Brady a stern look. "And if you'll calm down, and sit down, Rafe and I will explain."

To Kelsey's chagrin, Brady's blue eyes turned even stormier. Up till now, Brady had always been so easygoing, even in the tensest situations. She hadn't figured he had a jealous bone in his body. That showed how much she knew!

"The only explanation I want to hear from you is going to be at home," Brady told her in a low tone that brooked no arguments. Brady took her by the elbow.

Kelsey shook off his grip and tilted her chin at him. "I'm not leaving here, Brady. Rafe and I have a date tonight—"

Looking as if he had just been pushed to the absolute limit, Brady stared at her. "And you see nothing wrong with dating him while you're married to me?'' he queried coolly.

Given the fact they had yet to exchange anything except a few heated kisses and a lot of empty promises? ''As it happens, no, I don't.''

Sensing trouble, Rafe stood, too.

His nervousness of just moments before gone, he looked at Brady like the calm, personable elementary school principal he was. ''Brady, I think you should listen to her,'' Rafe advised quietly.

''Oh, you do, do you?'' Brady countered sarcastically as heads turned all around them, and all other conversation in the room ground to a halt as the diners gawked at the three of them.

''Yes,'' Rafe replied urgently, on Kelsey's behalf, beginning to sweat. ''It's all perfectly innocent.''

Brady shook his head and continued to look as if he longed to punch something.

''If you think that, you're as messed up as she is….'' Brady swore at Rafe in a low, furious voice.

The maître d' hovered behind them, like the referee in a boxing ring. ''Please, folks. No scenes.''

Brady turned around grimly. "Don't worry. There isn't going to be one," he told the maître d'. "I've seen all I need to see." Ignoring Kelsey altogether, he turned on his heel and walked out of the restaurant.

"YOU NEED TO GO AFTER HIM," Rafe whispered as soon as Brady had bolted out the door.

Kelsey sat down at the table. She was so embarrassed her face felt as if it were on fire. She had always hated it when people underestimated her, or thought the worst of her, without first taking the time to try to understand what was going on with her. Her sisters had been doing it for years. When they weren't jumping to conclusions, they were assuming she would fail at whatever she attempted. Only Brady had been different.

From the very moment they met, he had ignored what everyone else said about her, or thought about her, and accepted her for what and who she was. That was one of the reasons she had found herself willing to form a partnership with him, and also why she had begun falling in love with him.

But now he was like everyone else.

Automatically thinking the very worst of her.

And it hurt. A lot.

But maybe that was what she got, Kelsey thought, for opening up her heart to him, and making herself vulnerable.

Well, no more.

He was either going to have to clean up his act and go back to trusting her again or go back to wherever it was he had come from. And she was going to tell him that as soon as she caught up with him again.

Meanwhile, she had a vow of her own to keep. She looked at Rafe and smiled. "I promised you I would help you get over your jitters and I will. Now, let's just sit here and have dinner and a nice conversation and I'll tell you if I see any red flags about the way you intend to carry out your date with Patricia...."

As Kelsey had suspected, Rafe was not nearly as rusty as he thought.

He forgot to ask her if she wanted dessert before he consulted with the waiter, and he stepped on her toes several times when they were dancing after dinner, but all in all, he was fine. And a lot more confident at the end of their two-hour date than at the beginning of it. The two of them said good-night, and then, her stomach in knots as she thought about seeing Brady again, and probably continuing the fight that they had started but not really finished in the restaurant, Kelsey drove back to the ranch.

Brady's truck was out front, but the ranch house was dark and silent. She went inside, wondering if he was already in bed for the night, even though it was barely ten o'clock, but he was nowhere to be found.

She went out to the barns and looked around. He wasn't there, either.

Kelsey went back to the house and sat down to wait.

One hour passed, then another. Finally, around midnight, she heard the sound of an approaching rider on horseback. She looked out and saw Brady ride into the yard next to the stables. He swung down off the horse, and then proceeded to take off the saddle and rub down the animal, before turning him out to pasture for the night with the other horses on the ranch.

His strides heavy but purposeful, he disappeared into the stable with the rest of the tack. Another five, ten, fifteen minutes passed and he still didn't emerge.

Tired of waiting for him, Kelsey walked out to the stables. She heard the sound of water running as soon as she was inside the cement-floored building with the wooden stalls.

She headed down to the stable manager's office. Brady had turned it into his private quarters when he moved out to the ranch. There was still a desk and file cabinets there, but he had pushed those to one side of the room. The other side of the small room held an old-fashioned iron cot, made up with white sheets and green wool blankets. The original bathroom with sink and commode had been left intact, but Brady had put in the kind of utilitarian metal-walled shower stall they used in high school locker rooms beside that.

He was currently in the shower. He had obviously stripped off his clothes the moment he walked in—they were hanging over the sides of the stall. Kelsey thought about backing out of the room, then decided against it.

They were married.

And she'd already seen him naked.

She could handle this. His intimate parts were shielded from view. All she could see from her vantage point were his legs, from his calves on down, and his head and shoulders above the metal sides.

He turned to glare at her as she came in, then, his mouth clamped shut furiously, finished shampooing his hair in utter silence. He ducked his head under the stream, rinsed off, and then shut off the water.

The silence that followed was broken only by the sounds of the water running down the drain next to his bare feet.

Her heart pounding at the showdown to come, Kelsey stayed where she was until he emerged from the shower stall, dark blue towel slung low across his hips, in a way that made his broad shoulders and muscled chest look even sexier and more buff. With difficulty, Kelsey tore her eyes from his slicked-back hair and damp skin. "What do you want?" he said.

"Exactly what you'd think," Kelsey replied, mocking his sarcastic tone to a T. "To talk to you."

He quirked a discerning brow. "Without your boyfriend?"

Kelsey's temper flared. There was nothing she hated more than having those close to her simply suppose the worst about her, instead of taking the time to understand. She smiled at Brady tightly and moved away from the wall. "Rafe is not my boyfriend."

Brady shrugged and went over to the sink. He lathered up his face and began to shave. "Could have fooled me and everyone else in that restaurant." He looked at her in the mirror. "Or do you hold every guy's hand like that?"

Determined to set the record straight, Kelsey moved closer yet. She continued to hold Brady's eyes in the mirror while he shaved with quick, precise strokes of the blade. "I was doing him a favor."

Brady finished and rinsed his jaw. He patted his face dry with a hand towel, then said in a low, bored tone, "Maybe you really shouldn't tell me any more."

Clamping her lips together in frustration, Kelsey stalked even closer. "It was a pretend date, Brady."

"Well, that's a new one," Brady drawled as he slapped on a generous amount of wintry-smelling aftershave.

Ignoring his sarcasm, Kelsey propped both her hands on her hips and continued explaining her actions in the most matter-of-fact tone she could manage. "Rafe wants to ask Patricia Weatherby out and he came to me for help. He thought if he had a trial run of the evening he planned for himself and Patricia, the real date with Patricia would go a lot more smoothly. All I was doing tonight was giving him dating tips. There was nothing of a romantic nature going on."

Finished, Brady turned to face her and leaned against the sink. His glance roved her mocha-brown stretch-velvet dress, taking in the way the fabric molded snugly to her every curve before swirling prettily to mid-calf.

"Yet you stayed at the restaurant with him," Brady said, his eyes roving the high neck and fitted long sleeves, before returning to her face. "Instead of coming home with me."

Kelsey shrugged and paced the room restlessly, her high heels clicking against the cement floor. She knew what Brady wanted, but she refused to apologize for not giving in to Brady's husbandly demands. "He's a friend and I had promised to help him," she said. As far as she was concerned, that should be explanation enough.

"Yeah, well—" Brady leaned closer as she strode past. He caught her arm and swung her around to face him, *"I'm your husband."*

"In name only," Kelsey corrected him icily, still seeing red over the way he was behaving, as she pried his fingers from her upper arm. "And where do you get off acting so possessive, anyway?" she demanded indignantly. "It's not as if we're really man and wife."

Brady's brow lifted in a manner that was all the more possessive. He backed her up against the wall, so his hips pressed into hers. "Well, maybe we should be," he said.

"What's that supposed to mean?"

Brady leaned in even closer. He let his towel drop to the floor and his hands came up to cup her shoulders. "What do you think it means?"

Engulfing her with the heat and strength of his body, he lowered his head and delivered a breath-stealing kiss. She moaned, and he kissed her again, shattering what little caution she had left. Her lips parted beneath the pressure of his as his tongue swept her mouth with long, sensuous strokes. He encircled her with his heat and strength until Kelsey's whole body was alive, quivering with urgent sensations unlike any she had ever felt.

"Brady—" Kelsey moaned again as his hands swept down her body, molding and exploring through the soft, stretchy fabric of her dress. It felt so good to be wanted and touched. It felt so good to be held against him like this. To have the barriers between them start coming down. Desire trembled inside her, making her tummy feel weightless, soft. She melted helplessly against him, thigh to thigh, sex to sex. She could feel his erection pressing against her, hot and urgent, his heart pounding in his chest.

"I'm through pretending I don't feel the way I feel. I want you, Kelsey," he whispered, raining kisses down her throat, across her cheek, her lips. Framing her face with his hands, he forced her mouth up to his. "I want you to be mine." He tunneled his hands through her hair, tilted her head back and kissed her with surprising tenderness. Lifting his head from hers, he asked in a low voice that seemed wrenched from his very heart, "What do you want?"

He was so strong and wonderful. He tasted so good, so undeniably male, so right. "You," she whispered, her hips moving against his as he continued to watch her in that unsettling way. "I want you...."

"No more holding back, then," he promised her softly. "This time we're really going to do this."

"Yes," Kelsey said, quivering at the tightening of his muscles beneath her fingertips and the heat flowing into his bare skin. She had never experienced anything like this intense, aching need. She didn't care if she was behaving recklessly once again. She wanted to see where the passion would lead them. Would it bring her as close as she wanted to be to Brady? Would making love link them forever, make them truly man and wife?

His legs pinning hers to the wall, he bent his head and kissed her with a passion so hot it sizzled. His tongue flicked across the edges of her teeth, before delving deep in a slow mating dance. Joy swept through her and Brady's hands moved behind her. The zipper of her dress slid down. The next thing she knew, he was pushing it off her shoulders, letting it fall to the floor. His whole body was quaking as he regarded her transparent black lace bra, thigh-high stockings and damp bikini panties. ''You are so beautiful. So sexy,'' he murmured, and then those came off, too.

Wanting to remember everything about this night, Brady let his glance sift slowly over her. Kelsey was gorgeous, no matter what she was wearing. But she had never looked more radiant than she did at that moment, with color blushing her freckled cheeks, and her cinnamon-red hair tumbling over her pale shoulders.

His gaze moved over her supple curves, her long slender legs and silky thighs, the shadowy vee. He knew they were far from solving all their problems, but he didn't care. He couldn't wait any longer. He had to make her his.

She trembled as he bent and kissed her ripe coral nipples one by one. She clasped his shoulders and sagged against the wall as his mouth moved urgently on her breasts. He slid down her body, kissing the hollow of her stomach, stroking the soft insides of her thighs. He traced her navel with his tongue, then dropped lower still, to deliver the most intimate of kisses, until she was awash in pleasure, shuddering.

Achingly aware of every soft warm inch of her, Brady laid her down on the cot and stretched out over top of her. Savoring the sweetness of her unexpected acquiescence to him, he closed his eyes, lowered his mouth to hers and let her lead him where she wanted to go. He groaned as their tongues twined urgently and his body took up a primitive rhythm all its own, until there was no doubting how much they needed each other, needed this. And then she was lifting her hips, pleading wordlessly for a more intimate union. He edged her knees apart, lifted her up and eased into her, past that first fragile barrier, not wanting to hurt her for anything. Her eyes widened in surprise, in pain, even as her body stretched to take him.

"That's it, sweetheart," he whispered, deepening his penetration even more as he kissed her slowly, thoroughly. "Take all of me."

Kelsey didn't think it was possible. He was so big, so hard. She was so tight. But as he slid one arm beneath her and arched his body up and all the way into hers, she found it was possible after all. Not only possible, but wonderfully sensual, hot and wild. Loving the tender but fierce way he was possessing her, she closed her eyes, awash in sensation. Brady kissed her again, his body taking up the same slow, timeless rhythm as his tongue. And then she was moaning again, moving against him, with him, able to hear the soft, whimpering sounds in the back of her throat, and the lower, fiercer sounds in his. What few boundaries that still existed between them dissolved. She ran her arms along his arms, across his shoulders, down his back. Their spirits soared as he pressed into her as deeply as he could go, withdrew, then filled her again. And they were lost in the ecstasy, free-falling into pleasure unlike anything Kelsey had ever known.

LONG MOMENTS PASSED as they clung to each other, still trembling, still in awe at what they'd done. Finally, Brady rolled onto his back. Kelsey had only to look at his face to see his regret. "It shouldn't have happened like that."

She rolled onto her side, disappointed he didn't look as happy about what had just happened as she was. She had thought this would change everything. Apparently not. At least not in the way that she had hoped.

She felt her defenses go back up, as surely and swiftly as they had come down. "What do you mean?" she asked warily, doing her best to hide her hurt that he could find anything wrong with what had just happened between them.

Brady turned troubled eyes to hers. "Here," he told her, not bothering to mask his guilt. "On a cot in the stable. In the midst of an argument. You are—were—a virgin, for heaven's sake. Not to mention, my wife. At the very least, it should have been in a real bed," he said thickly. "With candles and roses all around. Maybe even some champagne and strawberries or something."

The source of his worry identified, Kelsey smiled and began to relax. Brady's concern for her was sweet but hopelessly misguided. The fact was, had the consummation of their marriage happened any other way, except in such a hot, wild manner, Kelsey probably would have had time to think about it, weighed the pros and cons and lost her nerve. And that would have been a shame because, whether the two of them were really married or not, she wouldn't trade the experience for anything. She rolled over, so she was lying on his chest, looking up at him. Unable to keep herself from touching him even one second longer, she ran her fingers through the tufts of dark hair on his chest and looked up at him earnestly. "That was exactly the way I wanted it to happen, Brady. It was exciting and—" she flushed, but forced herself to continue "—wonderful...."

He smiled at her unabashed praise and reached over to gently brush the hair from her cheek and kiss the back of her hand. "Still—"

"Still, nothing," Kelsey interrupted, scooting closer yet. She draped one of her legs between the warmth of his. "I know I'm inexperienced here, Brady. Not as inexperienced as I was—" she grinned mischievously as one hand drifted playfully lower "—but inexperienced nevertheless." She paused, looked deep into his eyes, before continuing seriously, "But I'm also an adult who's been on my own for a long time now. I know what I wanted, Brady. And what I wanted was you," she said softly, earnestly.

"I wanted you, too. Still do, as a matter of fact."

He moved so he was on top of her once again. The possessive look in his eyes made her catch her breath. She could blame their first bout of lovemaking on a combination of passion and recklessness. If they made love again, the way he clearly wanted to make love to her, slowly and deliberately, it was bound to mean much more. It was bound to make her fall all the way in love with him.

Kelsey wasn't sure she was ready for that. She wasn't sure she was ready to let him all the way into her heart. Because doing that would make her vulnerable in a way she'd never been before. She swallowed around the sudden lump of emotion in her throat. "Brady—" she whispered tremulously.

"I'll be a lot more gentle this time," he

whispered, mistaking the reason for her unease. ''I promise.''

It was all Kelsey could do not to sigh at the languid nature of his touch. She pouted as his hands moved over her, butterfly soft, accommodating. ''I don't want you to be gentle.'' She didn't want him protecting her. She wanted to be his partner, his equal, in every way. But Brady, it seemed, had ideas of his own.

He grinned, already bending his head and kissing her thoroughly. ''Tell me that after, and I'll believe you,'' he teased. ''Until then, we'll do this on my time frame, my way.''

# *Chapter Ten*

"Brady's way" turned out to be wonderful, sensual and slow. By the time morning came, and they finally fell asleep, wrapped in each other's arms, Kelsey had never felt so well-loved, so treasured and wanted, in her life. And unless she missed her guess, Brady was just as happy with the way she made love to him, too.

So happy that when they woke the next morning, he couldn't seem to stop smiling any more than she could. "I think we should move all your stuff up to the house and put it in the master bedroom, along with mine," Kelsey said as they shared a breakfast of coffee and cinnamon rolls on the front porch and watched the sun rise.

"That's a pretty big step," Brady said, wrapping his arm around her.

Kelsey turned to him with a contented smile. "I know." But it felt right to her. And for now, that was all that was important.

Brady grinned and kissed the top of her head. "Well, just for the record, it suits me just fine."

Together, they brought his belongings—which consisted of a steamer trunk of clothes and books—to the house, and put them away. As they worked, Kelsey couldn't help but compare his meager belongings to the amount of stuff she had accumulated over the years. She'd heard about traveling light, but this was ridiculous, she thought. Surely he had more stuff somewhere.

And if not, why not?

"What are you thinking about?" Brady asked as he hung the last of his shirts in the closet, next to her shirts and jeans.

The last thing Kelsey wanted to do was put a damper on the happiness she'd found. She had a feeling asking Brady questions he had always been loathe to answer would do just that. She'd find out what she needed to know in time, she reassured herself firmly. All she had to do was be patient. Even if patience wasn't a virtue that came easily to her. "I was thinking about how much work we have to do today," Kelsey said, glancing out the window at the clouds gathering on the horizon. "The saddles and horses and cattle are going to be delivered this morning and it looks like a blue norther is rolling in."

Brady switched on the weather radio beside Kelsey's bed. It ran on batteries and only got one channel—the national weather service for their area. Forecasts were broadcast continuously.

"The cold front coming down from the north is bringing a twenty-degree drop in temperatures and a ninety percent chance of rain," the forecaster said. "The precipitation should continue throughout the night, ending by midmorning tomorrow...."

"Darn it," Kelsey said, shaking her head in frustration as she met Brady's eyes. "That means I'm going to have to cancel this afternoon's after-school riding lessons."

"What you need is a covered arena, so your lessons can go on no matter what," Brady said.

He took her by the hand and led her outside, and showed her where he thought it should go. "It probably wouldn't take long to build, either."

"If we had the money," Kelsey concurred, looking at the spot Brady had picked out behind the stables. She turned to him with a sigh. "We've just about spent everything Wade lent us." They had enough for feed and vet bills, to get them through until the real money started coming in, but that was about it.

"You leave that to me." Brady leaned over and kissed her tenderly on the lips. As the sky darkened ominously all the more, he led her back inside. "Right now we have more important things to think about," he said.

As Brady set about pouring them more coffee, Kelsey pushed away the memories the dark clouds brought. That was how the sky had looked the day her parents had been killed in the tornado. Even though no tornado warnings had been issued, she felt a sense of foreboding, anyway.

Pushing her superstitious fear away—nothing bad was going to happen—not when she had just found the kind of all-encompassing love she had always wanted, just like her sisters had. She rubbed her arms briskly, to ward off the chill that had overtaken her. She accepted the mug from Brady and forced herself to smile at him. "And what important things would those be—besides waiting for the delivery trucks that are bringing our new horses and cattle?"

He held out her chair for her, then snapped up a pad and pen off the kitchen counter, before he sat down with her at the kitchen table. "We need to figure out what our brand is going to be."

Kelsey had been putting off a decision on that for several months now. It hadn't seemed important since they didn't have much stock. Now that was about to change, she figured they were going to have to come to some decision. And soon. She hesitated, wondering if they were going to be able to agree about this. "We can't use the sideways L my parents used to have—we let the registration lapse when we sold the ranch years ago and it's since been taken up by someone else."

"Maybe that's for the best, anyway," Brady

said as he put up his arm, blocking her view of whatever it was he was drawing on the page in front of him. "Given the fact that the two of us are starting fresh and going into business together."

Kelsey studied him. Brady was one of the most deliberate men she knew. If he had brought this up, it was because he had made a decision. "You have something in mind, don't you?"

"Mmm-hmm." He continued drawing, then turned the page over so she could see. "What do you think?"

Kelsey studied the two interlocking hearts, with the arrow that went through them both. "Even sort of makes sense," Brady continued, then explained what he was proposing with a heart-stoppingly sexy smile. "Locked hearts. Lockhart."

Kelsey flushed at the unexpectedly romantic nature of his suggestion. "I like it. As long as it's not taken."

"It isn't." Brady sat back in his chair, looking confident as all get-out. "I checked. So what do you say?" He looked deep into her eyes. "You want to register that as our brand?"

Yes, Kelsey thought. *You don't know how much. Mostly because of how much it seems to indicate you care about me and think of us as a couple now.*

But almost as soon as she thought it, the practical side of her disagreed with the emotions of her heart. Adapting a brand like that set the bar pretty high for them. Since her parents had died, Kelsey had made a habit of setting the bar low, so she wouldn't be crushed if her hopes and dreams didn't match the reality of what actually occurred. She bit her lip, searching for an excuse that would allow him to back out gracefully, before they made even bigger fools of themselves than most people— including her family and the McCabe clan— thought she already had. "I don't know, Brady." Kelsey traced her finger around the rim of her coffee mug. "The other ranchers in the area might have a heyday with this."

Brady shrugged his broad shoulders affably, as confident he was going to get what he wanted in the end, as ever. "Let 'em tease me for being romantic. I don't care who knows you stole my heart, Kelse, 'cause you have." He leaned across the table, took her hands in his and kissed her, sweetly and tenderly. The next thing she knew she was sitting on his lap. His arms were all the way around her. And he was still kissing her with a passion and a gentleness she had never guessed might exist when they heard the sound of a vehicle rumbling up the drive. "That's probably one of our deliveries," Kelsey said, reluctantly starting to break it off.

"Let 'em wait," Brady murmured around another kiss. "Can't they see I'm busy here?"

Kelsey giggled and let him draw her even further into the embrace. Before she knew it, Kelsey had forgotten all about their visitor, and she was kissing him back, at first sweetly and tenderly, then with building passion. One kiss turned into two, two turned into three. Brady wrapped his arms around her more tightly, bringing her closer yet. She arched against him, her breasts crushed against the powerful muscles of his chest.

"Well, seems like I owe you five bucks after all," a familiar feminine voice said.

Kelsey and Brady turned to see Dani and Beau standing by the porch. Dani shook her

head, tacitly accepting blame where it was due.
"Beau's been saying for months now that the
two of you were seriously, romantically at-
tracted to each other," she said. "I was thinking it was just a friendship, and a pretty casual
one at that. Seems he was right," Dani continued as she and Beau came all the way up the
porch, an overflowing gift basket in hand.
"And it also seems I owe you an apology, Kelsey." Hand to her pregnant tummy, she backed
into the chair Beau held out for her and set the
gift basket on the kitchen table. "I am so sorry
I got upset about the computer."

"It's okay." Kelsey waved off her older sister's concern as she slid off Brady's lap. "I
shouldn't have broken it."

"You didn't break it," Brady interrupted,
pulling her right back into his lap and anchoring
his arms around her waist. "It broke on you,
remember?"

Kelsey wished she could be as sure as her
husband was about that.

"He's right," Dani said firmly, exchanging
matter-of-fact looks of apology with everyone
in the room. "That computer has been giving

me trouble off and on for months now. I just didn't take the time to get it looked at. And I'm really sorry I started crying and everything.'' She teared up again just talking about it, and fished for a tissue in the pocket of her chic maternity pantsuit. ''I've just been really emotional the past few months.''

''I can attest to that,'' Beau said, gently patting Dani's shoulder. ''She's even started crying at the commercials on TV.''

''Well, some of them are pretty sentimental,'' Kelsey pointed out in Dani's defense.

''The ones about floor wax?'' Beau teased.

''Beau's right. I have been weeping a lot at strange moments,'' Dani said. ''The doctor says it's hormones. Anyway…'' Dani handed over a basket of goodies for Kelsey and Brady. It was filled with an assortment of gourmet cheeses, wine and fruit, as well as a freshly baked loaf of sourdough bread. ''I wanted to make sure we were okay, 'cause I don't want to fight with you, Kelsey.''

''I don't want to fight with you, either,'' Kelsey said.

The two stood, and Kelsey and Dani hugged

as best they could around Dani's pregnant tummy. Dani looked at Kelsey as they drew apart. "You really are happy, aren't you?" she said softly, looking as pleased as Kelsey was about that.

"Yes," Kelsey smiled. "I am."

And no one was more surprised about that than she was.

KELSEY AND BRADY SPENT the rest of the day making sure the cattle got unloaded to the appropriate pastures, the new horses put in the stable, and the saddles and tack stored for cleaning and repair as soon as they could get to it. They didn't eat dinner until after nine, and by 10:00 p.m., they were exhausted and ready for bed when the doorbell rang.

To their amazement, Rafe Marshall was standing on their doorstep. He was dressed in a suit and tie, and looked more miserable than Kelsey could ever recall seeing him. Rafe looked at Brady. "About last night—"

"Kelsey explained."

"Good." Rafe gave Brady a man-to-man look. "I wouldn't want to be responsible for any trouble between the two of you."

"You haven't been," Kelsey said.

"In fact, if anything, you helped us get a few things straight," Brady said, looking at Kelsey. He turned back to Rafe and shook his hand, then ushered him in out of the rain and chill November wind. "So it all worked out in the end."

"I'm glad," Rafe said, looking happy for them but no less miserable himself.

Kelsey took Rafe's overcoat and hung it on the rack next to the door to dry. She had only to look at his face to know he had bad news. "What's wrong?" she asked, concerned.

Rafe sat down in front of the fire Brady had built. "When I took Patricia to the Gilded Lily tonight, we had the same maître d' you and I had last night."

Kelsey tensed as she and Brady took a seat on the sofa. "The snooty, sarcastic one?"

"Yep. He recognized me instantly, and he pulled me aside before he seated us, and said he was glad to see me but that he hoped the woman I was with tonight was not married to someone else because he didn't want any more ugly scenes. Patricia overheard, and she marched out of the restaurant before we could even be seated."

Kelsey flattened a hand across her heart. "Oh, no."

"'Oh, no' is right," Rafe agreed miserably, looking at both Brady and Kelsey. "I tried explaining to her that it wasn't what she thought, but all she wanted to know was one thing, had I been with someone else last night who was indeed married to someone else. And when I confirmed that was so, she cut me off and demanded I take her home."

"Did you at least explain everything to her?"

Rafe shook his head, sighed heavily. "There was no point. She just wasn't going to listen. Besides, I didn't want to make things worse for you, and at this point, no one in Laramie knows what you and I did except Brady and he's not telling anyone. Are you?"

"I haven't," Brady confirmed. "But I do think you ought to just spill all to Patricia and let the chips fall where they may."

"I agree," Kelsey said. "Honesty is always the best policy."

"I'm sure she'll understand," Brady continued.

Rafe and Kelsey exchanged troubled looks.

"Okay, I'm missing something here," Brady concluded quickly. "What is it?"

"Patricia was involved with a married man before she came to Laramie," Kelsey explained. "The whole experience has left her kind of gun-shy when it comes to men."

"The bottom line is I blew it with her, just like I figured I would," Rafe continued. "I just wanted you two to know what happened, and that I protected Kelsey and her reputation. No one knows she was the woman there with me, and no one has to know."

"That's where you're wrong," Kelsey said. "Someone has to talk to Patricia and set her straight. And it's going to be me. I'll go and see her first thing tomorrow morning."

RAFE MARSHALL LEFT shortly after. Brady would have thought that would have been that, as far as Kelsey was concerned, since nothing more could be done that evening, but it wasn't. Her mood was as down as Rafe's had been.

Figuring there was something there that needed to be talked about, Brady added another log to the fire in the fireplace to ward off the chill of the evening and brought out the bottle of wine that had been in the basket Beau and Dani had delivered earlier in the day. "Okay, tell me what's on your mind," he coaxed as he poured them both a glass of chardonnay.

Kelsey was a complicated woman. Brady wanted to understand her as badly as he felt she secretly wanted to be understood. But that wasn't going to happen unless she let him. And right now, for everything she said to him, she still kept twice as much to herself. Of course, he could hardly criticize her, given what he had yet to tell her about his identity and his past, Brady thought.

"It's nothing," Kelsey insisted. She took a sip of her wine, then put it back on the coffee table in front of her.

"It is something if it has you looking that unhappy," Brady disagreed as he sat down beside her.

Kelsey gave him a look that let him know she didn't appreciate his goading. Tough, Brady thought. He wasn't giving up until he found out what was bothering her. "If you want to play twenty questions, we can do it that way."

Kelsey blew out an exasperated breath and leapt up from the sofa. Both hands shoved in the back pockets of her jeans, she began to pace.

Abruptly, she whirled to face him and said in a low, dead-serious tone, "If you're smart, you'll get out while the going is still good."

Brady blinked, sure he hadn't heard right. "What?"

Kelsey lifted both hands in a helpless gesture, then let them fall again to her sides. Moisture gleamed in her pretty green eyes. "I'm jinxed." She swallowed hard and, her eyes locked with his, continued explaining sadly, "You've heard of Wade McCabe, and how everything he touches magically turns to gold?" she asked softly. "Well, everything I touch turns to rust."

Brady would have laughed at the ridiculous notion, had she not been so pale. "You're serious," he whispered.

Kelsey nodded. She wiped her damp eyes

with the back of her hand and said in a low, trembling voice, "And with good reason. This situation with Rafe is only the last in a long line of catastrophes, the only common denominator in all of them being me." The tears she had been suppressing fell in a torrent, spilling over her cheeks and chin. "My parents died because I wasn't where I was supposed to be and they were out looking for me."

"That was a random act of fate, Kelsey."

"I might believe that, too, if it were only that incident." Kelsey shoved her hands through her hair. "But there have been dozens of them since."

"Such as…?"

"I knew about Jenna's botched elopement to Jake when they were teenagers. I could have stopped it, Brady. If I had, his parents might never have found out about it and taken action to separate them, and they might never have been apart."

Brady hadn't been around when that happened, but he had heard the story at the time Jenna and Jake had gotten married this past summer. "That was years ago, Kelse. You were just a kid yourself."

"So? There's no age limit on jinxes, Brady. I'm bad luck, pure and simple." She studied him in obvious frustration. "You don't believe me, do you?"

Brady shook his head. "No." He stood and tried to take her in his arms, but she pushed him away.

"Maybe you would if you had been around when Meg delivered Jeremy."

Brady leaned against the mantel. He studied the color in her face and the anguish in her eyes. Was this guilt the root of her recklessness? Was it fear behind her legendary fickleness, instead of just an inability to make up her mind or commit to any one person or thing? "What happened there?" he asked calmly, wanting—needing—to know how all these pieces fit together for her.

Kelsey sat down again on the sofa. She gulped her wine. "Meg went into premature labor when we were returning home from a shopping trip together."

Brady watched the way her fingers tightened on the stem of her glass. "I suppose you did something to Dani, too?"

Kelsey nodded, her knuckles turning as white as her face. "I'm the one who talked Dani into going off to Mexico with Beau Chamberlain to help settle their feud." She took another gulp of wine. "They came back married."

Brady shrugged and countered calmly, "They look happy enough now."

"They weren't at first!" She set her glass back down on the coffee table. Distress tightened the pretty features of her face. "In fact, due to some weird happenings down there, neither of them could even remember saying 'I do.'"

Brady had heard about that, too—everyone in Laramie had. "The fact they both had amnesia about their wedding was not your fault," Brady said sternly. Guessing what she was about to say next, he said, "And neither was the fact her laptop broke while you were using it."

"Yeah, well—" Kelsey shivered, looking as if she would never be warm again "—tell that to her the next time something happens and it can't be fixed so easily. Tell that to Rafe, who probably had a clear shot to Patricia Weatherby's heart until I got involved.'' New tears spilled down Kelsey's cheeks.

Brady went back to the sofa and sat down beside her. He shifted her resisting body onto his lap and cuddled her against him. He pressed a kiss into her hair. ''You're going to fix that tomorrow, we both are, when we talk to Patricia and tell her straight out what happened and why.'' Brady paused. He tucked his fingers beneath her chin and tilted her head up to his. ''As for everything else, in every life a little rain must fall. You can view the catastrophes that come up as problems and give up. Or you can view them as challenges and take 'em on, one right after another.'' He flashed her a crooked grin designed to lift her spirits. ''You know what I prefer.''

She let out a wistful breath and slowly began to smile. ''You like the challenges.''

''Yep.'' Brady threaded his hands through her hair, glad she had come to her senses once again. ''And most of all, I like you. You're my favorite challenge, Kelse,'' he told her solemnly, loving the way she nestled against him. ''The one I want to win, and dedicate myself to, more than anything else.''

Warm amusement sparkled in her eyes as she splayed her hands across his chest, rubbing, stroking. Reckless as ever, she said, "You think you've won me."

Brady noticed she didn't quibble with his desire to dedicate himself to making her happy. Deciding it was time they curtailed the talk and switched to action that would better prove the way he felt about her, he shifted her so she was lying against the back of the sofa. He stretched out beside her, cupped her cheek and gently ran his thumb along her lips.

"Famous last words," he teased. "Especially since there's not a challenge that's gotten the best of me yet. You included, sweetheart."

Kelsey grinned all the more. "Well, maybe I'll be the first," she murmured softly, already unbuttoning his shirt.

"I don't think so." He took her face in his hands and kissed her with the same deep and abiding hunger she felt. Her lips softened under his, inviting him into her sweet, urgent heat. But when he wanted her undressed, it was Kelsey who took the lead, helping him with his clothes. Touching and kissing him with a wild sensuality that surprised him, even as it pushed him toward the edge. Not about to go without her, he shifted so she was beneath him once again. Together, they dispensed with her clothes. The orange-blossom scent of her hair and skin drove him wild, and their kisses, fed by a passion that had taken on a life of its own, took on an even wilder flavor.

"Now," she said, urging him closer.

"Not," Brady decided, "until I've had my fill."

She shut her eyes as he took her hands and anchored them on either side of her head. "I can't wait that long," she whispered.

"Yes, you can," he whispered back, loving how much she wanted him. "And I'll prove it to you."

Ignoring her hoarse exclamation of need, he held her wrists in one hand and used his other to touch, stroke, love. She trembled and he kissed her again, taking her mouth with his, until the mating of their tongues was an intimate act without an ounce of restraint. Her skin grew hot and flushed, and her thighs splayed wide to accommodate his legs. His sex pressed against her, and a fierce wave of tenderness swept through him. He hadn't expected her to be so vulnerable—ever. She was. He hadn't expected her to be so open to loving him. But she made him feel like he was hers and hers alone.

Knowing, even if she didn't, that she was the one who was conquering him, he flicked her nipples with his tongue and touched her with his lips and explored her with his hands, until she was silky wet and trembling. Ready. Wanting. Needing. Parting her knees with his, he braced a hand on either side of her and situated himself between her thighs. Her hands caught his hips, brought him against her, closed around him and guided him inside. The last of his restraint fell away as she drove him to the brink. He moved inside her, commanding everything she had to give, while at the same time availing every part of him to her. They were married. They were part of each other. And for the first time, the only time in his life, Brady learned what it was like to be with a woman, heart and soul. He hadn't known he could want like that. He hadn't known he could need. But he did. And so, he thought, as their climax inevitably came, did she.

They floated there, breathing hard and clinging to each other. Enjoying the aftershocks consuming their bodies, Brady touched his lips to her face, her hair. She was so sweet. So wild. And she was all his. Which left them only one thing to resolve. He shifted so he could see her face, and she could see his. "Still feel like a jinx?" he asked her softly.

"No." Kelsey let out a trembling sigh as she pressed a kiss into his palm, gratitude and affection shimmering in her eyes. "Not anymore," she told him confidently.

"Good," Brady said, his satisfaction complete. He tightened his arms around her possessively. "'Cause you're the best thing that ever happened to me, Kelse." No question.

## Chapter Eleven

The phone rang the next morning as they were walking out the door. "Let the answering machine take it," Brady said.

"Okay, but I just want to listen to the message in case it's anything important," Kelsey said as the prerecorded message clicked on, followed by the beep and a man's voice. "It's Friday morning. This is Hargett. Brady, I want to talk to you about our...situation."

Frowning, Brady pushed by Kelsey and headed for the machine.

"Look, I know I said I'd give you the full two weeks you've got left," Hargett continued gruffly, "but I just can't. Not after the way we left things the other morning. I want to talk to you about the money and everything else you promised me, ASAP—''

Brady clicked the stop button on the machine, then turned the answering machine off entirely so no further messages would be recorded in their absence.

"Why did you do that?" Kelsey demanded as the phone began to ring again a few minutes later.

Brady pushed her out the door and locked it behind them. "Because I know what he's going to say."

"Well, I don't!" Kelsey argued.

Brady fixed her with a warning glance. "The message isn't for you, Kelsey."

"In other words," Kelsey guessed, unable to help but feel hurt at the way he was shutting her out of whatever was going on with Hargett, as the phone continued to ring, as insistently as ever, "I should mind my own business." And that hurt, because she'd thought Brady understood, accepted and appreciated her like no one else. Had she been wrong about that? And if so, what else was she wrong about? Kelsey wondered.

Brady sighed. Obviously realizing how upset she was, he closed the distance between them and cupped her shoulders gently. "Look, Hargett is a complex guy. What problems the two of us have are between him and me. I know you want to help me deal with him, but—" the hesitation was back in his voice "—the bottom line is, you can't."

Kelsey began to feel very uneasy. Brady was acting as if whatever Hargett said or did could somehow hurt the two of them and/or disrupt the happiness they'd found as man and wife. She swallowed hard. She wasn't worried about herself. She had the feeling she could handle Hargett. But she didn't want anything to happen to Brady. She cared about him too much. "Is he threatening you?" she asked warily.

Brady's mouth tightened into a grim line. His eyes took on a remote look. "Not the way you think," he said bluntly.

Kelsey thought about all the options and finally concluded, "He wants something from you, doesn't he? That's why he keeps calling and coming around."

Brady turned his brooding glance to her and

admitted, with a great deal of reluctance, "He wants me to go back to work for him."

"Doing what?"

"Just...business," Brady said vaguely, looking all the more evasive and uncomfortable. "It's not anything I want to do. And it's not important to the two of us, 'cause it's not going to happen."

Kelsey studied him wordlessly. There was something he still wasn't telling her. And didn't want her to know, Kelsey decided. "Maybe it's not important to you," she said, hurt at the way Brady kept refusing to confide in her.

Brady's lips tightened in exasperation. "There is nothing that Hargett has to say to me that won't keep until I'm of a mind to deal with him," he said grimly. "And that'll come soon enough."

Seeing the worry come back into his dark blue eyes, Kelsey felt her uneasiness grow by leaps and bounds. "Look, I know you've gotten in over your head. And I just want you to know I don't blame you," Kelsey continued hastily, putting up a silencing hand before he could interrupt her. "It could have happened to anyone who needed money and had nowhere else to borrow it. And heaven knows we've had to sink a lot more than we thought into the house, bringing it back to a livable state. But it's not too late, Brady. There's still a way out. There's always a way out."

Brady studied her with obvious admiration and gratitude. "You'd forgive me," he questioned thoughtfully, "even knowing I did something to compromise my future?"

"Yes," Kelsey said firmly. "I would."

"You're some kind of woman, Kelsey," Brady said with obvious admiration.

"Thank you." Kelsey beamed at his praise.

"But we still don't need to discuss this here and now," Brady decided firmly. "What we do need to do is hurry and get to town if we want to catch Patricia Weatherby before she leaves for work at the chamber of commerce. Otherwise, she's going to think we stood her up."

"All right," Kelsey conceded reluctantly, unable to shake the feeling that trouble was just over the horizon. "But just so you know, Brady, we're not finished talking about this."

BRADY KNEW HE SHOULD HAVE told Kelsey who Hargett was and what he really wanted from him, aside from going back to work for Hargett and the company, that was. But he hadn't because he knew she'd probably be furious when she found out everything he had been keeping from her and everyone else in Laramie. He was going to have to tell her, of course. And soon, given both the upcoming deadline he and Hargett had agreed upon when Brady had broken away, and the way Hargett was now breathing down his neck.

But he didn't want to tell her.

He didn't want anything to spoil the miracle the two of them had found. And he sensed, from the way Kelsey wasn't really pushing him to confess all here and now, that Kelsey didn't want anything to spoil their newfound love affair and "marriage of convenience," either.

Not when they had a chance to make it all as real and solid and wonderful as the ranch they were now calling home.

They caught up with Patricia at nine-thirty. Her daughter, Molly, was already in school. Patricia wasn't due to work over at the chamber of commerce until ten. "You're here to talk to me about Rafe, aren't you?" she said as she ushered Brady and Kelsey inside. She looked tired and stressed. "Well, you can forget it," she stated emphatically. "I'm not going to go out with anyone who sees a married woman on the side."

Glad she had wasted no time in getting to Patricia, Kelsey hastened to set the record straight. "I was the married woman Rafe was with that night, and it was not a real date, it was a practice date for his evening with you."

Patricia blinked in confusion. "I don't understand. Why would Rafe need a practice date?"

Kelsey rolled her eyes. "Because he's such a klutz and he hasn't dated anyone in a very long time and he has a wild crush on you and he really wanted everything to go just right. He thought if he had a trial run with me, I could critique him and then everything with you would go super smoothly. He really wanted to impress you. And he needed to get his confidence up to do that. That's all it was, Patricia."

"But the waiter said something about a husband coming in, being very upset—"

"That was me," Brady said, owning up to his actions matter-of-factly. "Kelsey neglected to tell me what was going on, and I got the wrong idea. So, yeah, I was pretty jealous until Kelsey explained the situation. The point is, Rafe and Kelsey are just friends, Patricia. I wouldn't be here, asking you to give Rafe Marshall a second chance, if there was anything else going on."

Patricia sat down, her expression bleak. "Oh, dear. What a mess. I imagine, if I'd only given him half a chance, Rafe would have told me all this last night."

"What happened in the past, including last night, isn't important," Brady said. "The future is."

"DID YOU MEAN WHAT YOU SAID about the future?" Kelsey asked Brady as they turned into the path that led up to the ranch house. "About it being more important than anything that happened in the past, even yesterday?"

Brady nodded as he parked in front of the ranch house and cut the motor on his pickup. He wondered what Kelsey was trying to get up the nerve to ask him.

"Because there's something I need to tell you," she said. She bit into her lower lip uncertainly. "Something important."

Before she could elaborate further, Brady heard another car. He turned and saw a familiar late-model Cadillac coming up the drive. He swore beneath his breath. Kelsey looked just as distressed at the ill-timed interruption.

"Let me take care of this," Brady said firmly. Darn it all. He should have known that Hargett wouldn't stop with a phone message, that he would show up here in person.

Brady climbed out of the pickup truck just as Hargett climbed out of the Cadillac. The two met halfway. Brady blew out an exasperated breath as he regarded their uninvited guest. "You want to see me, fine, but not here and not now."

"Then when?" Hargett demanded unhappily as Kelsey dashed out of the pickup and threw herself between them.

"To get to him, you're going to have to go through me," she vowed.

Hargett's brows drew together. As before, he was dressed in an elegant and expensive business suit, seemingly at odds with his rough-hewn appearance. "Is that so?" Hargett drawled, regarding Brady's wife with obvious amusement.

"Yes." Kelsey kept her arms out on either side of her and backed up until she was totally blocking Hargett's access to Brady. "Listen here, Hargett, I don't know what it is that you've got hanging over Brady's head, but I think you should just forget about getting him to come back to work for you, and go home."

Brady clamped his hands on her shoulders and attempted to move her, so she was no longer shielding him with her body. "Kelsey, you don't have to defend me here," he said, frustrated at the way Kelsey was digging in her heels and refusing to budge.

"Actually," Hargett interrupted, raising his brow and folding his arms in front of him, "I want to hear what this wife of yours has to say, Brady. I admire a gal with gumption. Plus, unless I am mistaken, and I don't think I am, this little filly really loves you."

"I'm not a filly, but you're right, I do love him," Kelsey retorted hotly.

*And I love you,* Brady thought. But he wasn't telling Kelsey that. Not here and not now. Not in front of Hargett. That could wait until they were alone and had a properly romantic setting, so he could kiss and hold Kelsey the way he wanted to kiss and hold her when he told her he loved her for the very first time.

"And I want to protect him from the likes of you," Kelsey argued hotly.

Hargett laughed.

Brady glared at him. Of all the times he didn't need the kind of interference Hargett was capable of, it was now. "I will talk to you later," he promised again, looking at Hargett. "Right now, you need to leave," he stated emphatically.

But instead of leaving, Hargett said, frowning, "You didn't tell her who I was, did you?"

At that, it was all Brady could do not to cringe. He swore beneath his breath. "No. I didn't. Not yet."

"Which means she doesn't know who you really are, either," Hargett concluded heavily, with a telling, sympathetic look at Kelsey. "Does she?"

HARGETT AND BRADY MIGHT as well have been talking in secret code, for all Kelsey was getting of their conversation. "Of course I know who he is!" Kelsey retorted, reassuring herself there was absolutely no need for her to panic, despite the secretive glances Brady and Hargett were exchanging. "He's Brady Anderson. My husband." She pressed a hand to her heart and continued in a low, fiercely emotional tone of voice. "And I love him with all my heart and soul."

"I think you've done enough damage here," Brady told Hargett tightly.

"I'm not the one who kept something that important from my wife," Hargett countered, looking Brady up and down. "But you're right, Brady. This is a discussion you and Kelsey should have alone. When you've finished, call me at the inn. Or come by and see me in person. Like I said on the phone, we have some very important business to discuss." He handed Brady a small card, with a phone number scribbled on the back. He tipped his hat at Kelsey, went back to his Cadillac, climbed in and drove away. Kelsey stared at Brady, waiting for the explanation to come.

Brady sighed, swept off his hat and slammed it against his thigh. His jaw was clenched. He looked and acted as frustrated and upset as Kelsey suddenly felt. "That was my dad." He pushed the words through his teeth.

As the meaning of Brady's words sank in, Kelsey felt like she'd just had all the air knocked out of her lungs. "Your dad," she repeated, stunned.

"Yes." Brady clenched his jaw all the more. He turned and looked Kelsey square in the eye. "His full name is Hargett Anderson and he owns the Anderson Oil Company."

Kelsey's knees grew weak. "Not the same company that owns all those gas stations."

"One and the same."

She leaned against the back of Brady's pickup truck. "And you're an heir to all that?"

"Not just an heir." Brady's midnight-blue eyes glimmered with barely checked resentment. "The *only* heir."

Kelsey worked to contain her hurt, even as she struggled to understand why Brady had done what he had. "Why didn't you tell me?" she whispered.

Brady slammed his hat back on his head and tugged the brim low across his forehead. "Because for the last two years I have been trying to live a normal life, the kind of life I never had the chance to live as a kid."

"Your father disapproved of that?"

"Yes. He grew up dirt poor. He had no connections. He had to do everything on his own and he sees no reason why I should have to do the same when he could hand it all to me on a silver platter."

"But you don't want to help him run his company."

Brady frowned. "I've got the talent to do it, no question."

Kelsey recalled what a fierce bargainer he was. How he cared about every aspect of the business, and always watched the bottom line.

"I just wasn't happy as an oil company exec," Brady continued, as if willing her to understand. "Dad thought it was a phase, that I would get over my need to be my own man and blaze my own path. But I knew that wasn't the case. I not only had what it took to be a cowboy, but to own my own ranch as well. Any-

way, I made this deal with my dad. He had to
stop pressuring me and totally stay out of my
life during the two years I was proving my mettle. If I couldn't do it, learn the business and
save enough money to purchase a ranch of my
own and make it a success, then at the end of
that time I would go back to Houston and spend
the rest of my life working for him and the
company again.''

''So that's why you were so desperate to go
into partnership with me and make this ranch
work,'' Kelsey supposed slowly, ''even if it
meant borrowing money from Wade McCabe to
stock it.''

Brady shot her an irritated look. ''I could
have bought a ranch of my own.''

''Not one this big,'' Kelsey countered, mocking his mildly irritated tone. She glared at him,
not sure whether she was more hurt or angry,
just knowing she was both. ''Not without my
seed money, too.'' How could he have kept
something this important from her, even after
Hargett started coming around and while he
knew she was worried about Hargett's interference, the way he seemed to be pressuring
Brady?

Brady stubbornly held his ground. "I thought we'd be good together. I wanted this ranch to be a success for both of us, Kelsey."

"When were you going to tell me?" Kelsey demanded.

"Soon," Brady said vaguely.

"Today?" Kelsey pressed, as impatient to get to the truth as he was reluctant to give it.

Brady shrugged, as if that hardly mattered. "I probably would have waited a few more days," he conceded after a minute.

"Or in other words, as long as possible," Kelsey guessed.

"Or until I'd gotten my trust fund."

Kelsey's heart sank. Just when she thought it couldn't get any worse, she found out there was yet another element to Brady's duplicity.

"I'm due to come into my trust fund in a little over a week now—that's the deadline Hargett keeps referring to," Brady continued. "My getting the funds was contingent upon my being a success as a rancher. That's why I wasn't worried about paying Wade McCabe back, or building an indoor arena or anything else, because I knew I'd have the money to do anything we wanted to do here if I just made it a few more weeks.''

''You must've really wanted this,'' Kelsey said as a chill descended over her heart.

Brady nodded affirmatively. ''There's a lot we can do with those funds to continue to fix up this place, Kelsey. Heck, with that kind of money, we could go state-of-the-art on everything and make the Lockhart-Anderson Ranch a real showplace.''

Kelsey had once thought Brady's ambition and ability to dream big were laudable. That was before she had been used to further both. ''Well, I have to hand it to you, Brady,'' Kelsey said bitterly. ''You made a complete and utter fool out of me. Here I thought you'd done all this because you wanted me as your partner so we could build something real and lasting. When all I ever was was the means to an end.''

Brady released a short, impatient breath and gave her a look that said she was making this unnecessarily hard on them both. ''You can't seriously believe that,'' he said.

The problem was, she did. Not once, Kelsey recalled, had Brady ever said he loved her. Or even could be falling in love with her. Not once had he hinted that he wanted their marriage to be anything more than a furthering of the business arrangement and the friendship they already had.

Once, she'd thought those things would be enough to make her happy. But that had been before she'd fallen in love with Brady. Now she needed him to love her, too. If he didn't... Well, Kelsey didn't see any reason to continue on with an arrangement that was only going to devastate her in the end. She looked at him steadily, wanting him to come to grips with the harsh reality of the situation, too. "You needed me to make your dreams of owning your own ranch come true."

Brady's face hardened. "I needed you for a lot more than that, Kelsey."

"Yeah," Kelsey agreed sarcastically, remembering how wonderful it had been when they'd been together in bed. "You needed me for passion. Fun. Companionship." But not as a real wife. Tears stung her eyes. "No wonder your father was so disapproving and so upset to find you here with me. He knew all along what you were up to even when I had no clue." It was funny, in a sad sort of way. For so long she'd been afraid to give her heart to anyone, for fear she'd get hurt. When she finally had put that fear aside and given her heart to Brady Anderson, she'd ended up devastated, anyway. How ironic was that?

"Don't use my father as an excuse. Yes, he's a pain. But Hargett's not the problem here, Kelsey. You are. You don't even have to tell me. I can see it by the look on your face. You've got one foot out the door already, don't you?"

Kelsey didn't want to hear Brady spout off what everyone else already thought—that she was so naturally fickle she couldn't be trusted to love anyone. Because that wasn't what had happened here. Brady had betrayed her, not the other way around. "You can't seriously expect me to stay in this marriage, knowing what I know now!"

Brady glared at her. "You just told my father that you loved me," he reminded her grimly. "Or was that all a lie?"

Kelsey hurt, just thinking how quickly she had jumped to his defense. She stared at Brady in confusion. "I didn't even know who you really were," she reminded him quietly, abruptly feeling as confused and adrift as she had when she and Brady had first met the previous summer, when they had both been ranch hands on Travis McCabe's ranch. "So how could I love you?" she asked him sadly. "How could I love anything we've done together or been to each other when none of it, absolutely none of it, has been real?"

Brady looked away a long moment, before returning his gaze to her. "Great excuse, Kelse. But it doesn't wash with me. You're just looking for a way out because you're scared to make a commitment."

Kelsey didn't feel that way at all. But, she figured uneasily, maybe he did. And that hurt her more than she could possibly say. "You'd like to blame this all on me," she stated angrily, "but I'm not going to make it that simple for you. You know what I think?" Kelsey demanded, stomping closer, not stopping until they stood toe-to-toe and nose-to-nose. "I think you're the one who wants out of our marriage of convenience, Brady. Not telling me who you were was just a way of providing yourself with the insurance to do just that, once you had met your father's terms and gotten your inheritance, of course."

Brady regarded her stoically. "I'm not that cold-blooded, Kelsey."

"Maybe not consciously," Kelsey allowed, feeling as if her heart were breaking. "But the bottom line is still the bottom line, in ranching or relationships or anything else." Able to see he still disagreed, she pushed on deliberately, "You told me yourself how much you like a challenge. And there's no greater challenge around here than winning my heart. It was probably a real test of your mettle, wasn't it?" she asked, unable to keep the bitterness from her voice. "After all, you've gone where no man has ever gone before."

"You asked me to marry you, remember? You invited me to your bed! Furthermore," Brady thundered on brusquely, giving her no chance to interrupt, "I've been a good husband to you."

Kelsey had once thought so, too. But that had been before Brady's father had showed Kelsey just how superficial and shallow her relationship with Brady really was. "Good husbands don't keep secrets from their wives," Kelsey shot back tightly. Good husbands had confidence in their wives.

And damn it all, Brady had known how much his pretending to be something other than what he was, how much his keeping something that important from her, even after they'd started to get close, would hurt. But he had gone on and done it anyway.

Kelsey clamped her arms in front of her and continued to regard him angrily. "Face it, Brady, if you had really cared about me, if you had really wanted this marriage of ours to work, you would never have shut me out this way."

But he had, and that spoke volumes about what was in his heart. The bottom line was he didn't trust her enough to confide in her. And without trust, there could be no love. And love and trust were the two things she wanted most of all.

Brady hooked his thumbs through the belt loops on his jeans and stared down at her with resentment. His mouth tightened into a thin line. "You're saying it's over?"

Kelsey looked at him with unbearable sadness. "Don't you see?" she said quietly. "It has to be."

# Chapter Twelve

"You should have told her who you were before you married her, son," Hargett told Brady later the same day, when Brady went to see Hargett at the country inn where he was staying.

"I think I figured that out already, Dad," Brady said with no small trace of irony in his low voice. Not leveling with Kelsey had been the biggest mistake of his life. He took off his hat and sat down opposite his dad, in one of the wing chairs before the fireplace. "Not that it matters, anyway."

Hargett's eyes narrowed in concern. He gathered the business papers he had been studying when Brady got there, then put them aside. "What do you mean?" he demanded.

Brady's jaw tightened as he thought about what his wife had said to him. Feeling more restless and discontent than ever, he shoved a hand through his hair. "Kelsey's decided to move on to greener pastures."

"And you're just going to let her go?" Hargett asked, disbelief etched in the craggy lines of his face.

Brady didn't see what choice he had. He was hardly going to hog-tie his wife to keep her by his side. Right now, that seemed like the only way he could keep Kelsey. Ten to one, she was booting his belongings out of the house and onto the porch right now.

"So you're just another in a string of guys that have passed through her life," Hargett guessed.

Brady nodded, silently telling himself he would get over this. "Right."

"Bull." Hargett got up and went to the minibar in the corner of the room. He got out two bottles of Lone Star beer, handed one to Brady and twisted off the cap on his own. "I saw the way that wife of yours looked at you, the way she threw herself in front of you to protect you, when she thought I was there to do you harm. That gal loves you, son.''

Brady twisted off the cap on his beer and sat with it cradled in his hand. ''Whether she does or not is immaterial,'' he countered, the icy chill of the glass seeping through to his palm. ''She doesn't want to stay with me.''

Hargett took a long, thirsty drink. Regret colored his eyes an even darker hue. ''Don't make the same mistake I made with your mother.''

Brady paused with the bottle halfway to his mouth and put it back down without taking a drink. ''What are you talking about?''

Hargett wiped his mouth with the back of his hand. ''Your mother was convinced I didn't love her, not the way I should. Instead of making sure she knew how much she meant to me, I told her if she wanted to go she should go. And darn it all if she didn't up and do just that. I should have gone after her. But I didn't,'' Hargett emphasized in a brusque tone with an even blunter look, ''because I was too stubborn and proud. I figured in time she'd come to her senses and come back to you and to me. Next thing I knew—'' Hargett shook his head, recalling ''—I had divorce papers in my hand. And sole custody of you.''

Some of the old hurt and confusion came back to hit Brady, full blast. ''If she had loved us, she wouldn't have left us, Dad,'' Brady said bitterly. If she hadn't left, she might not have moved to California and died in that multicar pileup on the interstate when Brady was five.

''And maybe your mother was just scared,'' Hargett countered in a calm, compassionate way that let Brady know his father had at last put the past to rest the way it should have been retired, years ago. ''Maybe if your mother and I had just tried, we could have worked things out,'' Hargett said evenly. ''The point is, I used my battalion of lawyers and made it impossible for her to come back. I boxed her in, the same way I boxed you in with the terms of the trust. And she died, thinking what I wanted her to think, that you and I were much better off without her, than with her. When it simply wasn't true.''

Brady swallowed. ''You're saying she might have wanted to come back to us?''

Hargett shrugged. ''I'm saying I don't know.

I never gave us a chance to find that out. And now it's too late. We can't go back and fix things with her, or give you the mother you should have had all those years. But there are business and financial matters that can be put to rights and that's why I came to see you this morning. I wanted to talk to you about that deal we made when you left nearly two years ago."

Brady looked his father straight in the eye. As long as they were speaking what was in their hearts, he figured he had to tell his dad this, too. "I don't care about my inheritance, Dad. I never have. All I've ever wanted was to be my own man, same as you."

"And you've done that," Hargett replied, with no small amount of pride in his voice. "Which is what I came to tell you this morning. I talked to my lawyers. I'm giving you your inheritance, free and clear. No more terms, no more restrictions. It's yours to do with what you wish."

Brady studied his father. This was a big change, one that had been long in coming. It also meant he had finally proved himself to his father. "No more pressure to come back to work for Anderson Oil?" he asked.

Hargett shook his head as he clamped an affectionate hand on Brady's shoulder. His eyes were serious. "I've put the idea of the two of us working side by side away. I realize now you don't have the passion for it that I do, and it takes real passion to run a company or build up a ranch. I want you to follow your dreams, son. I want you to follow your heart."

"I WANT TO THANK YOU," Patricia Weatherby said when she caught up with Kelsey at the ranch late that afternoon. She cast a curious glance at the stack of Brady's shirts draped over a porch chair. "I talked to Rafe Marshall a little while ago. He explained everything and we're going to try it again tomorrow night."

Kelsey moved a stack of Brady's blue jeans so Patricia could sit down. "Are you going back to the Gilded Lily?" she asked.

"No, we figure that place is jinxed as far as the two of us are concerned. We want to do something more our style, so we're going to go to the Armadillo and have chili dogs and sodas and play putt-putt golf. I think it'll be a lot of fun and so does Rafe. He is such a nice man, Kelsey."

"I've always thought so." Kelsey moved a box of Brady's belongings off a chair and sat down, too. She looked at Patricia seriously. "I'm glad you're giving him another chance."

The corners of Patricia's lips curved up ruefully. "I almost didn't, you know. My experience with Cal, Molly's father, left me pretty gun-shy when it came to men."

Kelsey nodded and sighed. She knew that feeling. Given what she had just been through with Brady, the way he had turned her heart upside down and then stomped on it, she didn't think she'd ever love again. Not after the way he had heartlessly used her, all so he could collect his inheritance. Not that she wouldn't have helped him had he been straight with her. She would have. It was the fact that he hadn't trusted her enough to tell her the truth, about the trust or his father, that really stuck in her craw.

Patricia continued sadly, shaking her head, "I was such a fool, Kelsey."

"Been there and done that, too," Kelsey said. She couldn't believe the way she had opened herself up to Brady, only to have it all thrown right back in her face.

"Cal kept promising me he would get a divorce and marry me."

"But then didn't," Kelsey said, recounting what she already knew.

Patricia nodded grimly. "He said his wife wouldn't give him a divorce, and he couldn't leave his other kids. He had five back in Louisiana. So I just let it go. I was just so desperate to give Molly the father she wanted and needed, that I let Cal talk me into believing we could have a family life in Houston without really being married or him actually getting divorced. He traveled back and forth between the places all the time, anyway, for work. I convinced myself the legalities didn't matter as long as Molly was happy and had a father to love her. When he died, without having made provisions for us, I was devastated."

"Why didn't you fight to keep the house you were living in, and the car Cal had leased for you?" Kelsey asked curiously.

Patricia frowned. "I thought about it, but I knew it would involve years of legal wrangling, a lot of money for lawyers. Plus, Cal's family was very powerful and well-connected. They had threatened to drag both Molly and me through the mud if we contested the will and made a claim on Cal's estate, and I didn't want Molly to have to go through that. So instead I decided to start over and make a new life for us and we ended up here."

Kelsey knew Patricia wasn't confiding all this to her now, just for the heck of it. "You're trying to tell me something, aren't you?" Kelsey guessed after a moment.

Patricia nodded. "I loved a man who was so wealthy, who had such a sense of his own entitlement, he didn't care who he hurt or who he lied to as long as he made sure all of his needs were met. Brady's not like that."

Kelsey sighed. She studied the look on Patricia's face. "You heard he's an Anderson Oil Company heir, didn't you?"

"Yeah. Everyone in town has. He's been telling people himself, and walking around introducing Hargett Anderson as his dad."

Kelsey paused to digest that bit of news. "That's good. I'm glad they've worked out whatever the difficulty between them was." She wanted Brady to be close to his father.

"Which leaves only one problem," Patricia said as Dani drove up, parked her car and got out. "The difficulty between you and Brady, whatever that is."

"My thought exactly," Dani Chamberlain said, coming up on the porch to join them. "I heard the news about who Brady is, and wondered how you were taking the news." Dani looked at the belongings stacked on the front porch. "Guess this answers my question."

Kelsey cleared a place beside her, so the pregnant Dani could sit down. "You know how fickle I am," Kelsey said, doing her best to make light of the situation.

"You stopped being fickle the day you hooked up with Brady," Dani argued.

Kelsey lifted a brow.

"Think about it," Dani continued. "You said you wanted to be a rancher last summer. You did that. You've overcome tremendous odds and a lot of family dissension to make this place a success and you've done that. And through it all, Brady has been by your side, first as your friend and the person who shared your same dreams, then as your partner, and finally as your husband."

"He only married me and went into partnership with me because he wanted to get his inheritance. And he had to own a ranch, and make a success of it, to do that."

"Hogwash," Dani said. "He could have gotten Wade McCabe, or even Travis McCabe, to help him there. He went into partnership with you because he wanted to be with you, period. I'm not saying he didn't make mistakes along the way. From what I've been able to see, you both did that. But he never stopped loving you or caring about you, and he still does, otherwise he wouldn't be driving up the lane now."

Kelsey's heart skipped a beat as she followed Dani's gaze. Sure enough, Brady was driving up the lane in his pickup truck. And he wasn't wasting any time about it, either.

Abruptly, she wished she had never taken all of Brady's belongings and carried them down to the porch. But she had, and it was too late to rectify it.

Her heart in her throat, she watched as he parked his truck so it wasn't blocking anyone else's vehicle, and climbed out. His eyes locked with hers, he kept right on coming, not stopping until he was just in front of her. He tipped his hat at Patricia and Dani. "Ladies, good to see you, but I need to talk to my wife."

Patricia and Dani nodded. Both looked at Brady and Kelsey as if wishing them luck on working things out, then headed off to their respective vehicles. Kelsey waited until they had both driven away, before she said, "Uh, about your stuff—"

He eyed her thoughtfully. "Looks like you have been doing some rearranging."

Wasn't that the understatement of the year, considering everything he had left in the house was now sitting on the front porch, while everything she owned was still inside. "A little," Kelsey confirmed. "But I'm not finished yet." If things went the way she hoped, she'd be putting it all back, pronto.

"I would hope not," Brady said, in the same crisp, matter-of-fact tone he always used when they talked about ranch business. "But we'll get to that in a minute. Right now I've got something more important to say." He paused and looked her straight in the eye. "I was wrong not to tell you about the terms of my inheritance, Kelse. And I swear on everything that's good and right in this world that I will never do anything like that again, because there's no room in any true partnership for secrets. In addition—"

Kelsey studied the documents he handed her. "You paid off the mortgage to the ranch?" That, she hadn't expected.

Brady nodded, and continued gruffly, "As well as what we owed Wade McCabe. My father gave me the money he had set aside for me, free and clear."

Kelsey swallowed. She wasn't sure if he was trying to make up with her, or break up. She only knew that the financial reasons that had existed for Brady to be with her no longer were in play. Knowing whatever happened, whatever he said, she wasn't letting him go without a fight, and a victory, Kelsey said cautiously, "Obviously, you have a plan here—"

"Don't I always?" Brady shot her a rueful, sidelong grin as he sat down beside her. He took her hand in his and let both rest on his thigh. "I may as well tell you straight out," he continued with a seriousness that made her heart turn somersaults in her chest. "I think we made a mistake, Kelse, getting married the way we did, pretending to everyone else it was a love match so we could get the money, while we were telling ourselves it was a strictly business arrangement. I've come to the conclusion that circumventing the truth or doing anything in halfway measures is never a good idea, no matter what the reason."

"I have to agree with you there. We should have been honest with each other from the get-go. 'Cause if I had been..." Kelsey said, taking a deep breath and getting to her feet. Brady stood, too. She grasped his hands in hers before continuing determinedly, "I would have told you that I've been in love with you, almost from the first day we met. I just didn't want to admit it to myself."

Brady's midnight-blue eyes took on an even darker hue as he swept her into his arms. "But you're ready to admit it now?"

"With all my heart," Kelsey confirmed, wreathing her arms around him. Going up on tiptoe, she clung to him tightly, and Brady lowered his head and delivered a long, soul-searching kiss that left them both breathless and shaking.

"Well, that's good, darling," Brady said when the languorous caress finally came to a halt, "because I'm head over heels in love with you, too." He tenderly cupped her face in his hands. "Which brings me to what I came here to say," he whispered with all the romance and the love she had ever wanted. "I think we ought to do more than just stay married, Kelse," he told her hoarsely. "I think we ought to get married all over again. Only this time," he continued firmly, "we're going to do it right. In front of all our family and friends."

"KELSEY, WILL YOU PLEASE stand still?" Jenna demanded as she put the finishing touches on Kelsey's wedding gown. "You're going to be walking down the aisle in five minutes and you've still got two buttons undone."

"Not to mention the fact we haven't given her something old, something borrowed, something blue or something new," Meg continued as six-year-old Alexandra smiled shyly and presented her Aunt Kelsey with an antique gold heart to wear around her neck.

"And here is something borrowed—" Meg gave Kelsey the white handkerchief she had tucked into her sleeve on the day she married Luke.

Dani handed Kelsey a satin garter. "Something blue—"

"And the something new," Jenna said, kneeling and helping Kelsey slip on a pair of brand new white leather cowgirl boots, made especially for that day.

"Looks like I'm all set." Kelsey beamed at her three sisters and her niece. Outside, in the chapel, the organ began the strains of the wedding march. It was time.

"Nervous?" Jenna asked.

Kelsey shook her head. "With Brady out there, waiting for me? Not one bit." She knew she could handle anything as long as the two of them were together.

Hugs and kisses were exchanged all around, and then Alexandra picked up her basket and proceeded out into the vestibule and into the church, strewing flowers all along the way. The pregnant Dani was next, followed by Jenna, and then Meg. Finally, it was Kelsey's turn. John

McCabe held out his arm and walked her down the aisle.

Kelsey's heart and eyes were brimming as John officially gave her away, in her father's stead, and Brady took her hand in his. Together, they turned to face the minister and spoke what was in their hearts. "I, Kelsey, take thee, Brady, to have and to hold from this day forward...."

"For better for worse, for richer for poorer, in sickness and in health, to love and to cherish, till death do us part," Brady said, fitting the ring on her finger.

When the minister pronounced them man and wife, and Brady took her in his arms and kissed her, the whole church erupted in soft oohs and aahs, then rambunctious applause. And the celebrating continued well into the night, at the reception John and Lilah gave them at the McCabe ranch.

"Well, you did it," Meg Lockhart told John and Lilah admiringly as the guests kicked up their heels. "You helped all four of your sons find the ultimate happiness with the loves of their lives, and now all four of us Lockhart women, and your nephew Sam McCabe, have made the leap into matrimony, too.''

John and Lilah looked over at Sam McCabe and Kate Marten, who were busy enjoying the reception with their five sons, too.

''I wasn't sure we were going to be able to manage it,'' Lilah McCabe admitted with a relieved smile.

''But we did,'' John announced happily as he wrapped his arm around his wife's waist and tenderly kissed her cheek. ''And now they're all settling down, right here in Laramie, and building families of their own.''

''And we're happier than we've ever been,'' Meg added honestly as she looked at John and Lilah, who were still beaming proudly as any parents over their accomplishment. Gratitude filled her heart, as she looked at them soberly. She knew she was speaking for all of them as she continued, ''I don't think any of us realize how much we had missed being near each other, until we moved back here, and were together again. But as good as that was, being close to family and old friends, in the community where we grew up, there was still something missing—for all of us.''

"And that was the kind of love you only get from the person you're destined to marry," Lilah guessed.

Meg nodded. "Thanks for being there, to guide us through the rough spots," she said.

"Our pleasure." John grinned and gave Meg a hug.

"And for the record," Lilah added, leaning over to kiss and hug Meg, too, "we'll continue to be here for all of you girls, whenever, however you need us. Because that's what family is for."

On the dance floor that had been erected on the lawn, Brady tugged Kelsey even closer, luxuriating in the feeling of holding his new bride in his arms on the beautiful Indian summer night. "Have I told you how beautiful you look tonight?" he murmured, the soft surrender of her body against his like a balm to his soul.

Kelsey blushed, looking even prettier in her white satin gown, with her cinnamon-red hair swept up on top of her head. "Only about a thousand times," she admitted.

And the way she looked at him then, with a combination of lust and love and tenderness, had him feeling like the luckiest man alive. "Have I told you how much I love you?" he asked, even softer.

Kelsey nodded, her emerald-green eyes darkening seriously. "I love you, too, cowboy," she whispered throatily, "so very much."

Brady tightened his hold on her possessively, knowing she was making all his dreams come true. "Our lives are just starting now. And as good as things are," and they were incredibly good, Brady amended silently, "they're only going to get better."

Kelsey nodded her agreement as she rose on tiptoe and kissed him, with all the passion in her heart. "I can't wait."

\* \* \* \*

*Look for* Cathy Gillen Thacker's
*next exciting novel,* Their Instant Baby
*– out in November 2007!*

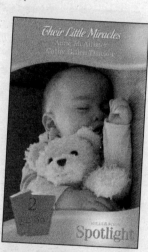